SHE TASTED OF SALTWATER AND SUGAR, HEAVEN AND HELL, TEMPTATION AND SALVATION . . .

Impulse ruled him. He cupped the side of her face in his hand. She didn't move but her eyes questioned him. He had no reasonable answer.

Leaning closer, he brought his face forward and she closed her eyes. He knew she wanted his kiss as much as he wanted to sample the ambrosia of her. Her lips trembled under his, then parted on a sigh. Desire flashed through him with the intensity of a lightning bolt.

Julienne kept her eyes closed, wanting his mouth to continue its seduction. Her body craved him while her mind reeled in bewilderment. Then the tip of his tongue traced the shell of her ear. And all rational thought turned to dust.

If You've Enjoyed This Book,
Be Sure to Read These Other
AVON ROMANTIC TREASURES

COMANCHE WIND *by Genell Dellin*
FORTUNE'S MISTRESS *by Judith E. French*
HIS MAGIC TOUCH *by Stella Cameron*
THEN CAME YOU *by Lisa Kleypas*
VIRGIN STAR *by Jennifer Horsman*

Coming Soon

SHADOW DANCE *by Anne Stuart*

MASTER OF MOONSPELL

DEBORAH CAMP

An Avon Romantic Treasure

AVON BOOKS ◆ NEW YORK

MASTER OF MOONSPELL is an original publication of Avon Books. This work has never before appeared in book form. This work is a novel. Any similarity to actual persons or events is purely coincidental.

AVON BOOKS
A division of
The Hearst Corporation
1350 Avenue of the Americas
New York, New York 10019

Copyright © 1993 by Deborah E. Camp
Published by arrangement with the author
Library of Congress Catalog Card Number: 93-90115
ISBN: 0-380-76736-8

First Avon Books Printing: August 1993

AVON TRADEMARK REG. U.S. PAT. OFF. AND IN OTHER COUNTRIES, MARCA REGISTRADA, HECHO EN U.S.A.

Printed in the U.S.A.

RA 10 9 8 7 6 5 4 3 2 1

Each that we lose takes part of us
A crescent still abides,
Which like the moon, some turbid night,
Is summoned by the tides.

—EMILY DICKINSON

Chapter 1

Standing near the prow of the ship, Julienne Vale pressed her face to the wind and sea spray. The thrill of adventure sizzled through her veins to warm her blood and fire her spirit.

Home, she thought as the sloop rode the waves of the Atlantic. Her eyes hungered for familiar sights as she gazed lovingly at the land slipping by on her right. The Florida Keys. Wild, unpredictable, dangerous; a place of pirate kings and their hot-blooded concubines, of suspicious shipwrecks and stolen treasure. Julienne could already feel a change in temperature. She could smell the tangy scent of citrus and exotic flowers and the promise of rain on the horizon.

She looked toward the bank of low, dark gray clouds. A silver veil of rain floated from it to the water's surface. Thunder rolled across the ocean, making the air quiver with expectation. Was this vessel swift enough to outpace the storm?

Her gaze drifted to the figurehead of the *Coral Queen,* and it reminded her of the pirate tales she'd grown up hearing from her father. The carving was of a beautiful woman, her face thrust into the sea wash, her arms pressed to her sides, pieces of coral clutched in her fists. A crown of stars and crescent moons adorned her wavy black hair.

A ship fit for a dark pirate prince, she thought,

1

smiling. Anticipation zipped through her like lightning.

"The captain has another sloop named the *Golden Conch*," the skipper shouted above the noise of the snapping sails. "And he has a grand schooner called the *Treasure Chest*. Oh, she is most beautiful!" He grinned, showing off two glinting gold teeth amid his other snowy white ones.

Julienne could picture the gold-toothed skipper aboard a real pirate's ship. Cesare Gomez's dark Cuban coloring was the stuff of fantasy. His black eyes flashed with mischief. He'd parted his iron gray hair in the center and gathered it into a queue tied with a red leather thong. His blue breeches stopped just below his knees, and his buttonless red shirt hugged his beefy torso.

Privateers and pieces of eight had been swimming in Julienne's mind ever since she'd been told by the mother superior that her new position as governess would be on Pirate's Key and her new employer was none other than Buccaneer LaFlamme. Good heavens, his name fairly oozed with dash and daring! In the civilized year of 1879 it was exciting to know that men named Captain Buccaneer LaFlamme still existed.

"How long has it been since you've seen the keys?" Cesare asked, breaking into Julienne's thoughts.

"I left after my father died," she called back. "Ten years ago."

"And you lived with him on Key Largo?"

She nodded. "That's right. We had a couple of acres, but we lived off the sea mostly. I'd heard about Pirate's Key, but I've never been here before."

"Sail much?"

She shook her head. "Hardly at all. We had a small fishing boat. No sail. Paddles!" She pantomimed paddling a canoe and received another broad grin from Cesare. "Since then I've been virtually landlocked at the St. Augustine abbey. I can't begin to tell you how thrilling it is to be on the ocean again."

"You lived at the abbey?"

"Yes, in a small room behind it. I was the cleaning woman, and I helped in the orphanage next door."

Cesare returned his attention to the riggings. The wind had picked up with the approach of the storm. Thunder rolled again and a streak of lightning blazed on the horizon.

"Will we be able to make it to shore before the storm hits?" she shouted into the wind.

Cesare glanced at the dark sky. "It will be close. You mind getting wet?"

She laughed. "Not one bit! I just hate to meet my new employer looking like a drowned rat."

"You can always go below. It is comfortable down there."

Julienne shook her head and faced front again, her eager eyes scanning the shore. Coconut trees leaned toward the ocean, casting shadows over the strip of dazzling white sand. Cesare sailed the swift sloop a safe distance from the shore to avoid the treacherous coral reef that had spelled death to many a brash sailor.

Suddenly a horse and rider burst through the brush and took the beach. The mighty chestnut sent up sprays of sand as it raced along the shore, parallel to the sailing ship. The wind skinned back the equestrian's thick black hair, and droplets of sea spray shone like diamonds in it. He leaned over to press his face against the horse's sleek neck. Julienne couldn't make out his features, but he reminded her of something wild—like a panther or a . . . a pirate! Yes. All he needed was an eye patch. What was that glinting along his side? A saber? No, it must be a jewel-encrusted sword snatched from a defeated foe. Only such a weapon would be worthy of a true cutthroat, she thought. A strangely luscious feeling spiraled through her midsection and she gripped the handrail to watch the pirate's thundering ride.

His white shirt billowed out behind him like a sail. He rode bareback, holding on to the horse by the sheer power of his legs, encased in tight brown breeches and knee-high boots.

"That's him!" Cesare shouted.

"Who?" Then Cesare's meaning flashed through her, taking her breath for a second. "The captain?" she asked, getting Cesare's nod before fastening her gaze on the horse and rider again. "Captain Buccaneer LaFlamme," she breathed, enthralled, enraptured, ensnared.

"Hey there, Buck," Cesare called, swinging one arm above his head in a grand wave that was lost on the equestrian. "He's probably hurrying home to greet you himself!"

"Or outrun the storm," she murmured.

Thunder cracked, followed by the zigzag of a lightning bolt that seemed to split the sky. Captain LaFlamme tipped back his dark head and laughed up at the firmament. His deep-throated, booming laugh rode the wind to her and sent a chill down her spine.

It's as if he's laughing at the devil, Julienne thought.

Trepidation gripped her for an instant. What kind of man would ride with such abandon and laugh at the threatening sky? Would he approve of her? Or would he think Mother Superior had sent the wrong person to oversee his five-year-old daughter, Alissa? What had Cesare called him?

"Buck?" she repeated, looking at the skipper to catch his nod.

"*Sí.* Buccaneer is too much of a mouthful!"

She frowned slightly, not caring for the shortened name that changed a pirate into a cowboy. His name fit him perfectly and shouldn't be trifled with, she thought. Buccaneer LaFlamme. Ah! Now, *that* was a name that conjured up many a favorite fantasy. She wondered about the captain's parents and why they had decided on such an unusual moniker. She turned toward the shore again and was dismayed to find that the horse and rider had vanished.

"Buccaneer . . ." she whispered, feeling oddly bereft. "How long has the captain lived on Pirate's Key?"

Cesare moved closer so that he could be heard. "All his life. His grandfather was given the whole key, but he sold off some of it. He was one of the last of the pirates here in the Florida Straits. Black Pierre, he was called."

"I've read about him," Julienne said. "Wasn't he killed for salvaging ships without a wrecker's license?"

Cesare nodded. "Got himself run through for boarding and looting ships he'd wrecked on the reefs." Cesare gestured toward the shore. "He used to set out lights along there on moonless nights and lure the ships in to wreck on the reef. One night he wrestled with the wrong skipper and got skewered with a length of cold steel."

He paused in his story to execute a lunge and slice the air with an imaginary sword. He laughed at Julienne's wide-eyed stare.

"His son, Gaspard, inherited all his wealth and property," Cesare continued. "Gaspard is the one who named the estate Moonspell, in honor of Black Pierre's sly bewitching." He scowled, his eyes trained on the dazzling white beach. "Don't think Pierre was the only one doing such things. This place crawled with pirates back then, and their favorite game was to lure ships in with lights. On a black night any kind of illumination

casts a spell over shipmates. Nobody knew that
better than the privateers. They lived by the sea
and didn't see anything wrong with dying by the
sea—as long as it was somebody else doing the
dying!"

Julienne shivered, thinking of the poor sailors
who had guided their ships into the jagged coral
reef, lured there by a pirate's greed.

"Is Gaspard still alive?" she asked.

"No, he died quite a few years ago."

"And the captain's mother?"

"She died a long, long time ago when Buck was
a baby." Cesare glanced at her, his gaze thorough,
as if he read every nuance of her expression.

"Is something wrong?" Julienne asked, sensing
it. "Did something happen to his mother?"

Cesare shook a finger at her, and his smile was
forced. "You've heard those crazy stories, haven't
you? Don't you believe them."

Julienne stared at him, confused. "Stories?"

"Gaspard didn't kill his wife. It was an accident,
I am sure."

"Oh, dear." Julienne gripped the handrail more
tightly. "He killed her," she repeated. Some of the
romance she'd been steeped in evaporated.

"Buck didn't murder either one of his wives either," Cesare said, almost crossly. "You should
close your ears to such nonsense, señorita. There is
no reason for you to be afraid."

Stunned into silence, Julienne gaped at him.
Murder? The mother superior hadn't mentioned
anything about murder! Perhaps it had been an in-
tentional omission so that Julienne would have no
reason not to come to Pirate's Key. She forced her
mouth closed and swallowed hard. It was one
thing to hear tall tales concerning her employer's
father, but quite another to learn that evil rumors
circled Buccaneer LaFlamme as well.

"Who . . . That is . . . people think the captain

murdered his wives, too? Both of them?" she ventured.

Cesare scrutinized her. "You had not heard this before?"

"I . . . I've lived a rather sheltered life among the Sisters."

"Ah, but of course." He shrugged. "Then forget what I said. It is of no importance." He flapped a hand. "Idle gossip."

Julienne acquiesced, reluctant to tarnish her dashing image of Captain LaFlamme any further. But, she remembered that her father had often said that where there was smoke, there was fire. If people talked like this about Captain LaFlamme, then there must be a reason for it.

"Gaspard raised Buck by himself," Cesare added.

Just like Papa and me, she thought, feeling another link with her new employer. They'd both lost their mothers when they were babies and had been raised in the wilds of the Florida Keys by their fathers. She felt better having found common ground with him.

Cesare began trimming the sails to reduce their speed. As they were nearing the moorings, Julienne noticed a young man sitting on an outcropping of jagged rocks. The tide was in and the boulders were surrounded by the sea. She waved, but the rock-sitter only stared at her.

"Who's that?" she asked, pointing the man out to Cesare.

Cesare shaded his eyes with one hand. "Ah, that is Ootay."

"Ootay? That's odd-sounding."

"Probably means something witchy." Cesare's gold teeth flashed. He let out the anchor alongside a stretch of pier. "He lives on the edge of the estate with his grandmother, the witch."

"You don't believe in such things, do you?" Julienne scoffed.

"Señorita, I am Cuban. I would be crazy if I did not believe." He tossed thick ropes onto the pier, then sprang out of the sloop with the agility of a youngster. He tied the sloop securely before offering his hands to her. "Let me help you, señorita. Be careful, now. Take your time."

"Thank you, Cesare, and please call me Julienne."

"As you wish."

Julienne lifted her black skirt with one hand and settled her other in Cesare's. He'd brought the sloop steps to the edge of the pier, so it was easy to leave the bobbing vessel for more solid ground. When she'd gained her balance she released Cesare's hand and tried vainly to brush the wrinkles from her traveling ensemble. The black skirt, gray blouse, short gray jacket, and scuffed high-top shoes were serviceable, but hardly fashionable. But what did one need with fashion at an orphanage and abbey? She fit her ash gray hat securely over her dark auburn hair. She could feel places where the velvet had been rubbed slick along the crown and short brim. The black bow and chin strap had been so moth-eaten, she'd torn them off and clutched the hat in her lap during the voyage. Her hair, she knew, was a mess, having been thoroughly windblown, so she piled it up under the sad-looking chapeau.

"We will go to the house and I will leave you with Rosa. She'll see that you are settled in."

"Rosa . . . Is that the housekeeper?"

"*Sí.* She has been with the family since before Isabelle."

"Was Isabelle the first or second wife?"

"First. Buck's second wife was Magdalena, and she was quite beautiful." Cesare lifted her satchel and hatbox, then offered her his arm. "It is a short walk to the house. If we hurry, we will beat the rainstorm." He nodded ahead to a bridle path cut through the dense foliage. "Do you feel at home here already? This must look familiar to you."

Julienne nodded, the crying of gulls in her ears, the smell of wild orchids filling her head. "Oh, yes," she breathed. "I feel right at home. It's wonderful to be back in the Keys."

The pathway was bordered by majestic royal palms fronted by the smaller queen palms that swayed in the wind, their fronds whispering urgently. Cesare pointed out groves of avocado, guava, papaya, and banana trees. Yellow-blossomed prickly poppies and flame-colored spider lilies grew thick under the bordering palms. A kingfisher swooped from branch to branch, and a skink, as long as a man's foot, darted across the path ahead of Julienne.

"Don't be frightened," Cesare said. "It's a harmless lizard."

"I know. Remember, you're talking to an island girl, born and bred."

"Ah, but of course." Cesare winked. "I forgot for a moment. You probably know the names of all these plants, while I am ignorant of many. For instance, what is that one with the yellow flowers?" He pointed out a bushy plant.

"Why, that's a yellow elder," Julienne replied.

"And that one . . ." Cesare indicated another. "That one with the little green and red blooms. It's very pretty."

"Those are some of my favorite flowers. Papa called them cathedral bells, but I've heard other people call them air plants."

"I like your papa's name for them better." Cesare focused his attention ahead of them again. "And here we are at the heart of Moonspell Estate."

Julienne's stride lengthened as she was drawn

to the imposing two-storied structure at the end of
the bridle path. Dingy white against the green and
gray backdrop of earth and sky, the house was
surrounded by palms. Dead brown vines draped
the front of it. Terraces ran all around the outside
on both floors, except for the north side, where a
small house had been attached. The smaller structure reminded Julienne of an adult-sized doll-
house, and she could tell by the architecture that it
has been constructed later—an afterthought, and a
rather intrusive one at that.

Overall, the estate was in decline. Paint peeled
away from the front columns and the window
sashes. Wild vines, tall weeds, and last year's
leaves covered the stone steps. Flower beds held
only a few courageous blooms, but were mostly
honeysuckle vines. If a home reflected its owner,
then Moonspell Estate's had his mind elsewhere,
because the house had been neglected.

Julienne climbed the front steps and stared at
the anchor-shaped knocker, but before she could
lift the brass ornament, the door swung inward
and a stiletto-thin woman divided the entryway.
No smiling greeting, no extended hand. Not from
this dour-faced woman. She glared at Julienne
with eyes that looked like chunks of coal, and her
frown deepened.

"I am Rosa. Come inside." She gave a curt nod
at Cesare and took Julienne's things from him. "I
will take over from here."

"And I will return to the fields." Cesare touched
two fingertips to his forehead. "I hope you enjoy
life with us, señorita."

Julienne knew a moment when she wanted to
clutch Cesare and beg him to stay, but she forced
a cheerful smile and strode into Moonspell's
marble-floored foyer. A staircase curved upward
to an open, airy second floor with all doors shut
against prying eyes. A pearly gray haze drifted

through an oval skylight where pots were suspended on chains and pulleys, but the pots were barren. More neglect, Julienne thought, imagining them filled with lacy ferns and dripping blossoms. Must have been lovely at one time.

The first fat raindrops splashed on the overhead panes. Rosa clapped loudly, giving Julienne a start. A young maid raced around a corner upstairs and bolted into view.

"*Sí*, Rosa? Aha, so she's here!" The maid wiped her hands on her white apron. "Welcome, welcome, señorita!"

"Thank you," Julienne called up to her. "*You're* very kind." She glanced at Rosa, hoping the woman caught the implication. If she did, she took no notice of it.

"Ursula, come take her satchel and show Señorita Vale to her quarters." Rosa faced Julienne. "I am the housekeeper here. Ursula is the upstairs maid. I have been taking care of the child, too."

"Please, call me by my first name, Rosa." Julienne offered her hand. Rosa ignored it. "So nice to meet you. Where's Alissa?"

"Napping. You will meet her when the captain wishes it and not before."

"Very well. Is Captain LaFlamme here?"

"He is in the tobacco fields. He will deal with you later." Rosa handed Julienne's belongings to Ursula, then without another word, spun on her heels and marched toward the back of the house.

Ursula giggled, drawing Julienne's attention. "She's got no manners."

"Where is she going?"

"Back to the kitchen, I guess. She's the cook here, too. Come along, señorita. Captain Buck says to put you in the Bride's House."

A door closed upstairs, drawing Julienne's attention. A beautiful woman glided toward the stairs and descended them with the grace of a dancer. Her skin reminded Julienne of café au lait, and she admired her glossy black hair and sloe eyes. As the woman came closer, Julienne noticed the delicate lines at the corners of her eyes and mouth, and realized that the beauty was a few years her senior.

"And who is this?" she asked, eyeing Julienne. "Oh, but of course, the little governess sent by the nuns." She extended a limp hand. "I am Señorita Selena. I'm visiting Buck."

"She lives in Cuba," Ursula supplied.

Selena's glance at Ursula was sharp and swift. "When I want your contributions, I shall ask for them." She pulled her hand from Julienne's and surveyed her with a mixture of amusement and disdain as she smoothed the lacy collar of her own coral pink dress. Her gaze slid to the satchel and hatbox Ursula held. "I suppose you should wear some kind of uniform like Ursula's. That outfit you have on simply will not do."

Julienne shrugged. "I shall be most happy to if the captain wishes it."

Selena's smile was meager. "Then I shall tell him at once that you are to wear uniforms. You see . . . little governess . . ." She leaned closer with a conspiratorial air. "I have the captain's ear—among other body parts." Straightening, she laughed at Julienne's high color, then made a shooing motion. "Go on, go on. Take her to the Bride's House, Ursula, and then bring two glasses of sherry and a bowl of fruit to the north veranda for me and Captain Buck."

"Is the captain back from the tobacco fields?" Julienne couldn't disguise the eagerness in her voice.

"Not yet, but soon." Selena sent her another sweeping glance. "He will deal with you . . . eventually." She glided away, her slippers barely making a sound on the marble floor.

Ursula made a scoffing sound under her breath.

"That one! She was Magdalena LaFlamme's cousin and she would love to be the next mistress of Moonspell, but don't let her big talk fool you. She has no claim on Captain Buck. Body parts!" Ursula laughed. "The only times she has her hands on his body parts are in her dreams."

Julienne cleared her throat to ward off a laugh. "I don't think we should be talking like this about our employer. Could you show me to my quarters now?"

Ursula nodded, smiling brightly. "This way. You'll like the Bride's House. It's better than just having a bedroom upstairs. Cesare was the one who talked Captain Buck into putting you in it. 'No need to make a shrine of it,' he told Captain Buck."

"Is it that house built onto one side?"

"That's right. This hallway connects it to the main house. You'll school little Alissa in there, too. It has a bedchamber, a parlor, a private dressing room, and a garden room."

"It sounds quite grand." Julienne thought of the six-by-ten-foot room she'd been living in behind the abbey since her father's death. The only window had been near the ceiling, letting in light but providing no scenery for a girl who had been raised among the greens and golds of the Florida Keys. Once in a while she could smell the ocean, and the salty perfume of it had sent waves of homesickness through her.

Ursula led the way and opened the heavy oak door. She stepped back for Julienne to go inside first.

Julienne smiled at the dark-eyed maid. "Are you from Cuba, too?"

Ursula shook her head. "Mexico, but my parents moved to California when I was a baby. I came to Florida to be with my oldest sister. She worked for a friend of Captain Buck's. That's how he came to hire me."

Julienne was barely listening as she moved slowly around the impeccably appointed parlor. This was a grand lady's room, and Julienne felt like an interloper. A musty odor hung in the air, giving evidence that these rooms hadn't been used in months. Ursula must have smelled it, too, for she set down Julienne's belongings and went to open the French doors that gave access to a small patio partially enclosed by ornate wrought iron.

The wind gusted in, bringing rain with it. Ursula shrieked and shut the doors.

"Aiee! I didn't know it was blowing so outside! Not to worry. These early spring rains last only minutes."

Julienne stared out the door panes, thrilling to the sight of the whitecapped ocean in the distance, the wind-whipped trees, and the slanting curtains of rain. "I love the rain," she whispered to herself, then looked back at Ursula. "Often it's scary, especially when you're out at sea, but I like being scared sometimes." Her heart raced as she gazed at the tumult outside.

"The bedchamber is right through here," Ursula said. "And the dressing room, too. Oh, and through here . . . Señorita?"

Julienne faced her. "Yes?"

She opened another set of French doors. "This is the garden room. It hasn't been used in years. Captain Buck's first wife loved flowers, but his second wife wasn't interested in them."

"I like to garden." Julienne admired the small, sunny room with its many shelves and empty terra-cotta pots. Cane chairs and tables were piled in one corner. "Do you think the captain would mind if I planted some things in here?"

"Of course not, señorita. He'll want you to feel right at home."

"You like him, don't you? Is he a kind man, a fair employer? From what Cesare said, the captain has a rather tragic past." Julienne watched Ursula's reactions to her questions—enthusiastic nods, followed by a sympathetic frown.

"He's a kind man, but his past has been most sad." She made a sweeping gesture. "This place is part of his unhappiness."

"How is that? These quarters look lovely to me."

"The Bride's House was built for the first wife because she didn't want to live with Captain Buck."

"Really?" Julienne surveyed the parlor, confused. "Didn't she love him?"

Ursula closed the doors of the garden room. "I've been told that the marriage was never ... Oh, what's that word?"

Julienne knew the word was "consummated," but she held her tongue, uneasy with the personal nature of the conversation.

Ursula flung up her hands. "Anyway, the poor woman wanted separate rooms, and Captain Buck built this place for her."

"The Bride's House," Julienne said. "So, that's how it got that name."

"Yes, and even the second wife moved in here."

"The second wife, too?" She frowned. "But that marriage produced Alissa."

"It wasn't all that happy either, I guess. Señora LaFlamme was living in these rooms when she died."

"She died in here?"

"No, no." Ursula patted Julienne's arm. "She died out there in the ocean. Come and look at the bedchambers."

"Everything is beyond my wildest dreams," Julienne assured her as she followed Ursula into the bedroom. The talk of death and unhappiness distressed her, but her mood brightened again at the color scheme of white and pale pink. "Oh, this is so ladylike!" She admired the private dressing area with its discreetly curtained chamber pot and washstand. The French-style furniture was so delicate-looking that Julienne was almost afraid to touch it. "It makes me glad I'm a woman," she whispered, awed.

Ursula opened the chiffonier and began placing Julienne's clothes—two blouses, one skirt, a few undergarments—in it. "This is all, señorita?"

Julienne laughed. "That's all. I'm as poor as a church mouse, yet rich in many other ways."

Ursula clucked her tongue. "I thought I was the poorest of poor, but I have more clothes than this!" She flung a hand at the nearly empty chiffonier. "You should ask the captain to buy you some more."

"Oh, no, I couldn't do that. I'll buy some material with my first wages."

"There is a good seamstress in Key West. The captain has Alissa's dresses made by her."

"I'm sure I can't afford to pay a seamstress. I'm not that gifted with a needle and thread, but I'll manage to stitch something together."

"I will help, if you wish." Ursula planted her hands on her hips. "If there is nothing else, I'll leave and see to the sherry and fruit Señorita Selena wanted."

"Yes, please go on with your other work. I'm fine. Thank you so much, Ursula. You've been very kind."

Ursula's smile was one of the happiest Julienne had ever seen. It was nearly impossible not to reciprocate. "I hope you like it here."

The history of the Bride's House invaded her thoughts again. "Ursula, how long has it been since Mrs. LaFlamme's death?"

"She died ten months ago. These rooms haven't been used since then."

"She drowned?"

Ursula's smile faded a little. "He had nothing to do with it. No one will ever make me believe that Captain Buck could be so cruel." She drew in a deep breath and regained her sunny disposition. She fingered a bellpull near the door leading into the corridor. "If you need anything, just pull this."

"Thank you. Do you think the captain will see me today?"

The click of heels sounded in the corridor, and both Julienne and Ursula peered toward the sound. The black-clad Rosa emerged from the deep shadows. Her expression was still unfriendly.

"The captain has returned from the fields. He will see you in an hour in his study. I will come then to take you there. Be ready."

Julienne clamped both hands over her hat, knowing she looked a mess. "An hour? I must hurry and make myself presentable." She caught sight of her reflection in the chiffonier mirror and gasped. "Good heavens! I'll frighten the captain if he sees me looking like this!" She pulled off the pitiful-looking hat, but her disheveled hair wasn't much of an improvement.

"The captain is not interested in how you look, señorita. Your vanity will be lost on him."

Julienne bit her tongue and wrestled her temper under control. "Nevertheless, I'll make no apology for wanting to make a good first impression." She saw Ursula's sassy smile over her shoulder in the mirror, and returned it. "I'll be ready in an hour, Rosa." She was glad when the sour-faced housekeeper left with the grinning maid.

Staring at her reflection, Julienne drew in a deep breath. "Oh, Captain," she whispered, her heart hammering. "I do hope I won't disappoint you."

Chapter 2

By the time Rosa escorted Julienne to the study, the rainstorm had passed and the sky had tossed off its cloud cover. Left alone to await the captain, Julienne took a few deep breaths to allay her nerves. She opened the terrace doors an inch to let in a breeze. The scent of hibiscus and oleander soothed her.

Her hand trembled slightly as she smoothed a few wispy strands of her mahogany-colored hair back from her temples. After giving her hair a thorough brushing, she'd braided it and wound it into tight circles at the back of her head. Severe, she thought, but it made her look older and wiser. She looked like a governess in her dark clothing. Neat and mature. Just the sort of person to supervise a child. She hoped.

She stared at her reflection in one of the shiny swords crossed on the wall behind the desk. Her brown eyes reminded her of a frightened doe's. She stepped back a little to admire the swords, one jewel-handled, the other bearing beautiful scrimshaw on ivory. She touched one blade and found it sharp—almost as if it were still used. She backed away to survey the other weapons lining the walls: guns, pistols, bows and arrows, cutlasses, knives. Julienne released a shaky sigh, puzzled by the show of force.

18

Why anyone would collect weapons was beyond her. Her gaze drifted to the desktop, where an ornate pistol rested amid a few papers and quill pens. Even on his desk, he kept a weapon! Did he feel threatened all the time? Did he think the world was a dark, bad place? Her thoughts circled to the humorless Rosa, the slinky Selena, the tales Cesare and Ursula had told of murder, and finally of the captain laughing up at the growling, snapping sky. What sort of child would Alissa be, surrounded by this bizarre collection of people?

Two flags flanked the desk—the Stars and Stripes and the pirate's Jolly Roger. Julienne pinched one corner of the Jolly Roger and lifted it out to inspect the skull and crossbones. She wondered if the captain's forefathers had kidnapped fair maidens and ravished them, only to return them, ruined, to their grieving families. When she released the flag, it whispered into silken folds.

Movement outside caught her eye and drew her to the terrace doors again. A dark-haired girl of about five or six sat under a coconut tree, not far from the house. Alissa. Julienne admired the girl's frilly white dress and laughed to herself when she noticed that Alissa was sitting in a soggy patch of monkey grass. Just like me, Julienne thought. No matter how many times Papa tried to make me look like a little lady, I managed to end up looking like a ragamuffin.

Alissa's black hair fell in ringlets down her back. She seemed to be studying something in her lap. A picture book perhaps or a new toy, Julienne guessed. She wanted to approach the child, but decided she should wait for the captain to make introductions.

A tall man in a white shirt and black riding breeches strode into view. Knee-high boots lent him a sense of power, and the saber swinging at his side added a dash of danger. In profile, his fea-

tures were striking, and Julienne wished he'd turn
her way so that she could get a better look at his
straight-bridged, bold nose and deeply set eyes.
He'd combed his inky hair straight back from his
wide forehead, and it tumbled over his collar. He
pursed his full-lipped mouth as if he were debat-
ing something. Julienne fancied that he could be as
kind as he could be cruel, for there was something
about this mouth . . . a touch of ruthlessness . . . a
hint of cynicism.

He moved with catlike grace, reminding Julienne of the time she'd seen a wildcat on Key
Largo. It had attracted and frightened her. She'd
known an insane desire to reach out and stroke it,
although she knew it could slice her to ribbons
with one sweep of its powerful claws.

Stopping near Alissa, the man withdrew the saber from its scabbard slowly, methodically.

"What's he doing?" Julienne murmured, then
gasped when he raised the vicious weapon above
his head. "Good Lord!"

She reacted without thinking. She grabbed the
pistol off the desk and wrenched open the doors.
Standing with her legs braced apart, she grasped
the pistol with both hands and aimed it at the
man's head as he began swinging the saber down
toward the innocent child.

"Stop!" she shouted. "Stop, or I'll fill you full of
lead!" Where on earth had she learned that? she
wondered irrationally, even as the man froze the
saber in midswing and turned to glare at her. His
eyes glinted like the curved blade in his hand. "I
swear it!" Julienne added, just in case he didn't
believe her. "I'll kill you dead. Now, drop your
weapon or pay the consequences." She was having
difficulty keeping the pistol pointed at him, and
she wished that her aim were as steady as her
voice.

The child screamed, scrambled to her feet, and threw her arms around the brute's legs.

"Don't kill my papa!" she begged, then broke into heartrending sobs as she pressed her face against his muscled thigh.

Papa? Julienne lowered the pistol, inch by inch. The man sheathed his weapon and gathered the crying child into his arms.

"Cap ..." Julienne swallowed and tried again. "Captain Buccaneer LaFlamme?"

"In the flesh." He patted the back of the child's head. "There, there, Alissa. Stop your hysterics."

"Don't hurt me, Papa!"

Frowning, he inched back his head to look at his daughter's tearstained face. "Now, why would I hurt you? When have I ever laid a hand on you?"

She sobbed more loudly and hid her face in the curve of his neck. Her little hands clutched at his hair. He swung his disarming gaze to Julienne. She saw that his eyes were gunmetal gray and that he was devilishly handsome.

"You must be the governess."

"Yes, Captain." For some reason she couldn't fathom, she curtsied, and garnered a scowl from him. "I ... I thought you were going to harm her and I ..." Her gaze drifted to where Alissa had been sitting, and she felt like a fool when she saw the coconut lying there. "Oh, I see the nut now. You were going to chop it open for her."

"And you were going to shoot me for it," he added.

"No," she scoffed. "I wouldn't have *really* shot you. I—I—"

"I know you wouldn't have. That pistol isn't loaded." He shifted the child to a more comfortable perch against his left hip and noticed that the back of Alissa's dress was grass-stained and damp. "Rosa isn't going to be happy with you,

Lissa. You've soiled this pretty frock Selena gave you."

"I don't care." Alissa wiped her runny nose on the puffed sleeve.

Julienne laughed softly, but quickly sobered when Buccaneer's hard glare slammed into her. She retreated into the study as he advanced on her. Without looking, Julienne dropped the pistol onto his desk. The child continued to sob brokenly.

"Alissa LaFlamme," he said, exasperated, and the child's face crumpled again.

Realizing she was close to being shipped back to St. Augustine, Julienne focused her full attention on the distraught child.

"But this can't be Alissa LaFlamme."

"It can, and she is. Alissa, stop your bawling, please." He jiggled her a little, but her sobs didn't abate.

"Captain, I'm confused," Julienne said. "You told me that your daughter has the courage of ten pirates and the beauty of twenty fairy princesses. While she is a beauty, to be sure, where's this courage you bragged about?"

Buccaneer LaFlamme looked at her as if she'd lost her mind, but Alissa stopped crying and raised her head from her father's shoulder.

"You see, Captain, I came here to be governess because I am quite timid and would like to be brave. Your description of Alissa made me hopeful that she could teach me courage while I taught her reading, writing, and her numbers."

Alissa wiped tears from her cheeks and looked at her father. "Did you tell her I was b-brave like ten pirates, Papa?"

For a moment, Julienne thought he'd deny it, but then he must have noticed the pleasure radiating from his daughter's eyes, for he nodded.

"Now that I think about it," Julienne continued, "she did display courage. When I threatened you, she came to your defense. She shielded you from me and ordered me not to shoot." Julienne smiled at the cherub-faced child. "You were very brave indeed. I'm impressed." She slid a finger down Alissa's damp, dimpled cheek. "My name is Julienne. I'm happy to make your acquaintance."

"Hello." Alissa trained her big, silvery gray eyes on her father again. "Papa, did you say I was pretty like ten princesses?"

He smiled, and Julienne decided she'd been wrong. His mouth held no trace of cruelty. "I believe it was twenty fairy princesses, Lissa. Ten isn't adequate."

Alissa wrinkled her button nose and giggled, then she grew shy and pressed her face against his neck again. She mumbled something Julienne couldn't understand.

"Sleepy, are you," Buccaneer said. "It's past your nap time, I suppose." He eyed Julienne for a moment, and she felt as if he were sizing her up. "You may go back to you quarters now. I'll speak with you later." He smoothed his daughter's hair back from her face. "Let's go to your room, Lissa, and I'll read you a story. We haven't done that in a long time, have we?"

Alissa ran a hand up her nose. "You're always too busy, Papa. You don't like me anymore."

"What? Don't talk like that."

Alissa cowered from him. "I'm sorry. Don't get mad." The child looked pleadingly at Julienne. "You come, too."

"Not just now," Buccaneer said, turning away. "There will be plenty of time for you and the governess to be together." He swung back to Julienne, his gaze moving from her hair to the tips of her shoes. "The correspondence said you were twenty."

"That's right."

"Then why are you dressed like that?"

She glanced down at her dark clothing. "Like what, Captain?"

"Like a matron or a grieving widow."

"I don't have many clothes. Señorita Selena said I was to wear uniforms."

"Is that so?" He lowered his brows over his deeply set eyes. "What shall I call you?"

"Julienne will be fine, Captain."

He opened the study door and waited for her to go ahead of him, then he shut it with authority. "Can you find your way back to the Bride's House, Julienne?"

He didn't just say her name, he caressed it with his lips and tongue. Julienne had to take a deep breath before she could trust her voice. "Yes, I believe I—"

"Good." Abruptly he pivoted. Alissa waved to Julienne over his broad shoulder.

Julienne waved back, then stared at the study door, tempted to go back inside just to spite him. No, she told herself firmly. You've acted childishly enough for one day. Her face grew warm as she recalled how ridiculous she must have looked holding a gun on him. So much for making a good first impression. She shrugged. At least she'd calmed the child and saved herself from being asked to pack her bag before she'd even spent one night on Pirate's Key. She shuddered to think what Mother Superior would have said if that had happened. After all, her last words of advice to Julienne had been, "Think before you act, dear one. The Lord placed your brain above your eyes for a reason."

Wandering along the hall, Julienne admired a landscape painting by a French artist, and then another, this one depicting a shipwreck. It was marvelous to be in a real home again after ten years of living in tight quarters. The one she'd shared with her father had been little more than a hut, but it had been a cozy nest. She wondered if it still stood in the clearing on Key Largo and if another child looked out the back window and built castles in the air.

She noticed that a door stood ajar. Peeking in, she could see a crystal vase full of white and mauve peonies sitting on a piecrust table, and she inched closer until she was over the threshold. She found herself in a parlor, its walls covered in creamy, tufted leather. Julienne's shoes made no sound on the plush wool rug as she moved to the center of the room, drawn by a portrait hanging above the fireplace.

It was more than the striking beauty of the woman in the portrait that mesmerized Julienne. There seemed to be the crackle of fire in her eyes—eyes as green and mysterious as a cat's. Her inky black hair lay in waves upon her head and down her back. A rosette bloomed behind her ear, holding her glossy black hair away from the side of her face. The rosette was the exact same shade as the red dress that hugged her every curve down to where her toes peeked out from under the lacy flounce. It was a Spanish-style dress, tight-fitting with a scooped back and a black lace train pooling behind her. A necklace of rubies, onyx, and emeralds dangled from her fingers.

The woman's Spanish heritage was evident in her dark coloring, high cheekbones, and seductive posture. A pair of castanets lay near her bare feet. Julienne could swear she could hear them clicking. Then they stopped. Not castanets, footsteps! Julienne whirled to find Rosa standing behind her.

"I was on my way back to the Bride's House and I saw this portrait and I thought . . ." She took a breath and scolded herself for allowing Rosa to intimidate her. "Who is that?"

Rosa's face softened and her frown actually disappeared. "Magdalena LaFlamme, the captain's one and only love."

"Magdalena was his second wife," Julienne said.

"Second wife, but first in his heart," Rosa stated, the frown returning. "He will never love another as he loved Magdalena. Alissa is her daughter."

Julienne examined the portrait again. "Yes, I can see some resemblance."

"Some? Alissa is her image, her twin!"

Julienne recalled the child's wide, gray eyes and curvy-lipped mouth. Julienne wished her first meeting with the captain hadn't been so unorthodox so that she would have had time to really look at him. Her lasting impressions were of a tall, darkly handsome man with a voice that reminded her of a distant foghorn—husky, deep, comforting. "Alissa resembles her father, too."

"Speaking of which . . ." Rosa's tone sharpened. "Captain Buck has left orders for you to remain in your quarters. He'll speak to you after breakfast tomorrow. I will bring you a dinner tray later."

Julienne sighed. "Very well. Did he tell you about my misunderstanding? You see, I saw him raise his saber over—"

"He told me that you are a high-strung young woman. I have no doubt that he is reconsidering his decision to hire you."

Julienne pressed her fists just under her thudding heart. "Oh, dear. I . . . It was a silly mistake. I'm quite capable of taking care of his child."

"You can tell him that tomorrow morning. Now I will take you back to your quarters."

Julienne followed behind the stiff-backed housekeeper, her heart beating dully in her chest, her spirits drooping around her like broken wings. Why couldn't the captain have seen the absurdity in the situation? The man obviously had not one shred of humor in his body. For no reason other than that, she'd be good for Alissa. The poor child was stuck in this neglected house full of grumpy people.

Rosa opened the door to the Bride's House. "You stay in here until Captain Buck sends for you. If you need anything before I bring in your dinner tray, use the bellpull."

Julienne narrowed her eyes at the bossy woman. "Captain's orders?"

"*My* orders," Rosa corrected with a haughty lift of her chin. "You are not a guest here, señorita. You have been hired to work at Moonspell, and I am mistress over the workers in this house." She stared hard at Julienne. "You remain here unless you are sent for by the captain." Then she shut the door in Julienne's face.

Hours later Julienne sat on the terrace outside the Bride's House and admired the seascape. She had already fallen in love with the place, and she'd hate to leave it. When she saw the captain again, she'd simply have to put on her best face. She could work wonders for Alissa and this household if he'd only give her a chance.

She heard a door close inside the Bride's House and reluctantly left her ocean lookout to go inside. No one was there, but a tray had been left on a table between two wing chairs. Julienne examined the domed plate, glass, and carafe of water. She lifted the silver lid, and her throat tightened. The meal was all white and did nothing to entice her. Steamed rice, a couple of sprigs of cauliflower, paste gravy, and a paper-thin slice of chicken breast that looked as dry as parchment had been dumped—not arranged—on the plate.

"They call this dinner around here?" she said, her glance straying to the chunk of bread resting on top of the gravy. Green flecked the edges. "Mold!" Julienne lifted the bread, saw the green growth on the underside, and dropped the crusty mess back into the sticky gravy. "I won't be treated like this." She wiped crumbs from her hands as she marched toward the door. Nor will I remain in here as if I'm an unruly child either, she thought.

With a lift of her chin, she opened the heavy door, half expecting a massive ogre to block her path, but no one stood guard. Julienne moved along the corridor and through a maze of rooms, one as spacious as the next, but all as quiet as tombs.

Finally she heard a snatch of conversation and followed the sounds. They grew stronger until she could identify Selena's sultry purr and Cesare's wheezing laugh. Julienne approached a carved archway and peeked into the brightly lighted dining room, dominated by a long cherrywood table. Cesare sat to the right and raised his wineglass. Alissa sat at one end of the table, her back to Julienne. Two huge, leather-bound volumes stacked in the chair seat boosted Alissa to table level. Selena, sitting on the left, laughed, her glossy hair spilling down her bare back. Her dress, Julienne noted, was expensive and meant to attract the masculine eye with its daring dips, both back and front. Julienne resisted the urge to glance self-consciously at her own breasts, which were small and high compared to Selena's lush, full ones.

Instead, her gaze was drawn to the man holding court at the head of the table. Buccaneer relaxed in the big chair that his tall, wide frame filled easily. He smiled at Cesare and lifted his wineglass for a long sip. His throat flexed and his long, square-tipped fingers caressed the fragile goblet with controlled strength. When he set the glass back down, his lower lip glistened. Julienne had a sudden urge to lick the leftover wine from it. He brought up a linen napkin to dab at his mouth, thus removing the temptation.

His black shirt had long, voluminous sleeves, and silver disks festooned his black vest, joining the two sides. Candlelight shimmered over his midnight hair, reminding Julienne of moonlight on ocean waves. His penetrating gaze suddenly located her, and she felt her heart drop like a stone to her feet, then soar up again to lodge in her throat.

"Look who has joined us," he said, breaking into Cesare's comment about wine tasting better straight from the barrel. "You must be feeling better."

Julienne stepped into the room, his attractive voice sailing a shiver down her spine. "P-Pardon me?"

He tented his fingers and stared at her over the tips. "Rosa said you requested dinner be brought to your room because you were feeling under the weather. Have you decided to join us, after all?"

Rosa had lied! Julienne smothered an urge to tattle on the devious housekeeper, and managed to hold her tongue. Just then, Rosa whisked through a swinging door into the dining room. She held a platter heaped with steaming roasted chicken and wild rice. The aroma alone made Julienne's knees weaken and her stomach growl. The housekeeper stopped in her tracks and glared at Julienne.

"You are supposed to be in your room, señorita. Go back there at once!"

Anger clamped down hard, and Julienne matched Rosa glare for glare. "I won't! I'm tired of being shut up in there like some . . . some prisoner!"

Buccaneer lounged back in his chair. "Rosa, set another place for the governess." His tone was lazy, but held authority. He nodded past Cesare. "Over there, next to Cesare, please."

Cesare rose and helped Julienne into her chair. "I'm glad to see you have recovered from your seasickness."

Seasickness? Julienne flashed Rosa an annoyed frown. Enough was enough! "I have never been seasick in my life," she stated. "And I feel as frisky as a filly, thank you very much."

"Her hair makes one think of a horse, as well," Selena noted.

Running her hand over the top of her head, Julienne wished she hadn't gathered her hair into a long tail and tied it with an old dress sash. She felt herself color with self-consciousness and figured her skin looked like a boiled lobster. Why must Selena be such a spitting cat? She treated her as a competitor, but for what were they competing?

"I . . . I loosened my hair because I didn't think I'd be sitting down to dinner with anyone . . ." Julienne's feeble excuse died when her gaze locked with Buccaneer's. A tremble raced through her, and she couldn't help but question the powerful emotions he seemed to arouse in her. The heat in her face increased. Never had she felt so inadequate, so unsure of herself. His gray eyes seemed to be magnets, pulling her, holding her so tightly, she could hardly breathe.

"Actually, I prefer her hair this way." Mercifully he shifted his gaze to Rosa. "You may serve dinner now." He draped the linen napkin across his lap. "Julienne, we dress casually for our meals at Moonspell, and there's no required hairstyle that I'm aware of." He glanced sideways at Selena, a smile hovering at the corners of his mouth.

"Why is she taking meals with us? She's house help, Buck, not a guest."

"It's important that she spend time with Alissa and teach her correct manners."

"I'll teach her manners."

The smile tipped up one corner of his mouth. "You possess manners, Selena? Wherever have you been hiding them?"

Cesare chuckled, and it was all Julienne could

do not to laugh aloud. Selena batted a hand and her lashes at Buccaneer.

"Stop your teasing, Buck. I'll take Alissa under my wing and make a lady of her."

"No need. I've hired Julienne for that."

Julienne went limp with relief. So he wasn't going to dismiss her, after all! Another of Rosa's lies, she deduced. She wouldn't believe anything else the housekeeper said. That should make her life easier at Moonspell. For some reason the housekeeper had decided not to like her. Mother Superior would probably tell her to treat Rosa with constant good cheer and kindness, but Julienne thought it would be prudent to avoid the housekeeper whenever possible. She began by ignoring her when Rosa served her portions of the succulent chicken and moist rice.

"*This* meal looks very appealing," Julienne noted, feeling Rosa's hateful frown.

"By the way, you said earlier that you have few clothes," Buccaneer said.

"Yes, Captain," Julienne confirmed. "I'm afraid my wardrobe is meager. I'll buy some fabric with my first wages. Ursula said she'd help me make a few skirts and shirtwaists."

He waved a fork, dismissing the plan. "I'll have some bolts of fabric sent to you in a few days."

"What about the uniforms?" Selena persisted. "Black dresses with white aprons . . ."

"She's not a maid, Selena." His tone brooked no further argument. "I told Cesare about you almost shooting me earlier, Julienne. He said it was a pity the pistol wasn't loaded."

Cesare drained his wineglass. "Sometimes a plug of lead strengthens a man's character. Pass the wine, Buck."

"This is quality, not sour mash." Buccaneer handed over the carafe. "Go easy, my friend."

"You wound me, Buck. I mean to be a gentleman and fill Julienne's glass, and you accuse me of gluttony!"

"No, please." Julienne covered the goblet with her hand. "I really shouldn't ..." She looked at Buccaneer. "Should I?" His teasing smile made her dizzy-headed for a moment.

"Even Jesus drank wine, mam'selle."

The foreign word fell off his tongue naturally, making Julienne more aware of his heritage. He might be surrounded by Cubans, but he was French, through and through. He even spoke with a slight French accent. Julienne removed her hand from the goblet. "So he did," she conceded, and Cesare poured the pale burgundy into the sparkling goblet.

Before Cesare set down the carafe, he half filled his own glass, ignoring Buccaneer's chiding regard. Julienne unfolded her dinner napkin and placed it on her lap, mindful of Alissa's intense scrutiny. The child watched her every move, and Julienne knew that she was forming an opinion of her. It was important in these first few days to earn the child's trust. Minding her manners, Julienne tasted the chicken and rice. Where the earlier plate of food had looked bland, this meal burst with seasonings and spices, and she had to force herself not to give Alissa a bad impression by gobbling her food.

She reached for the wineglass and filled her mouth with the sweet liquid. It warmed her all the way down. She didn't realize she was smiling until she heard Buccaneer chuckle. Even his laughter caused her heart to trip-hammer. Was there nothing about him that didn't trigger a reaction in her?

"Good, isn't it?" he asked, and she nodded. "It's older than you. We opened a special bottle tonight to celebrate Cesare's news."

"News of what?" Julienne asked Cesare.

"We heard today that my other daughter back in Cuba is engaged."

"Congratulations, Cesare," Julienne said. " 'Other' daughter, you say?"

"*Sí*, I am papa to six children. Four sons and two daughters." He lifted his glass and smiled across the table. "Selena is my youngest daughter."

Julienne released a sound of surprise. "I didn't know you were related." She digested this tidbit. Cesare was Magdalena's uncle! He must believe wholly in the captain's integrity, she thought, to work for him even as others gossiped that Buccaneer had murdered Cesare's niece.

Throughout the meal, they chatted about the young man who would soon be Cesare's son-in-law. While Buccaneer conversed with the others, Julienne admired his features, his voice, his gestures. Everything. Sister Mary Constance would say that she was "besotted," and perhaps she'd be right, Julienne admitted.

He had an exotic face, sensual in every detail from his wide forehead and his heavy brows to his square jaw, shadowed with the emerging stubble of beard. His eyes were almond-shaped and hooded, framed with thick, straight lashes. And then there was his mouth. That generous, expressive mouth. Every time she looked at it, something corkscrewed in her stomach and shameful questions bombarded her. How would his lips feel on her skin? Were they soft? Would they taste as sweet as this wine? How many women had swooned when touched by them? Had Selena known the pleasure of his kiss?

Julienne closed her eyes against the pounding questions and forced herself to gain control of her burgeoning fantasies. Why was she so obsessed with kissing? She tried to recall the last time she'd received one, but couldn't.

She opened her eyes and found Alissa regarding her intently. Sensing that the child craved attention, Julienne plucked the linen napkin from Alissa's lap. Deftly she folded and twisted and tucked the square of material as Sister Mary Constance had taught her. When she was finished, she'd fashioned a swan, which she set in front of Alissa.

"Do you know what that is?" Julienne asked.

"A bird!" Alissa picked it up gingerly as if it were made of spun glass.

"Not just any bird. It's a swan. Have you ever seen one?"

Alissa shook her head.

"They're white with long, beautiful necks. They glide on the water so smoothly, so gracefully, that one can't help but think of ballet dancers. Have you ever been to the ballet?"

"I'm afraid that growing up in the isolation of the Keys has deprived my daughter of many things," Buccaneer said. "Ballet being one of them."

"Captain, you're talking to a child of the Keys, and I don't feel deprived at all. My father taught me to appreciate the arts. He told me about ballet, opera, theater, literature, sculpture, paintings. I'll be most happy to teach Alissa what I know."

"Your father was a learned man? Where did he receive his education?" Buccaneer sat forward and his shirt gaped open at the neck to reveal a patch of dark, curling hair.

"From books, I suppose." She stared at her plate, finding it difficult to look at Buccaneer and keep her mind on the conversation. "He was a dreamer and a lover of all beautiful things. I think he might have seen an opera or ballet once, because he described them in such detail ..." She shrugged. "But maybe not. He had such a way with words that he could make you believe he'd traveled around the world and seen everything under the sun."

"What happened to him?" Buccaneer asked.

"He died in his sleep. His heart gave out, I think."

"I don't think it's wise to tell a child tall tales," Selena said. "What good will that do? Children have enough trouble keeping their imaginations under control without *encouraging* them to make things up."

Julienne squared her shoulders, accepting the other woman's implied challenge. "I beg to differ, Señorita Selena. I believe an imagination is an asset. I know that the trips I've taken in my mind have entertained me during many a lonely night."

The sheen in Selena's eyes made Julienne want to take back that last divulgence, but before Selena could stick in a verbal knife, Buccaneer noisily pushed back his chair.

"Cesare, let's have a smoke on the terrace." He stood and offered his hand to Selena. "Would you care to join us, or will you object to the aroma of our cigars?"

"I love the smell of cigar smoke, and you know it," Selena said, slipping her hand in his.

"Perhaps you could take Alissa to her room and prepare her for bed, Julienne," Buccaneer suggested.

"Of course, Captain."

They filed out, leaving her alone with her new charge. Julienne released a long sigh and raised her hands to her flushed cheeks. Goodness, the man certainly could cast a spell over an unsuspecting heart!

"Lady?" Alissa tugged on her sleeve to get her attention. "What's your name again?"

"Julienne."

"Julienne, Papa says you got spanked."

"Spanked?" Julienne stared at the child, trying to comprehend. "He said I was *spanked*?"

"Uh-huh. He said you got lots of spanked."

Julienne mulled this over. "Are you sure he didn't say I had lots of *spunk?*"

Alissa's eyes widened. "That's it! He said you got spunked."

"Did he now?" Julienne enjoyed the compliment for a few moments before offering Alissa her hand. "Come along, ladybug. Will you give me directions to your room?"

"Uh-huh, but I want my bird first!"

Julienne let Alissa pick it up. "It's a swan, remember? During your bath, we'll see if it can swim." She captured Alissa's free hand, and as she turned on her heel, she caught a glimpse of Rosa's face in the crack of the swinging door. Julienne left the dining room without looking back, having endured enough of Rosa's fierce frowns for one day.

Chapter 3

S itting in bed, Julienne looked around the strange room and willed sleep to come.

It eluded her.

"Oh, bother!" She flung off the covers and reached for her overwrap. What she needed was a book, she told herself. A novel, preferably. She'd always had a stack of books in her abbey room, and it had become her habit to read nightly until her eyes refused to remain open.

The new surroundings coupled with her nervous agitation over embarking on her duties tomorrow had succeeded in keeping her wide-awake. If she was to rise early as was expected, she'd have to get some sleep tonight.

She padded barefoot to the big door, holding a lamp aloft. Releasing the bolt, she pushed it open and stumbled into the corridor. Pale moonlight shone ahead of her, and she hurried toward it. She tried to remember the route to the parlor where she'd seen a few bookshelves full of leather-bound volumes. The study and adjoining library were the captain's private rooms, Ursula had told her earlier.

Finding the front parlor easily, she congratulated herself as she moved toward the bookshelves to scan the titles. The leather-covered walls lent the room a pungent perfume. She selected a volume of poetry and a novel about high-sea adventure, then paused to examine the portrait of Magdalena LaFlamme again. The rich swirls of oil paint and the skill of the artist entranced her. Of course, she'd heard it said that an artist was only as good as his subject, and Magdalena was certainly a perfect model. Her sparkling eyes and curvy figure were pure inspiration. The Lord was certainly in a generous mood when He created her, Julienne thought.

Something moved in a far corner of the room. Whirling, she saw a form rise from a wing chair. She plastered a hand over her mouth to catch the scream before it could rend the air.

"Admiring Maggie the Magnificent, I see."

Her momentary fright dissipated, and she removed her hand from her mouth. "Captain, you scared ten years off me!"

He moved forward into the light. The laces on the front of his shirt were loose to expose most of his chest. Dark hair swirled over dark skin. Power emanated from him. As he approached her, Julienne felt as if the room shrank. He loomed before her, and she caught his scent—woodsy, mixed with tobacco. His mussed hair fell across his forehead. She realized her breathing had grown shallow and she wondered if she'd ever be able to behave normally around him.

"What have you got there?"

She followed his gaze to the books in her hand. "I hope you don't mind. I'm a passionate reader and I . . . well, I couldn't seem to fall asleep."

"Passionate, you say?" He stopped scant inches from her to take the books from her unresisting fingers. His felt warm, even hot, and slightly callused. He examined the books, then his gaze lifted, flicking over her like a hungry flame. "Passion." His lips stroked the word. "What does a girl raised by nuns know of that, I wonder?" He handed the books back to her, and she was careful not to touch him, because every time she did, he sent a tingle through her like a static charge. He looked up at the painting. "She knew all about passion. It ruled her."

"You must miss her terribly."

His smile lifted only one corner of his mouth. "Terribly. Yes, that's a good word for it."

Julienne swallowed, her throat suddenly tight with nerves. She found it hard not to stare at him as she would a piece of art. She made herself look at the painting again. "Was she a dancer? The castanets suggest—"

"They're part of her heritage."

"And the necklace she's holding?"

"A wedding present using the colors of Maggie. Black for her hair, red for her lips and fiery spirit, green for her eyes. When I proposed marriage, I vowed to replace her castanets with jewels."

Julienne smiled, thinking it was the most romantic story she'd ever heard, but surprised that he could be sentimental. He clasped his powerful hands behind him and moved closer to the portrait.

"Maggie was a she-devil, a Siren luring men to the rocky shores of her heart." His voice, like rough velvet, tugged at the heart.

While his poetry enchanted Julienne, his description also held a tinge of bitterness. She wasn't sure he meant to flatter his former wife. But then, maybe he liked difficult women. Perhaps, to his mind, a she-devil was the highest form of flattery.

He turned and leaned back against the mantel, his lazy virility filling her senses again. "So it's been ten years since you've been in the keys. Glad to be back?"

She nodded. "This afternoon I was afraid you were going to send me back to the abbey."

"I decided to give you the benefit of the doubt.

My daughter needs another woman in her life. Rosa tries, but she's too strict, and I'm not pleased with the way Alissa is acting. She . . ." He glanced away, and confusion marred his features. "Sometimes she acts as if she's afraid of me."

"I noticed that."

"I swear I've given her no reason to be afraid."

"Losing her mother is hard on any child, Captain. Perhaps she isn't afraid of you, but of losing you, too. I often worried that my father would be taken from me. He was all I had, and I couldn't imagine life without him. I'm sure Alissa will grow out of this behavior."

"I hope you're right. So the nuns took you in after your father died?"

"I was placed in the St. Augustine orphanage. When I was old enough to leave, the Sisters allowed me to stay in a room behind the abbey. I cleaned the church and helped with the orphans for my board." She moved aimlessly to a side table and placed the lamp there, all the while aware of his keen regard. "Were you asleep here in the dark?"

"No. Just thinking."

"I saw you riding along the beach right before the storm." She chanced a quick look. His eyes glittered in the feeble light cast by the lantern. "I used to ride like that—flat out—on Key Largo. I'd come home with flecks of blood on my cheeks and arms from being scratched by branches and thickets. Papa would scold me and tell me I should ride like a lady instead of a heathen."

"We have several horses stabled here, and you're free to ride whenever you want."

"May I, really?"

"Of course." He shrugged one shoulder. "Bareback, if you wish."

She laughed. "It's been so long since I've been

astride a pony, I'd better take it slow. I'm not a girl anymore."

He quirked an eyebrow, and his eyes sparkled with interest. "No. You're a woman. I bet you could handle a spirited mount." He stepped closer. Shadow and light played across his face, and Julienne's pulses quickened. "You told my daughter that you're timid, but I think not. Just in coming here, you've proven your courage."

Tension built within her until she found it hard to breathe. "I was most happy to come here, Captain. I need the work and I love the keys."

"Didn't the Sisters tell you about me? Surely you've heard the rumors that swirl about me like a black fog."

"I . . . don't listen to idle gossip, Captain."

"How do you know it's idle? Who's to say it's not true?" His husky voice slipped over her like a silken shroud. She warded off a shiver as he bent closer until his lips grazed the top of her ear. "They say I murdered both my wives in cold blood."

A nervous twitter rattled from her throat as she moved to avoid him, but he grabbed her upper arm to keep her in place. His hand was so warm, she thought his skin would burn hers, and his grip was just short of painful. She tried not to wince or show fear, but she thought he might have seen a flicker of it in her eyes, because his fingers loosened ever so slightly on her arm.

"That's silliness, Captain. I heard that your wives drowned at sea." She was proud of herself for not stuttering.

"One did, yes. The other was killed and then dropped in the ocean." He widened his eyes, mocking her. "Didn't anyone tell you about that? Perhaps my first wife didn't drown, after all. Perhaps she was killed and then dumped in the bay. Maggie washed up on the coral reefs in the same place Isabelle was found. It would be wise of you to stay out of my reach. A monster never knows his own strength until it's too late."

She wrenched free of him. Although her heart pounded in her breast, Julienne managed to retrieve the lamp and move with a measure of poise toward the doorway. "I'm not afraid of you, Captain. I won't listen to this nonsense."

"Yes, you will!" His voice took on a hard edge that stilled her protests. He loomed before her, the width of his shoulders blocking out the light. His eyes glittered with dark fire. "I would rather you hear this from me than from someone else. Ursula is a fine housemaid, but her tongue flaps on both ends." He noticed something in her expression and his gaze sharpened. "I see she's already been talking."

"She believes in your innocence, Captain."

"She's in the minority. Most think I regretted marrying my first wife, so I killed her."

"What really happened to her, Captain?"

He sighed wearily and ran a hand through the inky waves of his hair. "I believe she killed herself. She walked into the ocean to escape me and our marriage. So, in a way, I was responsible for her death."

Julienne stared at him, wanting to console him, but not knowing how or if she should. He dropped his head forward, and the only sound in the room was the ticking of the mantel clock. When he looked at her again, his expressive eyes shimmered like starlight.

"Isabelle was a frail thing, you see. So unhappy. She wanted to be a nun, but her father wouldn't hear of it. Our marriage was arranged. Actually, she would have made a devoted nun. Forcing her to marry was like a death blow to her. No matter how hard I tried to make her feel at home here, she resisted. I built the Bride's House so that she'd have private quarters. It wasn't enough. I had only to walk into the room and she'd grow as pale as a ghost and shiver all over. She made me feel like a demon."

"Poor dear."

"Me or her?" he asked, his tone sardonic.

"Both, I suppose. You were both unhappy. How old were you when you married her?"

"Barely seventeen. She was fifteen."

"Her father arranged the marriage?"

"Both of our fathers arranged it. Her father was a shipbuilder. For a wedding present, he gave us a sloop. The *Treasure Chest*. I still have it. Isabelle's father was having trouble finding her a suitor. My father and his father before him saw marriage as another form of commerce. Love never had anything to do with it. He offered me as a husband if Isabelle's father would build him a sloop to his liking. They shook on it. Isabelle and I were but pawns in their business deal. Isabelle's father married her off, and my father got a beautiful sloop."

"How long were you married?"

"A few weeks shy of a year."

"And then you met your second wife?" Julienne looked from him to the portrait. "Magdalena."

"Yes, I met Maggie a few years later."

"What happened to her, Captain? Was she shot or . . . ?"

"She was strangled and thrown into the ocean. After her death, I became the prime suspect. She'd moved into the Bride's House months before her death."

"Why did she do that?"

He cut his gaze at her. "Perhaps I *am* a monster. Maybe it was a mistake for you to come here, mam'selle. You know, women don't leave Moonspell—alive."

She had the impression that he was testing her mettle. She looked him squarely in the eyes.

"Lucky for you, Captain, I'm not fainthearted or superstitious."

He thrust his face close to hers; so close that she could feel his breath and see the true colors of his eyes, gray with black pupils and silver rings around the irises. Beautiful, seductive eyes, she thought. Strange, disturbing eyes. Contradictions. The man thrived on them. He towered over her. A pulse throbbed below his left ear. His breath wafted over her face again, and she smelled liquor on it. Had he been doing more than thinking here in the dark? How much had he had to drink?

"I wonder how brave you are, little orphan girl. Would you sport with the devil?" He ran a finger-tip down the side of her face, sending goose bumps skittering across her flesh. That odd, spiral-ing feeling entered her stomach again and sailed down between her thighs. She gasped, gripped by a sugary weakness, and stumbled backward to break free of his potent spell. His smile was more of a taunt.

"I'm not afraid of you," she whispered. Did her voice shake? Did he notice? Could he detect the tremble in her knees? "I hope you're not disap-pointed."

"Not afraid?" His voice boomed and he stamped one boot. It sounded like a gunshot.

Julienne swallowed a shriek and dashed from the room, but not before she heard his cruel laugh-ter and his taunting "Where's your courage now, little orphan!"

Forcing herself to stop, Julienne stood in the cor-ridor until she had command of herself again. She would not leave him thinking he'd humiliated her! Resolutely she turned and went back to the parlor. He was standing in front of the portrait again, and he raised a glass of liquor in a mock toast.

"Congratulations, Maggie. It appears that you still rule the monster."

Julienne hesitated, vacillating between tiptoeing back to her quarters or confronting him again. Finally her stubborn streak won out.

"Captain."

He spun around, and whiskey sloshed over the sides of the glass. Frowning, he switched the glass to his other hand and shook off amber droplets.

"What now? I thought you'd run off to bed like a good little girl."

"I just wanted to say that I know you're drunk and I hope you don't display such behavior in front of Alissa. If you do, I have no doubt why she cowers before you."

Surprise flitted across his face, followed by dark anger. He lowered his brows and stared at her from beneath them. "I am not drunk, little governess, and when I want your opinion, I will ask for it!" He shook his dripping hand again. "Now, get out and leave me be!"

"With pleasure, Captain," Julienne rejoined, whirling away from his glowering visage. She used every scrap of her courage to walk sedately from the room.

She made two wrong turns before finding her way back to the Bride's House, but she took heart that she was navigating better and would know every nook and cranny of Moonspell within a couple of days. While it was large, its design wasn't intricate. When she'd put Alissa to bed earlier, she'd gotten a peek at the upstairs. Alissa had pointed out the captain's quarters at the south end. The door to his private sanctum had an etching of a ship's anchor in it. Alissa's room was next to his.

Downstairs contained a front and back parlor, sun-room, kitchen, pantry, dining room, study, and library. The Bride's House was connected to the back parlor by a short hall. Wall sconces defied the darkness, but made Julienne feel uneasy, too, because they were in the shape of grinning gargoyles, peering down from ledges with candles clutched in their claws. While she welcomed the light, she didn't appreciate the macabre touch. Stepping into her quarters, she felt a sense of security. In this brooding place, these rooms were hers. All hers. Perhaps Isabelle and Magdalena had felt the same.

Julienne removed her overwrap, folded it, and placed it in the chiffonier drawer. She paused to rearrange her few articles of clothing, and something pricked the palm of her hand. Gasping, she held her hand to the lamplight and removed a thorn. Now, where had that come from? She shook out the clothes, and a twig from a rosebush fell out.

Rosa, she thought, then felt guilty for jumping to that conclusion, but the thought persisted. Rosa did this, an inner voice repeated, and Julienne's heart concurred. Why did the housekeeper resent her arrival? And why play pranks on her? Was this her way of showing that Rosa had thorns, too?

Julienne threw the thorny twig outside and doused her hand in a basin. Her blood appeared as pink threads in the water. Had Rosa resented the other women who had claimed the Bride's House? Not Maggie, she thought. Rosa had obviously adored Maggie. But what of Isabelle? Had Rosa made Isabelle unhappy? And did the captain condone his housekeeper's evil tricks?

She dried her hands and went to the French doors. Crossing the threshold, she gloried in the cool, rain-freshened breeze and the canopy of glittering stars. The ocean murmured sweet nothings to her. Julienne closed her eyes and saw the captain—so tall and dark and dangerously handsome. Did his heart hammer in his chest when she drew near? Did his mouth go dry and his throat constrict when she looked into his eyes? Did he ache to touch her hair, her lips, her cheek?

She drew a deep, shaky breath and released a smile with it. Oh, these wonderful, scary feelings! Was this love or lust? All she knew was that she felt alive when she was around Captain LaFlamme. Even when he was slightly drunk and rude. Even when his gray eyes turned cold as stone. Even when his mouth twisted with scorn. There wasn't a time when he didn't stimulate every fiber of her being. He charged her atmosphere.

Thunder rumbled, and Julienne opened her eyes. Stars winked at her. The storm must be distant, she thought, then wondered if it was going away or approaching. She went back inside. Was the captain asleep or was he listening to the storm with her? Did his thoughts stray to her as hers continued to stray to him?

What was that?

Julienne whirled and stared at the unbolted door leading to her quarters. She strained to hear past her beating heart, certain she'd heard footsteps. Was Rosa sneaking around or . . . could it be the captain? Her heart galloped and blood roared through her head. Spellbound, she watched as the door inched open on squeaking hinges. For a moment she thought a ghost had pushed it open, because no one appeared, then she dropped her gaze and saw a round, frightened face. Julienne released her breath with a laugh and motioned Alissa into the room.

"Come in, Alissa. Why didn't you knock?"

The child shrugged. She looked like an angel in her long white nightgown. Her eyes were as large as silver dollars. Thunder spoke to lightning again, and lightning responded with a blaze of white. Alissa dashed across the room and threw herself at Julienne. She wrapped her arms around Julienne's legs, nearly knocking her off balance.

Julienne stroked the child's hair. "How sweet of you to check on me, Alissa. You're very brave."

"I'm not," Alissa said, her breath hot through the thin fabric of Julienne's nightgown.

"Didn't you come here to make sure I wasn't frightened by the storm?" She pried Alissa's arms from around her and knelt to be face-to-face with the child. "You must have known that I might be afraid in this strange house during a noisy storm." Julienne framed Alissa's face in her hands and wiped away the child's tears with her thumbs. "Your father was right. You're a brave girl." She kissed her forehead. "Would you rather go to your father's room?"

Alissa shook her head. "I want to stay in here with you. Don't make me go to Papa. He'll be mad."

Julienne stood up again and took one of Alissa's hands in hers. "I doubt that."

"He would. He doesn't like me much."

Julienne led her into the bedroom, picked her up, and settled her in the center of the big bed. "He not only likes you much, he loves you much, silly goose."

Thunder grumbled overhead and Alissa ducked under the covers and sobbed. Julienne joined her under the sweet-smelling sheet and placed an arm around her.

"My father told me once that thunder courted lightning. Thunder has a deep, manly voice and he asks lightning to join with him and be one. All that noise he makes shouldn't frighten us. He's only making sweet talk. Lightning smiles and giggles, as girls do, and her smile is so bright, it lights up the whole sky. When thunder and lightning finally get together, they release raindrops to nourish the earth. Their union makes trees and grass grow and flowers bloom and rivers flow." Julienne removed the cover from their heads. Alissa had stopped crying. Her eyes were still wide, but no longer with fright.

"But storms are bad. Storms can kill people."

"Not if people stay out of their way. Like us." She hugged the child to her side. "We're smart. We're in here out of the storm, all cozy and warm and friendly. I'm glad we're friends, aren't you?"

Alissa nodded. "Are you going to stay here?"

"Yes."

"Rosa said you'd be gone soon."

Exasperation nipped at Julienne, but she managed to conceal it from Alissa. "Rosa is wrong. We're going to have many wonderful days together, Alissa. I'll teach you all kinds of things— not just reading and writing and such. I'll teach you about shells and plants and stars. You can teach me, too."

"What could I teach?"

"Oh, let me see." She glanced up in consideration. "You could teach me games and how to have tea parties with dolls. Do you have dolls?"

Alissa nodded. "I got one named Vanessa and one named Molly and one named Winnie."

"What lovely names. I can't wait to meet them. Maybe you could introduce them to me tomorrow."

"Okay. You got any?"

She thought to correct the child's grammar, but decided Alissa didn't need a teacher tonight. Tonight she needed a friend. "I used to have one doll, but I lost her."

"What was she called?"

"I named her Ella. That was my mother's name."

"My mama's named Maggie. She gave me Vanessa for Christmas once."

"And who gave you the others?"

"Papa gave me Winnie, and *Tía* Selena gave me Molly just yesterday."

"Oh, so Molly is a brand-new baby? That's wonderful. Do you love her already?"

"Um-hmmm. She's a rag doll." Alissa snuggled into the downy mattress and rested her head on the pillow. "She's got red hair."

"She sounds pretty. Are you getting sleepy now?"

"Kinda."

"Would you like me to tell you a story?"

"I guess." Her eyes widened a moment. "My mama used to tell me stories."

"Did she? Do you have a favorite?"

"She wrote stories, too." Alissa's eyelids slipped down and her words began to slur. "She kept them in the fireplace."

"The fireplace? You mean she burned the stories after she wrote them? Alissa?"

Alissa stirred and shifted onto her side, never opening her eyes. Julienne marveled how children could drop into a deep sleep within seconds. She tucked the covers around Alissa and lay down beside her. Before she turned out the lamp, she admired the child's beauty. Her face was a perfect oval, her skin a lovely shade of cream. After extinguishing the lamp's flame, Julienne watched shadows creep across the ceiling. The sound of rain drifted to her. She thought about the captain again and wondered why Alissa questioned his love for her. It was troubling, especially since Julienne wanted to find reasons to like the captain and justify her attraction to him.

However, there was no escaping the disturbing fact that his only child would rather take refuge in the arms of a stranger than in his.

Violence seemed to permeate Moonspell. Rooms full of weapons, a child begging her father not to hurt her, rumors of murder, a child's belief that storms could kill. Where there's smoke, there's fire, her father would have said. Beware! Beware of the devil behind the flames.

Chapter 4

After entering the pungent interior of the stables, Julienne stood a few moments to let her eyes adjust to the dimness. She heard the rustle of hooves in hay, and she smelled the musky aroma of horseflesh. Glad to finally claim a few hours of daylight for herself, she strolled from stall to stall, admiring the horses.

Her first full week at Moonspell had resulted in a comfortable routine, but left little time to explore the new territory. Mornings were taken up with tutoring Alissa, whom Julienne found a willing and intelligent student. However, like her father, Alissa suffered from mood swings. Most of the time she bubbled with questions and observations, but occasionally she descended into a morass of distrust and self-interest. Julienne managed to break through her moodiness, but couldn't divine what brought it on. Alissa evaded questions about why she was withdrawn. However, Julienne knew from working with children that a child's natural disposition was carefree. Woes were burdens placed on them by adults.

Taking her evening meals with the others had given Julienne a chance to observe the adults in the house, and she decided that Alissa's moods were tied to Buccaneer LaFlamme. One frown from him dashed her joyful smiles and giggles. Julienne wondered if the captain realized the strength of his influence, not only on his daughter, but on every inhabitant of Moonspell, herself included. Everyone sought his approval, his smile, his burst of laughter. One scowl or criticism from him settled a pall over the entire household that only he could lift by word or deed. Sometimes it felt to Julienne as if they were marionettes, and Buccaneer LaFlamme was their puppet master.

Following her strange confrontation with him on her first night at Moonspell, the captain had kept his distance from her. The next morning he had detailed her duties. That had been the last time he'd spoken to her, except during dinner. Even then, he rarely said her name or encouraged any conversation. He treated her like a hired hand, and it galled her, although she knew it was ridiculous to feel slighted.

After Alissa's nap each afternoon, Julienne had entertained the child with games, playacting, and storytelling. This afternoon, however, Selena had announced that she was going to instruct Alissa in needlepoint. Alissa hadn't seemed interested, but had gone quietly with Selena, leaving Julienne on her own for the rest of the day. Julienne's first thought had been the stables. There was no better way to explore Pirate's Key than by horseback.

The groom helped her select a sturdy bay gelding called Seabiscuit and pointed out the bridal trails to her. She took the one that eventually emptied onto the stretch of beach where she'd first seen Captain LaFlamme riding, wild and free. The trail cut through dense woods where banyan and mahogany trees mingled with every species of tropical palm. The afternoon was warmer than she'd thought, and she removed her jacket and plucked at the front of her gray blouse.

Ursula had taken her measurements yesterday morning, having been instructed to do so by Captain LaFlamme. New clothes were to be made for her by a woman in Key West, Ursula had told her, adding that the captain said he'd select some material himself. Julienne wondered if this was common, but had been too uneasy to ask Ursula. If this was special treatment on his part, she assumed it was to excuse himself for his rude behavior that first night at Moonspell.

Riding sidesaddle made her wish she'd instructed the stableboy to outfit the gelding with only a pad and bridle, but she persevered and tried to ignore her complaining leg and back muscles.

Sidesaddle was the most awkward way to sit a horse, she thought, pressing a hand against the small of her back. A man must have conceived of it, for no woman in her right mind would invent such torture for her sisters.

Still, she enjoyed the trek through the palmetto and cypress fields. Hindered by the saddle, she kept the gelding reined to a slow gallop, although she longed to let the horse chase the wind. Greenery flashed by. Birds fluttered overhead. The sun played peekaboo with her, slanting through tree branches to find her, then losing her under the thick canopy, only to find her again and spear her with hot, golden shafts.

Eventually, however, the awkward sidesaddle sapped her strength. By the time she reached the beach, her clothing stuck to her sweaty skin and pain shot from her ankles, straight up her back to her neck. She dismounted with a groan and touched her toes to unkink her knotted muscles. Seabiscuit shook himself all over, but wasn't winded or overheated. Julienne reached into her skirt pocket for the apple she'd pilfered from the kitchen earlier, and gave it to the big horse. Velvety lips stroked her palm as he plucked the treat from her fingers and chomped noisily on the juicy fruit.

Spotting a long piece of driftwood, Julienne walked Seabiscuit closer to it and wrapped the reins around the smooth, white wood. She remembered the horse she and her father had shared on Key Largo, an ancient roan named Nell. She'd often tied the docile animal to driftwood or anchored the reins with a big rock. Anything, however flimsy, tethered Nell, for the fat mare had no desire to bolt and run.

She kicked off her shoes and removed her stockings, then sat for a while in the sand, letting the sea foam roll over her bare feet, then her ankles. It had been ages since she'd splashed in the ocean, and she yearned for the old days when she could doff her clothing and jump into the turquoise water. She wasn't a child anymore, she reminded herself. It would be unseemly to swim in her altogether. Still ... one more time. To feel the salt water all over her, to experience the freedom of a sleek dolphin gliding through sun-warmed water. One more time, for old times' sake.

Sweat trickled down her aching back, between her breasts and thighs. The sun heated the top of her head, her face, her neck and arms. Julienne flung back her head, eyes closed, and imagined the coolness of the water, the taste of salt in her mouth. Ooo, to be a child again and be able to splash in the surf!

Julienne glanced around at the deserted beach. Seabiscuit stared at her, then turned his head. She smiled. Even the horse was giving her some privacy! The lure of the ocean grew stronger until Julienne flung up handfuls of sand in frustration.

"Oh, why not," she declared with a cavalier shrug. "No one will see. This is private property."

Having convinced herself, she began unfastening her clothes and folding them into a neat pile on the white sand. She removed the last of her underclothes quickly and dashed into the ocean. The water felt cold at first, but wonderfully so, cooling her overheated body and washing away the sticky perspiration. Julienne dove underwater, wetting her hair thoroughly before stretching into a lazy swimmer's crawl. The salt water unknotted her muscles magically, and the twitches of pain ceased. She floated on her back, enjoying the sun's stroking rays. Memories of her father and Key Largo swam through her mind.

Seabiscuit tossed his head, and the reins slithered off the driftwood. He cantered across the sand and into the glade. He moved farther away from the shore and chomped at patches of clover, then farther still, to a berry bush. A whiptail lizard raced across the path, inches from his nose, and startled him into a gallop. Seabiscuit crashed through a patch of low-growing brush and veered off the bridle trail to avoid a chestnut stallion and rider.

Buccaneer reached out and snagged the trailing reins. "Whoa, there. Where are you off to?" He reined in the flustered gelding and ran a hand over its heaving ribs. "Easy, now," he murmured, examining the sidesaddle. "Did you toss her off, you ornery son of a gun?"

Just like a female, he thought, to brag about her horsemanship and then get thrown like a loose shoe the first time out. He chuckled, thinking ahead to how embarrassed Julienne would be when he brought Seabiscuit back to her. Relishing that, he clicked Blaze into a trot, with the runaway following.

Figuring that she'd ridden to the beach, he expected to spot her ahead of him on the trail at every curve. Worry nipped at him as he grew close enough to hear the pounding surf. The horse must have thrown her on the beach, he thought, reining his mount as they neared the edge of the woods where the bridle trail ended in the sugary sand. Blaze stopped and shook his mane to discourage a dragonfly that floated too close to his eyes. Leaning sideways to dodge the insect, Buccaneer caught a glimpse of his quarry out in the ocean. She looked like a white lily floating on the blue surface.

He sucked in a breath, surprised to see that she was naked. Gloriously, brazenly naked. Touching his horse's sides with the toes of his boots, he signaled Blaze to back up into the camouflage of the palms and palmetto. Seabiscuit retreated, too. While the horses settled into the shadows, Buccaneer never took his eyes off the governess. He knew he shouldn't spy on her, but damn propriety! He wanted to see her, admire her.

After all, he hadn't seen a woman nude in six months. He shook his head, trying to rid himself of that awful memory. In a world of hurt, he'd succumbed to the entreaty of a Key West whore and had regretted it the moment he'd spent himself in her. He'd felt nothing good. Not even gratification. His only emotions were unholy, unclean ones, and he hadn't been able to leave the empty-eyed whore and her dingy, smelly room fast enough.

But was that a decent excuse for peering through palm fronds at his daughter's governess? He shrugged. Excuses were frail things when faced with a beautifully naked girl.

He sensed her sudden comprehension a second before she looked frantically around her. Buccaneer grinned. Yes, superb horsewoman, where *is* Seabiscuit? he snickered to himself. He heard her call for the horse, then whistle before she started for shore. A tingle erupted between Buccaneer's legs as his anticipation mounted and the water line on her body receded.

Her breasts were small, but round and firm with blushing pink centers. Her narrow waist could be spanned by his hands. Her hips flared attractively. Her legs were long, tapered, sleek. His gaze lingered on the triangle of dark brown curls below her navel, and the tingle in his groin intensified. He felt himself begin to stiffen and swell.

Had he called her a girl before? This Venus walking straight toward him was a woman, by God! No wonder he'd felt light-headed the other night when she'd stood close to him in the parlor and gazed at him with those almond-shaped eyes of hers. He'd blamed it on a mixture of wine, whiskey, and ghosts, but now he knew differently. It had been her, for even now he could recall the exact shade of her eyes—chocolate brown—and the shape of her lips—a plush, pink valentine. Admiring her piquant face, he had known an insane desire to press a kiss to the curve of her neck and breathe her name against her sweetly fragrant skin. *Julienne . . . Julienne . . . little jewel.* She might be fresh from the convent, but she knew how to look deeply into a man's eyes and make his blood thicken with need.

As he watched her tug on her clothing, he imagined himself nuzzling her breasts and laving her nipples. The mother superior certainly wouldn't approve. She'd sent word that Julienne Vale was a young, unsophisticated, eager-to-please girl, who was excellent with children and animals, but knew nothing of men and the mayhem they could cause. He trapped a low laugh in his chest, thinking he might enjoy instructing the governess in the ancient art of seduction and surrender.

He hadn't craved another woman since Maggie, but he found he ached to slake his thirst for Julienne's lips, breasts . . . her whole luscious body.

After Maggie, he'd promised himself never to fall for another woman's charm. That promise lost importance as the sun struck Julienne's wet hair, summoning the red highlights in it. Buccaneer tapped the heels of his boots against Blaze's sides, and the stallion pranced onto the beach.

"Good afternoon, Julienne. Have you lost something?"

Julienne's heart crammed into her throat, but slowly slid back into place when she recognized the captain. She went limp when she saw him leading her horse. "You found him! Thank you." She pulled her blouse away from her damp skin. "I tied him to some driftwood, and I guess he worked himself free."

He lifted one brow. " 'Tis the nature of the beast."

"The horse we had back on Key Largo always stayed put."

"You're not on Key Largo now, little orphan girl, and that horse is long since dead."

Her cheerfulness faded. "I know that, Captain." Her voice was carefully modulated. "And please stop calling me that stupid name. Little orphan girl. I'm not little and I'm not a girl."

He smiled, and she blushed furiously. He could almost see the wheels turning in her mind.

"How . . . Did you see me before?"

"Before what?" he taunted.

"I was swimming."

"I can see that." He let his gaze slip over her, finding the pink stain of her nipples against her wet blouse particularly fascinating.

"Did you see me . . . swimming?" She grabbed her hair and wrung salt water from it.

He stared out at the ocean, wondering if he should lie or construct something more clever. "What were you swimming in?"

She flung her hair over her shoulder. "The sea.

I didn't think anyone would come along and bother me."

"It's a good thing I was close enough to *bother* you or you'd be without a horse right now." He smiled tightly, enjoying the upper hand. "You must be careful around Pirate's Key, Julienne. There are many men on this key. A lady must conduct herself with decorum, even in the remote isles."

"Thank you for reminding me of that, Captain. The only men I've been around were my father and priests, so I'm ignorant of their moral turpitude."

Was she teasing him, tempting him? Her guileless brown eyes convinced him that she didn't have a devious bone in her whole curvaceous body. How refreshing to speak with a female who possessed no outward vanity or artiface. Before he knew it, he was smiling at her.

She spread her arms wide. "But then, what man in his right mind would want a woman who looks like a drowned cat?" She sighed and turned her back on him to face the ocean. "I heard the waves murmuring my name, calling me out for a swim, and the sun was so dreadfully hot! I just couldn't resist. I'm ever so grateful to be here. Pirate's Key is gorgeous. It must be the closest thing to Eden on this earth."

His smile broadened at her sincerity. Neither Isabelle nor Magdalena had appreciated Pirate's Key, and it was gratifying to hear a woman expound on his home's many virtues.

"Eden, you say? Well, I must agree, but my wives swore this was the last outpost to hell itself."

"Did they?" She glanced over her shoulder at him, then returned her attention to the sun-splashed surf. "They probably didn't like the remoteness."

"Exactly."

"I thrive on it." Excruciatingly aware of him behind her, Julienne tried to slow her thrumming pulse. Why did he have to be so dashing in his tight riding breeches and black shirt? She liked his voluminous, long-sleeved shirts. They had pointed collars and deep, V-shaped necklines with laces, which he invariably left loose to reveal a portion of his bronze chest with its slick, black hair.

"Have you visited Spirits Cove yet?"

"No," she answered, swinging about to face him. "Where is it?"

He nodded in the general direction. "About a mile down that way. There are boulders out in the water."

"I remember that place! A young man was sitting on one of them. Cesare said he lived on the edge of your property. He had an odd name."

"Ootay, probably."

"That's right! So that place is called Spirits Cove." Julienne moved a little way from him, pretending to gaze into the distance. The frankness in his eyes unnerved her. She felt more naked now than she had when she hadn't been wearing a stitch of clothing!

"Spirits Cove is one of the more colorful places on the key." He admired the curve of her back. She was a little thing, really. Her shoulders were narrow, but nicely squared. A breeze fluttered her skirt, showing him her sandy ankles and calves. The way she stood, feet apart, hands on hips, made her look ready to take on any challenge. And made him think of ways he'd like to challenge her.

"I bet you kept your father on his toes, didn't you?" he observed, and she pivoted to face him.

"I followed him like a shadow, and I yearned to be just like him. Being a girl was a great disappointment for me."

He chuckled. "And for him?"

"No." Her father's face floated before her, a trick of her memory. "Nothing about me disappointed my father." She regarded the man astride the horse, her curiosity aroused. Could the same be said for Buccaneer LaFlamme? Did he find her lacking in some way? "Funny, I was just thinking of dear Papa. You must have read my mind."

He hoped to heaven she couldn't read his, because he was thinking of how she looked naked—delicate and disarming, her skin like strawberries and cream, that dark patch of curling hair hiding her innermost delights. He cleared his throat and yanked on Seabiscuit's reins.

"Here. Take your horse." The suggestion came out as an order. He winced inwardly as she took the reins from him, her eyes reflecting her hurt feelings.

"Thank you, Captain. I'm sorry to be a trouble to you." She stared at her sand-covered feet.

Irritation consumed him, more from his own actions than hers, although her sudden timidity incensed him. "Stop that!"

Julienne brought her head up, and her gaze crashed into his. What had angered him? Why couldn't she be what he wanted?

"Stop that sniveling and shuffling your feet. It's not becoming."

"I assure you, Captain, I am *not* sniveling! As for shuffling my feet, they itch. Begging your pardon, sir!" How dare he accuse her of such behavior! The man was impossible. Simply impossible!

He admired the flags of anger flying in her cheeks and eyes. God, she was a beauty when her temper found the best in her. Throwing a leg over, he slipped off Blaze and landed directly in front of her. She blinked, startled by his sudden move. For a magical moment, he saw his reflection in her eyes and was caught in the smoky topaz jewels.

"How are you and Alissa getting along?"

She blinked, glanced away for a few moments, then swung her gaze back to his. What kind of game was he playing? "Fine. Just fine."

"She seems to have taken to you."

"She needs a friend. I'm glad to be one for her."

He lowered his brows, feeling as if she'd just insulted him, but not understanding quite how. "She needs a friend, does she? I thought I'd hired you to be a governess."

"You did. I'm her friend for free. No extra wages required, sir."

He fumed inwardly. "It seems we are adept at talking at cross purposes."

"And I'm sure it's all my fault, being the stupid little orphan girl that I am, Captain, sir."

Anger surged, then magically receded. Regarding the imps dancing in her eyes, Buccaneer feared he'd been bewitched. "You, mam'selle, have a tongue like a whip."

A smile teased the corners of her mouth. "And you, Captain LaFlamme, are often begging for a flogging."

Impulse ruled him. He cupped the side of her face in his hand. She didn't move, but her eyes questioned him. He had no reasonable answer for her, and he didn't wish to scrutinize his actions too closely. He might lose his nerve, regain his senses.

Leaning closer, he brought her face forward and she closed her eyes. That's when he knew that she wanted his kiss as much as he wanted to sample the ambrosia of her. She tasted of salt water and sugar, heaven and hell, temptation and salvation. Her lips trembled under his, then parted on a sigh. Desire flashed through him with the intensity of a lightning bolt. Buccaneer wrapped an arm around her waist and swept his tongue over her soft, warm lips. He kissed her cheek, her chin, her earlobe.

Julienne kept her eyes closed, wanting his mouth to continue its seduction. Her body craved him, while her mind reeled with bewilderment. Was this really happening? Should she allow it or should she escape him before it was too late ... before he changed her from a governess to a conquest? Then the tip of his tongue traced the shell of her ear, and he blew a line of flesh bumps down the side of her neck, and all rational thought turned to dust.

"Captain ... my captain," she whispered, her voice so young, so rife with confusion, that it sent clarity splashing through his mind like a cold ocean wave.

He set her away from him, consumed with guilt for taking advantage of her innocence. She stared at him, her beautiful mouth glistening from his kiss, her large eyes glazed. He picked up the reins again and placed them in her hand, then curled her fingers around them.

"Go on with you." He cleared his throat, trying to think of how to explain his actions. Stumped and tongue-tied, he swung onto Blaze's back again. "Forgive me, mam'selle. I forgot myself ... That is, I lost myself." He stared at her, wanting to add that he'd lost himself in her eyes, but too cowardly to speak such a bald truth.

"Have I ..." She gathered in a breath, trying to clear her mind and heart of him. "That is, I can tell you're displeased with me. I shouldn't have allowed you to take liberties. I'm sorry, sir."

He chewed his lower lip until his urge to rail at her passed. "Julienne," he said with admirable aplomb, "I'm the one who took advantage of you, but now that we've both given this a second thought—"

"I've been dismissed," she finished, jutting out her chin. "I understand, Captain. Mother Superior told me that men are ruled by instinct. I shouldn't have allowed—"

"Julienne, please—"

She shook her head, unable to bear his attempt to excuse her unfortunate display. A lady of breeding would have slapped his face, not opened herself to him like a blossom straining for sunlight! "Captain, let's just forget this whole encounter."

"Very well." He squared his shoulders, hoisting an invisible weight that seemed to have landed on them. Damn it all, he couldn't leave it like this, with her feeling chastised. "Let me show you Spirits Cove."

"Now?"

"No. I'll take you and Alissa there tomorrow afternoon."

Her gaze shied away from his. "You don't have to feel obliged, Captain."

"Believe me, I don't." Obliged, no, he thought. Hot, tight-skinned, and bursting at the seams, yes. He forced his gaze away from her delectable mouth. "Good afternoon." Then he wheeled the big chestnut around and coaxed him into a fast walk toward the bridle path.

Gritting his teeth, he wondered how he'd be able to face her over the dinner table tonight and act as if he hadn't seen her naked and didn't ache to see her that way again.

Chapter 5

Back at the house, Julienne went upstairs to check on Alissa. She was surprised that Selena was still with the child, but she wasn't surprised that both Selena and Alissa seemed bored to tears. Needlepoint notions lay scattered over the canopied bed and on the window seat, but had been abandoned in favor of watercolor paint and big sheets of white paper. Selena and Alissa sat on the floor, hunched over their individual artistic efforts. Alissa sighed. Selena covered a yawn with one hand. She looked up from the vase of flowers she had sketched and narrowed her dark eyes.

"Just where have you been all afternoon?"

"Is there a problem?" Julienne responded, smiling a greeting at Alissa. "Hello, ladybug. Have you already learned how to needlepoint?"

Alissa wrinkled her nose in distaste. "I don't like it. I like painting better."

"I thought you were supposed to be supervising this child!" Selena stood and pressed a hand to her spine. "Rosa said you'd left the house. Disappeared off the face of the earth without telling a soul!"

Julienne smiled at Selena's fit of temper. "You said you wanted to spend the afternoon with your niece, so I went horseback riding."

"Where to, Key West?" Selena eyed her critically. "Your hair's wet."

"I went swimming, too."

"My, my!" She clasped her hands and turned wide eyes on Alissa before looking at Julienne again. "You had yourself a holiday, didn't you? You should have stayed closer to the house. Even though Alissa was occupied, she might have needed you. Buck will be interested to know that you've been riding his horses all over creation."

"He already knows, so there's no point in you tattling to him, señorita." Julienne savored Selena's smoking glare. "I met up with him out on the beach." She directed her attention to Alissa again. "How would you like to go riding tomorrow with me and your papa?"

Alissa turned back to the paints and dabbed the narrow brush into a pot of red. "I guess so." Her lack of enthusiasm couldn't be missed.

"You shouldn't impose on Buck. He's a busy man."

"He suggested the outing, not me."

"He did?" Selena regarded Julienne coldly. "He wants to be with his daughter, not with you."

"Certainly. I wouldn't suggest anything else."

"Then why don't you stay behind and let him and Alissa ride together?" Selena's eyes glinted and she gave a happy laugh. "I'll tell you what!" She squatted in front of Alissa. "I'll go with you. Wouldn't you like that?"

Alissa shrugged. "I don't care."

Disappointment and panic ran roughshod across Julienne's nerves. "Señorita, you should consult the captain first before making these plans. After all, it's his invitation to give or rescind."

"I'll speak to him this evening," Selena announced with a gleam in her eyes. She moved closer to Julienne. "Need I remind you that you are hired help and shouldn't be setting your sights on a man like Buccaneer LaFlamme?"

Julienne felt her eyes widen. "Me? I never . . ." The memory of that kiss on the beach brought scalding color to her face.

"Stay away from him," Selena whispered, her expression fierce. "I'm going to be the next Señora LaFlamme, and I won't let anyone—especially a goldbricking little governess—get in my way! You hear me?"

"What . . . what makes you think the captain would even look twice at me?" Had he said something to Selena about her? Julienne wondered. Had he revealed an attraction that she hadn't sensed until the kiss on the beach?

"Because he's a man, and every man likes to pluck ripe fruit off the tree of life, take a big bite, then toss it aside when his hunger is momentarily satiated." Selena illustrated, picking an imaginary fruit from the air and throwing it away with a flick of her wrist. "You think you're the first servant to dream of snagging the master's attention?" She laughed scornfully. "He'll dally with you because you're so readily available, but he won't marry beneath his station. Buck will marry a lady. Me." She hitched up her chin and swept past Julienne. "Moonspell will be mine. *My* children will inherit this land and these holdings. So don't flatter yourself by thinking that Buck is interested in anything other than what's underneath your skirts!" Selena sashayed from the room in a rustle of silk organza.

Julienne gasped at the crude reference and glanced uneasily at Alissa. She was relieved to see that the child was engrossed in her painting and hadn't paid attention to Selena's whispered warnings and degradations.

She was about to sit on the floor beside Alissa when Rosa stepped into view and motioned for Julienne to join her outside the room.

"Yes, Rosa?" Julienne asked, partially closing the bedroom door for a measure of privacy.

"I heard what Selena said to you."

"You were eavesdropping?"

"I was cleaning." She nodded toward a mop leaning against the wall and a bucket of soapy water. "She is right. I have known Captain Buck many, many years. I have seen him use women for his pleasure and then turn his back on them. His heart will always belong to Magdalena."

"But she's dead."

"She does not rest, and as long as her spirit lives, the captain shall not know any peace." She inched closer. "You want to keep this job?"

"Yes, of course."

"Then don't let him have his way with you. Once he has bedded you, he won't want you around his daughter. You understand? He would have no respect for you."

Julienne retreated and looked the older woman squarely in the eyes. "I suppose you want Selena to be the next wife."

Rosa made an ugly face. "Bah! That one is a *puta!* She wants only Captain Buck's money so she can lie around all day and do nothing but issue orders to the servants. She thinks she is as beautiful as Magdalena, but she is a hag next to her cousin!" Rosa shook a bony finger at Julienne. "Hear me! Captain Buck will never be happy with another woman! Never, never, never."

Julienne pulled herself up to her full height and looked down the bridge of her nose at the stern-faced housekeeper. "I won't gossip like this about the captain, Rosa. I'm the governess here, and the captain's personal life is none of my business. Nor, I might add, is it any of yours."

"You sneaked out to meet him today," Rosa fairly hissed at her.

"I did no such thing!"

Rosa narrowed her eyes to slits. "You have been warned."

"And you have been listening at too many keyholes, Rosa." Julienne gave an arch smile before turning her back on the nosy old woman. She joined Alissa again and was glad to see Rosa move on, away from Alissa's room. *That woman is a bad influence,* she thought. *I certainly wouldn't want her around a child of mine!* She crouched beside Alissa and examined her painting.

"Who is this?" she asked, pointing to the figure of a man standing to the far left.

"Papa." Alissa pointed to a small person on the far right of the paper. "That's me."

"And this?" Julienne touched the black-clad figure in the middle.

"Rosa."

Julienne scrutinized the painting. "Where would you put Cesare?"

Alissa thought a moment, then pointed next to her papa's likeness.

"And where would you place Selena?"

Again, Alissa pointed to the man figure.

"And where would you put me?"

Alissa regarded her solemnly before indicating her own small rendition.

"Beside you?"

The child nodded, a tiny smile nudging her mouth.

"Why are you standing so far away from your papa? Is Rosa keeping you from him?"

Alissa shrugged. "I'm s'pose to go to Rosa if I want something, not to Papa. If I want something, I got to ask Rosa and then Rosa asks Papa for me."

"It's not 'got,' ladybug. It's 'have to.' You *have to* ask Rosa." She ran a hand over the top of her charge's silky, black hair. "Did your papa tell you to ask Rosa first?"

"I guess. That's just what I got . . . have to do."

Julienne examined the picture again. "Well, it's a lovely painting. Did you enjoy playing with Selena?"

She held up her forefinger. "I stuck my finger with a needle!"

"Oh, dear." Julienne studied the tiny, pink pinprick. She gave it a quick kiss. "There! All well."

Alissa giggled. "That won't do nothing!"

"No? You just wait until morning. You won't even know it's there. Didn't you know that sugar kisses heal scrapes and cuts?"

Alissa shook her head.

"Well, they do. First the person has to love you or like you a whole, whole lot." She lowered her voice. "Like I like you."

"A whole, whole lot?"

"That's right. Then when that person kisses the other person, poof!" She snapped her fingers. "All well. No more hurt." She noticed that Alissa looked past her, and a shadow seemed to fall across the child's face. Julienne swiveled around. Buccaneer stood over them, tall and broad-shouldered. His smile bordered on tenderness and made Julienne's heart tumble over itself. "Oh, Captain! I didn't know you were there."

"Is Alissa hurt?"

"No, she was learning needlepoint and pricked her finger, that's all." She laughed, embarrassed that he'd overheard her fanciful conversation with his daughter.

"Let me see." He reached out, but Alissa shook her head and scrambled to stand behind Julienne.

"Alissa," Julienne scolded. "Don't misbehave. Let your papa see your finger."

"That's all right," Buccaneer said, clasping his hands behind him. "It's not that important."

Julienne hated the pain in his eyes and wished she could insist that Alissa apologize.

"I just saw Selena, and she said you invited her

along on our outing to Spirits Cove tomorrow?" He lifted his black brows, questioning her, silently asking for an explanation.

"She did? She said that?"

"She did. What have you to say about it?"

Julienne didn't know if she should call Selena a liar to his face or be discreet. Discretion won out. "She mentioned that she wanted to come along and . . . Well, it's up to you, Captain. I'll even stay here and you can take Alissa and Señorita Selena to the cove. I leave the decision to you, sir."

He delivered a lopsided smile. "Then I think we should stick with our original plan."

"Buck, here you are." Selena swept into the room. Her glance at Julienne cut like a knife. "Shall I tell Rosa to pack a basket for us tomorrow? I thought it might be nice if you and I shared a bottle of wine while Alissa ran off and played in the caves with the governess."

He shook his head. "Selena, you're no good on a horse. I think you should stay here at the estate while we explore Spirits Cove. I assure you, it's not your cup of tea."

Selena's smile faltered and she laid a hand on his sleeve. "Why don't you stay here with me and let the little governess take Alissa to the cove?"

"Because it was my idea to go there in the first place. Neither Alissa nor Julienne knows the way there."

"If this is going to be a problem, Captain, then I—"

"Why don't you call me by my first name?" he interrupted Julienne. "Hearing you call me 'Captain' and 'sir' is getting tiresome."

Selena stared at him, her eyes wide with alarm. "Don't be foolish, Buck! She just wouldn't feel right being so familiar with you! Why, she couldn't possibly call you by your first name!" Selena swung around to Julienne. "Could you?"

she demanded, and it was clear which answer she expected. "Tell him!"

Julienne conjured up her courage and faced her employer. "Actually, I think Buccaneer is a beautiful name, and I will be most happy to use it."

He chuckled. "You have to be the first to find my name anything but odd." He dipped his head. "You can call me Buck, if you wish."

She looked away from his glittering eyes, suddenly shy. "I prefer Buccaneer."

"Then by all means—"

"How sweet," Selena drawled, stepping neatly between them. She rested a hand on Buccaneer's chest. "Buck, you are too, too kind to the hired help. Next you'll be showering them with affection, if someone doesn't stop you." She pushed at him, half-playful, half-malicious. "Lucky for you, I'm here to keep you on the straight and narrow."

Julienne cleared her throat. "Alissa, we need to get ready for dinner. Let me help you put away these paints." She knelt and started corking the little pots of paint.

"Buck, may I speak to you alone?" Selena said, a hard edge to her voice. "Now?"

"Of course." Buccaneer touched the crown of his daughter's hair and waited for her silvery eyes to find his. "May I see your painting later?"

Alissa nodded, solemn, wary.

"Good." Buccaneer motioned for Selena to lead the way.

After they were gone, Julienne studied Alissa's slight scowl. "Alissa, why didn't you want to show your papa your finger? He would have given it a kiss, too. He loves you."

Alissa shrugged.

"Please talk to me. Don't you believe that your papa loves you?"

Alissa stuck out her lower lip. "He didn't love Mama."

"We're talking about him loving you. You love him, don't you?"

"I guess."

"Has he been mean to you? Does he spank you?"

Alissa shook her head and sighed. "He took Mama away and she's never coming back. He could take me away, too, if he wanted. I don't want to go!"

Julienne gathered the child close, realizing Alissa was trembling. "There, there, where do you get such ideas? Your papa didn't take your mama away, and you certainly don't have to go anywhere."

"Promise?"

"Promise."

"I don't have to go tomorrow?"

"You mean to Spirits Cove?" Julienne asked, and Alissa nodded. "But it will be fun. You can ride behind me on my horse, if you want."

"I don't want to go there with him. Please, don't make me!" Her voice climbed to the brink of tears.

Julienne stroked her hair. "Hush now. We'll talk about this later. Let's get ready for dinner now. Put your paints back in the box, and I'll do something with the needlepoint and sewing notions." She set the child away from her and moved to pick up the scraps of fabric, needles, threads, and spools.

How was she going to tell the captain that his own daughter was frightened of him and would rather stay alone in her room than spend an afternoon with him?

Selena arranged herself on the parlor settee and gave Buccaneer a calculated smile. "Finally, we are alone, *caro mío.*"

Buccaneer stood with his back to Magdalena's portrait. "Selena, I want you to feel comfortable at Moonspell while you visit your father—"

"Oh, I do! It feels like home. I might never leave."

He stared at the toes of his boots. "Yes, but Moonspell isn't your home. You're a guest here, Selena. It has come to my attention that you're . . . How shall I put it? Throwing your weight around? Passing yourself off as the mistress of Moonspell?"

Selena rested a hand between her breasts, and her dark eyes rounded. "I was only trying to help you, Buck! As Magdalena's cousin, I want only to ease your heartache and make life easier for you."

"Thank you, but I can handle life on my own."

"Like just now when you encouraged that governess to call you by your first name? I want to talk to you about—"

"Be careful, Selena. I'm a grown man and I won't take kindly to being lectured by you."

Selena arched her shapely brows. "*Sí, sí*. You don't have to tell this woman that you are a fully grown man." Her gaze flickered away. "Nor do you have to tell that governess."

Buccaneer tamped down his rising anger. "Speaking of which, I would prefer it if you'd stay behind tomorrow afternoon."

"Will you seduce her in front of your daughter?"

His anger broke through his calm like a fist. Before he realized he'd even moved, he had jerked Selena to her feet. His throat tightened and his voice emerged in a harsh whisper. "Don't push me, Selena! I'm trying to be a genial host, but you're making it damned near impossible."

Selena clutched his upper arms. Her nails dug into him, nearly poking through the material. "Buck, can't you see that I'm crazy with jealousy? You're the only man for me. I came here not just to see my father, but to make *you* see *me*." Her gaze grew languid, suggestive, and she flattened herself against him. Her pelvis rocked against him. "A man like you shouldn't be without a woman. Send that governess back to St. Augustine and let me take care of you and Alissa." She moved one hand down between their bodies and cupped him.

He stared at her, unmoved. "I'm not in the market for a caretaker or a wife."

"I don't believe you." She rose on tiptoes and spread her other hand at the back of his head to bring his mouth down to hers while she squeezed him.

Buccaneer allowed the kiss and meant to allow no more than that, but Selena's soft curves appealed to the loneliness within him, and her hand seduced his indiscriminate masculinity. She rubbed him, massaged him. He speared her mouth with his tongue, and she moaned and tried to unbutton his fly. The months of deprivation crashed over him, and he closed his eyes and let temptation reign.

Behind his eyelids he saw a face ... an elfin face with an upturned nose, nut brown eyes, a mouth so soft and sweet, it could bring a man to his knees. Julienne.

Startled by the vision, Buccaneer tore his lips from Selena's and set her from him. He backhanded his mouth. Selena retreated, then squared her shoulders and tossed her black hair.

"What's wrong, Buck?" she whispered. "You liked it. I know you liked it. You miss Magdalena." She ran her fingertips down the front of his shirt. "I can take her place. You have only to say the word."

He shook his head, trying to rid himself of Julienne's image and Magdalena's haunting.

"You poor man." Selena stroked his sleeve up to his shoulder. "Let me hold you, let me heal you."

"Selena, stop it!" He jerked away from her and made for the door. "I'm not a wounded animal, and I certainly don't need a woman's charity." He strode from the room and kept going until he was outside.

Leaping onto the back of his horse, he kicked Blaze into a flat-out run toward the tobacco fields. His gut churned and his manhood throbbed. God, yes! He wanted a woman, but not Selena.

He reined Blaze beneath the cool canopy of a buttonwood tree and dismounted. Blaze munched on grass while Buccaneer paced, his breath rasping in his throat, his insides seething, his groin tingling, coming alive after months of dormancy.

"Damn it to hell!" he bellowed, then sank back against the tree trunk. "Damn it to hell," he whispered, his frustration dying to embers. He was in a sorry state, he thought, lusting for a governess when a temptress like Selena was his for the taking.

But he knew Selena's affections came with a price. A hefty one. She and Magdalena had that much in common—both liked the finer things in life. He remembered how Selena couldn't get to Moonspell fast enough after receiving word of her cousin's death. She'd coddled him, tried to comfort him, but hadn't been blatantly on the husband-hunting trail. However, this visit was different. She openly campaigned for him, and he didn't relish the role of spoiler.

Staring into the middle distance, he contemplated the events that had led him to this moment in his life. First Isabelle. Poor, trembling Isabelle. He'd never forget how she'd been frozen with fear when he'd kissed her or how she'd fallen to her knees before him on their wedding night and begged him not to touch her. Tears had streamed down her pale face, and her small, clasped hands had shaken as she'd stared imploringly up at him and pleaded to keep her virginity intact. Rape was not in his repertoire, and Isabelle had died a virgin less than a year later.

Between his marriages to Isabelle and Maggie, he'd sampled many of the available women in the Keys and in Cuba. He'd had no intention of marrying again and he'd enjoyed being an eligible bachelor. Sex had become a sport, a pleasure, and he had become a legendary cocksman. A wicked grin overtook him as he conjured up a vision of himself swaggering from port to port and from woman to woman. He'd been happy then and supremely satisfied.

Then came Magdalena. Like a witch's spell, she'd descended on him, making him regret his life of variety and yearn only for her lips, her affections, her fiery temperament. He'd seen her dancing in Havana in a bawdy cantina, but he'd been told by the proprietor that she wasn't of common blood. She was a rebel, a black sheep of an aristocratic family. Buccaneer had stalked her like a hunter hot on the trail of a flash of red fur. Looking back, however, he wondered if he might have been the fox and she the hound, because ultimately he had been her prisoner. Even now, on this bright spring day, her shadow darkened his heart; the memory of her laughter mocked him. Was she the one sin from which there was no salvation?

He slammed his fists back against the tree trunk. "Goddamn you, Maggie! Leave me be!"

Blaze raised his head and stared at him, making Buccaneer laugh at his own theatrics. He smoothed a hand down the stallion's blazed face.

"No, I haven't lost my mind . . . yet," he assured the horse. Although, he thought, sometimes he felt as if he were on the verge of doing so. Like earlier today on the beach.

He closed his eyes and leaned his forehead against Blaze's neck. Immediately the memory of Julienne's naked beauty consumed him and his mouth went dry, his heart kicked, that tingling returned in his loins. That kiss. He shouldn't have . . .

Straightening, he dismissed his guilt. She certainly hadn't fought off his advances. She'd offered herself to him. He'd done nothing other than kiss her. He might have done more, but he'd remembered his place and hers. She was here for Alissa, not to satisfy the aching between his legs.

Then why had he suggested the outing to Spirits Cove? Why had he picked that place, the most secluded on his property?

He swung up on Blaze again, having no desire for answers to those questions. Besides, Alissa would be along, too. He smiled with irony, finding the idea of using his child as a chaperon just short of sheer lunacy.

Chapter 6

"It's too bad that Alissa wasn't feeling well enough to join us," Buccaneer said as he and Julienne walked from the house to the stables.

"Yes, well, are you sure about this? Maybe I should stay with her."

"No, she's resting." He glanced at her, wondering if his eagerness to be alone with her was apparent. Clearing his throat, he added, "That is, Rosa will keep an eye on her, so we needn't worry. Besides, you've been with her all morning. Even governesses deserve holidays now and then."

Julienne lengthened her strides, feeling the need to distance herself from him in case he noticed her uneasiness. She knew Alissa had no stomachache, but she hadn't wanted to insist that the child join them. If Alissa felt it necessary to lie, then Julienne didn't want to force her hand. She'd talk with Alissa later and pry out of her the real reason for her refusal to go with them to Spirits Cove.

She examined the captain from the corner of her eye. He seemed younger this morning and not quite so imposing. The breeze played through his hair and fluttered the sleeves of his charcoal gray shirt. He glanced at her and smiled briefly. Julienne chided herself for worrying how it would look for them to go off together on a trip. After all, he was merely being a gracious host and employer. No sense in her reading anything else into his gesture. Still, was it proper? Should she have refused? He glanced at her again, his gaze swift but thorough.

"I see you've worn the riding skirt I had sent to your room this morning."

She wiped her moist palms on the russet gabardine split skirt. "This is far more comfortable than what I would have worn. Thank you, Captain."

"Captain?" he repeated, dipping his head to catch her eye.

"I mean, Buccaneer."

He nodded, obviously pleased.

"Who did this skirt belong to? It's a little full in the hips, but I managed to fold a few tucks into it."

"It was Maggie's."

Maggie's? She felt strange wearing the woman's clothes.

"It's a tad too long, I see." He stared at the skirt brushing the tops of her shoes. "It stopped a good three inches above Maggie's boot tops."

"You've kept her clothes?"

He quirked an eyebrow. "You find that odd, do you? I kept only a few articles of her clothing. Is that permissible?"

"Yes, of course. I wasn't judging you."

"The hell you weren't," he snapped, his voice suddenly hard. He jerked his head around, looking away from her. His jawline tightened. "However, I'm used to people judging my every move."

She opened her mouth to apologize, but he lengthened his strides and outdistanced her.

"I instructed the stableboy to outfit Seabiscuit with a western saddle. Can you sit on one?" he asked when she caught up with him again in the stables.

"Yes. In fact, I despise those sidesaddles."

"Next we'll have to secure you a pair of boots."

He raised a hand, greeting the stableboy, who brought two saddled horses. "Thank you, Danny. We'll take them from here." Buccaneer went around to help Julienne into the saddle.

He spanned her waist between his hands easily, and she had to concentrate hard on getting her foot in the stirrup. His touch unnerved her, made her heart frolic and the blood roar in her ears. When she hoisted herself up, his hands slipped from her waist to trail ever so lightly along her hips. She sat astride the big horse, knowing that her face had turned cherry red and that the captain was sure to notice. Nothing got past his thorough gaze.

"Comfortable?" he asked, laughter brimming in his voice.

She nodded, not trusting herself to speak. Grinning, he swung himself onto Blaze's back.

He indicated the trail ahead. "We'll take this path. It winds along the edge of the beach and empties onto Spirits Cove."

The bridle path was wide enough for two horses, so he maneuvered his big chestnut alongside Seabiscuit. Lush vegetation bordered the path. Occasionally one of the horses tried to strip a dangling branch of its leaves. Early afternoon light slanted through the woodsy canopy in bright, golden bars. The scent of the ocean and the call of the gulls floated to them, drawing them to their destination. The sun's rays brought out the sharp aromas of horseflesh and leather. Gradually Julienne relaxed and felt her normal coloring return. She chanced a quick look at him. He rode easily, his back straight, his fingers relaxed and curled over the reins. His cutlass was in a holder strapped to the saddle, instead of around his waist. A pirate king, she thought with an inner smile. Tearing her gaze from his impressive profile, she focused on the adventure ahead of her.

"Why is it called Spirits Cove?" she asked him.

"Because that's where pirates hid their loot, my grandfather, Black Pierre, among them. Supposedly the spirits of those pirates return to the cove to search for the gold they buried." He cut his eyes at her. "Have you ever seen a ghost?" he asked in a low voice.

"Certainly not," she scoffed. "Black Pierre. He sounds like a rascal."

"He was," Buccaneer agreed with a rueful smile. "People around here still talk about him. I think he was a little bit crazy, but my father, Gaspard, insisted that *Grandpère* was merely a man who was against all flags, his only allegiance being to himself."

"What was your grandmother's name?"

He furrowed his brow. "Well, there were several grandmothers. My father's mother was a woman named Constella Dupree. *Grandpère* was married four or five times before he died."

"Good gracious! What happened to all his wives?"

"They died." His silvery gaze shimmered with mystery. "I told you that women have trouble staying alive around the LaFlamme men. And things at Moonspell have trouble staying dead."

She made a face, trying to ward off the shivers he seemed determined to inspire. "Am I also supposed to believe that spirits actually inhabit the cove? I have a healthy imagination, but I know the difference between pretense and reality." Julienne ducked to avoid a low limb and decided to avoid any other unsavory talk of ghosts. "You must be so proud of Moonspell. How long has it been in your family?"

He chuckled, acknowledging her change of subject matter. "Since 1813. It was given to Black Pierre as a bribe. The government said he could have the key if he'd quit wrecking ships on the barrier reef. He lured them in with lights on moonless nights, then he killed the crews and took what he wanted off the ships."

"Begging your pardon, but I don't think your grandfather is residing in Heaven after that kind of life."

"Nor my father, for that matter," Buccaneer agreed, giving another huge shrug. "Nor will I."

"Don't say that," Julienne protested.

"And why not?"

"I refuse to think the worst of you."

He guided Blaze ever closer until his thigh brushed Julienne's. "Can you change this sinner into a saint, mam'selle?" He laughed at her heightened color. "The LaFlamme men have black hearts. My father was no better than his father before him. Ill-gotten money and jewels were buried all over this island, and my father uncovered most of the loot to obtain women and ships and any other thing that caught his eye. He was notorious for his trading. He never made a fair one. Gaspard LaFlamme could spot a fool a mile away, and he never failed to take advantage of the simple-minded or naive. No deed was too dastardly for him. I once saw him steal gold coins off a dead man's eyes."

Julienne stared at him, aghast, and Buccaneer grinned. "You're jesting," she accused.

"Oh, no." He shook his head, part of him wanting to deny his ancestry and part of him glorying in it. "He was a pirate at heart, and pirates aren't known for being genteel. They'd rather dance with the devil than be serenaded by a choir of angels." He urged his mount ahead of hers. "The cove is right up here. Mind your head. This branch is low." He ducked under it and looked back to see that she cleared it easily.

"Low for you," she said, smiling. "Just right for me."

He laughed. "Try to keep up, small stuff." With that, he dug in his heels and Blaze surged forward, throwing up sand as he raced along the beach.

"Hey, no fair!" She kicked Seabiscuit, sending him after the chestnut stallion.

Buccaneer tipped back his head and laughed. "Pirates never play fair!"

Julienne held on tight. The wind lashed her, stinging her cheeks, mussing her hair, making her eyes water. Seabiscuit couldn't gain on Blaze, but managed to keep the stallion in sight until the horse veered around a jutting cliff and disappeared. Julienne leaned over Seabiscuit's neck and urged him on. The elbow of land loomed. When she cleared it, she reined in Seabiscuit. The big bay pranced in his traces, almost sending Julienne flying over his head. Blaze was grazing on a patch of sea grass, his reins dangling in the sand. At first Julienne didn't see Buccaneer, then she spotted him lying on his back in the shade of a palm, his hands making a pillow for his head, his eyes closed against the sun's glare, and a long sprig of sea oats bobbing between his lips.

Julienne dismounted. "Clever, but unconvincing."

He opened one eye. "Ah, so you've finally arrived." He yawned hugely. "I was beginning to think you'd gotten lost or something."

She walked Seabiscuit closer to Blaze. "Your talents don't lie in the theater, Buccaneer LaFlamme." Propping her hands on her hips, she surveyed the cove. "So this is it, huh? I don't see any ghosts."

"You can't see ghosts during the day, silly. They only pop up at night. You can hear them during the day, though."

"What do they say?"

"They mostly moan." He leaped to his feet, agile as a cat. "Being a spirit must be gruesome." He reached out and cupped her elbow. "Come on. Maybe we can hear them today."

Julienne let him guide her to a cave opening and motioned for him to go in first. He took her hand in his and pulled her behind him as he moved deeper into the earth. In the gray interior, she could see the whites of his eyes and teeth, but little else.

"It's so dark!"

"And scary," he added in a voice that was lower than normal.

"I didn't say that, you did."

"Shhh. Listen. They're calling to us."

Julienne held her breath and heard a low moaning. At first she thought it was Buccaneer trying to unnerve her, but then she realized it was the wind sighing through the cave opening.

"It's only the wind."

Buccaneer squeezed her hand. "You sound relieved."

"I'm not frightened. Sorry to disappoint you."

"Not much scares you."

"That's correct."

"Except me."

"You?" Her heart stuttered. "Never."

He released her hand, and she couldn't see his glinting eyes or teeth anymore.

"Buccaneer? Where'd you go?"

Panic blew through her, but she fought the urge to scream at him. Instead, she devoted herself to listening until she heard his breathing ahead of her. She moved forward, taking small steps.

"I hear you, Buccaneer, so you might as well stop this silly game of hide-and-seek."

She saw the glint of his teeth as he smiled, and like a ship sailing toward a flash of light, she charted a course straight for him. Lifting her arms, she groped and her fingers brushed against skin.

"Buccaneer, say something." Her fingertips

found bare skin again. Had he removed his shirt or rolled up his sleeves? Gradually her agitation evolved into fear. Had he undressed? Was he planning to . . . ? She stumbled backward. "Buccaneer? Please, stop teasing me."

"Julienne, whatever is keeping you?"

Julienne whirled in the direction of the voice behind her, confusion fogging her senses. "Buccaneer?" But if he was outside the cave, then . . . who . . . ? She whipped back around, her hands out in front of her, groping madly, but touching nothing but cool air.

Something landed on her shoulder and she screamed. The sound bounced off the cave walls and returned in waves. Spinning toward the mouth of the cave, she saw the shoulders and head of a man silhouetted against the daylight.

"What the devil? I thought you said you weren't scared."

"Oh, Buccaneer!" She wrapped her arms around his middle, and he cradled her against him. "I . . . Someone else is in here with us!"

"Don't be ridiculous."

"I'm not! I heard him breathing."

"You heard me breathing."

"Behind me? Back there?"

"Come outside." He guided her toward the light and examined her features carefully. "You stay here and I'll go inside and see if I can find this other person."

"No!" She clung to him, then noticed that his sleeves were rolled up past the elbows, and she backed away. "I mean . . . don't bother."

He frowned. "Did your imagination run wild, or do you think there's someone else in there?"

"I don't know. It was probably my imagination." She walked away from the cave. "Let's just forget it." Had he tried to frighten her? she wondered, but she didn't want to pursue the answer by making him go back inside the cave. Now that she was out in the sunlight again, she began to doubt herself. Had she really heard breathing or had her mind played tricks on her? And she probably hadn't touched skin, but had brushed against the damp cave walls.

"Julienne, are you all right?"

"Yes, of course." She tried to laugh, then looked around at the secluded cove. "This is a lovely place. I can see why the pirates decided to hide their treasure here."

"The scenery had little to do with that." He stopped behind her, his chest touching her back. "Out there—" he extended an arm past her, pressing even closer "—there is a break in the reef, just wide enough to let through a good-sized sloop or a small schooner. They could haul in their loot by ship, you see. That's impossible anyplace else on this key. My father built the long pier and harbor for his own vessels, but before that, there was only this place. Otherwise, you had to weigh anchor far out there and row in."

Still shaken from the cave, she could barely concentrate on what he was saying. She squinted against the glare of the sun and brought into clearer focus a jumble of beams and tattered cloth. She shaded her eyes with one hand.

"It's a shipwreck." Buccaneer answered her unspoken question.

"Recent?"

"No. It happened months ago during the last hurricane."

"Did anyone survive?"

"Only two were lost. The captain and crew came ashore, nearly drowned, and passed out here on the beach. The next morning they trudged to the estate. I gathered a few men and sent them to help salvage the ship, but when they arrived, someone had beat them to it. Quite a bit of their gold and other valuables were already missing."

"Who took it?" She turned to face him again.

Buccaneer shrugged. "Could have been almost anyone passing by."

"Passing by? Here? That seems unlikely."

His eyes darkened. "You think I had something to do with it?"

"No, I only wondered—"

"It was a wild night, and the storm helped the ocean carry bits and pieces of the shipwreck all along the straits for others to notice. Word of a shipwreck spreads like wildfire among these dots of land."

"So someone outside of Pirate's Key could have sailed here and stolen things off the ship?"

"Or it could have been someone on Pirate's Key. I'm simply saying I have no idea who took their belongings."

"Buccaneer, I'm not accusing you," she hastened to add, sensing his mounting irritation. "I was only curious."

He picked up a bit of broken shell and tossed it toward the foamy surf. "We helped them salvage the rest, and I instructed Cesare to take them to Miami aboard the *Treasure Chest*. They were happy to be alive and didn't fret too much about the lost cargo."

She cut her eyes in his direction, calculating whether or not he was telling her the unvarnished truth. Why couldn't she simply trust him? she wondered.

"I'm thirsty. What about you?"

Julienne nodded. "Did you bring a canteen?"

"I did better than that. I brought a skin of wine."

"I'd prefer water."

He sent her a chiding glance before he strode toward his horse. "We'll have wine and then traverse the rocks for a better look at the wreck."

Her excitement with the excursion returned. "Yes, I'd love to see it."

He unhooked the wineskin from around the saddle horn. "Not much left to see, you understand. The sea has claimed most of it."

"There are some sails left."

"She was a brigantine. Her foremast was square-rigged and her mainmast was fore-and-aft-rigged. She was called the *Seaworthy*, but she wasn't on that night."

Julienne watched as he uncorked the wineskin and squeezed a long stream into his mouth. "I understand about half of what you just said. Ships are mostly foreign to me."

"Then I'll have to teach you a few things about them. And about other things, as well." He passed the skin, shaking it at her when she hesitated. "Come, come, little governess. Where's your sense of adventure now? Drink some wine and unfurl your riggings."

Accepting his challenge with a hefty measure of trepidation, she squirted some of the heady juice into her mouth and swallowed it. It was fruity and sent fumes through her head. She coughed and handed the wineskin back to him. His face blurred as tears built in her eyes.

"That . . ." She swallowed and tried to find her voice. "That is stronger than the wine we had the other night."

"So it is. This is homemade."

"Who made it?"

"A woman who lives nearby. She stomps the grapes herself and ferments them with utmost care. Have some more." He extended the wineskin and laughed when she shook her head vehemently. Aiming the skin at his open mouth, he squeezed off a generous font, swallowing several times before he was done. "Ahhh! That'll cure what ails you."

"You appear to be ailing something fierce. Perhaps we should get back to the estate and put you abed."

A rakish grin tilted up one corner of his mouth. "Perhaps we should!" His eyes glimmered dangerously. "You might be good for what ails me. You might even cure me . . . after an hour or so."

Julienne's breath caught in her throat and she turned away from him to look toward the ocean. She had the sensation of drowning. "You . . . you're very humorous. Shall we explore the wreck now?"

His laughter was more like a purr. After hanging the wineskin on the saddle horn again, he tethered the horses securely to the low branches of a banyan tree. Grabbing Julienne by the hand, he strode across the sand toward the portion of shore that nosed out into the sea.

"Are you limber?"

"Why?"

"Because we'll have to hop from boulder to boulder to get a good look at the wreck."

"I can jump like a rabbit," she boasted.

He cast her a dubious glance. "Good. Then you won't need me to assist you."

Julienne looked ahead at the widely spaced boulders and wished she hadn't been so quick to brag. He went first, leaping from the shore to the first, flat-topped rock. She followed easily. The next boulder was rounded, and the footing wouldn't be so sure. It gave Buccaneer no trouble. Julienne held her breath, bunched her muscles, and jumped. She barely made it. Buccaneer didn't wait to see if she was all right. He was already on the next boulder. Julienne judged the distance and the sharp coral below the surface. She knew the coral would cut like a knife if her bare flesh touched it, scraped it. Waves lapped and slapped the boulder, leaving lacy foam and seaweed in their wake. She looked at Buccaneer, wanting to ask him to catch her, but he stood with his arms folded and didn't seem disposed to being a gentleman.

He motioned with agitation. "Come on, come, rabbit. Jump!" He started to turn away and leap to the next rock.

"Buccaneer!" Julienne called, and he twisted back around to her. "You might have to help me. I . . . that is . . ."

"I'm sure you can make it. I did."

She glared at him. "You're not going to let me fall in . . . are you? Well, are you?"

He grinned with cocky arrogance. "What do you think?" He glanced around at the sharp coral and rough-hewn rocks. "You can swim, can't you? I don't see any sharks out there today, but that coral could smart."

"I don't know what to think when you act like this."

"I suppose you'll have to test me."

"You're not funny."

His smile vanished in the blink of an eye. "You're right. I'm not. You've been defending me ever since you arrived; telling me not to think poorly of myself, not to listen to the local gossips, not to speak of my black heart, and so on and so on. If you believe in my goodness so much, then come on. Jump!"

She flinched at his sharp, rapping order. He won't let me fall, she told herself. He won't. He's only trying to unnerve me, make me doubt him so that he can tease me about it later. She drew in a breath and backed up a couple of steps. She let out her breath and ran hard, leaping at the last possible second into the air. Her feet hit the side of the next rock, and her left shoe slid out from under her. She fell against the boulder, and air rushed from her lungs. She made a wild grab at the smooth rock, finding nothing to hold on to. Then, miracle of miracles, her hands located Buccaneer's ankles and she latched on to them.

"Buccaneer!" she called to him, barely aware that her voice broke his name in half.

She felt herself slipping down the side of the boulder. The sea wet her shoes and the hem of her riding skirt. She expected to feel the stinging slice of the coral when Buccaneer's strong hands closed on her wrists. He lifted her as if she were weightless and deposited her onto solid rock beside him. A moment of relief was quickly followed by a burst of fury. She pushed at his shoulders, wishing she could knock him flat, but knowing she couldn't even make him wobble.

"Just what do you think you're doing?" she demanded. "I could have been hurt!"

"You said you could jump like a rabbit."

"So you stood there and let me get wet just because you . . . you—" She raised her hand again to him, but he grasped her wrist and brought her hand abruptly to her side.

"Take care, Julienne." He held her fast, his face so close to hers that she felt his every breath. "I caught you, didn't I?"

"In the nick of time," she pointed out, and wrenched her wrist from his grasp. "You test my patience."

"And you test mine." He inclined his head, and his eyelids drooped seductively as his gaze focused on her lips. His mouth covered hers for a few blissful seconds and then he stepped back from her.

Julienne stared at him, her feelings in turmoil, her lips tingling from the contact with his. She passed the tip of her tongue across her mouth and

tasted salt water, wine, and temptation. Buccaneer
cleared his throat and turned away from her.

"Here's the wreck you wanted to explore."

She forced herself to move, stepping gingerly to
the edge of the boulder so that she could see the
remains of what must have been a mighty ship.
Her knees trembled and her heartbeats drummed
in her ears. She sat down, trying to regain her
equilibrium.

The wreck leaned against the rocks. A school of
parrot fish sailed over the submerged deck. The
bow nosed above the waterline, and Julienne
leaned closer to read the gold-lettered name—
Seaworthy—and admire the figurehead of a mer-
maid, her fishtail looped around an anchor, her
bare breasts jutting out in all their brazen glory.

Buccaneer sat beside her, close but not touching.
"Do you know your ropes, sailor?"

She shook her head. "I can make a square knot,
but that's about it."

He crouched beside her. "A square knot isn't
much good on a ship, mate. Do you know about
your namesake?"

"There's a knot called Julienne?"

"No." He stared intently at the wreck, but one
corner of his mouth quirked. "But every sailor is
familiar with small stuff."

She wrinkled her nose, playfully, and some of
her nervousness ebbed away. Giving him a poke
in the ribs with her elbow, she laughed lightly.
Why couldn't he always be this way, so light-
hearted, so easy to talk to and laugh with? "Very
funny, Captain LaFlamme."

"Small stuff is any cordage less than an inch in
circumference. Rope, on the other hand, is an inch
or more in circumference, with three twists."

She nodded, only half listening to his lesson,
and pointed with her toe at a mast sticking out of

the water and the platform built around it. "Is that the crow's nest?"

"Yes, but that one's too large for a nest. It's a maintop, built for half a dozen men, if needed for watch."

"And when they see land they yell, 'Land ho!' "

He smiled. "Yes, but they're mainly put up there to watch for other ships. Enemy ships."

"Could they defend themselves? I don't see any cannons on board."

"She was equipped with them, but they've sunk into the sand below. No ship of any size would cast off without several cannons."

A crab scuttled near her hands, and Julienne stood and stepped away from the shipwreck. "I wish I could have seen her afloat. I have such a fascination for ships. I suppose it's because I used to watch them sail by when I lived on Key Largo, and I imagined they were headed for exotic lands and unbridled adventure. So often I wished I could go along, but I didn't want to leave Papa."

"Why not take him along?"

She sighed. "Papa didn't care for sea journeys. I could barely get him in a dinghy! He had motion sickness."

"That's easily cured."

"And he couldn't swim."

"Can you?"

"Yes, I taught myself by watching dolphins and porpoises."

Buccaneer shook his head. "A man who lived in the keys and he couldn't swim? Sounds as if he was afraid of the water."

"Not afraid, just overly respectful of it. He loved to look at it, but he didn't like to be in it any farther than knee-high. Nevertheless, he was a giant to me. A fearless giant."

"I hope someday my daughter recalls me with such devotion." He frowned out at sea. "However,

I'm beginning to seriously doubt if that day will ever come."

"Of course she will. Just give her time."

"She has no stomachache or any other ailment, does she? She simply didn't want my company."

Julienne decided not to trouble herself by denying it. "Do you know why she shuns your company?"

"No. Do you?" He swiveled around to face her, anxious for her to enlighten him, but her expression dashed his hopes. "You have no idea why she trembles if I touch her?"

"Have you ... That is, you've never beat her?"

"No. Never."

"Then she's reacting to the loss of her mother. That's the only explanation. Unless ..."

"Unless what?"

"Unless someone is influencing her by telling her lies about you."

He shook his head. "I doubt that."

"Has she always withdrawn from you?"

"No. It began after Maggie died. I tried to comfort her at the funeral, and she pulled away from me and flung herself in Rosa's arms."

Rosa. Julienne wondered if she should share her doubts about the housekeeper with him. She opened her mouth to speak, but he'd already turned away. He leaped to the next slippery boulder, then held out his arms to her.

"Come on," he called. "I'll catch you, small stuff."

She gathered her nerve, backed up, then ran and jumped. Her aim was true and she fairly plowed into him, but he was solid as the rock on which he stood, and took her weight easily. Her skirts fluttered as a breeze swept across her. The activity had loosened her braid from its pins, and it hung down her back.

"I don't know my own strength," she whis-

pered, achingly aware of his arms circling her
waist and the heat of his body against hers. "Why
did you almost let me fall into the sea?"

"I wanted to know if you truly trusted me."

"You could have asked."

"You could have lied."

"No. I won't lie to you."

His eyes smiled into hers. "I might be a fool, but
I believe you." He stroked her face and caressed
her from shoulders to wrists, then linked his fingers through hers. Her eyes reflected her wavering
indecision on whether she should encourage or
discourage him. He smiled, because it didn't matter. His mouth descended to hers. He licked the
salt water off her lips and tried to coax them apart.
Didn't she know he craved her whole mouth and
not just her trembling lips? He slipped the tip of
his tongue through the soft seam. She made a startled sound in her throat, and her tongue touched
his before retreating hastily. Buccaneer deepened
the kiss, finding her tongue again and stroking it
with his. She moaned and wilted in his arms.

The eerie howl of a wolf pierced the air and shattered the passionate encounter. Buccaneer swung
toward the misbegotten sound and scanned the
shore. What the hell . . . ?

"It's a timber wolf," Julienne said, running her
hands over her hair. Curls fell upon her forehead,
damp with sea spray. Her insides fluttered like
butterfly wings. He had kissed her again . . . and
she had allowed it . . . again. Why couldn't she resist him? Why couldn't she at least put up some
pretense of resistance?

"It's no wolf," Buccaneer said, scanning the
shoreline. "There are none on Pirate's Key."

"Then what . . . ?" She followed his eyeline, but
saw nothing amiss on shore. "Or who?"

Buccaneer saw that he'd worried her, so he

placed an arm around her narrow shoulders. "Maybe it's a ghost!"

Was he going to kiss her again? she wondered, then seized the moment before it was too late and pulled away from him. Barely keeping her balance, she bounded to the next rock and had to scramble to keep from pitching headfirst into the drink. Buccaneer followed. He reached out to steady her, and she edged away from him, afraid that one touch and she would be in his arms again, begging for the caress of his lips and tongue.

Buccaneer frowned at her. "If you don't want me touching you, say so. No need to break your neck to keep yourself away from me." His gray eyes were storm-tossed. He grabbed her elbow when she would have jumped to the next rock ahead of him. "Take care. You wouldn't be the first woman to die trying to escape me."

She shivered, and he laughed. Julienne watched, stunned, as he sprang from one boulder to the next until he was ashore. She cast off her tremors and followed, but more slowly and carefully. He didn't even wait for her on shore, but strode to the horses and was astride Blaze by the time she came to claim Seabiscuit.

"Follow that trail back to the estate," he said, pointing the way they'd come.

Julienne lifted herself into the saddle. "Where are you going?"

"I want to scout around here for that . . . wolf."

"I'll help—"

"No," he said, rejecting her offer almost before she'd finished making it. "Go back to Moonspell."

"Buccaneer, please listen to me. I'm flattered that you find me attractive . . . in some way." She gathered in a breath, wishing he would look at her instead of scan the area in search of . . . of what? She knew that she'd angered him and wished he could understand that she had difficulty keeping up with his moods and handling her own. "A poor girl like me receiving any attention from an intelligent, wealthy—"

"Enough!" He swung his gaze to bear on her, cutting her off. "Are you trying to praise me into a better mood?"

"No, I'm only saying that I'm flattered, but that I—"

"Rosa warned me that you might try to entice me and thus secure your place at Moonspell."

Julienne gasped. "That's a lie!"

He chuckled, motioning her toward the trail. "Go on. Our afternoon adventure has ended."

Julienne started to quietly obey, but her stubborn spirit wouldn't allow it. "Why are you angry with me? Who has planted these seeds of doubt in your head about me? I've done nothing to—"

"I'm not angry," he interrupted, his gaze insulting, his smile coldly cruel. "I'm simply bored. So run along, young one. Run along."

Pride tipped up her chin and straightened her spine. "Gladly, Captain LaFlamme. If you are bored with me, imagine my effort to endure your rudeness!" And she dug in her heels and sent Seabiscuit flying.

For a smoking instant, Buccaneer thought to run her aground and give her a tongue lashing before kissing her senseless, but the moment passed and he swung Blaze toward the dense foliage where he'd seen a rustle of leaves earlier. He hoped to find a wolf hiding there—a wolf that walked upright and enjoyed spying on his brethren.

After an exhaustive search, Buccaneer found no wolf, but he did find tracks made by big feet. Just about every man on Pirate's Key went barefoot, so the search was fruitless. He'd have to set a trap to catch the barefoot beast, he thought. And soon.

Chapter 7

The cranks bolted on either side of the front door were rusty, but Julienne managed to get them working to lower the big earthen pots down from the skylight. She blew against the bottom of one, and dust swirled to reveal a signature in the terra-cotta. *Isabelle*.

"Just what do you think you're doing!" Rosa demanded as she strode angrily across the foyer to Julienne. "You have no business nosing around this house! Where is Alissa?"

"She's having her nap," Julienne answered, using all her patience to keep her voice mildly pleasant. "Was Isabelle a potter? Her signature is on the bottom of this—"

"Yes, she made them. Pull them up at once and go back to the Bride's House."

Julienne filled her lungs and counted her blessings as the Sisters had taught her. Her ire lessened. "Rosa, I'd be most grateful if you'd speak to me instead of yelling at me. Where's the captain? I want to ask him if I can plant flowers in these."

"You can't. I have enough to do around here without adding gardening. I won't have them dropping leaves all over this floor."

"I'll be responsible for their upkeep, and I'll sweep the floor if any leaves should fall upon it.

Where's the captain? Ursula said he'd returned from the fields."

"He is busy. You can't plant the flowers. I say so."

"Rosa, must I find the captain by myself? Shall I stand here and shout his name? I will, you know. I'm an ill-bred orphan with no notion of what's accepted in a manor house."

Rosa glared at her, her eyes resembling small pieces of coal. "He is in his study and he doesn't want to be disturbed."

"I'll trouble him only a moment." She cranked up the pots and saw Rosa scurry in the direction of the captain's study. The woman reminded her of a quarrelsome crow, swooping from one hapless victim to the next. Resolutely Julienne followed in Rosa's angry wake and wasn't the least bit surprised to hear her whispered, poison-laden voice floating from the captain's study as she approached.

". . . and I won't have her taking over as if she's mistress of the manor, Captain Buck. First flowers, and then she'll want to draw up the menu. Selena is enough for me to worry with. Must I fight off yet another of your strutting hens?"

Strutting hens! Julienne armed herself with her humor instead of her anger as she stepped into the room. Buccaneer sat behind his desk, and Rosa stood to one side, one fist pounding into her open palm as she made her points.

"*Braaaa, brak-brak-brak-brak, brak-brak!*" Julienne let loose her imitation of a hen's cackle, earning both Buccaneer's and Rosa's astonishment. "This strutting hen would like to speak to the cock of the walk, if he wouldn't mind."

Rosa's eyes burned with malice. Buccaneer lifted a hand to hide his smile.

"The captain says you are not to plant any flowers!" Rosa announced, her face set in a thunderous frown.

"What in heaven's name is wrong with flowers?" Julienne asked, spreading her arms wide as she advanced into the room. "I happen to know that Moonspell once burst with blooms. It's evident everywhere one looks. Empty flower beds surround this place, and the pots in the foyer aren't there just to gather sunlight! My own quarters has an entire room devoted to flowers and plants, although it's been sadly neglected. I can say the same for this whole estate. This place needs a little color and something growing near it besides tobacco and weeds."

"She thinks that if she fills your pots with flowers, she can eventually fill your bed and heart," Rosa stated with a smug smile. "But you, Captain Buck, aren't the fool she takes you for."

The gross insinuation crumbled Julienne's vow to remain cheerful. A gasp escaped her and she strode toward Rosa, not knowing exactly what she intended, but strangulation wasn't out of the question.

"Why, you old—"

Buccaneer stood, his looming masculine presence dominating all else. "Rosa, thank you for your advice. Let me speak to the governess alone now." He patted the older woman's shoulder. "It will be all right."

Rosa pivoted and walked past Julienne without another glance.

"And close the door behind you," Buccaneer called out, and the housekeeper obeyed. He arched one brow. "You have a penchant for stirring up tempests in teacups, Julienne."

Julienne spread a hand above her heart. "Me? I ask to plant flowers and am accused of trying to seduce my employer, and you point the finger at me?" She laughed, but without humor. "If seduction were my aim, gardening skills wouldn't be the first arrow I chose from Cupid's quiver."

His eyes twinkled before his laugh filled the room. "Cupid's quiver?" He laughed again. "Something you read, no doubt. Ah, you are quaint. Uncommonly quaint." He rounded the desk and sat on the corner of it, one long leg swinging nonchalantly. "Which arrow would you select first, as a matter of curiosity?"

The anger went out of her, doused by his laughter. "I don't know," she confessed before a thought struck her. "Maybe I'd cook a big meal for you."

"You can cook?"

"I can try."

He lifted one dark brow, and his gray eyes sparkled with humor. "You've never cooked?"

She nodded. "Never, but I'd love to learn. Papa cooked for us, and I don't know who cooked at the orphanage, but whoever did was terrible at it. I count myself as being fairly intelligent, so I imagine I could learn culinary skills without too much trial and error."

"While I am a man with a healthy appetite, I'm not sure cooking would make my heart beat faster." He propped his fists on the desktop and leaned toward her, eyes all atwinkle. "Haven't you any other skills?"

She swallowed, her mouth suddenly dry. She had the feeling she was wading into deep, deep water. "I can sew."

"Sew?" He spread his arms out from his sides. "Do I look like a man in need of a tailor?"

She examined the perfect fit of his clothing on his lean, muscular body. "No."

"Then what else can you offer me, mam'selle?" His voice was low, his intention clear as his gaze roamed her body.

Julienne cleared her throat and decided to wade right in. "Well, I give a fine massage."

Interest glimmered in his smoky eyes. He folded his arms against his chest, and a smile tugged at one corner of his wide mouth. "And where, pray tell, did you learn that?"

"Papa taught me. Massages are one of the things he missed about Mama, so I learned to give them. I can work the kinks out of a man's muscles and have him purring like a kitten in no time."

He stared at her long and hard and made a move toward her. Julienne tensed, but stood her ground. Her senses clamored for his touch, her lips ached for his. Suddenly he squared his shoulders and leaned backward as if straining away from her enticement.

"We shouldn't be ... That is, I've digressed." His gaze lingered momentarily on her heaving breasts. "And why have you come in here looking like that?"

Puzzled, Julienne glanced down at her simple, modest dress. "Like what? I'm wearing what I usually wear during the day."

He frowned and yanked his gaze from her, then whirled toward the bookshelves. When he removed a ledger, Julienne noticed a tremor in his hand. He kept his back to her. "You wanted something, Julienne?"

"Wanted ..." For a few moments, she totally forgot what had sent her into his study, but it flooded back and she snapped her fingers. "Of course! I want to plant flowers in the foyer pots. The ones Isabelle made? And I'd like to plant a few outside, too. Rosa acted as if I were asking to plant bombs instead of bulbs, and then she ran in here to tattle on me and get you to side with her. She's determined to make my life miserable."

"Rosa has been Moonspell's housekeeper since I was a boy. My father hired her. She's used to running this house with an iron fist, and I appreciate her hard work and dedication."

"Then you won't allow me to plant flowers?"

"Yes, go ahead, but you have to tend them. Rosa won't."

"I wouldn't expect her to."

"And no more treading on Rosa's territory, Julienne. She's the senior domestic around here. When it comes to this house, she's boss."

"You're taking her side? You think her attitude toward me is proper? She stood here a minute ago and insulted me! I've done nothing to provoke such behavior."

"She's simply looking after my best interests. She is well aware that I'm a target for women aiming at a life of leisure."

"I'm not such a woman, I assure you."

"Just stay out of Rosa's way."

"And what if she insists on standing in my path? Must I constantly choose another route? You hired me to govern your daughter, but Rosa fights me at every turn. I think she even lies about me to Alissa to make the child doubt me."

"That's ridiculous. Rosa loves Alissa."

"But she doesn't love or even like me. When it comes to Rosa, you are blind."

"And you are overstepping your bounds." He tossed the ledger onto his desk and spun around to glare at her. "Plant your flowers and supervise my daughter. You have your orders; now, go."

"That's another thing," she said, her aggravation with him for taking sides against her growing by leaps and bounds. "I don't like being ordered about by you, and I certainly don't like it when Rosa speaks to me as if I were a hound underfoot!"

"Need I remind you that *I* own this estate, Mam'selle Vale?" he thundered, jerking a thumb toward his chest. "I run a tight ship here. I prefer a strict regime. When I give an order, I expect everyone to obey me without question."

"Even Alissa?"

"Even Alissa. If you can't handle that, then I suggest you find work elsewhere."

Fury pumped courage through her veins. "Shouted orders and stormy glares are no way to raise a child. You might be a sea captain, sir, but Alissa and I aren't sailors!"

"That will be enough!" He pounded the desk with his fist.

"No, it's not nearly enough!" She thrust her face close to his and settled her fist on his desk. "What are you so afraid of that you must hide behind your housekeeper's skirts and scowls?"

He clenched his jaw, and his face fused with bright color. "You are dismissed! To your quarters, mister!"

The last word hung in the air between them, slicing through the heat of the moment with rapier precision.

Buccaneer retreated first, stunned that his temper had exploded so violently that he'd completely forgotten to whom he was talking and about what. He pushed all ten of his fingers through his hair. God, what had happened? He felt drained, oddly defeated. How could a slip of a female with almond-shaped eyes reduce him to such a sorry state? It had been two days since their trip to Spirits Cove, and nearly every night he had awakened from dreams of her; dreams that had drenched him in sweat and trussed him in the bonds of unrequited lust. Selena had even started to look good to him! But he knew in his gut that bedding Selena wouldn't sate his hunger. His craving was for someone else. Someone he'd just yelled at as if she were an insubordinate shipmate.

Mortified, Julienne touched her shining mass of rich brown hair just to make sure she still had it. *Mister?* Never had she felt so gawky, so inadequate. He looked at her and saw *a boy?* No won-

der he had dismissed her so abruptly the other
day at the cove. He hadn't been joshing when he'd
confessed his boredom. He'd kissed her and had
been so *unmoved* by it all that he ceased to see any
femininity in her at all! She made a sound of remorse and waved a limp-wristed hand, words fail-
ing her.

"Julienne . . . I . . ."

She shook her head and took her leave, anxious
to be done with the uncomfortable confrontation.
Her feet moved, but she was barely aware of the
walk back to the Bride's House. Once inside, she
crossed to the full-length mirror.

A waif stared back at her. A big-eyed, pert-
nosed, small-breasted, scant-hipped waif. Oh, why
couldn't she be a bright flame like Selena or
Maggie? Why did she have to be a dying ember
like Isabelle? Buccaneer had been unhappy with
Isabelle, and he probably thinks of that poor puri-
tan whenever he looks at me, Julienne fretted.

No, that's not quite right. When he looks at me,
he sees *a boy*.

Her brown eyes filled with tears and her lips
quivered with sadness. She'd been an imbecile to
entertain the notion that she might truly attract the
captain's eye. A tear tracked her cheek. Rosa
would be so pleased when she discovered that
Captain LaFlamme was safe from the clutches of
the new governess!

"But I still get to plant my flowers," she said,
seeing Rosa's face instead of her own for an instant. "So there, you old crow!"

Rain beating on the windows awakened Julienne. She lit the lantern on the bedside table and
padded into the parlor. She looked out the French
doors at the sheet of rain and wondered if Alissa
was upstairs trembling in her bed. Maybe she

should check on her, she thought as she reached for her thin robe.

Taking the lantern with her, Julienne left her quarters and tiptoed through the quiet house to the staircase. She moved the lamp close to the face of the grandfather clock in the foyer and saw that it was coming up on four in the morning. She ascended the staircase and padded silently to Alissa's bedroom to tap on the door. When no one answered the summons, she opened the door a crack and peeked in. Alissa was sound asleep, her breathing even, her dreams deep enough to block out the fury of the storm. Julienne closed the door quietly.

Unable to resist, she glanced toward Buccaneer's room. The lamplight shifted across the carved anchor on the door, and Julienne held her breath for a moment. The door had moved! Had he been watching her? She moved closer to listen, but could hear nothing except her own erratic heartbeat. She paused to admire the intricacy of the carving and wondered what artist had chipped and sliced this nautical motif into the smooth, white wood. Perhaps she'd imagined the movement of the door ... No. She shook her head. It had been ajar, and someone had shut it. Oh, well. She shrugged and went downstairs. The ticking of the grandfather clock seemed uncommonly loud in the quiet house. The rain continued to fall in great sheets, pecking against the windowpanes and skylight as if begging to come in.

Standing at the bottom of the stairs, she thought of Alissa's sweet face and the shadows of her lashes lying like black crescents on her rosy cheeks. A beautiful child, she thought. And a troubled one. Julienne looked up at the same instant that a bolt of lightning blazed, illuminating the interior of the house for a split second. In that crumb of time she saw a figure standing at the top of the stairs—a woman . . . or a man wearing a long coat. Swallowing a garbled scream, Julienne lifted the lantern over her head, and the light swung in a bigger circle.

"Who's there? Who is it?" She advanced up the stairs again until the edge of the light circle reached the place where she'd seen the person a moment ago. But no one was there.

Julienne backed down the stairs slowly, afraid to turn around until she'd reached the first floor again. She lowered the lantern and took several deep breaths.

I didn't see anyone. My eyes deceived me.

Somewhat bolstered by her own reasoning, she crossed the foyer and tried not to run, although she wanted desperately to be inside the Bride's House again with the door bolted behind her. As she reached the threshold to the parlor, she heard a door shut upstairs, and she whirled around and stared up at the second landing. Again, nothing stirred. Julienne released her breath in a burst of frustration. Who was trying to rattle her? And why?

Whoever played these silly games wouldn't succeed in frightening her, she vowed, continuing on her way to the Bride's House. Inside her quarters again, she barred the door and set the lantern on the bedside table. She turned down the wick, but didn't extinguish the flame. The light comforted her, and her heartbeats returned to normal.

Lightning crackled and thunder boomed overhead. Julienne plastered a hand across her mouth to keep from screaming, then she chided herself. Maybe she should take refuge in Alissa's room this time, she thought, laughing off her nerves. So someone had stood at the top of the steps, and she'd spotted him . . . her. Or, more likely, nobody had been there in the first place. Certainly the incident didn't warrant such a reaction! She shivered, suddenly chilled.

What she needed were cheery flames leaping in the grate, she told herself, moving purposefully to the fireplace. The wood was already stacked, ready for a match. Julienne opened the flue, added kindling, and blew at the embers until flames shot up to feed on the dry wood. She placed a hand against the brick facing to help propel herself up from her kneeling position, and felt one of the squares shift. She pulled her hand away and discovered a loose brick. The mortar had been chipped away so that it came out easily. She peered into the black hole left behind and saw something tucked inside. Gingerly she reached in and removed a roll of paper tied with two lengths of red ribbon.

She stared at the parcel, knowing she had stumbled upon a secret. "Should I or shouldn't I?" she murmured, sitting cross-legged in front of the hearth. She plucked at the ribbon, feeling guilty, yet goaded by her curiosity. The bow unraveled and the ribbon fell into her lap. "Well, I'll just take a quick look and then put this back where I found it," she vowed, giving herself permission.

After straightening the papers in her lap, she brought the lamp near to examine the scrawled handwriting on the first page. Magdalena LaFlamme's name leapt off the paper. Julienne's heart climbed into her throat.

"This is her diary!"

Julienne rolled the paper up again as a voice inside her told her this was private and not for her eyes. That other, more persistent voice urged her to take one quick look. Where's the harm? it cajoled. Who will know if you read a few passages just to make sure it is a diary?

She unrolled the sheaf of papers and flipped through, stopping at random. Magdalena's handwriting was easy to read.

He's as tempestuous as the sea. He told me that he will tame me. I have learned that he is a hunter and I am his prey, but I can control him by purring his name and stroking his vanity. Sometimes I fear him. His temper bursts like a storm on the land and makes me tremble.

Lightning popped overhead again. Julienne jerked spasmodically. She stared at the paper in her hands. Was this Maggie's impression of Buccaneer? It must be, she reasoned. He certainly had a temper, but why would Maggie think of herself as his prey? Julienne didn't like the sound of it, but maybe Maggie did. Perhaps Maggie enjoyed the imagery of being stalked. She read the part again about purring his name and stroking his vanity. Was this the way to his heart?

Julienne sighed, wishing she knew half as much as Maggie had about how to attract a man. Something deep inside made her ache to curry favor with Buccaneer. But she was woefully inept when it came to catching a man's eye and keeping his interest. Especially a man like Buccaneer LaFlamme—so worldly, so handsome! He even thought she was after his money and landholdings. What an impression she must have given for him to leap to that conclusion!

As she rolled the papers, it occurred to her that this was the book Alissa had been talking about her mother writing and keeping in the fireplace. She should probably turn it over to Buccaneer . . .

Maggie the Magnificent.

Buccaneer's description of his wife returned to haunt Julienne, and she hugged the roll of paper to her chest. This could be an instruction book on how to woo and win Buccaneer LaFlamme! Would she dare to read it and follow Maggie's tried-and-true ways? It seemed that she did everything wrong when it came to Buccaneer, and Julienne realized that she wanted desperately to please him.

His kisses had awakened in her a profound yearning. She'd never before been so aware of her femininity and her unfulfillment as a woman.

When she had been more than willing to stay in St. Augustine and devote her life to caring for orphans and cleaning churches, the mother superior had insisted that she travel to Pirate's Key and work for Buccaneer LaFlamme. God had intervened, she told herself. He had placed Buccaneer in her life's path for a reason, hadn't He? She wasn't here just to care for Buccaneer's child. She knew that. Since the first time she'd heard his name, she'd fallen under his spell. If nothing else, Maggie's diary could give her insight into the complexity of his nature, and that would aide her in mending the rift between him and Alissa.

Buoyed by her inflated logic, Julienne tied the ribbons around the papers and replaced them behind the brick. First she'd read the diary—only those places pertaining to Buccaneer's personality—and then she'd give the diary over to him.

She felt her face heat with shame for using another woman's memories for her own benefit, but she blocked out the guilt. She wasn't hurting anyone, she argued. The good Lord had placed this book in her hands so that she could learn from it.

Julienne grabbed a poker and jabbed at the smoking logs. She had little patience with those who would use the Lord to justify their every questionable deed, and she greatly feared she had just joined their ranks.

Chapter 8

❝I can't believe you've never been to see where your papa works," Julienne said as she buttoned the back of Alissa's dress. "This will be a nice surprise for him."

"What surprise?" Selena asked, lounging in the doorway of Alissa's bedroom.

Julienne barely hid her grimace. Why did she have to show up now? she bemoaned. Another minute or two and she and Alissa would have escaped without having to answer to anyone.

"We're going to the fields," Alissa said, smiling. "It'll be a surprise for Papa."

"*Sí*, it certainly will." Selena's gaze hardened when it landed on Julienne. "You might get a surprise as well. You might see Buck blow like a volcano."

Alissa shivered and moved closer to Julienne. Placing an arm around the girl, Julienne sent Selena a scathing glare.

"He won't mind if we drop in on him for a few minutes," Julienne said, giving Alissa a quick, reassuring hug. "I've never seen tobacco fields. Alissa and I can learn about the crop together."

Selena didn't budge from the doorway. She looked from Alissa to Julienne, studying them as if they were flesh-and-blood puzzles. Abruptly she straightened from the doorframe. "You wait. I'll go with you." Then she pivoted sharply and strode toward her upstairs room.

Julienne exchanged a look of regret with Alissa. "Well, I suppose we must wait for her. It's only polite."

Alissa made a face. "I don't want her to go with us."

"I know, but we can't be rude, Alissa." She touched the girl's shiny hair. "You need to wear a hat. Where do you keep yours?"

Alissa pointed to the curtained-off area where her clothes were stored. "On the high shelf."

Julienne selected a straw boater and squatted before Alissa to tie the black velvet bow under her short chin. Impulsively she kissed the child's cheek.

"You're a sweet thing," Julienne said, grinning. "And your kisses are sweet as sugar, too." She swiped another one, bussing Alissa's cheek. "Ooo, you're going to make me as fat as a pig!"

Alissa giggled. "Can I kiss you back?"

"Why, of course, angel face!" Julienne tapped her cheek with a forefinger. "Plant one right here and we'll see if freckles grow there later."

"What?" Alissa eyed her with wonder.

"You've never heard of that? My papa always said that sometimes freckles grow where you've been kissed by someone who loves you. And if a bad person kisses you, a wart grows there!"

Alissa screwed up her mouth. "Ewww, warts! I hope freckles grow right here." She kissed Julienne's cheek.

"I've always wanted a freckle right there." She tugged at the black bow under Alissa's chin before standing again. "Ready now? Let's go hurry up Selena."

They walked, hand in hand, to Selena's room, but the woman emerged just as they reached the door. She'd changed into a frilly, ruffled white frock and she carried a matching parasol. Julienne glanced down at her own charcoal-colored dress and scuffed shoes. Ursula had given her the straw hat, but it was a little too big and rode her eyebrows. She'd found one of Alissa's older dresses and made the child change into it, not wanting Alissa to soil any of her good clothes. She and Alissa looked like poor relations of Selena. The sloe-eyed beauty strode ahead as if she were ashamed to walk with them.

"Is the wagon waiting outside?"

"Wagon?" Julienne repeated. "We'd planned on walking to the fields. They're not very far from here, I'm told."

"I'm certainly *not* walking!" Selena tipped her nose high in the air. "I'll tell the stableboy to hitch up the wagon and drive us to the fields."

"Very well, but I can drive a team. No need to bother the stableboy for that."

Selena regarded Julienne for a few moments, her gaze resting on her hands. "You can drive a team?"

"Yes. I learned how at the abbey." Julienne clasped her hands behind her, suddenly ashamed of her short fingernails and tanned hands. "They sent me into town for supplies once a month."

Selena shrugged. "If you want to drive them, I'll not stop you. But I hope you are strong enough to control the horses. I don't want to be jostled."

A good jostle would do you a world of good. Julienne nodded. "I'll do my very best."

They followed along behind her ... a good six feet behind her. Selena swept into the stables, her parasol held high, her nose jabbing the air.

"Boy! Boy! Hitch two of the horses to a wagon. We're going to the tobacco fields."

The stableboy leaned a pitchfork against the wall. "Which horses, ma'am?"

"I don't care. Hurry. We're anxious to be off."

"Yes, ma'am." He trotted off to do her bidding.

While the stableboy readied the buckboard, Julienne took Alissa from stall to stall, introducing her to the horses.

"Haven't you seen any of these before?" Julienne asked when Alissa questioned her about one.

"Uh-uh. Papa says I'm too little to ride a horse."

"Oh, posh! I was riding bareback when I was your age. I'll speak to him and see if I can't get his permission for you to begin riding lessons."

"Who will teach me?"

"I will, of course. I'm your tutor, aren't I?" Julienne glanced up and down the line of paddocks. "Which would be best for you, I wonder? Maybe that gentle white mare they call Dumpling. She's small enough, I think. You could handle her."

"I'd be scared."

"A girl with the courage of a pirate scared?" Julienne scoffed. "I think not."

"Ten pirates," Alissa corrected with a grin. "I'm as brave as *ten* pirates."

Julienne laughed. "And certainly not afraid of a horse named Dumpling. After a day of riding her, you two will be best friends, I guarantee it. The wagon's ready. Come along, Alissa."

The stableboy gave Selena a steady hand as she climbed up and then lifted Alissa onto the buckboard. Julienne let him assist her, although she didn't require it. He seemed surprised when she took up the reins.

"Ma'am, don't you want me to drive you?"

"No, I can do it. Which horses are these?"

"The gold one is Saint and the black one's Sinner."

She smiled. "I ought to be able to remember that." She flapped the reins. "Let's go. Giddap thar!" she called in her lower register.

The horses responded as she'd hoped. They rotated their ears to catch her deep tones and then set off with a jingle of harness and a creak of the wheels. She felt Selena's sharp regard, but kept her eyes focused ahead. Alissa sat between her and Selena, her small body tense with excitement.

The child's cloistered life perplexed and peeved Julienne. The captain's and Rosa's strict rules stifled Alissa. Didn't they see that? She'd lived all her life on this key, and she'd seen precious little of it. Alissa had not been to Spirits Cove or the tobacco fields. Where *had* she been? Just in the manor house and the immediate grounds? Like Moonspell, Alissa had been neglected since Magdalena's death. Julienne's conviction to correct that solidified.

"Alissa, you remember how we've been studying Florida? Well, do you know how it got its name? It means 'abundant flowers.' When Ponce de León came here seeking the fountain of youth, he was dazzled by all the flowers growing here. And do you know how many isles are in the key chain?"

"No." Alissa turned to Selena. "Do you?"

Selena sighed. "No, nor do I care."

"Ten thousand," Julienne answered, ignoring Selena's bored tone and frowning countenance. "I bet we have a million different flowers in the keys, not to mention all the trees in these parts. Mangroves and cypress, mango and tamarind. Take a deep breath, Alissa. Smell the keys."

Julienne and Alissa filled their lungs with air. Selena stared straight ahead, refusing to participate. Suddenly Julienne smelled something she couldn't identify. A strange, sweet smell. She sniffed again and the scent struck her senses sharply.

Then the wagon lumbered over a rise and Julienne gasped at the sight before her as the sweet aroma embraced her, enveloped her.

"Oh, my!" she breathed, staring at the sea of white cloth stretching out before them. "This is beautiful!"

Acres and acres of white tents billowed over the land, all propped up with poles so that it looked as if someone were growing tree stumps. But Julienne knew she'd find tobacco plants in between the posts and under the miles of white cloth. She could see a few people milling underneath it. Horses were tethered near several sheds on the perimeter of the field. A chestnut pranced into view, and the man astride it rode with a regal bearing, his white shirt tucked into tight riding breeches, his panama hat shading his face.

"There's Buck," Selena said, waving madly. "What are we waiting for? Why have we stopped?"

Julienne clucked her tongue, and the horses set off again, moving carefully along the narrow path that snaked down to the fields.

"Isn't this beautiful, Alissa?" Julienne asked, nudging the child with her elbow. "I never dreamed the tobacco fields would look like this! I wonder why they cover them with cloth."

Selena glanced disdainfully at her. "It is shade, dunce."

"Pardon me?"

Selena sighed. "It is shade tobacco." She eyed Julienne's puzzled expression. "It's the best there is, grown for cigars. Cigarette tobacco is grown out in the sun and called broadleaf."

Julienne smiled. "You know a lot about it, don't you?"

"All I want to know. I have been raised around the smelly mess."

"That's what I've been smelling! It's sort of pungently sweet like the incense they burn in church sometimes."

Selena nodded and curled her upper lip. "Tobacco."

The sound of the wagon and horses must have reached the field hands, because work stopped as all faces turned toward the newcomers. Buccaneer reined in Blaze and stared in their direction. Selena waved grandly, but Buccaneer didn't return the greeting. Apprehension stole through Julienne, making her fear that Buccaneer would indeed not want them there. He probably had rules about visitors intruding, she thought with a frown. The man was a font of regulations. She directed the team straight for him and reined them alongside Blaze.

"I told her not to come, but she insisted," Selena said, apparently sensing Buccaneer's displeasure and jumping at the chance to blame Julienne. "She says it is time Alissa saw the fields, and I came along to assure you that I tried to stop her from bothering you, but she absolutely *ignored* me, Buck. You must speak to her and remind her of her place at Moonspell."

Julienne waited a moment and arched an inquiring brow at Selena. "Finished? Good." She turned her attention to Buccaneer. His expression wasn't as hard-edged as she'd feared. "We didn't come here to pester you. I only wanted Alissa to see what you do. Children are curious about such things. It's only natural." She eyed Selena. "And I fail to see why I should be shot at dawn for venturing out here."

Selena squinted menacingly at Julienne. "Buck, did you hear her? I will not tolerate impertinence from the household staff!"

Buccaneer's lazy gaze drifted to Alissa. A smile poked at the corners of his mouth. "Good morning, Lissa. Want to ride on Blaze with me?"

Alissa shook her head and burrowed against Julienne's side. Julienne firmly pushed the child away and made Alissa look at her.

"Go on and ride with your father." When Alissa

shook her head, Julienne lowered her voice. "Alissa, you are princess of this land. Your papa is the king and you are the princess. Now, the king has asked that you ride with him and survey your holdings. It's your duty as princess." She kissed Alissa's forehead. "Not to mention being a great honor. Go on, now. Do your duty."

"What a pile of rubbish," Selena scoffed. "You act loco sometimes, governess girl. Completely loco!"

Alissa scrambled over Selena's feet and held out her arms to Buccaneer. He lifted her easily and sat her sideways in front of him. She slipped her arm around her father's waist and grabbed a handful of Blaze's mane with her free hand.

"That's a good girl." Buccaneer reined Blaze in a tight circle. "Off we go, Princess Alissa. Your subjects await you."

"What are we supposed to do?" Selena called after him. "It is hot out here and we are thirsty!"

If Buccaneer heard her, he showed no sign of it. Julienne guided the team to a shady place under a canopy of tree limbs and tied them off there. She gathered her skirts and climbed down from the buckboard seat.

"Where are you going?" Selena demanded.

"I'm going to explore." She admired the crop and spotted Cesare striding toward her. "Hello, there! Selena, it's your father."

Selena offered her hand, and Cesare helped her down from the wagon. "Papa, Buck is ignoring me. He is mad because we've come, but it is not my fault. *She* insisted. He's punishing me, though."

"Nonsense," Cesare chided her. "True, he doesn't like for you to be here, but he's not doing you any harm."

"Why doesn't he want us here?" Julienne asked.

"Because this is a man's place." Cesare waved

an arm. "See? No women. The men are here to work, and Buccaneer doesn't want a woman around to divert their attention." He shrugged. "But since you are here, what would you like to see?"

"The water bucket," Selena said, holding the parasol high to give herself more shade.

"Don't worry, daughter. The sun won't melt you."

"I'd like to see the crop up close," Julienne said. "I'm fascinated by this. Why haven't more people grown tobacco in the keys?"

Cesare stood between Julienne and Selena and hooked his arms in theirs, then guided them toward the acres of tents. "You can't grow tobacco just anywhere, but when I saw this land, I told Buck that I thought a crop might take root here. It is doing well, so far. We had a pretty good harvest last year. This year will be even better."

A young man emerged from under one of the canopies. He was shirtless, and his teak-colored skin gleamed with perspiration. Julienne noted his black hair and eyes and guessed he, too, was from Cuba.

"This is our foreman, Lorenzo," Cesare said. "Lorenzo, have you met the new governess, Julienne Vale?"

"No." Lorenzo smiled, showing two rows of straight, white teeth. He dipped his head in greeting, and his gaze slipped over Julienne with oily efficiency. "So pleased. So *very* pleased," he almost purred in a heavily accented voice. His gaze meandered to Selena. "And here is the beautiful Señorita Selena. You must carry a stick to beat off her suitors, Cesare."

"If I did, you'd have a knot on your head by now," Cesare noted. "Selena is thirsty. Could you take her to the water truck?"

"But of course! What about you, señorita?"

"No, thank you," Julienne said, clutching Cesare's arm more tightly. She didn't like the way Lorenzo looked at her. He made her feel as if she weren't wearing a stitch!

Selena fit her hand in the crook of Lorenzo's arm and they strolled in the opposite direction.

"Lorenzo is the local Romeo," Cesare said with a chuckle. "I'd worry if he were romancing anyone but my Selena. She can handle him. In fact, it's Lorenzo I'm worried about."

Julienne laughed with him. "Cesare, I don't know anything about tobacco, but it looks as if it's a difficult crop to grow."

"Ah, sí. The most difficult." He raised a hand, motioning for Buccaneer to ride closer. "The young governess wants to know about tobacco, Buck. You tell her while I take this one to the water wagon. Want a cool drink, Alissa?" He raised his arms for Alissa and helped her slide off the horse. "I want to show her off to the others," he told Buccaneer. "Also I must chaperone my daughter. She's with Lorenzo, trying to make you jealous."

Buccaneer pursed his lips to keep from grinning. Julienne looked from him to Cesare and wondered if Cesare wanted his daughter to succeed in snaring Buccaneer.

"Chico has made some dolls you might like," Cesare said, patting the top of Alissa's perky hat.

"Dolls?" Alissa echoed.

"Sí, tobacco-leaf-and-straw dolls. Very nice. He might give you one for the price of one smile." Holding Alissa in his arms, Cesare walked away, chatting amicably to the child.

Julienne angled her gaze up to the man still sitting astride the chestnut stallion. "I suppose you'd rather eat a bucket of rusty nails than entertain my questions."

A smile teased the corners of his mouth and he

swung a leg over the horse and dropped lightly to the ground. "This isn't the place for young women. Hard work goes on here."

"So I can see. It's just that I thought Alissa should see where you work. This is her home, and she knows so little about it." She tipped back her borrowed hat to get an unobstructed view of the field. "Why do you cover them?"

"Because they have to be protected. They're like children. You must shelter them until they grow big."

Like your daughter, Julienne thought, but managed to keep the observation to herself.

"Selena said that the kind that's uncovered is called broadleaf."

"Yes, it's not as fine. This crop is to be used for the best cigars." He glanced at her from head to foot. "It's good you dressed accordingly. Selena, on the other hand, looks as if she's going to church instead of a dirty tobacco field. She should know better."

"Perhaps she's trying to impress someone."

He looked at Selena and Lorenzo lounging near the water wagon. "Then she succeeded."

Julienne had meant that Selena was trying to catch Buccaneer's eye, but her arrow had missed the mark. "Cesare says this is a tricky crop to grow."

"He ought to know. He's been around it all his life. He's one of the best cigar makers in the world. Lorenzo . . . you met him?"

She nodded. "The foreman. I take it he's also from Cuba."

"Yes. Cesare brought him over. Lorenzo has the touch."

"What's that?"

Buccaneer rubbed a thumb and forefinger together in illustration. "That uncanny touch . . . a knowing. He knows his crop. He knows when to plant, irrigate, harvest."

"You don't have this knowledge?"

"I'm learning." He removed his hat and drew his forearm across his brow. His hair gleamed like a raven's wing in the sun. "Once you plant the crop, then it's the boss. It's out of your hands. You've got to keep it warm, keep it sheltered, and worry, worry, worry. Is it too wet, too dry, too hot? Are there bugs, disease?" As he talked, he moved toward the tented fields, and Julienne fell into step beside him. He ducked under the cloth and into the sultry shade and brushed a hand haphazardly through his hair before putting his hat back on.

"I helped the Sisters tend a vegetable garden, but it was the size of a lady's kerchief compared to this!"

"Yes, and anything can happen and wipe out the whole crop. One field burned to a crisp the first year we planted. Somebody must have thrown a match near it, or maybe it was struck by lightning. We came out that morning to a black field."

He stopped to examine some thickly bunched plants. "These need to be thinned out. The big ones will be planted in another row to let the smaller ones grow."

Julienne rubbed one of the sticky leaves, then leaned closer to sniff. "I could smell them before we saw them. The scent is distinctive."

"I don't even notice it anymore. Last year worms attacked the fields and took out six rows overnight." He untied the red bandanna from around his neck and mopped his brow with it, then crammed it into his back pocket. "That's what makes farming a misery. Fate. She points her finger, and overnight something is ruined beyond repair."

"That's why you enjoy it, too. It's a challenge."

She stroked another fuzzy leaf. "And it's quite an accomplishment when you harvest a good field of tobacco."

"Harvesting is just the beginning! Then the damn stuff has to be dried to perfection in those sheds." He swung an arm to take in the small structures. He'd rolled his shirt sleeves up past the elbows, and Julienne couldn't help but notice the muscles rippling under his deeply tanned skin. She caught the scent of him—earthy, warm, distinctly masculine. So unlike any other smell she'd experienced. Her nostrils flared in response. "If you do one thing wrong, everything is ruined," he continued. "You might as well burn the leaves to ash."

Julienne wrenched her attention back to the leafy plants. "My, it is a temperamental crop. No wonder you picked it to be your passion."

He eyed her. "And what does that mean? I feel as if I've been lectured . . . or perhaps ridiculed."

"You must admit you're temperamental, and this tobacco seems to take up much of your time . . . if not most of it. It's good that you have such a keen interest, but your daughter would grow just as wonderfully as this crop if you'd give her a bit more of your attention."

He squinted at her, but she felt no anger emanating from him. In fact, his eyes held silvery lights. "Were you this outspoken around the nuns?"

"Oh, much more so! Mother Superior threatened to gag me once."

He grinned. "I don't doubt that for a second. It's a wonder she didn't make good on her threat."

"She sent me here instead and asked that I think before I speak, but it's difficult for me. I'm rather opinionated."

"No!" He widened his eyes, mocking her. "Opinionated? You?"

She grinned back at him, enjoying his teasing. "I'm glad you're not angry that I brought Alissa to the fields."

"Just don't make a habit of it." He gestured toward the water wagon, where the workers had gathered around Cesare and Alissa. "As you can see, the field hands look for any excuse to quit their work."

"Alissa seems to have charmed them. I take it they rarely see her."

"Some have never seen her."

"Why do you keep her prisoner in that house?"

"She is not a prisoner." He rounded on her, his eyes flashing. "Why do you think it's your place to criticize the way I choose to raise my child?"

"I'm not—"

"You are, and you will cease." He angled closer so that she couldn't miss the mounting fury in his eyes. "Do I make myself clear?"

"Yes." She looked away, acknowledging the power of his personality. Still, her stubborn streak wouldn't let her remain silent. "Still, the whole key is her home, and she knows so very little about it. It seems a shame."

He drew in a deep breath, as if he were gathering his willpower so as not to lash out at her. "I don't want her to be a wild child. I want her to be raised a lady."

"Wild child?" The accusation stung. "You were raised similar to me. Do you think we're heathens?"

"I didn't say you were a heathen. Although I don't think my upbringing was particularly grand. Look how I turned out."

She examined him with a swift, encompassing glance. To her eyes, he looked magnificent with his shirt molded to his wide chest and muscled arms, and his legs braced apart. "Not too bad from my standpoint."

He angled closer, the brim of his panama hat touching the brim of hers. "Oh, no? Most people think I killed my wives."

She inched backward, a tremble feathering through her body. She knew he was testing her again, trying to rattle her and make her admit that he frightened her and that she didn't trust him. But it wasn't true. A small part of her might be frightened, but mostly she was titillated by his challenge and angry that he would doubt her sincerity. What did she have to do to prove herself to him?

"Having second thoughts, mam'selle?" he taunted.

Julienne shrugged. "Hardly. Idle minds make idle gossip."

"Don't be so hasty to dismiss it."

She rested her hands at her waist and gave him a level stare. "You expect me to believe that you murdered your wives?"

"Other people are convinced of it."

She sensed he was interested in her rejoinder, so she chose her words carefully. "I'm not other people, Buccaneer. And I wouldn't work for a man I thought was a murderer. Furthermore, I would try my best to remove Alissa from a murderer's home. I think Alissa needs you, and you need her. She's nervous around you because you don't spend enough time with her."

"I see her every morning."

"For half an hour at the most. Usually it's for ten minutes and then you're off to work."

"I see her during the dinner hour."

"And you talk to Cesare and Selena and rarely address Alissa."

Anger smoked his eyes. "I hired you to be governess to my daughter, not to supervise me!" He started to turn from her, but she grabbed his sleeve.

"I brought her out here so that she could be with you, Buccaneer. She's shy around you because she doesn't know you, and most of the time you act as if she's a nuisance."

"I have never given her that impression."

"You give her that impression daily! You hired me to fill a gap I can't fill. I can't give Alissa a father's love. Only you can do that."

He jerked his sleeve from her grasp. "You try my patience, Julienne. I love my daughter, but she pushes away from me. You've seen it with your own eyes."

"And I'm trying to tell you that it won't get any better if you allow her to push you away."

"I frighten her. I make her uneasy. Just as I did Isabelle—and, later, Maggie."

She frowned. "I hate to disappoint you, but you're not a monster." She faced his puzzled expression. "And don't act as if you don't know what I'm talking about. Sometimes I think you cultivate the image of yourself as a plunderer, a murderer, a monster. Your daughter wants your love. The only thing monstrous she sees in you is your reluctance to embrace her, kiss her, rejoice in her childhood. My father—"

"I knew it." He propped his hands on his hips and swayed back to glower at the blue sky. "Any time talk turns to parents, I must be compared to that paragon you called Papa."

"He had his faults, but he never made me feel like baggage." She knew she'd gone too far even before his lips thinned to white and his eyes darkened to charcoal. "Buccaneer, I didn't mean to hurt your feelings or to—" She clamped her lips shut since she was speaking to his back. He strode angrily along the rows, gathered Blaze's reins in a tight fist, and sprang onto the horse's sleek back.

Go ahead and turn your back on me, Buccaneer LaFlamme, she fumed inwardly. But eventually I will break through your defenses and I'll find that heart of yours. And I'll bet a month's wages it isn't black or void of emotion.

Taking a deep, calming breath, she glanced around. She'd hoped the trip to the tobacco fields would bring Buccaneer and Alissa closer, but she'd managed to drive them further apart by pointing an accusing finger at Buccaneer. He certainly didn't need more blame piled on his head, she thought. He blamed himself for enough already.

Chapter 9

Pushing aside the tray of food she'd asked Rosa to bring upstairs to her, Julienne stared at the red spots mushrooming over her arms and hands. Her face started to burn, and she balled her hands into fists to keep from clawing at it.

Poison ivy? Had she walked through a patch during her excursion to the tobacco fields earlier that day? She smothered a groan, dreading the hours ahead.

Poison ivy. How could she have not noticed it? She had a good eye for finding rash-giving plants before they found her. Her mind raced ahead. Who should she tell? Could she suffer through the rash by herself? Unlikely, she thought. Sooner or later, someone would notice.

Her cheeks stung mightily. "Not my face, too!" she moaned. The itching intensified to the point of intolerance. She paced and scratched at the red spots on her arms, although that seemed to make the itching worse instead of better. She framed her face in her hands and felt the skin heat her palms.

Miserable, she sat in the armchair again. Think, think. There must be something she could do to help herself. Maybe a cold bath would ease the fever attacking her body. If only she knew what had caused this deplorable state! She tried to remem-

129

ber where she might have walked through the poison ivy, but couldn't.

Someone rapped at the Bride's House door, and Julienne clamped a hand over her mouth to keep from crying out. Now what? Oh, please, let it be Ursula coming to her aide.

"Julienne?" Buccaneer called through the door.

Julienne pressed her lips together. Maybe he'd go away.

"It's Buccaneer LaFlamme. May I come in?"

"No! Please, I . . . I can't see you now."

"Are you ill?"

"Yes."

"What's wrong? Maybe I can help."

"I'm just ill, that's all."

"Are you sure you're not pouting? We exchanged some heated words this afternoon, but certainly it wasn't so bad that you can't show yourself at dinner tonight. You've worried Alissa."

"I'm sorry. I . . . I'm fine. I'll see you all tomorrow."

"Julienne, I won't leave until you tell me what ails you. Open the door, please."

"I can't. I'm not decent."

"Then get decent," he commanded.

She sighed, wishing he weren't as stubborn as a mule. The swelling had moved to her face, making her lips and eyelids tingle. What if she needed a doctor! "Julienne, must I break down this door?"

"No, don't do that." She rolled her eyes, surrendering to his single-mindedness. She knew he meant every word. He wouldn't hesitate to break down the door like some barbarian. "Wait a moment." She reached for a wrapper and tied it at her waist before going to the door. She opened it a crack to tell him all was well and he could leave her alone, but he pushed the door and her out of his way. "What are you . . . ! Am I afforded no privacy?"

He moved farther inside, then turned to face her. He dominated the room and her. For a few moments, she forgot all about the bedeviling rash. He stared at her hard, uncompromisingly. "Now, what seems to be the trouble with you?" His gaze drifted to where she scratched furiously at her thigh. He grabbed one of her wrists and jerked up the sleeve of her loose wrapper.

"Stop that!" she protested, trying to tear her wrist from his grasp, with no success.

He examined the angry red spots on her forearm, and his grip lessened. A smile softened his features. "Julienne, didn't you handle tobacco leaves today?"

"Yes. Why?"

He let go of her. "You're tobacco-poisoned."

"What?" She stared at her hands, her palms, her arms. "I thought it was poison ivy."

"It's similar to that." He took her by the shoulders and turned her toward the bedroom. Resting a hand between her shoulder blades, he guided her there. "You lie down and I'll have Rosa mix up some soda and aloe paste. It'll draw the heat and sting out of your skin."

Julienne shook her head. "I don't want Rosa tending to me."

He gave a conceding nod. "Ursula, then." He flung back the top sheet. "Get in."

She hesitated, feeling vulnerable and not sure she wanted to be flat on her back with him in the room. She stared at the bed. Had he made love to Maggie in this bed?

He arched one brow at her. "Well? Must I place you in bed myself and tuck you in as I do Alissa?"

"No." She slid quickly between the sheets, bringing the top sheet up to her chin.

"When Ursula brings in the paste, spread it everywhere you itch, and you'll be much better in the morning."

"Why didn't you warn me?"

"About what?"

"This!" She flung out her spotted arms.

"I didn't think about it. Some people are affected by the tobacco and some aren't." He shrugged as if it were of no consequence.

"How long will it last?"

"Only a day or two. I remember the time I was afflicted." He stood at the foot of her bed, tall and potently masculine in this, her feminine corner of his world. "I was miserable, but too proud to tell anyone I had contracted some damnable disease. Cesare caught on, though, and spread a balm on me from head to foot. I let the rash go for a couple of days before Cesare intervened. If I'd simply confided in him, it would have tormented me only a day instead of a week." His smile comforted. "You'll feel much better tomorrow."

She released a long, shaky breath. "You can be rather nice when you let your guard down."

His gaze drifted from her face down the length of her. Julienne felt exposed. She pulled the sheet up higher again and crossed her arms over the front of her. His gaze snapped back to her face. "Have Ursula help you if there are places you can't reach. I'd offer my services, but I know you wouldn't accept them." He bent closer to her. "You're still mad about today, aren't you? Soon you'll realize that I don't take well to lectures or unsought advice."

"I was only trying to—"

"Yes, I know, but stop trying and we'll get along better. Believe me, you can't change me. Others have tried and failed. I know you'd like me to fit your image of a good father and loyal citizen, but save your breath." He started to turn away, but stopped. "Why don't you like Rosa?"

"I don't trust her."

"Don't be ridiculous," he scolded, moving toward the parlor. "Rosa is completely trustworthy."

"Maybe toward you," Julienne called after him. "She treats mongrels better than she treats me."

He was in the parlor, but he paused halfway to the door leading to the rest of the house to look back at her. "She's protective of me and my family. I appreciate her allegiance."

"I don't appreciate her assuming that I'm a moneygrubbing guttersnipe."

"You exaggerate."

"Are you blind to her rudeness or do you simply condone it? The only people she's nice to are you and Alissa. She thinks everyone else is out to steal your money or marry into it."

He sent her a dark scowl. "You sound just like Selena." He left her, shutting the door with a bang.

She winced. What hurt worse? she wondered. The rash or being likened to Selena?

Standing before the mirror in her bedroom, Julienne touched the raw, tender spots on her face and neck. The soothing paste had conquered the itching, but patches of her skin still stung. Why hadn't Buccaneer warned her about tobacco poisoning?

A timid tap at the door drew her attention from her polka-dotted face, neck, and arms. Ursula peeked around the door facing. "Yes, come in," Julienne said. "It's better today, but the welts are tender."

Ursula's smile was all compassion. "I am one of the lucky ones. The poison never took me."

"I wish it had passed me by. I wanted to learn more about the crop, but it looks as if I can't even get near it again."

"Oh, no, señorita." Ursula rushed into the room. "The poisoning, it comes only once. Now you need not worry. It is over." She flicked her fingertips off her thumbs, making a soft exploding sound. "Like a spell, it has been cast and can never visit you again. The pink spots will be gone by tomorrow. The itching, it is already gone?"

"Yes. The medicine worked miracles." She turned away from the mirror. "Is Alissa still eating her breakfast?"

"*Sí*, and Captain Buck wanted to know why you didn't come down. I told him you were too spotted. He laughed." Humor sparkled in her dark eyes. "Oh, he did laugh."

Julienne grimaced. "I bet he did. Selena probably laughed even harder."

Ursula shrugged. "*Sí*, but don't you waste worry over that one." She clutched one of Julienne's hands. "I bring you some things!"

"What things?"

Ursula squeezed her hand. "Captain Buck, he told me to bring them to you. He said they would make you forget your spots."

"I doubt anything can do that."

"These will." Giving her a secretive smile, Ursula hurried out the door, but returned within a minute, her arms full of colorful fabrics.

"What's this? The material the captain promised me?"

"Better than that," Ursula said, heading for the bed to drop her armload onto it. "Ready-made clothes!" She whirled and headed for the door again. "There is more."

"M-More?" Julienne moved slowly toward the bed, almost afraid to blink for fear the room would dissolve like a dream.

Ursula returned, this time carrying a stack of white garments and footwear. She laid the things on the bed with the others. "Undergarments, so you'll be well dressed from the skin out. He must be pleased with your work or he wouldn't have gone to such trouble for you."

Julienne counted five dresses and one night-gown. The latter brought a flush of warmth to her already stinging cheeks. She couldn't think about him considering her underthings or she'd start itching again. She trailed her fingers over the dresses of yellow, blue, rose, cream, and peach. She wondered what the mother superior would say about this. "I can't accept these."

"Of course you can, and you will," Ursula insisted. She grabbed Julienne by the shoulders and forced her around for a confrontation. "You can't throw Captain Buck's generosity back in his face! You need new clothes, and he has provided. Take them and be grateful."

"But they're too fine," Julienne protested. "I expected house dresses!"

"These are house dresses."

"No, they're . . . I've never had such lovely things."

"He wants you to dress like this in this house, so at Moonspell these are house dresses. He could have gone along with Selena and made you wear uniforms." She glanced at her own crisp uniform and frowned. "Be glad he didn't!"

"Yes, I am glad, but I thought he was going to give me a bolt of cloth and I would make—"

"This is better," Ursula interrupted. "Which will you try on first?" She whirled back to the bed. "Look at these underclothes! Such nice fabric, and with pretty ribbons laced through the ruffles. This satin chemise will feel light as a feather against your skin."

"Satin . . ." Julienne shook her head, feeling dazed. "I've never worn anything made of satin." She admired the shoes—a sturdy brown pair and black kid leather high-tops. She recalled his amazement when she'd disclosed that she owned only the pair of shoes she wore. Well, he'd remedied that. Never had she owned such fine footwear. Never had she dreamed she ever would!

"Why has he done this?"

"So that you will be a good example for his daughter," Ursula answered.

"Yes, that's it. He did this for Alissa."

"And for you. He likes you."

"He likes you, too, but he hasn't spent his money on a new wardrobe for you. No, he did this for Alissa. He doesn't want to be ashamed for her to be seen with me in my orphanage hand-me-downs."

Ursula smiled. "If that is what you wish to believe . . ." She shrugged grandly. "He gave orders for you to rest today. I will put more aloe on your blisters. He says you can join them for dinner if you are feeling up to it."

"I can't laze about here today. Alissa will be—"

"Alissa is going to the fields with Captain Buck."

"She is?" Julienne looked up from the cream dress she was admiring, struck by this morsel of news.

Ursula pulled the rose gown from the others to examine it more closely. "Señorita Selena said she'd watch over Alissa, but Captain Buck said no. He wants to spend more time with his child."

"He does, does he?" Julienne smiled, savoring the small victory. The bright colors and exquisite fabrics tempted her and she surrendered, gathering up the bright yellow dress. She held it against the front of her and pivoted toward the mirror. "Oh, Ursula! Am I dreaming? I'm almost afraid to believe that these things are mine."

"Look them over while I prepare the medicine. I want to see you in all of them. Which will you wear this evening at dinner?"

"I don't know. They're all so pretty. Why don't you try them on, too?"

"Me? They wouldn't fit. I am too tall and my shoulders are too broad—not to mention my chest sticks out much farther than yours!" Laughing, she headed for the privy area. "Did you notice the French lace on the collar and cuffs of the night-gown?"

"French lace on a nightgown? Whoever heard of such extravagance?"

"You should have seen the things Señora Maggie used to wear," Ursula said, her voice drifting from the partitioned-off area. "Satin and lace and new dresses every season. She thought nothing of ordering half a dozen dresses at once, and she hired only the best seamstresses in St. Augustine and Jacksonville. One time she went on a shopping trip to New Orleans and came back with twenty-five new gowns. She gave Selena and her other girl cousins some of them."

Twenty-five gowns! Julienne couldn't imagine why a woman would buy so many at once, and how much had they cost? Buccaneer LaFlamme must have more money than Julienne could fathom, and Magdalena must have been less than wise when it came to spending it. She stroked the rich tapestry of old rose, admiring the way the color complemented her skin tones. She tried not to feel unworthy of Buccaneer's unexpected generosity.

"Julienne! Julienne!" Alissa called, running into the room. She wore play clothes and a floppy hat.

"Good morning, Alissa," Julienne greeted her, laying aside the gown. "I hear you're going to work with your papa today."

Alissa stopped in front of her and nodded, solemnly, gravely. Suddenly tears built in her silver eyes.

"Alissa, what's wrong?" Julienne crouched before her. "You're not crying because you're going to spend the day with your father, are you?"

Alissa shook her head.

"Then what?"

The child touched a trembling finger to Julienne's cheek. "I did that."

"What? You mean the rash? Now, how could you have given me a rash?" she chided.

"I kissed you there and g-gave you a wart! I'm a bad, bad girl. Don't tell Papa I'm bad! Please, don't tell him."

She wrapped her arms around Alissa and rocked her back and forth. "You didn't give me warts, silly goose. The tobacco plants did! Ursula says it happens all the time, but you only get it once. The tobacco didn't bother you because you are the princess of this land, and it and everything on it knows that." She smiled at Alissa and was given a smile in return. "That's better." Kissing the girl's button nose, Julienne realized she was growing more than fond of the child.

"Do you hurt?"

"No. I'll be fine by the time you get back from the fields. I'm almost well now." She moved her thumbs across Alissa's damp cheeks. "You must learn to save your tears and use them only when they'll do the most good."

"When is that?"

"It's one of the things females figure out for themselves." She pulled Alissa back into her arms for a quick, hard hug. "I expect to find a new freckle on my cheek as soon as these awful blisters are gone."

"Alissa?" Buccaneer's voice drifted up to them from somewhere downstairs.

"Your father is waiting. Go on and have a wonderful time."

"I wish you could come."

"I'd only be in the way. He wants to spend the day with *you*. He loves you." She gave Alissa a gentle push toward the door. When the child stopped on the threshold to look back at her with a wistful expression, Julienne made a shooing motion. "He's waiting! I'll see you this evening, and you can tell me all about your day."

"Alissa!" Buccaneer boomed again, and Alissa scampered out of the Bride's House like a frightened rabbit.

Julienne sighed and sat back on her heels. She prayed that the day would strengthen the bond between father and daughter. Whether they knew it or not, they needed each other's love desperately.

Standing, Julienne joined Ursula behind the curtained partition. "Ursula, have you noticed how reluctant Alissa is to be alone with her father?"

Ursula stirred soda and aloe juice and water, making a paste. "*Sí*, but it was not always so."

"Things were different when Magdalena was alive?"

Ursula's sideways glance revealed her surprise. "How did you know that?"

"Just a guess. Many things changed around here after her death, I imagine. Did she dote on Alissa?"

Ursula knitted her brow. "No. Never that."

Surprise made her gasp softly. "You mean she wasn't close to Alissa?"

"Alissa loved her, but Maggie didn't give the child much of her time. Sometimes at night she would read Alissa a story, but that was not often. I do not like to speak poorly of the dead, but she was not so good a mother. I don't think she even wanted to have a child. She told me once that she had Alissa to keep Captain Buck happy."

"Now I'm confused."

"Take off that wrapper and I'll smooth this medicine on your spots."

Julienne shrugged out of the thin robe and held out her arms to Ursula. "I thought Alissa was withdrawn because she missed her mother, and

Buccaneer hadn't paid much attention to her while Magdalena was alive."

"I have no answer. All I know is that I did not notice Alissa being so skittish of her father until after her mother died. Why she avoids him, I can't say."

"Do you think he is . . . well, mean to her?"

"No," Ursula said with a quick shake of her head. "Not Captain Buck. He barks sometimes, but he would never hurt Alissa."

"Perhaps he doesn't realize his strength. Maybe he disciplined her and didn't realize that he'd been too rough."

"This, I can't believe. He is so gentle with her. It pains him that she has pulled away from him this past year."

Julienne pivoted so that Ursula could dab the white paste on the raw places on her back. "What about Rosa? Do you trust her?"

"I withstand her as I withstand sickness and bad weather."

Julienne laughed lightly. "That's a good way to put it. She seems to have taken an instant dislike to me, but I understand she was totally devoted to Magdalena."

"Ah, yes. Maggie could do nothing wrong as far as Rosa was concerned. She was a saint to Rosa."

"Was she related to Rosa?"

"No, but she was everything Rosa wished to be. Beautiful, fiery, passionate. She was a man's woman, you understand? She brought men to their knees."

"Rosa must have been crushed when Maggie died."

"She didn't cry. That is strange, eh? I could tell that she was sad and wanted to cry, but she was like a zombie, going about her work, taking care of Captain Buck and Alissa, not allowing any of us to mourn in front of them or her. She made up all these rules, and Captain Buck turned things over to her."

"And what about the captain? Did he change?"

"*Sí.* He changed the most. When it was discovered that Magdalena had been strangled, he locked himself in his quarters for three whole days and would see no one, would eat nothing. When he emerged, he ordered that most of Magdalena's clothes be taken into Key West and given to the poor. He gave Rosa some of Maggie's jewelry and kept a few items back to give to Alissa when she's older."

"Has no one tried to find out who killed Magdalena?"

"The marshall questioned Captain Buck. Captain Buck ordered him off his land. It was said that the law thought Captain Buck had murdered her."

"But you don't believe that." Julienne turned around to face Ursula again and could see the answer in her face.

"Captain Buck is no murderer, although he probably had good reason to wish his wife harm."

"Why?"

"She moved out of his bed, didn't she?"

"But that's no reason to kill someone!" Julienne argued.

"There are other reasons." Secrets shone in Ursula's eyes. "But I will not speak of these things." She smiled suddenly. "Go put on the yellow dress first!"

Julienne nodded and moved back to the bed, where the new clothes looked like a fallen rainbow across the coverlet. She ran her fingertips across the bright fabrics and noticed that none were what Buccaneer had called "the colors of Maggie." No black, no green, no fiery red. She remembered him standing before his dead wife's portrait, lifting a glass of whiskey to her in a toast, congratulating her on still being in control of the monster that was in him. Was Magdalena still in control of the people living at Moonspell? Could a soul be so strong it could reach up from the grave and—

A hand landed on Julienne's shoulder and she released a short, piercing scream. Ursula fell back a step, staring at her, then laughing with her.

"What did you think had hold of you?"

"You don't want to know," Julienne said, embarrassed to have let her thoughts run wild. "I think the tobacco has poisoned my mind, too." She pressed a hand to her forehead. "Maybe I have a fever."

Ursula held out the yellow dress. "This will cure you. Nothing like a pretty dress to put a lady to rights again."

"I wouldn't know," Julienne admitted, filling her hands with the luscious sun yellow fabric. "But I'm about to find out, thanks to Buccaneer LaFlamme."

Chapter 10

❦

Buccaneer was away three days, having sailed with Cesare to New Orleans for supplies, but mostly, Julienne suspected, for a little masculine carousing. She'd overheard Selena begging to go with them, and Buccaneer's teasing reply that she'd hinder them.

He and Cesare returned early on the fourth morning. No one had to tell Julienne. She felt it in the air. A vibrancy had returned and everything moved faster ... even time. He sent for Alissa immediately, but not for Julienne. She tried not to feel slighted, but didn't completely succeed. Alissa returned within the hour, and they resumed her lessons.

"Did your father bring you something back from New Orleans?" Julienne asked, closing the primer. Alissa nodded, still bent over schoolwork. Julienne waited until Alissa had finished copying H-O-R-S-E, the last of the new spelling words. "What did he bring you?"

"A box."

"What kind of box?"

"A keepsake box. It's made of wood and has carvings all over it. It's got blue velvet inside."

"That sounds pretty. I'd like to see it sometime. What will you keep in it?"

She shrugged. "I dunno. Nothing, I guess."

Julienne glanced up with an expression of supplication. "Alissa, did you thank your father for the gift?"

"I guess."

"You either did or you didn't. Which is it?"

Alissa shrugged.

Julienne cupped Alissa's chin in her hand and forced her gaze up. "Talk to me. I thought you and your father were getting along better. He took you to the tobacco fields with him before he left on his trip, and you said you had a wonderful time."

"Then he left." Alissa pushed out her lower lip. "He didn't ask me to go. I never been to Norleans."

"Your papa was on a business trip, and it's called New Orleans," she said, pronouncing the city's name slowly. "Besides, New Orleans isn't a place for children. Someday, when you're old enough, he'll take you there during carnival."

"What's that?"

"A big party for grown-up men and women." She squeezed Alissa's chin affectionately. "Are you angry with your father because he left you behind?"

"I thought he liked me again."

"Princess, he loves you and he never stopped."

"He took Mama to Nor— Orleans."

"Did he? You remember that, do you?" Julienne patted her lap, and Alissa climbed up into it. She wrapped her arms loosely around the child, sensing that Alissa needed the contact. "Are you afraid sometimes that your papa might leave and never come back like your mama?"

"Mama died."

"Yes, that's right. And are you scared that your papa might die, too?"

"He will die. Everybody does."

Julienne frowned. "Who told you this?"

"Rosa. It's true. She said it's true."

"Yes, it is true, but you shouldn't think about that." Julienne kissed the top of Alissa's head and wished she could give Rosa a swift kick in her flat behind. "You'll be all grown-up and most of the people around you now will still be around you. We'll be here to love you now and later. You'll see." She released Alissa long enough to remove the silver chain and silver and ivory cross from around her neck. "I have something for you to put in your new keepsake box. Hold out your hand."

Alissa obeyed, and Julienne pooled the necklace in her small palm. "You don't want this no more?"

"This was given to me by the mother superior when I was twelve."

"Who's that . . . your mother?"

"No, princess. The mother superior is a nun. You've seen nuns."

"Uh-huh. They came to see Mama when she was buried. A priest came, too. You don't want this no more?" she repeated.

"I want you to keep it for me in your new, pretty box from New Orleans. You can wear it if you want. It will be something we share. It's pretty, don't you think?"

Alissa nodded. "I'll put it in the box right now." She slipped off Julienne's lap. "Thank you."

"You're welcome. I hope you said the same thing to your father."

Alissa puffed out a sigh. "I would have, but *Tía* Selena came in and kissed him all over, and he told me to come back here." She examined the cross, stroking the ivory with a fingertip. "*Tía* Selena is always kissing on him, and I don't like it."

Julienne smiled. "Why not, princess?"

"Just 'cause." She sighed again. "Want to see it?"

"The box? I will later. It's nearly dinnertime.

You'd better run upstairs and put on a pretty dress."

"You, too?"

Julienne nodded, and Alissa skipped from the Bride's House. Since receiving the new gowns, she'd worn one of them every evening for dinner, although Alissa had been her only companion. Selena had taken her meals in her room, not bothering to come downstairs since Buccaneer wasn't present at the table.

Julienne's nerves stirred in the pit of her stomach. Tonight he would see her wearing one of the gowns he'd given her! As she gathered up the books and other items she used to teach Alissa, Julienne found herself wondering, as she had countless times since he'd left, if Buccaneer had met a woman in New Orleans. Did he already know someone there or had he trysted with a stranger? Although she didn't like thinking about him being with someone else, she was pleased that he'd refused to take Selena along. He must not take Selena's advances too seriously.

"What do you care who he takes seriously?" she asked herself, angry that she'd forgotten her recent decision to keep her distance from him.

During the past few days, she'd counseled herself that she shouldn't read too much into his kisses and the new gowns. He was a tease where women were concerned, and he wanted her to look her best to give Alissa someone to pattern herself after. If he cared anything for her, he wouldn't have sailed to New Orleans without so much as an adieu. She hadn't even known he was gone until Alissa had told her during lessons the next day. She'd felt abandoned, which was ridiculous, she knew. She'd spent the evenings reading Magdalena's diary, although she found she could read only a few passages at a time. Too often the diary was upsetting, describing a Buccaneer Julienne had never even glimpsed. Maggie's stories also haunted Julienne at night, filling her dreams with images of Buccaneer kissing and fondling another woman.

Another woman. As if she had the right to call anyone else in his life that! Only betrothed women or wives had that right. She was neither. But then, neither was Selena. Julienne pursed her lips to keep from grinning impishly. It gave her a delicious thrill to be rid of the notion that Selena had some kind of claim on him.

But Selena kissed him all over, and he sent Alissa out of the room, a taunting voice reminded her. *He hasn't gone out of his way to see you since he's been back, has he? He's said hello to everyone but you.*

She clamped her hands over her ears, trying to block out the voice, but it wriggled into her mind. *And he wasn't anxious to see you in any of those dresses. He left right after he had them delivered to you. He only kissed you because you made yourself available. It meant nothing to him. You mean nothing to him.*

Julienne sat on the side of the bed and stared at the fireplace where Magdelena's diary waited to be thumbed through by an eager pupil. She'd been devouring every word, trying to glean what she could from it about Buccaneer's likes and dislikes. However, the more she read, the more she became convinced that she could never be someone he truly desired. The man described on the diary's pages was foreign to her. He had been to Magdalena a totally different man from the one he showed her. With Magdalena he'd been primitive, explosive, demanding, and even, on occasion, brutal. It had been his custom to make her beg for his kisses and plead for his attentions. Often he made Magdelena crawl to him on hands and knees and kiss his feet before he made love to her. Those descriptions made Julienne shudder with revulsion. She found it difficult to imagine such behavior from Buccaneer, but then she reminded herself that she didn't know him well at all.

If servitude was what he wanted in a woman, if humiliation fired his desire, then she should think herself lucky he'd gone to New Orleans for some sport. Julienne wanted to fall in love, but she wanted the man to be gentle, tender, and respectful. None of those characteristics was illustrated in Magdelena's diary. The very things that thrilled her appalled Julienne.

"If Magdelena is the moon, I'm the sun," Julienne murmured. As different from each other as night and day. He could never love me. Besides, she hadn't come here to fall in love. She'd come to Pirate's Key for Alissa.

Forget Buccaneer and concentrate on his daughter, she told herself firmly. Leave Buccaneer to women like Selena and Magdalena. She-devils, he called them. She-devils for a man with Satan's charm.

"H-O-R-S-E," Alissa finished, then smiled grandly when Buccaneer applauded her achievement.

"You've learned to spell many words since I've been away," Buccaneer acknowledged, pride swelling in his chest. "I'm impressed."

"Where is the little governess?" Selena asked, tapping her fingernails impatiently on the linen tablecloth. "Must we wait for her if she's late? After all, she's only a servant."

"And she's only a couple of minutes tardy. We'll wait a few more." But even as he spoke the last words, Julienne swept into the candlelit room. The golden light bathed her face and struck a fire in her lovely eyes. Her gaze swept over them and settled on him.

"I'm sorry to be late, Captain," she murmured, hovering on the threshold like a spirit.

Buccaneer felt his heart bump against his ribs. For the next few heartbeats he allowed his gaze to devour the beauty before him. The yellow gown revealed a figure he had felt with his hands and now could enjoy with his eyes. High breasts, a long, narrow waist, slim hips—they were all there, and he wished he were alone with her so that he could trace her shape with his hands. She'd evidently run from her quarters, because her breath soughed past her parted lips, and her breasts rose and fell provocatively. A pulse beat wildly at the base of her throat, and Buccaneer knew an urgent need to kiss it.

"Well, sit down," Selena snapped, breaking the spell. "We've waited long enough." She snatched up the bell near Buccaneer's right hand and rang it. "Rosa, Her Highness has *finally* joined us!" she called in the direction of the swinging door.

Julienne sat down, smiling nervously at Cesare and then at Buccaneer. "I'm terribly sorry. I couldn't fasten this dress by myself, and it was a few minutes before Ursula could come help me."

Buccaneer drank some wine, needing something to do besides drink her in with his thirsty eyes. If the nuns could only see her now! The wild child had become a ravishing woman. The late bloomer had burst open in all her glory.

Rosa pushed through the swinging door, carrying a tureen of soup. She served the women first, then Cesare and Buccaneer, who sniffed the aroma and sent her a grateful nod.

"Turtle soup, one of my favorites. Thank you, Rosa."

"It was hotter a few minutes ago," Rosa grumbled, her face set in an unforgiving scowl.

"It's hot enough now."

"That's my very favorite dress," Alissa said, her eyes bright with devotion as she looked at Julienne.

"Mine, too," Julienne confided, reaching out to gently tug one of Alissa's dark curls. The child wore the silver cross that she shared with Julienne. "Eat your soup, princess."

Buccaneer stared at his daughter's bright expression and the tenderness etched on Julienne's piquant face. They'd grown close, he realized, and knew a stab of jealousy. It had been a long time since Alissa had responded so openly to anyone, and it did his heart good to see the animation on his daughter's face and the sparkle of love in her eyes. If only she were as open with him . . .

"I haven't had the opportunity until now to thank you for my new wardrobe," Julienne said, her smile warm but reserved. "They are far more splendid than I expected."

"Highly impractical, if you ask me," Selena said.

"I'm glad you like them. Do the shoes fit?" Buccaneer asked.

"Perfectly."

"Never saw a governess dressed like that," Rosa grumbled.

"I am glad you said that." Selena's eyes raked Julienne with blazing hostility. "Giving her such things will make people question your motives, Buck."

He chuckled. "You expect me to care about that, Selena? People can think no worse of me than they already do."

"If you care nothing for your reputation, then what about hers?"

He looked from Selena to Julienne and back again. "What about hers?"

"You want people to think she's your pillow friend?"

Julienne gasped and glanced at Alissa. Anger, hot and quick, pumped through Buccaneer, and he slapped his open palm against the table, giving the glassware the shivers and making the people seated around him jerk with surprise. He glared at Selena, and her face went white. Her eyes widened with fear and . . . Was that excitement in their depths? Revulsion wrenched his stomach. Just like Maggie, he thought. Selena had that same streak of oddity about her. He had no doubts that if he slapped her right this minute, she'd melt in his arms and beg him to bed her. Just like Maggie. His stomach lurched again.

Cesare told Selena in Spanish to shut her trap, and Selena clamped her lips together, but her eyes blazed with spite.

Buccaneer took a deep breath, grappling for self-control. He started to tell Selena exactly what he thought of her loose tongue, but he noticed that Alissa's rosebud mouth quivered, and he feared she would burst into tears, as she usually did when he let his temper reign. He forced back his heated words for his daughter's sake. Julienne reached for one of Alissa's hands, and the contact acted like a sedative on the child. She relaxed, examined Julienne's reassuring smile, and gave her one in return.

Buccaneer let the ensuing silence prevail. The relationship that had evolved between Julienne and Alissa intrigued him. In truth, he envied his daughter's strong bond to the enchanting governess. Selena's outburst, however, reminded him of his tattered reputation. He should watch himself around Julienne. He would never forgive himself if he brought her shame and had to send her away from Alissa and Moonspell.

Cesare began telling Selena about the New Orleans trip and how the busy coastal city reminded him of Havana. Buccaneer struggled to concentrate on something besides the beauty at the other end of the table.

The second course arrived—stuffed crab legs and stewed potatoes. Cesare and Selena continued to dominate the dinner conversation. Buccaneer nodded occasionally to give the impression he was following the discussion, but he found himself hard-pressed to concentrate on anything other than Julienne's almond-shaped eyes and the gleam of candlelight on her mahogany hair. He'd thought of her often—too often, he admitted—while in New Orleans. Surrounded by beautiful women of every color and persuasion, he'd been irritated when his thoughts had kept circling back to her. He'd drunk too much and flirted with too many, all the while wishing for one woman in particular.

"Buccaneer, you have no objection if a few of the hands throw a little engagement party tonight?" Cesare asked.

Buccaneer shook his head, mostly to clear it.

"Good. I'll tell them," Cesare said.

"Who's getting married?" Julienne asked, her bright eyes focused on Cesare.

"Pedro, one of the field hands. He received word that his childhood sweetheart is willing to come here from Cuba and marry him. She's on her way, I believe, so we'll soon have a wedding."

"That will be fun," Julienne said.

"For those invited, yes," Selena noted, her eyes as frosty as her smile. "Have you even met Pedro?"

"Well, no." Julienne dropped her gaze, and color dotted her cheeks.

"Pedro will want the whole key to witness his marriage," Cesare said. "Quit being such a shrew, Selena."

"Papa!"

Cesare shook a finger at her. "And stop acting as if you've suddenly gone stupid. You know you behave badly. If your mama was alive, she'd swat you good."

"Don't talk foolish, Papa. I'm a grown woman,

and nobody's going to swat me." She pushed back
her plate. "Are we not having dessert?"

"I hope so. You need something to sweeten you
up." Cesare laughed at his daughter's thunderous
frown and his teeth flashed gold. "Here comes
Rosa now with—" He sniffed and grinned. "Ah,
can it be cobbler?"

"Sí. Just for you," Rosa said, with a tight, swift
smile. "I know you can eat the whole thing by
yourself, Señor, but you get only one big helping."

"And I will be thankful, Rosa. And I might
sneak into the kitchen late tonight and get another
portion." He laughed at her halfhearted frown.
"No one else can bake cobbler like you. The crust
melts in my mouth."

Buccaneer made a pretense of eating the dessert,
but couldn't stir up much enthusiasm. Selena
reached under the table and patted his knee, and
he drew it away from her, giving her a quick
scowl. Would she ever give up hope of being his
next wife? No matter how many times he insulted
her by pushing her away, she came back for more.
Just like Maggie. If it weren't for Cesare, he would
have sent Selena packing weeks ago.

"That was a wonderful meal," Julienne said,
glancing at Rosa, but she got no acknowledgment
from the housekeeper, so she shrugged and looked
at Alissa. "Ready to go upstairs, little one?"

Buccaneer was sorry to see her go. He would
have relished another minute or two watching the
expressions flit across her face.

"Perhaps you would like to join the celebration
tonight after you've put Alissa to bed," he said,
before thinking how it might sound. He felt
Selena's smoking glare and Cesare's curious one.
"That is, feel free to do so, if you wish."

"Thank you. I might do that." She took Alissa
by the hand and left the dining room.

"Why did you invite her?" Selena asked, her tone having the sting of a whip.

"I was being polite. You may join the festivities as well, Selena."

"As your guest? On your arm?" she prodded.

Buccaneer pushed back his chair. "I believe I'll turn in early tonight. The trip has tired me. You and Cesare will have to convey my regrets to Pedro."

"Convey them yourself." Selena threw down her napkin and stood up. "I'm not going without an escort."

"What about me?" Cesare asked, spreading his hands across his chest. "Won't I do?"

"Papa," she said, petulantly. "You are ... you are ... my papa!"

"And a fine one, he is," Buccaneer said, grinning. "Good night to you all."

"You're retiring *now*?" Selena asked, and Buccaneer nodded. "But I haven't seen you in days! I thought we could take a stroll."

He trailed his fingertips down her soft cheek, trying to calm her. "Tomorrow, Selena. Good night."

"I am also tired," Cesare said. "I will stay only a little while at the party and then toddle off to my bed."

Selena dropped into the chair again and folded her arms across her breasts. "You two are as much fun as wet firecrackers!"

Laughing, Buccaneer strode from the dining room and took the stairs two at a time to gain the second landing. He went to his room and stripped off his shirt, then pulled off his boots. Opening a window, he leaned out to allow the breeze to tickle his skin.

His eyelids felt heavy. Perhaps he'd take a nap and join the party later, hopefully after Selena had retired to her room to sulk. He closed his eyes, recalling how Selena had thrown herself on him when he'd returned. He'd given Alissa the keepsake box he'd bought in the French Quarter and had gotten a quick kiss on the cheek from her, which he'd treasured. Then Selena had interrupted, flinging herself into his arms and covering his face and neck with kisses. She'd embarrassed him in front of his daughter, and he'd sent Alissa away before making it clear to Selena that she was *never* to behave in such a way in front of Alissa again. He didn't want to give the child the wrong impression.

Selena hadn't liked his lecture, but he didn't give a damn. The woman was becoming impossible.

Leaving the window, he crossed the room to the wardrobe. Rosa had unpacked his traveling satchel and had laid the hat he'd purchased on the chair. She probably thought he'd brought it back for Selena, but he hadn't. He picked it up and admired the short, curled brim and splash of peacock feathers and blue and pink ribbons. Julienne would look enchanting in it. He dropped the hat in the chair again and stretched out on the bed, questioning the wisdom of the purchase.

Flinging one arm across his eyes, he listened impatiently to the voice inside calling him every kind of fool. Eventually he fell asleep and his mind wove erotic dreams of Julienne in her yellow dress and the new hat, riding bareback along the beach. The wind kicked up her skirts to reveal her creamy legs all the way up to her hips. Her hair was loose and flowing like water. Innocence shimmered over her like sunlight. God, had he ever been that pure?

He dreamed that he was kissing her lips, plundering her mouth. She tasted sweet ... sweet as sin. He took the hat off her and let it sail on the wind. She laughed up into his face, and he kissed her again and again and again.

Groaning, Buccaneer awakened and sat up in bed. He blinked at the darkness around him. Sweat trickled his skin and he ran a hand down his damp chest as he looked toward the open window. Stars winked at him, and he could see the tip of a crescent moon. He'd been asleep a couple of hours, he guessed. Must be nine or ten o'clock.

He placed his feet on the floor and waited for the tatters of the dream to leave him before he left the bed to put on a freshly laundered shirt. He combed his hair and splashed on a bit of cologne. Before going outside to the party, he decided to check on Alissa. She awakened when he bent over to kiss her.

"Will you tell me about Norleans?" she asked sleepily. "New Orleans. It's *New* Orleans, Julienne says. Is it brand-new, Papa?"

"No, Lissa, it's old." He sat on the edge of the bed. "What would you like to know about it?"

Julienne stepped outside and looked up at the velvet sky and sliver of moon. She smiled as the sprightly music introduced itself to her soul and asked her feet to dance. After dinner she had read Alissa to sleep and then had gone to her quarters to remove the yellow gown. She'd dressed for bed and curled up with Magdalena's diary, having found a fascinating passage about Maggie and Buccaneer finding a buried treasure chest at Spirits Cove. She'd wondered why he hadn't mentioned it to her. From Maggie's writing it appeared that the treasure was bountiful—jewels, gold doubloons, several bars of gold, and two of silver.

The lilting music had seduced her and she'd finally deserted the diary for the party. She had put on some of her old clothes—a gray, high-waisted skirt and a mustard-colored blouse—because they were more comfortable and she felt more herself in them. She shivered, remembering how Buccaneer had looked at her when she'd entered the dining room. She'd been as nervous as a mouse spied by a big cat, not knowing if the cat was hungry or merely curious. She'd glanced at him several times during the meal, and always his eyes had been on her. Once she'd met his gaze levelly and her breath had whispered down her throat. The cat, she'd seen, was hungry.

Drawn by the music, Julienne moved nearer to the bonfire where shadows writhed on the ground, cast by the jiggling bodies of dancers. Two men played kettle and steel drums, and there was a guitar player and a woman with castanets and a tambourine. The music sounded like rain pattering on crushed-shell roofs and pathways, and like the ocean birds on a bright morning. It sounded like the keys.

As she walked closer, the music placed a sway in her hips. A smile curved her lips as she joined the people in the outer circle. They clapped in time with the music and laughed at the two young men spinning and ducking and stamping in a pantomime of a bull and bullfighter. The bullfighter flapped a small red handkerchief, and the other one pawed the ground and danced closer, forming horns with his hands at the sides of his head.

Hot breath fanned her neck. "You mess with the bull, you get the horns, eh, señorita?"

Julienne whirled to face Lorenzo's lopsided grin. His gaze moved over her face with insolence. He wore black trousers that barely covered his muscled thighs, and a red pull-over shirt with no sleeves. Perspiration glistened on his body and in his thin, black mustache. She edged away from him, darting around two or three men and finding a spot beside the woman with the tambourine.

Lorenzo followed slowly, a leering smile on his lips, his eyes glittering with dangerous intent.

The music and the gaiety lost its appeal, and Julienne started for the house, her bare feet sinking into the sand and grass as she picked her way across the yard. Why didn't Lorenzo just leave her alone? Infuriated with herself for allowing him to spoil her evening, she paused on the path and flung an angry glance over her shoulder. Apprehension feathered her spine.

Was he following her? She thought she saw a shadow, but then realized it was cast by a tree limb. She faced front again and saw red. The red shirt blurred into motion, and long fingers bit into her wrist. Panic combined with a burst of fear, and without thinking, she raised her hand to slap him hard across the cheek.

Chapter 11

He grabbed her wrist before her hand could connect with his cheek, and brought her arm down and back behind her. He pressed intimately against her. She struggled for a blind moment before her vision cleared and she found herself staring up into Buccaneer's face.

Her lips moved, forming his name, but her voice caught in her throat.

"I must warn you, mam'selle, that my response to being slapped is not pleasant."

"Buccaneer!" Finally her voice whispered past her lips.

"What's this all about?" he demanded, his fingers still biting into her wrist and holding her arm bent behind her.

"I thought . . . I thought you were him."

"Him?"

"Lorenzo," she said with a sigh, then wriggled against her discomfort. "You're hurting me."

He turned his head to stare toward the bonfire. "He was bothering you?"

"Not really. I just . . ." She shrugged.

"Just what?" he asked, whipping his head back around to face her.

"Nothing. Please, let go." The solid masculinity of him assailed her. She smelled smoke on his skin and a musky maleness that made her want to

159

press her mouth fully, lavishly, against the glistening skin of his chest, exposed by the dipping vee of his collar. She knew he'd taste salty, succulent.

He let her go, but didn't step back from her. "Tell me. Has he taken liberties?"

"No, nothing like that." She knew she should move away, but her heart acted like a weight, keeping her in place. "He just makes me uneasy, that's all. He's rather flirtatious."

"If he ever oversteps his bounds, you come to me, and I'll deal with him." His voice held no warmth, no mercy. "I don't trust him."

"Then why do you keep him here?"

"I have my reasons." He'd rolled the cuffs of his black trousers a couple of times to expose his ankles. Like her, he was barefoot. "Cesare is a renowned cigar maker, and Lorenzo is Cesare's second cousin by marriage. Lorenzo knows everything about tobacco. He and Cesare make a great team and will eventually make me a great tobacco grower." He leaned closer, and his silver eyes bored into her. "But if he lays one finger on you, I'll break it and then all his others, one by one."

She grimaced. "Please, don't talk like that. I don't like to think of you resorting to barbarism."

The menace left his eyes. He stiffened and looked away from her. She realized she had somehow insulted him. Did he think she was calling him a barbarian? Oh, she wished she could read his complex mind and moods. Perhaps in time . . .

He cleared his throat. "Leaving the party so soon?"

"I . . . well, Lorenzo was following me, so I thought I'd just go back inside."

He held out his arm to her. "Why not give the party another chance? Lorenzo won't approach you while you're with me."

She hesitated before placing her hand on his proffered arm. "Very well."

He glanced at her from the corner of his eyes. "Back to your old clothing, I see."

"I didn't want to mess up the others."

"If you do, I'll buy you some more."

She started to argue and tell him she wasn't sure it was right for him to be buying her such beautiful clothing, but the music swelled and she forgot everything but the sounds of happiness. She squeezed Buccaneer's arm.

"Listen! It's so light and breezy. Doesn't it make you want to soar like a gull?"

She released his arm and ran ahead. When she whirled to face him again, laughter bubbled up from her heart, and her cautious love for him found strength in the moment. He had stopped on the path and his eyes glittered dangerously as they took her in, from her laughing face to her pink toes.

"Race you to the bonfire! If you catch me, you can keep me!" Then she spun about and kicked up sand.

She ran, overtaken by the joyous music and the dancing light of the bonfire. She stopped near the blaze where the musicians created magical sounds with their hands and tempered steel. Digging her toes into the sandy ground, she turned and sighed with exasperation at the sight of Buccaneer strolling toward her, a bored expression on his face. Anger shot through her. Why couldn't he let himself go and be human? she fumed. She wanted to erase the moodiness from him and replace it with laughter. But how?

She propped her hands on her hips and tapped one foot in disapproval. "What's the matter, Buccaneer?" she called to him, mindful that the others around her had stopped dancing and were watching her. She didn't care. She wanted to jostle him, unbalance him for a change, and make him enjoy the night, instead of merely observing it. "Are you afraid someone might discover you're not as grim as a lynching, after all? That you might even have a spark of life in you?"

His long strides ate up the ground, and he was on her before she could comprehend his intent. A hunger burned in his dark eyes, and Julienne knew that hunger was for her. Hooking an arm around her, he pulled her roughly against him and stamped his mouth with hers, hard and fast. She gasped and felt her whole body blush with embarrassment when she heard the murmurs around her. How could he do this in front of everyone?

"Hush your sassy mouth, Mam'selle Julienne," he rasped, taking her face in one hand and kissing her again. He ground his mouth against hers and tested the seam of her lips with his questing tongue. He eased himself away from her. His grin and the lusty chuckles around her spiked her anger and humiliation to new heights.

"Why, you . . . you . . ." Words failed her.

Buccaneer took her by the shoulders, spun her around, and patted her backside. "Now, behave yourself."

She rounded on him, her hands clenched in fists. A red mist swept over her eyes, and she knew that she had never in her life felt such anger toward another person. A dark-skinned man clapped Buccaneer on the back.

"Dat da way to shut a womon's mout, beeg boss. Dat da best way."

A caramel-colored young woman grabbed one of the man's hands in both of hers and tugged. "Dat so, braggin' mon? You bettah show deese people you not just talk, doncha tink?" She puckered up, and he kissed her soundly and lavishly while the others cheered and laughed.

Her anger finally freed Julienne's tongue. "If this is how you treated your wives, no wonder they moved out on you!"

Gasps and agitated murmurs erupted and everyone moved back a step, almost as if they thought Buccaneer might murder her on the spot. His eyes darkened to black, and Julienne felt his anger as keenly as she felt her own. She didn't retreat, although her whole being shrank from him.

Without taking his gaze from her, he spoke to the musicians in a language Julienne didn't understand. The music resumed, this time slow and throbbing. Buccaneer held out a hand and said something else in that odd singsong tongue. One of the men slapped the hilt of a knife across his palm. Julienne flinched. Good heavens, was he going to cut her? Buccaneer placed the blade between his white teeth, his gaze locked with Julienne's. She relaxed, although she wouldn't have turned her back on him at that moment.

Starting to edge away, she concentrated on getting far from the bonfire and the man who refused to release her from his penetrating gaze. But Buccaneer slid neatly in front of her, blocking her escape. The music throbbed through the night and he began to dance in a slow, sensual glide, circling her, caging her in. Each time she started to move away, he was there to keep her in place. As he continued with his disturbing dance, confusion reigned within her. She wished she could spit in his face or pummel him with her fists, but she was too afraid and too mesmerized by his glinting eyes. He clapped to the beat, which increased with the pace of her own heartbeats. Closer and closer, he danced, until she could feel his breath on her face and the heat of his body enveloped her like a hot breeze off the equator.

In a lithe blur of movement, he removed his shirt and tossed it to one of the women. His chest glistened with perspiration as he undulated to the music. His feet made patterns in the sand. His bared teeth reminded her of a dangerous animal.

Droplets shone like diamonds on his dark skin. He moved with a pantherlike grace, thrusting his pelvis, growling low in his throat, keeping her captive with his will.

Why is he doing this? she wondered, glancing at the rapt expressions surrounding her. Two people weren't so enthralled. Selena glared at her, hate blasting from her eyes. Lorenzo stood behind her, his dark eyes fastened on Buccaneer, antagonism marring his swarthy features.

The music grew frenzied and the drummers' hands blurred. Sweat poured down their dark faces. A couple of the women swooned. The men whirled in place, heads thrown back, arms outstretched to the sky. The women moaned, their eyes rolling back in their skulls.

A drop of fear rolled down Julienne's spine and she closed off her throat to keep from screaming at Buccaneer to stop circling her as if she were his prey.

Suddenly the incessant drumming stopped. Taking the knife in hand, Buccaneer flung it down. The scream emerged from her throat, cut off abruptly by the clamp of terror as the knife landed, hilt up, in the sand between her bare feet, its sharp blade missing her flesh by mere inches. Her gaze slammed up to his, anger and fear mingling to make her tremble.

"Just what do you think you're doing?" she demanded, her voice low and husky.

An insolent smile touched his mouth. "It's called the knife dance. It represents the power of the hunter over the hunted."

Her heart drummed in her ears. "Are you the hunted or am I?" She was afraid to hear his answer, so she whirled and strode toward . . . toward what? She stopped, realizing she was headed for the ocean. Hearing his approach, she spun about to face him. He still wore no shirt, and she had a devil of a time keeping her gaze from straying to his broad shoulders and hair-silky chest.

"You're running away, so you must be the hunted," he noted, then looked past her. "Where are you headed?"

"I . . . Nowhere." She shrugged. "Away from you."

"I make you nervous."

She tipped up her chin. "You deny that making me nervous is your intention?"

He smiled, slow and cunning. "My intention is to give you a taste of your own medicine."

She shook her head, confused.

"You accused me of not revealing any spark of life, when it is you who have experienced so little of it."

"That's not—" She broke off her protest as he moved closer until only an inch separated their bodies. He ran a fingertip down her cheek. She shivered.

"Didn't you feel more alive than ever during the knife dance? And right now . . . you're trembling with feelings." He bent his head, and his lips brushed hers once, then again. Rubbing, stroking, enticing.

She retreated, not trusting herself to endure much more of his soft assault. "I should be . . . That is, good night, Captain."

He caught her hand as she tried to rush past him. "What happened to Buccaneer?" he teased, then deftly tucked her hand in the crook of his arm. "Walk with me under the stars."

She shook her head, but he tugged her along. "I really shouldn't. It's getting late and I . . . I . . ." She glanced sideways, agonizingly aware of his bare, burnished skin. His scent wafted to her. Her nostrils quivered as she caught the aroma and breathed him in like a bouquet.

"I noticed that you and Alissa have become quite close."

Julienne swallowed hard. She knew he was steering her toward calmer waters and she let him, having no more will of her own. He covered her hand where it rested on his arm, and she felt captured. The hunter had cornered his prey.

He glanced at her. "I don't spend enough time with her. That's what you're thinking."

She smiled weakly and decided to let him believe that his child occupied her thoughts. "You took her to the tobacco fields with you. That pleased her."

He nodded, then gave her a sharp look. "What? You wanted to add something."

Julienne sighed, wishing she could read him as easily as he seemed to read her. "You left the next day, and she took it personally. However, I explained that your trip had nothing to do with her."

"No matter what I do, I only seem to disappoint Alissa. She searches for reasons not to like me."

"That isn't true. If she didn't love you, she wouldn't care where you spent your time."

"You have a point, I suppose."

He stopped and turned sideways, facing her. Lifting her hand, he dragged his fingertips across her palm, then tilted her hand until starlight illuminated the network of lines by which soothsayers discerned the future.

"You also have a long life line and a strong heart line. I see children in your future."

"I hope so, since I'm a governess."

"No. I believe you'll have your own someday."

She felt a smile nudge her lips. Children. Her? That would mean marriage. She dared not believe that such happiness could be hers. "You saw that in my hand, did you?"

"Clearly." His gaze clung to her face, missing nothing. "You believe in palm reading?"

"Not really, but I admit to a fascination for such things."

A burst of laughter wrested his attention. Julienne looked toward the bonfire, where one of the revelers bowed backwards and waddled under a broomstick. A woman went next, her skirt dragging behind her in the sand, her upthrust breasts barely clearing the broomstick.

"Where are they from, those people?" she asked.

"Jamaica."

"Have you ever been there?"

"Yes, several times."

"You've been many places, haven't you?"

He nodded. "All over the world. I spent a good deal of my younger years on my father's ships. He was a trader." He laughed harshly. "That's a polite way to put it. Actually, he was a thief. He traded worthless things for priceless things."

"How did he do that?"

"By sailing to remote areas where Western civilization hadn't reached. He traded glass baubles for real jewels; whistles and whiskey for gold and ivory."

Julienne frowned. "Quite a charming man, your father."

"Quite," he bit out, the memories flooding through his mind and the shame souring in his stomach. "He learned from the master, old Black Pierre. Now, there was a scoundrel. That man hadn't one scrap of decency in him. I recall sleeping in a bunk once with him in the hold of a ship. He made me sleep against the wall and told me that he wanted to be able to get out quick if there was a fire or the ship was sinking. He didn't want to waste time having to crawl over me."

Julienne gasped. "How horrible! How old were you when he told you this?"

"About Alissa's age, I think."

She shook her head. "The man should have

been horsewhipped for saying such a thing to a child—to his own grandson!" She sighed. "I used to think pirates were romantic, but your stories are forcing me to change my mind."

"They're like everyone else. They have their good points and their bad."

"Tell me the good points and salvage my original opinion of them," Julienne pleaded, smiling.

He glanced at her, caught her smile, and nodded. "Good points ... Okay. They are footloose, sailing from port to port—"

"And woman to woman," she interrupted with a teasing grin.

"Yes, I suppose so. I knew some who were married, but I never knew any who were faithful. They drank a lot and bedded whores ... raped any woman who resisted ..." His voice trailed off as the memory of his father raping one of the scullery maids on the butcher block table in the kitchen overtook him. When his father had turned to pull up his pants, he'd spotted Buccaneer and had laughed with glee, then asked if the nine-year-old spectator would like to have a go at the girl.

"You were supposed to list their good points," Julienne reminded him. "Drinking and whoring aren't my idea of sterling characteristics."

He shook his head to clear it. Running a hand through his hair, he strove to escape the blackened memories of his father, but he could dimly hear Gaspard's taunting voice as he'd tried to push Buccaneer toward the ravaged, sobbing maid. Buccaneer ground his teeth. God, how he'd hated that man!

"Buccaneer?" Julienne prodded. "Can't you think of one good thing about pirates?"

He sighed. "I'll try. Well, they sail the seven seas and they know no loyalty to flag or country." He warmed to the subject, and the bad memories scurried to the far corners of his mind. He stepped closer to a palm and leaned back against its trunk. "There's nothing better than being in the middle of the ocean on a clear night. The stars are big and bright, and the moon, fat and full. The sound of the ocean slapping against the sides of the ship is the sweetest lullaby. Many a night as a boy I lay awake up top and listened to the pirates sing of beautiful mermaids. I've watched dolphins break the waves and eye me curiously, then arch into the air and dive back into the inky water. I've swum with stingrays. I've ridden the backs of whales."

She gasped with delight. "Have you?"

He nodded. "I have."

"Oh, my!" She inched closer to him. "What was that like?"

"Exciting . . . and a bit scary. Actually, the whales are quite gentle. I don't believe they want to hurt men. I rode a porpoise once, too."

"Oh, Buccaneer, how grand!" She clasped her hands under her chin, and her eyes glittered like jewels in the night. "Tell me more."

"I've dived on wrecks and brought up handfuls of gold chains and coins," he related, his voice rough magic. "I've uncovered buried treasure chests with my father and squirreled the spoils away so that we wouldn't have to share them with his crew."

She remembered the part in Maggie's diary about the time they'd found buried treasure. Feeling guilty for hiding the diary from him, she bit down on her lower lip to stop from blurting out a confession. Not now, a voice inside her advised. Finish reading the diary and then hand it over.

"Looking back, I suppose it was exciting," he continued. "I can't count the times I stared death in the face. The 'canes and the violent storms at sea often drove me to my knees in supplication. Somehow we always sailed out of them."

"Did your grandfather make Key West his home before he claimed this land?"

"Black Pierre claimed no land until he was forced to give up his piracy and settle down or be hanged by the neck until dead." He tilted his head as if measuring her. "Know how Key West got its name?"

She nodded, full of confidence. "Because it's the most westward key, of course."

"Wrong." He grinned. "A Spanish explorer found sun-bleached skeletons littering the ground when he landed there, and he gave it the name *Cayo Hueso*."

She repeated the name to herself, but shook her head.

"Bone Island," Buccaneer translated for her. "Later it was Anglicized to Key West."

She smiled. "You're just a walking history book, aren't you?" She liked him when he was like this; allowing her to be on solid footing with him.

He shrugged. "I know many useless things." He gave a short laugh. "Such is my education."

"Knowledge is never useless, Buccaneer."

A smile broke across his face. "Spoken like a true governess." He narrowed his eyes, studying her so intently that she felt herself blush. Suddenly she was awash again, floating in the deep water of his eyes. "Why is it that I used to hate my name, but I like it when you say it?"

"You hate your name?"

He laughed bitterly. "It's totally ridiculous. My father named me Buccaneer just to infuriate my mother."

"I think it's a lovely name. It's the first thing that attracted me to you."

"The first?" He noted the color creeping into her cheeks and he knew he'd tripped her up, trapped her—again. "And what was the second?"

She swallowed convulsively and stared at her hands clasped tightly in her lap. Buccaneer took pity on her and eased a fingertip under her chin to bring her gaze to his. His heart bucked. His blood thickened in his veins. His groin throbbed from the pleasure she inflicted. Starlight found her hair and gilded it with silver. Flames flickered in the centers of her dark brown eyes. Her soft lips quivered slightly and the tip of her tongue darted out to moisten them.

"Ah, Julienne," he whispered, nudging her chin with his finger and drawing her to him with the sheer power of sexuality. "I tell myself not to be your ruination, but then I get too close to the fire of you, and my good intentions go up in smoke."

"Don't talk of ruination. I don't believe you're a rascal. I don't believe you'd ever hurt me, much less ruin me."

"I wish that were true." The temptation was too great and he claimed her lips, softly, tentatively.

She trembled, and he gathered her into his arms and slanted his mouth over hers. When her lips parted, the music became a dim memory, the world an insignificant speck. He ran his tongue over her lips and then dipped it within. It stayed there like a bee in a honeypot, momentarily stunned by its great good luck.

Julienne raked her hands through his midnight hair and clutched the curls at the base of his neck. If danger had a taste, he was it. Dark, delectable, divine. She had lived the past ten years cloistered behind walls and religion, and she was starved for the forbidden. Like Eve, she wanted to take a huge bite of the apple. Her teeth nipped playfully at his lower lip, and he growled deep in his throat and marched kisses down her throat. She flung back her head, giving him plenty of room. His lips pressed against the upper curve of her left breast where the skin fluttered with her heartbeats.

She wanted him to continue his onslaught. She caressed his shoulders, his back. He kissed her again and his tongue mated with hers. She'd never been kissed so boldly, so passionately, before. When he drew back to stare deeply into her eyes, her own inadequacy squirmed inside her.

"Tell me what you want, Julienne," he whispered, then kissed her mouth again and again until her lips felt swollen and bruised. "Tell me."

What did he expect from her? What would a worldly woman say or do?.... She recalled the diary and Maggie's descriptions of how she'd driven him wild with desire. She forced the words past her lips, hoping they sounded better than they felt.

"I'm yours. All yours. I belong to you. You are my master and I am your willing s-slave." The last word almost stuck in her throat.

He angled back, and his caressing hands slipped away. "Why did you say that?"

"Because . . . it's true?" She saw the disgust in his eyes, and cringed.

Buccaneer ran a hand through his hair and cursed softly under his breath. "I'll walk you to the house."

She wished she could take back the words. She wished she could turn back time. She started for the path. Buccaneer fell into step beside her.

"You don't have to walk with me," she said, wanting to escape him now that she'd made him aware that she wasn't the right woman for him. "It's obvious you don't want to be with me."

"Obvious?" He laughed harshly. "Hardly, Julienne." He jerked his head, indicating the place under the tree where passion had streaked and faded like a comet. "Why did you spout such nonsense back there?"

"I . . . I want to please you."

"You can please me by keeping such banalities to yourself."

She clamped her teeth together to stop from screaming at him that she'd never known a bigger oaf in life. She strode past him anxious to end this night of errors. "I think it's best if you just keep your hands and your lips to yourself!"

"I don't recall you struggling or protesting."

She pivoted. "I enjoyed your kiss, but I don't enjoy your critiques afterward. It seems I never please you and must suffer your pernicious lectures concerning my deficiencies. I can live without both, thank you!" Gathering her gray skirt, she whirled and flounced on ahead of him, her bare feet flinging sand in all directions.

The sway of her hips and hair enticed him into a better mood. He pursued and caught up with her a few strides from the Bride's House. Catching her hand on its backswing, he pulled her around to him. Her breath sawed in her throat, and her eyes glimmered with unshed tears.

"You're crying?" he accused.

"I certainly am not!" Even as she said it, a traitorous tear rolled down her cheeks, and she dashed it aside with her free hand. "You are the most infuriating man I have ever had the misfortune of meeting! No, let me go. I'm tired and must—"

He kissed her quiet again. She stiffened like a board, and he felt the heat of her anger. He didn't give a damn. She had the sweetest, hottest lips he'd ever tasted. Sucking gently, he tried to sneak his tongue inside, but she refused to cooperate. A scream of indignation vibrated in her throat and against his lips. Taking pity on her, he let her go. She stumbled backward, her eyes big and bright, her skin flushed rosy pink. Spinning away, she opened the French doors and crossed the threshold into the Bride's House. Turning back to him, she started to close the doors behind her.

"*Bonsoir*, little jewel."

She froze, the endearment flustering her. Then she closed the doors slowly . . . slowly . . . like the lid of a box extinguishing the luster of a rare, priceless gem.

Chapter 12

"**A**hoy, little jewel! Want to come with me and meet a witch?"

Julienne straightened from bending over the moonflower and morning glory vines she'd planted at the base of an arched trellis. Buccaneer sat astride Blaze. He wore tan riding breeches and one of his loose, buttonless shirts, this one a jungle green to nearly match the color of his wide-brimmed hat. The cutlass strapped to his side winked back at the sun.

"When?" Julienne asked, touching the back of her wrist to her damp forehead. "Now?"

"*Oui.*" He crossed his wrists atop the saddle horn. "Now."

She glanced down at her threadbare house dress. "I'd have to change first."

"You look fine enough to meet a witch."

She held out her hands, showing him the mud caked on them. "I'm filthy. I've been gardening most of the afternoon. Alissa and I have been crawling in the dirt and—"

"Where *is* Alissa?"

"Napping. I sent her inside a few minutes ago."

"You don't want to meet the witch?" he asked, looking down his nose at her.

She regarded his glittering eyes. "I simply can't go anywhere like this."

"Buccaneer, what are you doing here this time of day?" Selena asked, gliding outside and down the front steps, looking cool and spotless in linen white.

He frowned and threw a leg over Blaze, slipping to the ground. His gaze flickered to Julienne. "I'll wait. Make haste. I'm having Seabiscuit haltered for you, so wear a riding skirt."

Julienne saluted him. "Aye, aye, sir!"

Buccaneer was barely able to suppress a grin. He lowered his brows and jerked his head, sending her dashing past Selena and into the house.

"You certainly made a spectacle of yourself last night," Selena said, strolling toward him, her hands clasped behind her back. "Has the governess turned your head, Buck?"

"Has Lorenzo turned yours?" Buccaneer left Blaze to chomp sea oats and grass and brushed past her, heading inside. The moment he stepped into the cool foyer, his senses noticed something different. His nose twitched, and Buccaneer looked straight up at the skylight.

The pots were no longer empty. Mounds of hibiscus and petunias spilled over their sides. He smiled, remembering that flowers had given Isabelle her only comfort. She'd be happy that the blossoms were back, he thought, then realized that the empty pots had lent the foyer an air of incompleteness.

"Since you pointedly ignore me, why do you care if I cry on Lorenzo's shoulder?" Selena demanded, stopping beside him. She glanced up and made a disparaging sound. "Oh, look. Little Miss Sunshine and Flowers has been in here and left her calling card for the master."

"I like them." He brought his gaze down to Selena's frowning face. "That's what you've been doing with Lorenzo? Crying?" he countered, his tone calling her a liar.

"Why sip from grape juice when you can un-cork vintage wine?" she challenged, thrusting out her breasts and smoothing her hands down the front of her dress, over her belly to her thighs. "The governess has the sophistication of a child. Once you've dallied with her, will you send her back to the convent? Will the good Sisters accept spoiled goods? You think they'll send you another virgin to deflower? They don't have an endless supply, Buck."

Buccaneer narrowed his eyes and glared at her through the dusky curtain of his lashes. "Be very careful, Selena," he warned, his voice low, his temper high. He dragged his forefinger down her cheek. "Very careful."

Selena retreated a few steps. "I am trying to understand your game, Buck. If you want her to stay for Alissa's sake, then why do you toy with her? Do you think an unseasoned girl like her will remain in your employ once you have lain with her?"

Heels clicked sharply on the floor, alerting them to Rosa's approach. Her dark, furtive eyes took in Buccaneer and Selena, and Buccaneer knew the housekeeper sensed the animosity between them.

Rosa glared at the gently swaying pots overhead. "She goes out into the wilderness and brings in these weeds. I will not tend them." She pointed outside at the other flowers. "And I will tell the grounds keeper to cut those down."

"No, you won't." Buccaneer shook his head firmly. "She said she'll take care of the flowers, Rosa."

"She is supposed to be taking care of Alissa. Moonspell is *my* territory, not hers."

"Moonspell is *mine*." He looked from Rosa to Selena. "And I am my own man and have no need for advice."

Rosa blinked and her scowl softened. "Forgive

me, Captain Buck. I meant no disrespect. I will return to my duties, señor." She walked stiffly away, her heels echoing on the parchment floor.

Selena crossed her arms in a belligerent stance. "Where are you taking her, Buck? Another secluded cove? Your interest in her has people talking."

"Don't listen."

"I must. I worry about you. People are seeing a pattern. First Isabelle, then Magdalena. Both were innocent girls, seduced by you—"

"Maggie was hardly an innocent," he interrupted.

Selena shrugged. "But like Isabelle, she's dead, and the questions about you and those deaths dance around you like flames. I could snuff them out."

"Oh?" He propped his hands at his waist. "How so?"

"By marrying you, I will extinguish all speculation that you killed Magdalena. People will know that I would never wed the murderer of my cousin."

"You would do that for me?" He swept off his hat and ran his hand through his hair to lift it from his prickly scalp.

"I would do that and more."

He walked his fingers around the brim of his hat, his gaze downcast. "Are you so certain I didn't kill her?" His glance caught the tightening of skin around her mouth.

"I would not blame you if you had." She shrugged. "Magdalena was difficult. In a fit of temper, any man would ... might have ..." She flapped a hand. "But I know you did not. Papa says so."

He chuckled. "You have as many angles as a ship's mast, Selena."

Buccaneer heard Julienne's soft footfalls and

swung about, giving Selena his back. Julienne had changed into a split skirt and long-sleeved shirt-waist of burgundy. She placed a wide-brimmed straw hat on her head, and he remembered the one he'd bought for her in New Orleans, but hadn't given it to her. It was upstairs under his bed, and he couldn't make up his mind whether to present it to Julienne or throw the damn thing away.

"Am I presentable?" she asked, standing before him, the top of her head barely clearing his chin.

He reached for her hands and turned them over, inspecting them as he would a child's. "All clean. Yes, the witch will have no trouble reading your palms now."

"The witch? You're taking her to see Carmella?" Selena asked.

Buccaneer nodded and gently pushed Julienne out the open front door. "Keep an eye on Alissa for me, won't you?" he told Selena over his shoulder. "I should have the governess back before Alissa awakens from her nap, but one never knows." He winked, then laughed at Selena's rude gesture.

"Shouldn't we invite Selena to go with us?" Julienne asked, and received a quick scowl from Buccaneer.

"She doesn't ride, and I don't want to go by buggy or wagon."

She pulled on black gloves. "Who is this witch we're going to meet?"

"Carmella. She's Ootay's grandmother and Pirate Key's most colorful resident. Here comes Danny with Seabiscuit." He offered to help her mount.

Grabbing a handful of the horse's mane, she planted a foot on Buccaneer's rock-hard thigh and hoisted herself up and onto Seabiscuit's back. She settled comfortably while Buccaneer swung into his own saddle. The cutlass reflected rays of light.

"Why do you wear that thing?"

"What?" he asked, looking down at himself.

"That ... weapon." She wrinkled her nose in distaste.

"It comes in handy." He adjusted it on his belt. "Opens coconuts when I'm in need of a refreshing drink, clears away brush in my path, and it keeps impressionable young women at bay."

She laughed. "I didn't know you had to threaten Selena with a cutlass to prevent her from ravishing you!"

A slow grin conquered him and he wagged a finger at her. "There is that whipping tongue again."

She wagged a finger back at him. "You begged for its punishment."

"I can think of a better use for that tongue of yours." He laughed deep in his chest, enjoying her high color, then angled his head to the east. "This way to Carmella's. If you sass *her*, she'll put a spell on you."

Julienne widened her eyes. "Ooo! I'm terrified. Are you the one who has been filling Alissa's head with tales of death and doom?"

He slanted her a wary look. "Death and doom? What do you mean?"

"She seems overly concerned with such things," Julienne explained. "I've never known a child her age to talk so openly about people dying and how things can kill you. Storms, horses, wind, the sea, lightning; all these things are killers to Alissa." She regarded him for a few moments, realizing he hadn't been aware of his daughter's gloomy outlook. "I thought you must have talked about these things to her and made her afraid. Not that you'd meant to," she hastened to add. "But that's the result."

"I told you that Alissa has withdrawn from me, so we've had few conversations of any length. I certainly haven't dwelled on the sad, bad things in life."

"Then it must be Rosa."

"Rosa again. I wish you two would bury the hatchet and quit blaming each other for every wrong."

"She has influenced Alissa. You can't deny that."

"Rosa loves Alissa and wouldn't fill her head with talk of death."

"Then who has?" Julienne insisted.

"Alissa's mother died. That's why she is preoccupied with death."

"But what about being afraid of horses and storms and the sea? Those things have nothing to do with her mother."

He caught his lower lip between his teeth as the painful memories bobbed to the surface of his mind. "Her mother was thrown from a horse once and suffered bruises and scratches. And the night she died, it was storming, and it was at first presumed she'd drowned."

Julienne accepted his explanation, but it didn't answer all her questions. Someone had instilled a fear of experiencing life in Alissa. She was drawing out the child, but it was painstaking.

"I should never have married."

Julienne gasped. "Don't say that! I didn't tell you about Alissa's fears to make you think everything was your fault. Alissa is getting better. Haven't you noticed? She was as noisy as a magpie at dinner last night."

A smile flickered in his eyes. "Yes, but both my marriages were disasters, and I'm not a good father."

"You're a fine father, and you'll be a better one once you recover from the loss of your wife."

Irritation feathered through him, and he sent Julienne a dark glare. "Recover from the loss of my wife," he repeated, his tone just short of a sneer. "You think Maggie's gone?"

She stared at him, confused. "I don't understand." The sinister glint of his eyes and the insolent curl of his upper lip chilled her blood.

"I'll never be shed of her." He kicked Blaze, and the mighty horse lunged ahead, gobbling up the bridle path, shivering leaves as it whipped past hedges and flowering shrubs.

Julienne gave Seabiscuit his head and held on with gripping hands and knees. Greenery flashed past. She leaned over the horse's neck and squinted against the stinging air. Her hat fell back, held on by its chin strap, and her hair tumbled past her shoulders. She saw Buccaneer veer off the path, and she guided Seabiscuit with a sharp tug on the leathers. The gelding jumped over low bushes and trampled wild grass and flowers. She spotted a clearing ahead of them and saw Blaze rear on his hind legs and whinny. She pulled back on the reins, retarding Seabiscuit's pace to a gallop, then a canter, then a nervous prance.

Something tickled her cheek. Julienne removed her gloves and touched her face. She stared at the blood on her fingertips. Tears stung her eyes as the memory of younger days on Key Largo set her awash in emotion. Her gaze skipped to Buccaneer. His chest rose and fell as he sat astride his sweat-laced stallion. Understanding softened his features.

"Are you all right?" he asked, his voice a husky caress.

"Yes." She wiped at her cheek again and laughed softly. "Just like when I was a rowdy ragamuffin. Wooo, my heart is racing!" She laid one hand above her breasts. "It's been so long since I've ridden like that. I'd forgotten how ... how scary and magnificent—"

"Who goes there?" someone shouted in a warbling voice.

Julienne tore her gaze from Buccaneer and examined the ramshackle house squatting like a brown toadstool under a giant banyan tree. The roof needed fresh thatching. Palm fronds curtained the windows. A dingy cloth hung in the doorway.

"It's Buccaneer LaFlamme, Carmella."

"Cap'n?" A bony hand curled around the edge of the cloth door and pulled it aside to reveal a white-haired, dark-skinned woman with pale eyes. Her bright orange, shapeless dress was at least a size too big. She leaned on a crooked cane and motioned for them to advance. "I see you brought the Key Largo girl. Come, come. I have things to tell you."

Julienne's startled gaze flew to Buccaneer. "You've told her about me?"

Buccaneer grinned. "Not a word. Remember, she's a witch!"

Looking from him to the wizened figure beckoning them, Julienne experienced a moment of trepidation. If not for Buccaneer helping her slide off Seabiscuit, she might have reined the gelding about and headed home to Moonspell. While Buccaneer secured the horses, Julienne forced one foot in front of the other and approached the ancient woman, whose skin reminded her of wrinkled parchment.

"Hello, I'm Julienne Vale." She curtsied, and Carmella cackled.

"She be thinking I'm the queen, big Buck." She laughed and wheezed. "Come into me palace, little jewel."

Julienne glanced back at Buccaneer, who mirrored her startled expression. He shook his head at her silent question. He hadn't shared that endearment with the old woman? Then how did she . . .

Just a coincidence, Julienne told herself. Don't make so much of it.

Entering the woman's abode was like stepping into the cave at Spirits Cove, although not as dark. Little light found its way into the room, which was crowded with crudely built furniture. A table, draped with a fringed shawl, sat in the center of the area, and four rickety chairs surrounded it. Julienne sniffed at the wild, musty smell and heard the flutter of wings. She blinked, urging her eyes to adjust to the poor light, and spotted bird perches in every corner. Something scurried from a chair to a shelf, and Julienne inched closer to Buccaneer, but relaxed when she saw that the furry creature was a long-tailed monkey. The darting monkey disturbed an owl that had been dozing. The round-faced bird spread its wings and sailed to one of the frond-covered windows. It perched on the ledge and ducked under the fronds to escape outside.

"They come and go," Carmella said. "I share this land with them. Cap'n Buck, he think he own it, but he don't. Nobody own land. Just live on it, work it, curse it, and be buried in it." She eased herself in one of the chairs around the table. "Sit, sit. I know why you come."

Julienne sat in the chair Buccaneer held out for her. "Why did we come, other than for a visit?"

"To see far ahead." Carmella squinted her pale blue eyes and wiggled her fingers in front of her aged face. "Gots to look hard to see past years. I gots the knack. Gots it since I was a suckling at my mama's breasts."

Buccaneer sat beside Julienne. "You need anything, Carmella? Is your garden providing enough for your belly?"

She smiled, showing pink gums and only a few brown teeth. "My belly be so shrunk, a cupa tea fills it up. I gots alls I want. Alls I need. My garden grows, my chickens lays eggs, my goat gives milk." She shrugged. "I gots plenty."

"Then you won't want this." He pulled a small bag from his belt and tossed it to the center of the table.

"What that?" Carmella grabbed it, untied the neck, and peeked inside. A smile spread across her cracked lips. "Sugar!" She dipped in a finger and licked it clean. "I take this. Much obliged." She knotted the neck again and placed the sack carefully to one side. "You want for me to look at this lady's tomorrows?"

Buccaneer turned toward Julienne. "Would you like her to tell you what's in store for you?"

"You mean, read my palm?"

"Let me see your hands." Carmella captured Julienne's left hand, then her right. "Straighten out them fingers so's I can see them life lines, little jewel."

Julienne slowly uncurled her fingers. "The captain has already read my palm."

"Him?" Carmella scoffed. "Him knows palms like I knows ships." Her pale eyes laughed. "And I never been near one of them floating corks."

"Carmella is choosy about whose palms she'll read," Buccaneer said. "You should feel honored, Julienne."

She couldn't discern if he was teasing or not. The old woman bent over her hands, her gnarled fingers feeling like dried tobacco leaves brushing against Julienne's. Her pale blue eyes reminded Julienne of marbles stuck in fudge. She ran a dirty fingernail across Julienne's right palm, then across her left one. Julienne smiled, trying to take the edge off the flutter of nerves tormenting her. A brilliantly colored parrot squawked in one corner, and the monkey chattered happily. Julienne felt as if she'd stepped into a storybook. Nothing seemed real.

"I see a long life ... and a happy one." She peered into Julienne's palm as if it were made of glass and she could see through it and beyond. "I see something ... not quite right." Carmella passed a hand over her eyes and then focused them again on the web of lines in Julienne's pale pink palm. "There is a shadow here." She drew a line with her short, gray fingernail. "A long shadow falls across your life."

"What does that mean?" Julienne asked, examining the place on her hand that appeared to bother the old soothsayer.

"Trouble. It be trouble until that shadow is lifted. It be danger. Maybe cut your life line in two if it don't be swept away."

"How can it be swept away, Carmella?" Buccaneer asked, leaning forward slightly.

Carmella's glassy eyes found Buccaneer's worried expression, and she smiled. "You figure that out, Cap'n Buck. It up to you. This jewel gonna be crushed?" She shrugged her bony shoulders. "It all in your hands." Her smile slipped away. "Just like them other women. They be alive if not for you."

Julienne jerked her hands away from the woman's and glanced at Buccaneer. The pain evident on his face squeezed her heart. She placed a hand over his and was stung when he snatched it away.

"Carmella, you're babbling today. We should leave now, Julienne, before this poor, old witch gets worse."

The monkey became agitated, and Julienne looked toward it. A brown face staring at her from the window scared a startled gasp from her. The man ducked, and the palm frond whispered back into place over the window, leaving Julienne with the lasting impression of opaque eyes and reddish blond hair, eyebrows, and lashes, made all the more memorable against his coffee-bean-colored skin. Buccaneer looked toward the window, too.

"What's wrong?"

"There . . . there was a man there." She pointed to where the palm frond swung slightly. "He was staring at us."

"It be Ootay. He live here sometime."

"Sometimes?" Buccaneer asked. "Where else does he stay?"

"In the trees. On the land. Wherever him lays hisself down, I reckon. He be at home in the wild same as he be at home in this here place. Don't you pay him no mind, Key Largo girl. He just curious 'bout you."

"About me?" Julienne repeated. "Why didn't he come in and be introduced?"

"Don't want to, I reckon." Carmella's shoulders sagged. "It teatime. You go now. I sleep after I drink my tea."

"Just one more thing," Julienne said. "Did you see children in my future? The captain did, and I was wondering . . . my *own* children, did you see any?" Aware of Buccaneer's keen regard, she kept her gaze focused on the old woman.

"Chillen." Carmella's lids closed over her pale sky eyes. "You gots to get rid of that shadow afore they be any chillen. Dead women don't bear no chillen."

"Dead?" Julienne gasped. "Dead, me?"

"That's enough," Buccaneer said, standing. "Let's go. She's getting worse, as I feared."

"You be the mistress of Moonspell," Carmella said, her voice fading with her energy. "And all them mistresses die."

"No, I'm not the mistress of Moonspell," Julienne corrected her. "I'm Alissa's governess."

"You talks of today. I talks of tomorrow." She lifted a clawlike hand and let it drop heavily on the table. "There be more o' your blood spilt than that dribble on your cheek."

Julienne touched the dried blood, drawn from her wild ride through the brush.

Buccaneer squeezed Julienne's shoulder. "Let's go."

Julienne stood up, telling herself it was silly to put any stock in the old woman's ramblings. "Good-bye, Carmella."

The white head bobbed and Carmella snored loudly.

Outside again, Julienne shook off the remnants of the strange woman and her mysterious predictions. She went around to the side of the house where she'd seen the glassy-eyed man. The brush and grass had been disturbed, flattened by feet.

"Julienne?" Buccaneer called, and she hurried back to him. He helped her onto Seabiscuit's back and handed her the reins. "Pay no attention to what she said. I only brought you here for entertainment. I certainly didn't want you to believe the old hag."

"You don't?" She pulled on her riding gloves again.

"No."

She watched as he climbed into the saddle, thinking that his denial had been mild. She suspected he heeded the witch's warnings.

"Did she predict Isabelle or Maggie's death?"

Buccaneer released a harsh laugh. "How would I know? Her mind is going, has been for years and years."

"How long have you known her?"

"She's lived in that shack for as far back as I can remember. Her grandson used to work for me."

"He doesn't anymore?"

"Ootay is lazy. You can't depend on him. He hasn't shown up for work in a year or more. I guess he's living off the old woman." He held the reins loosely. "If you give Seabiscuit his head, he'll race home on his own. I'll be a gentleman and give you a head start. Are you game?"

She reined Seabiscuit to face the right direction, but shrugged indifferently. "Oh, I don't know. I've already scratched up my face and I probably shouldn't—" Then she dug in her heels, tore off her hat, and slapped the gelding's rump. "You're on!" she shouted into the wind, and heard Buccaneer's startled curse.

Seabiscuit laid back his ears and snorted. The big gelding plowed scrub brush, pounded saw grass, and stretched over the ground in long, sleek strides. Green and gold flashed past Julienne as she clung to the horse's mane and glued herself to his broad back. She heard the thunder of hooves behind her and knew that Buccaneer and Blaze were catching up and threatening to overtake them.

She yelled at Seabiscuit, urging him onward. Faster and faster they flew, but still the thunder rumbled behind them. Suddenly the grounds of Moonspell spread out before them. Seabiscuit's muscles bunched beneath her and his ears pricked forward. Home.

Julienne slapped his rump with her hat again, and the wind whistled past her ears and flattened itself against her face to burn her eyes and throat. She glanced back and then whipped her gaze forward again, alarmed to find Buccaneer and the red stallion just off to the side. Gaining. He was gaining!

The fence hurried toward them, presenting a most perplexing obstacle. Julienne sensed Seabiscuit's questioning and she tapped his sides, telling him to go over the fence instead of turning him toward the open gate. From the corner of her eye, she caught sight of Blaze veering toward that opening. If they could clear the fence, she'd win!

Julienne gathered Seabiscuit's mane in both fists and buried her knees in his sides. The big horse quivered, then he was up and flying. Julienne's heart soared into her throat, cutting off her breath. For a handful of moments, she was weightless and the world was utterly silent. Then Seabiscuit's hooves connected with the earth again, and the sky fell away with an alarming jolt that nearly unseated Julienne. Her breath jostled out of her, and her heart stuttered and began to beat again, pounding in her ears, flooding her veins with warmth.

In the blink of an eye, she was upon the stables and tugging back on the reins with what strength she had left. Seabiscuit reared up, then settled back on all fours, his sides heaving, his beautiful brown coat as wet as if he'd swum to the stables instead of flying there. Buccaneer arrived seconds later and barely waited for Blaze to stop before he dismounted and strode to Seabiscuit.

He reached up, his hands closing on Julienne's waist, and pulled her off the winded horse.

"You're insane, taking that fence the way you did! You could have broken your neck." He shook her slightly. Although he wasn't smiling, his tone was light.

"You have to take chances to win," Julienne rejoined. "And I won." She smiled up into his face. "It isn't often you're beaten soundly, is it?"

"No, not often . . . and never so pleasantly." His gaze devoured her face, and he ran a hand over the tumble of her hair. "You go to a man's head, little jewel."

"To his head?" she repeated. "Not to his heart?"

"If a man had one, of course."

She pressed a hand against his chest where his heart leapt. "What is that pounding in your chest, if not a heart?"

"Desire. Wild, barely fettered desire." He stroked

the pad of his thumb across her lips. His fingers touched the scratch on her cheek, and his thumb settled in the corner of her mouth. Instinctively she wet his thumb with her tongue. He quivered violently. His heart crashed against his chest, against her palm.

"I can hardly wait until our next adventure together," she whispered, beginning to comprehend the power she held over him.

His attention fastened on her mouth. "Neither can I." He leaned forward and his breath touched her waiting lips. Something snared his attention and he stepped back hastily, his hands slipping away from her. "Ah, yes, Danny. You can see to Seabiscuit, but I'm taking Blaze after I've given him a drink." Buccaneer glanced at Julienne, and humor lurked in his eyes. "Speaking of which, I could use a drink myself."

The stableboy gathered Seabiscuit's reins and led him away. Buccaneer retreated slowly from Julienne.

"I'm going back to the tobacco fields," he said. "I will see you at dinner tonight, mam'selle."

"Until then, Captain." Smiling, she placed her hat on her head and strolled toward the house. She felt his gaze on her the whole way.

Chapter 13

I used to think he would never hurt me, but now I'm not so sure. He looks so evil sometimes. He is a jealous man and he swears he'll kill me before he allows another man to have me. I laughed, but I wasn't laughing inside. He's capable of murder, and it wouldn't take much to send him over the brink. If I do one thing he doesn't like, if I rebuke him or criticize him once too often, he could easily break my neck. I find this chilling . . . thrilling!

Julienne closed the diary and put it back in its hiding place. A shiver of revulsion raced through her. Magdalena believed that Buccaneer could murder her? She curled herself into the wing chair. The more she read of Maggie's diary, the more troubled she became about how she should feel about Buccaneer LaFlamme. Allowing his advances might be the same as enticing Satan. Certainly he was a devil around Maggie. The difference between her and Magdalena was that Maggie liked the sinister streak and cruelty. To Julienne, Buccaneer was a *reformed* pirate, but Maggie's diary contradicted her. The man Maggie knew didn't make love, he raped and ravaged; and he didn't want a partner in life, he wanted a love slave. Humiliation was his idea of a game, and violence wasn't reserved for enemies.

The wind stirred the draperies, capturing her attention. Julienne pulled her wrapper more closely to her body and escaped outside. Fireflies winked in the night. She stood for a few minutes on the patio, drinking in the peacefulness of the grounds and the beauty of the night sky, then she heard a rustling nearby. Turning, she gasped when a shadow loomed before her, then took the shape of a man.

"Do not scream. It's only me." White teeth flashed in the darkness.

"Wh-Who?"

"Lorenzo." He stepped into the light that sailed through the open doors. "I have been watching you. You have something I want, señorita."

"Watching me? You mean, just now?"

"You are a beautiful woman. I love beautiful women, especially ones with bedroom eyes."

Bedroom eyes? She hadn't the foggiest idea what he meant, but it sounded dirty. She told herself not to let him know that he terrified her. "You have no business spying on me. I want you to leave me alone and stop following me or I'll tell Captain LaFlamme."

"What will you tell him?" he asked, propping an arm high on the outside wall, his hand dangling inches from her face. "Will you tell him that I want you just as much as he wants you? You should choose me over him. I will be good to you, and I haven't had two women die on me." He grinned and craned his face closer to hers. "Anybody ever teach you how to pleasure a man? I can show you, señorita."

Julienne retreated to the open doors, afraid to turn her back on him. "I don't find you amusing or attractive, Lorenzo. Good night." She slipped inside and closed the doors. As she bolted them, she heard his fist slam against the other side, sending vibrations skittering through the wood. Julienne swallowed a shriek and backed away, expecting another blow that would shatter the bolt. After a minute, she realized he was gone and she relaxed. She was about to turn away when she heard the wolf's howl. The moaning cry sent shivers through her. Just like at Spirits Cove, she thought. Lorenzo had been in the cave!

She'd explored that memory often, sometimes convincing herself it had been her imagination, sometimes that it had been Buccaneer playing tricks on her, sometimes that there had been another man in the cave with them that day. The wolf called again—*AaahWOOOooo*. So lonely. So completely out of place. Was it Lorenzo teasing her, just as he'd done in the cave?

Someone tapped lightly at the door, and she clamped a hand over her mouth to keep her startled scream inside. Swallowing hard, she set to mending her unraveling composure.

"Julienne?"

She smiled, recognizing Buccaneer's voice. "Wait just a moment." She belted her wrapper tighter and opened the door. Desire curled in the pit of her stomach at the sight of him—disheveled hair, half-lidded gaze, bronze skin, muscled body encased in tight black breeches, loose shirt, and riding boots.

"Good evening." She glanced toward the French doors. "Did you hear the wolf?"

"Wolf?" His eyes widened. "You heard a wolf? When? Where?"

"Outside. Just now."

Without asking for permission, he pushed inside and strode to the French doors. Unbolting them, he pulled them open and went outside. Julienne followed, waiting for him on the patio while he went around the side of the Bride's House. He came back within minutes.

"What is it, Buccaneer?"

"Who, you mean," Buccaneer said. "Someone is

howling around here, and I want to know who and why." He moved back inside, waited for her to join him, and then bolted the doors again. "If you hear it again, tell me immediately."

She nodded and thought about telling him she suspected Lorenzo, but decided against it, since she had no proof.

"I wanted to know if you'd be interested in a trip to Key West. I'm sailing there tomorrow for supplies."

"That sounds wonderful! Alissa needs to get out more. Does she like Key West?"

"Alissa?" He beetled his brow. "I hadn't thought . . . Alissa's never been sailing or to Key West. She might not want to go with us."

Julienne placed her hands at her waist and sent him an exasperated look. "The daughter of a sea captain has never been at sea?" She shook her head. "Well, it's high time she sailed, don't you think?"

"She's a bit afraid of the water."

"A bit afraid?" she echoed with a scoff. "Alissa is *a bit afraid* of nearly everything. My father always said that courage is found when facing fear. By the time we sail to and from Key West, Alissa will have found her courage and be in love with the sea, just like her father."

He smiled, but not convincingly. His attention seemed to stray from her and he surveyed the room slowly, carefully, before he strolled toward the fireplace. Julienne tensed and held her breath. Did he know about the secret compartment and the diary? He ran a hand over the side of the mantel, his fingertips caressing the bricks—*the brick*— then lifting to a blown-glass vase holding hibiscus.

"Isabelle so loved this house. *Her* house. And the flowers. She loved flowers."

"Did you ever love Isabelle?"

He shook his head. "No. Mostly I pitied her."

"Why did . . ." She bit back the question, realizing it wasn't her place to ask for private revelations.

"What?" He turned to face her.

"Nothing."

"No. You were going to ask something. Ask it."

"Why did Magdalena move in here?"

His eyes darkened to gunmetal gray, and muscles clenched in his jawline. "That's not what I thought you were going to ask."

"What did you think I'd ask?"

"Why I didn't have my marriage to Isabelle annulled."

She considered it and nodded. "That *is* a good question. Why didn't you? She could have still become a nun, if that's what she wanted."

"Oh, that's what she wanted, but our marriage was a business deal, and neither one of our fathers would have allowed us to renege. Even though Isabelle begged her father to dissolve the marriage, he refused. A deal was a deal. I knew Isabelle was unhappy, but I didn't know how miserable she was until . . ." He turned away and caressed a hibiscus petal with a gentle fingertip. "She was so fragile." He sighed and squared his shoulders. "You and Alissa meet me at the pier at six o'clock sharp and we'll shove off."

"We'll be there, Captain." She saluted him, and he smiled. "Which vessel will we be sailing on?"

"The *Golden Conch*."

"Oh, good. That's the sloop I haven't seen yet."

"Until tomorrow, then." He paused on the threshold and looked back at her, his eyes suddenly dark, his mouth pulled down at the corners. "Maggie moved in here because she was afraid of me. I threatened to kill her with my bare hands," he said softly, matter-of-factly.

Julienne's lips parted in a silent gasp. A few moments passed before she could muster up her voice. "Kill her, why?" But he was already gone, closing the door behind him.

The *Golden Conch* sparkled on the water like a jewel. It was painted gold with black trim; its figurehead depicted a conch shell with a sea serpent emerging from it. Alissa hung back, but Julienne tugged firmly on her hand.

"None of that cowering, Alissa LaFlamme. You are the daughter of a sea captain and you will act like it. We're going to be part of your father's crew today, so look sharp."

"I don't wanna go. I could get killed."

"You could, but you won't. Want to know why?"

"No."

Julienne looked heavenward for patience. "I'm going to tell you anyway. We will be perfectly safe because your father will captain our ship, and he's a splendid sailor."

"How do you know?"

"Everyone says so." Julienne spotted Buccaneer and waved at him. He rolled the rope ladder over the side of the sloop.

"Welcome!" he shouted.

"Permission to board, sir?" Julienne asked.

"Permission granted." He held out his hands to navigate them onto his ship. "Careful now. You first, Alissa."

Julienne had to push the child into his hands. He lifted Alissa into the air and then down onto the gleaming wood deck. Julienne slipped her hand in his and hitched up her skirts. She stepped onto the rope ladder, and Buccaneer steadied her as she climbed the two top rungs. Then he wrapped his free arm around her waist and lifted her up and over the railing. Julienne released a laugh of surprise. Gaining her balance again, she wedged her boater more firmly on her dark brown hair, which she'd piled high and secured with two strategically placed combs.

She'd chosen to wear one of her new dresses, the rose one with its apron front and lavishly full, pleated skirt to allow her liberated movement. Alissa wore a bright yellow pinafore dress, perky straw hat, and fearful expression.

"Papa, I can't swim," she said, yanking at his shirt sleeve.

"I know, that's why we're *sailing* to Key West." Buccaneer chucked her playfully under her chin. "Why the long face, Lissa?"

"We could drown, Papa. Like Mama, we could die out there."

Buccaneer's gaze bounced to Julienne before returning to his daughter. He gathered Alissa into his arms. "It will be a grand adventure. You'll see. You'll have a wonderful time, and I won't let anything bad happen to you."

Alissa's eyes filled with tears and her lips quivered. "Why do I have to go, Papa? Why are you making me go?" She buried her face in the side of his neck, and he looked to Julienne for help.

"Captain, how many pirates and princesses do you know who have never been out to sea?"

He blinked, then caught on. "None, that I can recall."

"Exactly. Wouldn't you say that it's the *duty* of the princess of Pirate's Key to sail at least once?"

"*Oui*. It is your duty, Princess Alissa." He bounced his shoulder, forcing her to raise her tear-stained face to look at him. "As your captain, I will protect you, princess. The sea can be a wondrous thing. Won't you let me show you?"

A smile teased the corners of Alissa's mouth. "Well . . . I guess." She wiped away her shimmering tears. "I like it when you call me princess."

He touched the tip of his nose to hers. "You *are* my princess. The princess of my heart."

Julienne's throat tightened with sweet sentiment and she averted her gaze from the father and daughter, feeling her own loss acutely. It had been ten years, yet she still missed her father's kiss, his voice, his wisdom, his laugh. If she accomplished nothing else here at Moonspell, she wanted to mend the tear in Buccaneer's relationship with Alissa. First she had to completely understand it. Someone wasn't telling her the whole truth. Alissa wanted to love Buccaneer, but something or *someone* was preventing her from trusting him.

"Shall we cast off?" Buccaneer set Alissa on her feet, but kept hold of one of her hands. "You come with me. You'll be my first mate."

Julienne looked around, getting her bearings. Two men, dressed in knee-length black pants and red and white striped shirts, scurried to cast off lines and hoist the anchor. All across the deck were coils of rope. She touched a length with the toe of her shoe.

"Looks like seaweed strewn about," she noted.

"Seaweed?" Buccaneer repeated.

"These ropes."

"Ropes!" He shook his head, his expression censuring. "Begging your pardon, landlubber, but these are *not* ropes."

She stared at the braided hemp. "Looks like rope to me."

"That's because you're not seaworthy yet. A sailor never calls this rope. Each piece, each coil, has a name and a purpose. Stays, shrouds, braces, and so on. Each has its function." He strode toward the bow of the ship, and Julienne and Alissa followed in his wake.

"I suppose those aren't sails." Julienne pointed to the sheets being raised into position by the crewmen.

Buccaneer glanced at the rigging and grinned.

"Sails? The devil, you say. Those are the ship's clothing."

Alissa giggled and skipped along beside him as he took her on a tour of the ship. From time to time he glanced back at Julienne to share a comment or check on her progress. She enjoyed hanging back to watch him relate information to his daughter. Alissa gazed up at him with an absorption only possible between a child and parent. A sharp, sweet pain speared Julienne and she recalled Buccaneer's prophecy that she would bear children. She dared not dwell on the possibility, she told herself. Remember, Carmella said nothing of children. That old witch spoke only of doom and gloom, of shadows and danger.

The ship glided from its moorings to open sea, and Buccaneer took his place at the wheel, with Alissa by his side. Julienne held on to a massive spar and listened to him entertain Alissa with tales of Jolly Roger and his cohorts.

"My *grandpère*—your great-*grandpère*—had a huge ship called the *Libertine*. When I was your age I learned to climb those rat lines—"

"What's that, Papa?" Alissa interrupted.

"The lines way up there running under the masts. See them?" He waited for her to locate them. "*Grandpère* would send me up the rat lines with two other boys to secure the rigging. The wind was often fierce and the sea was boiling, but you learned to climb on the windward side so that you were blown against the mast and not off it. Still, it was a clever trick to find a toehold on those foot ropes while the hull pitched to and fro and the wind tried its best to rip you off and throw you into the drink."

"People die out in the sea," Alissa said, solemn and round-eyed as an owl.

Buccaneer looked at Julienne, and his brows met in a frown, clearly baffled by Alissa's attitude.

"People also fall in love with the sea. I did. Even when I was hanging up there on the rat lines and praying I wouldn't fall, I loved it. Life isn't worth living, Alissa, if you waste each day of it being afraid." He removed his flat-brimmed hat, and the wind combed through the black waves of his hair. "Your *grandpère* crafted this hat." He handed it to her. "It's made from a ship's canvas and water-proofed with paint. If you decide you like sailing, I'll make one for you."

Julienne studied his attire, thinking he looked more piratical than ever in his sailor-cut trousers, white knit shirt, and black neckerchief tied in a square knot at his throat. His flat black shoes with silver buckles matched his belt, whence swung a short sword with an ivory and ebony handle. He stood behind the ship's wheel, legs braced apart. Placing Alissa's hands carefully on the wheel, he spoke softly to her, instructing her on how the ship was steered by sails and rudder. He noticed Julienne's interest and motioned to one of the crewmen.

"Potter, take the wheel," he instructed.

"Aye, sir." The agile seaman leaped to obey.

"Come along, ladies. Your tour isn't over. We must now explore below deck." Buccaneer picked up Alissa and motioned with his head for Julienne to follow. "This way. Mind your step and your head when going down. The stairs are narrow and the doorways are low."

Julienne ducked and followed them down into the hold, which was full of barrels. "What's in all of these?"

"Nothing, yet. We're going to fill them with staples in Key West. Alissa, see those covered circles?" He pointed along the walls at the four portholes. "Those are for cannons. We don't arm ourselves now, but we did back when your *grand-père* and great-*grandpère* were captaining the ships."

He pointed behind them. "Back there are the crew's quarters, and straight ahead is the captain's quarters."

"Where do the guests sleep?" Julienne asked.

Buccaneer arched a brow. "Well, if the guest refuses to stay in the captain's quarters with the captain, then I suppose she can bunk next door here in the officers' quarters."

Julienne felt her skin grow warm under his lambent gaze. Was he suggesting that she ... ?

"I want to stay in your room, Papa," Alissa piped up, and Buccaneer laughed.

"I'd have it no other way, princess." He opened the cabin door and stepped through. "Here we are. Captain's quarters. When I was a lad I dreamed of having my own private room on board. I always had to bunk with the crew on my father's or grandfather's ships, and that meant sleeping—or trying to sleep—in a swinging hammock. One good thing about it, I learned to sleep anywhere and anyhow. I could straddle a hurricane and nod off." He swung Alissa down to her feet. "Except lately, I've had trouble sleeping ..." His voice faded, then he drew himself up and glanced nervously at Julienne, obviously regretting his revelation. "What do you think, ladies? Does it meet inspection?"

Half the room was dominated by a bed, its cherrywood headboard depicting an elaborately carved conch shell on the ocean floor, surrounded by lacy plants and seaweed. Black satin draped the bed, and bloodred pillows added bold accents. A desk and captain's chair, a trunk, and a safe were the only other furnishings, all built-in or bolted to the floor. Julienne was delighted that it fit neatly with what she'd imagined. She examined a sandglass hanging from the ceiling and a brass bell near it, both very old and weather-worn.

"Relics from Black Pierre's pirate days," Buccaneer explained. "The sandglass was turned every half hour and the bell was rung. Sailors kept up with the number of bells to determine their watch shifts."

"I've heard of eight bells," Julienne said, snagging that bit of information from one of the countless stories she'd read of pirates and privateers.

Buccaneer nodded. "Eight bells is the end of a watch and sends seamen to their quarters for food and sleep."

"How far is it from Key West to Cuba?"

"To Cuba?" He crouched a little as he crossed the room to open one of the portholes. The ceiling brushed the top of his head. "About ninety nautical miles from Key West. Why?"

"You go there often."

"Yes, to trade and allow some of my workers to visit family they have there. The Ten Years War with Spain has been hard on that country. Independence, I suppose, always requires its full measure of spilled blood."

"But they've won their independence, so they can now look forward to rebuilding," Julienne said, but Buccaneer tossed her a chiding glance.

"We'll see. I fear there will be more bloodshed before we can say it's over, if that day *ever* arrives."

Someone stamped twice overhead, and he raised a finger to his lips for silence.

"By the dip four, Cap'n!" a man shouted above.

"What's that mean?" Julienne asked.

"The crewman has been heaving the lead." He smiled at their puzzled expressions. "It's a lead weight tied to a notched line that's thrown out to determine the depth of the ocean floor. We're out at four fathoms. I need to go topside again."

The ship rocked, sending Julienne against him. Buccaneer gripped her upper arms to steady her, but within an instant his touch changed to a caress. She looked up into his smoldering eyes, and her mouth went dry as desire built a fire within her. The ship seemed to undulate beneath her feet. She spread her hands upon his chest, feeling the muscled strength of him. He parted his lips, and she knew he meant to kiss her with unbridled passion, but then he seemed to come to his senses. He shook his head and put her from him with effort. Clearing his throat, he glanced at his innocent child.

"Papa, I'm thirsty," Alissa announced.

"We'll have mugs of punch topside, and I'll help the crewmen while you landlubbers learn your ropes."

"Ropes!" Julienne gasped. "There are no ropes on this ship, Captain. I have that on authority."

Pinpoints of light danced in his silvery-gray eyes. "It is most vexing to be gouged by one's own words." He placed his hands on Alissa's shoulders and sent her out of the room, but he turned back to Julienne and traced her lips with his fingertip. "Watch out, mate, or I'll make you my steward and have you satisfy my every need."

"Would that be possible?" Julienne whispered past the beating heart lodged in her throat.

"For you, yes." He stepped back, indicating that she should precede him.

Dimly Julienne heard Alissa climb the steps to the upper deck. She squeezed past Buccaneer, the front of her body pressed intimately against the front of his. She felt his desire and saw it leap like flames in his eyes. Just when she thought she would escape to the stairwell, his hand shot out to cradle her chin and bring her mouth up to his.

His lips claimed hers in a lush, openmouthed kiss that stunned her and then bewitched her. He circled her waist with one arm and tilted her head so that his mouth could fit more perfectly, more fully, upon hers.

"Papa?"

Alissa's voice drifted through the smoke of passion. Julienne pulled free of Buccaneer's velvet trap and shook her head, shocked by her own wanton behavior. Whirling, she hurried to the stairs and saw Alissa at the top, peering down at her.

"We're coming, Alissa," Julienne said, sounding breathless and bewildered to her own ears. It was a relief to see the sky and feel the brisk sea air. She grasped Alissa's hand, needing something to hold on to. Glancing back, she saw Buccaneer emerge from below deck, a knowing grin on his lips. She looked away from him and breathed deeply, trying to clear her head.

He's as intoxicating as homemade whiskey, she thought. One sip and she was reeling. And like all potent brew, one taste was not enough. Even now, with the voice of reason trying to be heard above the din of her traitorous heart, Julienne craved another taste . . . another long drink of desire.

Chapter 14

They weighed anchor at the Mallory Docks. While captain and crew made fast the ship, Julienne and Alissa took to the shore. Merchants crowded the square. Sailors milled, laughing and talking, winking at every woman who passed. Barrels and boxes of supplies littered the dock, waiting to be loaded as cargo.

The smell of fish permeated the air. At one end of the dock, men dressed out snapper and grouper while others sold shellfish fresh. Seagulls cried overhead and swooped to nab innards thrown by the anglers. Pelicans bobbed near the docks and fought one another for fish heads and tails. Nothing was wasted.

Alissa wrinkled her button nose. "Uggh. It smells awful here, Julienne. I don't like this place. Can we go home now?"

"No, we can't. All you smell is fish, and I know you like to eat fish."

"Yes, but I don't wanna have to smell it." She squeezed her nostrils shut with her finger and thumb.

Julienne laughed. "Quit being such a gray cloud. Look on the bright side. We made it to Key West by sea without being killed. I hope you're not too awfully disappointed, ladybug." Julienne gave Alissa a teasing smile and was glad when

Alissa finally giggled. She crouched in front of the child and straightened her hat and pinafore. "I'm proud of you for being such a brave girl aboard the ship. This trip means a lot to your father."

"How come?"

"Because he loves you and he wants you to love him."

Alissa stared at the seasoned wood under her feet. "I love him."

"Show him, Alissa. Trust him." Catching sight of Buccaneer bearing down on them, Julienne stood straight.

"The men will load the supplies while we stroll about Key West," he announced, reaching out to clasp Alissa's small hand in an unconscious gesture.

"Alissa thinks it stinks around here," Julienne reported with a smile.

Buccaneer laughed. "She's right. There's an eating establishment on Duval Street that serves wonderful steamed shellfish. I know Alissa can eat her weight in shrimp. How about you, Julienne?"

She pressed a hand to her middle and smacked her lips. "I can taste them already."

"We're off then." He held out his elbow. "Shall we?"

Julienne slipped her hand in the crook of his arm. "Thank you. As usual, Key West is as busy as a beehive." She stepped lightly along the street paved with crushed shell. A ship's horn bellowed and a bell clanged. Shouted orders drifted to them, some in foreign languages. A current of excitement rushed through Julienne as she was swept up in the activity of the port town.

Walking past a bar, Julienne peered into the darkness of the doorway, then gasped when a man came stumbling out. He fell into the street just behind them, rolled, and lay sprawled, his face to the sun.

"Stay outta here, you leech!" a man yelled from inside the tavern. "Sucking up my tonic and trying to pay me with old Cuban currency that ain't worth the paper they be printed on! You're lucky I don't blast your empty head off your scrawny shoulders!"

"Thattaway to tell 'im, Spunky," another voice crackled from inside. "Top off me glass, willya? I gotta get back to me ship after this one."

Buccaneer stooped and lifted Alissa into his arms. Her arms went around his neck and she looked over his shoulder at the man lying in the street.

"Is that the place where we're gonna eat, Papa?"

"No, princess." He chuckled under his breath and looked at Julienne to share his amusement. "That's no place for a lady."

"Why is that man sleeping in the street?"

"Don't worry about him. Look up ahead at all the pretty shops. Here's a dress shop." He stopped to let Alissa and Julienne admire the ready-made dresses and bolts of fabric in the window. "This is where I bought the material for Julienne's new clothes."

"It is?" Julienne turned wide eyes on him.

"I had the fabric sent to a seamstress I know here, and she whipped them up from my instructions." His gaze moved lazily over her. "That one looks particularly nice on you, Julienne."

Pleasure warmed her cheeks. "I'm glad you find the dress attractive."

"I find what's in the dress even more attractive."

She raised her gaze to his and told herself not to believe his softly spoken compliments, but her foolish heart soared. Several men approached from the opposite direction and tipped their hats.

"Good to see you again, LaFlamme," one of them said.

"Hello, Monsieur Blanchert," Buccaneer said,

pausing to shake hands. "How is the shipping business?"

"Busy, thank you."

Smiling pleasantly but quickly, they moved on. Julienne considered their behavior, recalling how men on the dock had greeted Buccaneer respectfully, but none had approached him or engaged him in conversation. Of course, Buccaneer didn't invite fellowship. He was a loner. Julienne had noticed how people moved out of his way as he approached and eyed him carefully after he passed. Did they think he was a dangerous character? Did they believe that Buccaneer LaFlamme had gotten away with murder?

"Hey, thar's the wife killer!"

The slurred voice dovetailed with Julienne's thoughts and she located its owner, a potbellied, unshaven man across the street from them. He swayed on his feet and belched loudly, making his two friends laugh uproariously.

"Hey thar, LaFlamme!" He gave a thumb's-up sign. "Atta way, buddy! You get tired of a silly bitch, you kill 'er. I like a man who don't put up with a fishwife. If more of us would strangle the life outta 'em and throw 'em to the sharks, we men would live longer."

"That's fer damn sure," one of his friends said, slapping him on the back. "Mebbe I can get LaFlamme to kill my ball and chain, seein' as he's so good at it."

"Hey, looks like he's got hisself another bride to float out on the reef," the skinniest of the three said, pointing out Julienne.

She felt Buccaneer's wrath before she witnessed his narrowed eyes and flared nostrils. The very air around her seemed to contract and vibrate. Buccaneer let Alissa slide down his body until she was standing.

"Why, you rotten bag of fish guts," he growled,

his hands bunching into fists. "How dare you say such things in front of my daughter."

He crossed the street in a blur and had rammed his fist into the stomach of one man, punched another, and grabbed the third by the shirt collar to hold him inches off the ground, all before Julienne could push Alissa up against a storefront, out of the way, and dash after him. She hesitated, fear crawling up her spine. Having never seen him in this state of rage, she wondered if he would know friend from foe. His eyes were glazed, and his fisted hands were weapons more dangerous than swords or knives. Unsheathed power rippled through his muscles. The man he held made a garbled sound and his eyes rolled up into his head.

"Buccaneer, stop it!" she yelled, afraid he might choke the potbellied loudmouth to death. The man's eyes bugged out of their sockets and his tongue lolled between his rubbery lips. Julienne grabbed Buccaneer's arm and pulled hard. "Stop it, Buccaneer! Not in front of Alissa, I beg of you!"

"Hey, mate, don't kill him," one of the other men said, rubbing his jaw where Buccaneer's fist had left its mark. He spit out blood and teeth chips. "He didn't mean nothing by it. Hell, he was only saying what everybody else thinks 'bout choo."

Buccaneer released the unfortunate man and whirled to glare at the other two, sprawled on the ground. A low growl escaped him as he started toward them, but Julienne stepped in his path.

"Get out of my way, Julienne," he commanded, clasping her shoulders to move her aside.

She clutched his shirtfront and tried to shake him, but she would have had more success trying to shake an oak tree. "Please, Buccaneer. Don't do this. They aren't worth it. Your daughter needs you."

"I'm doing this for her; now, step aside."

"Buccaneer, listen to me. You're scaring Alissa. Is that what you want? More nightmares for her?" She glanced across the street and saw that Alissa was crying, her little fists pressed against her mouth. "Look at her, Buccaneer!"

He shifted his gaze from the fallen men to the sobbing child, and something changed in his face. His eyes took on a gentle sheen and the flush of rage subsided. He groaned in self-deprecation and released Julienne to cross the street to his child. He held out his arms to Alissa, but she cringed from him. Julienne afforded the bleeding men a glance of sympathy before she raced across the street.

Alissa dashed to her, flinging her arms around Julienne's legs. The pain etched on Buccaneer's face tore at Julienne's heart.

"There, there, ladybug. It's all over now. Your papa just threw a temper tantrum." She smiled down at the child's upturned, tearstained face.

"Will you punish him for it?"

Julienne patted her damp cheek. "No, he's bigger than me." She looked at Buccaneer, trying to coax a smile from him, but he continued to stare at his child, his big hands flexing at his sides.

Pulling Alissa's arms away, Julienne turned her toward Buccaneer. "Go to your father."

"No!" Alissa sobbed louder.

"Alissa, your father wants to hold you."

"No!"

Buccaneer turned aside as if he couldn't stand to watch the fear on his child's face a moment longer. "Don't make her if she doesn't want to. She feels safer with you."

Julienne shook her head, dismissing his advice. She picked Alissa up in her arms and moved toward Buccaneer. "Your father wants to apologize for frightening you, Alissa, and you're going to listen and accept his apology." Her firm tone cut through Alissa's squirming and whining. She forced her into Buccaneer's arms. "There. You two are going to have to learn to talk with each other, understand each other, and forgive each other. I can't do it for you." She stood back, giving them a modicum of privacy.

Buccaneer cleared his throat nervously. "I'm sorry, Alissa. I lost my head . . . That is, those men had no business saying what they did, and I couldn't allow it to stand." He turned to look across the street, and his eyebrows shot up when he saw that the men were gone.

"You hurt them, Papa," Alissa said.

"Yes, but they hurt me first."

She pulled back in his arms, giving him a once-over with her big, gray eyes. "You're not bleeding like they were, Papa."

He smiled, and attractive lines creased the corners of his eyes and mouth. "Maybe I'm bleeding inside from what they said about me. A man can take only so much, princess, and then he must act. Do you understand?"

She shook her head. "I don't like bleeding, Papa."

He held her tightly, closing his eyes as he placed a kiss on her forehead. Julienne blinked back tears, the sight of the man holding the small child in his arms reminding her of her own relationship with her father.

He loves her so much, she thought, watching Buccaneer smooth a big hand over his daughter's dark curls. He'd give his life for hers.

"Alissa, your father has apologized. What do you say?" Julienne prompted.

"I sorry, Papa." Alissa pursed her lips in a babyish pout. "You don't scare me no more."

Buccaneer dropped a kiss on Alissa's button nose. "I'll try not to ever scare you again." He looked at Julienne, and his eyes sent her a debt of gratitude. She slipped her hand in the crook of his arm, accepting in kind.

"I'm hungry," she announced. "All this excitement hasn't stunted my appetite one whit, I'm afraid. If anything, it's heightened it."

Buccaneer's chuckle was lusty and deep-throated. "I'm not the least bit surprised by that."

Strolling beside him, Julienne thought of the impression they made—a family. A husband, his wife, and their child. She darted a glance at Buccaneer's handsome profile and wondered if he'd ever entertained such a fantasy about her—or if he ever would.

She was the most exasperating women he'd ever encountered, Buccaneer thought as he watched Julienne cradle his daughter and rock her back and forth. Alissa's eyelids drooped, and Julienne's sweet, clear voice lifted on the sea wind to him. The lullaby she sang tugged at his memory. Had his own mother crooned it to him? Somewhere, someone had, he was sure of it.

The stiff breeze combed through his hair and he tipped back his head and enjoyed the sky above, the sensual delights of the ocean, and the skill of his two-man crew. He gave the ship to them and lounged back on the bench, hardly noticing their course, because he knew his crew would make it true and they'd be home far too soon to suit him.

It had been a fine day, overall, save for that drunken lout's bellowing and the fight that had followed. He wished that hadn't happened, but damn it all, what was a man to do? That blasted woman didn't expect him to stand aside and allow that sot to defame him in front of his neighbors and kin, did she? It was one thing to hear it behind his back—he was used to that—but quite another to have it shouted on a city street for his daughter and all others to hear and snicker over. If he had to do over, he'd thrash them again.

Damn them to hell. Damn them *all* to hell! He knew that they smiled to his face and shook his hand and then called him a devil in the taverns and gaming rooms. Everyone said he should be in jail and that he would be if it weren't for his wealth and reputation. Let them talk. That's all most of them could do—talk. They dared not challenge him, because they valued their teeth and wished to keep them.

He'd had every right to defend his honor. Every right.

Then why did he feel as if his chin scraped the deck? That damnable woman, that's why. He felt as if he'd disappointed her somehow, and that rankled him. He wanted her to hold him in high esteem. What she thought of him meant more than what the whole damn lot of Key West thought. He jerked his gaze away from her. God, when had this happened? Why did her opinions begin to carry so much weight?

Selena and Rosa were right. This governess was getting out of hand. She should be reminded of her place . . .

The singing stopped and he looked at her. She was so beautiful that his heart slammed in his chest, sending hot, urgent messages to his loins. The sea breeze had spanked her cheeks a rosy pink and loosened her hair so that tendrils curled at her temples and nape. In that instant he wanted her more keenly than he'd ever wanted a woman, and in the next he felt ashamed because she was holding his child and trying to get him to help her with Alissa.

"Could we put her abed somewhere?" she mouthed, looking from him to the sleeping child in her lap.

He nodded and sprang to his feet, motioning

her to go below deck. He went first, letting Julienne follow him to the captain's quarters. He plumped the pillow and stood back so that Julienne could settle Alissa on the bed. She murmured something, turned onto her side, and dropped into a deep sleep.

"She's exhausted," Julienne whispered. "Will she be all right in here by herself, do you think?"

"Yes." Buccaneer opened a porthole to let in the sea breeze. "You can check on her from time to time. We should be home before she wakes up."

Julienne stood at the side of the bed, looking down at the angelic face. Buccaneer stopped beside her to admire his daughter's long, sooty lashes and perfect features. He looked at Julienne, and emotion knotted in his throat. He thought of her bearing children, raising children, laughing and playing with children. Not just her charges, but her own offspring. She'd make a loving mother . . . a passionate wife.

He cleared his throat and mind and turned away from her. They tiptoed from the room. Buccaneer left the door open, hooking it against the wall to make it stay that way. Julienne opened the next door and went inside.

"So this is the officers' quarters," she said, strolling around the small room with its two narrow bunks and chest of drawers. "Does the first mate stay here, and the captain's steward?" She sat on one of the cots.

He leaned against the doorjamb, recalling his playful threat earlier to make her his steward. "That's right. Which would you rather be, the first mate or the steward?"

"I believe Isabelle beat me to the first mate position." She smiled, taking the sting from her words.

His smile was rueful. "Actually, no. That would

have been Maggie. Isabelle and I never mated, so to speak. So you'll be my steward?"

She shifted on the bed, and the neckline of her dress gaped open to reveal more of her delicate throat and the curve of her breast. "I'm sure you already have one."

"No, I don't." Damn it all, did she have to look so delectable?

She removed her hat and gingerly pushed her fingers through her hair, lifting the dark auburn locks so that the meager light played over them in glossy splendor. She smiled at him, and his heart lurched. Did she know what that smile did to him? Had she any idea how lovely she looked with that shaft of dusty light falling across her body and the pleasure of the sea voyage evident on her face? He wanted to strip the hat from her hands so that those soft, cool fingers could massage his overheated skin. God, he was burning up!

She rose from the bunk and struggled to push open the porthole. It creaked and gave way suddenly, making her lose her balance. The hand with which she held her hat burst through the opening. The wind whipped it from her fingers.

"My hat!" She wilted and turned to face him, her expression as crestfallen as if she'd just lost a diamond-studded tiara. "I lost my hat."

Thank God! He looked at her hands, already feeling them on his chest, his stomach, his throbbing sex. He cleared his throat and jerked his gaze up to her face. "Really, Julienne. It's not much of a loss, is it?" He thought of the other hat under his bed, the one he'd bought for her but hadn't found the courage to give her.

"No, I suppose not."

He opened his mouth to tell her he'd give her the one he'd purchased in New Orleans, but then a breeze dashed in, throwing strands of her hair across her mouth and eyes. She lifted a hand and pulled a lock away from her lips. The gesture was inconsequential, but somehow incredibly sexual. Desire clenched in Buccaneer's gut and he reached for her. His arm hooked neatly around her waist and he brought her against him, bowing her body into his so that her head tipped back and her lips parted in shock.

"We shouldn't," she whispered.

"I know," he agreed, then slanted his mouth over hers. He wet her lips. "Give me your tongue, Julienne."

She shook her head.

"Give it to me," he demanded, craving the taste of her. He clutched the lower part of her face in one hand and positioned his lips expertly upon hers. He filled her mouth with his tongue and waited for her to return the favor. She trembled. "Do it," he whispered against her mouth. "Now."

Finally the tip of her tongue ventured forth and breached his lips. He opened his mouth wider to take her in and suckle gently. She tried to wriggle from his arms, but he tightened his hold by sliding his hands down to cup her hips. Her buttocks nestled in the palms of his hands and he kneaded her firm flesh and pressed his pelvis against her. He was already swollen, hot, and uncomfortable. Little sounds of wonder and trepidation vibrated in her throat and spurred him on. He captured one of her hands and brought it down between their bodies to flatten her palm against him.

"Oh, no. Oh, my." She snatched her hand away, and he laughed. "Don't laugh! You shouldn't . . . I can't t-touch you there!"

"You just did." He took her mouth again to silence her. As he suspected, her outrage was only skin-deep, for she melted against him and her arms snaked around his neck.

Her tongue darted into his mouth and collided with his own larger, bolder one. He showed her how he liked it, deep and slow, and she mimicked him admirably. A quick learner, she had him moaning in no time and lusting for a more total union. He raked his fingers through her hair. It felt like heavy silk and looked like fire floating over the backs of his hands. Gradually he moved his hands to cover her breasts. He felt her nipples harden in his palms.

"I want you," he told her, finding the combs in her hair and casting them out.

"No, we can't." She closed her eyes and sighed as he nibbled lightly along the side of her neck, then took the lobe of her ear between his teeth. "Oww, you devil," she said, laughing a little and inching away from him. "Stop, Buccaneer. We must stop." She brushed his hands away from her breasts. "This isn't right."

"Right, be damned. I don't give a fig for what is right or wrong. I know what I want, and it's you. I'll have you now." He heard himself talking like a barbarian, but he didn't care. His member throbbed painfully and he wanted to bury it inside her. Somehow he knew it would find a most wondrous pleasure in her—more wondrous than any other.

A plaintive cry separated them, jostling them from their world of two. Alissa's voice floated down the corridor.

"Papa? Julienne? Where am I?"

"Here I come, ladybug!" Julienne fairly flew from the quarters to the captain's cabin.

Buccaneer moved closer to the porthole and let the wind slap him sharply and bring him to his senses. A dull throbbing bedeviled him. The woman is a witch, he thought. He heard a sound behind him and turned to see Julienne.

"Where's Alissa?"

"She went back to sleep once she remembered where she was and that she was perfectly safe."

She didn't step into the room, but remained in the corridor. Her gaze lifted. "I think I'll go topside now. I'll check on her again in a few minutes."

"Afraid I might seduce you again?" he jeered.

She shook her head. "You know as well as I do that we shouldn't be familiar with each other."

"Why not? Where is that written?"

"It's not. It's understood. You . . . You're a widower and I'm an unmarried governess and we . . ." She sighed away the rest. "You are grieving for your wife and looking for another. Alissa needs a—"

"I'm not looking," he interrupted again. "And I know what Alissa needs better than you."

"I doubt that."

He narrowed his eyes, angered by her cheekiness. "Believe me, I know a hell of a lot more about this world and what's in it than you. I don't need your advice, nor do I appreciate it, so please silence your opinionated tongue."

Her expressive eyes sparkled with fire. "You begged for my tongue a few moments ago, Captain."

He drew himself up, tall and straight. "When a woman is willing, a man takes what he can get off her."

She sucked in a breath. Shock, then anguish, chilled her eyes. Buccaneer fought off a shiver of regret. He swallowed the apologetic words that crowded into his throat. She turned to go, and he clamped his lips together to keep from calling her back. But she paused and looked at him, her gaze steady but shadowed.

"Who do you think killed your wife?"

The question unnerved him, but he managed to sound sarcastic. "Which one?"

"You don't suspect that Isabelle was murdered, do you?"

"That's what they say. I murdered both of them."

"I'm not interested in what others say. I'm asking you. Who killed Magdalena?"

"Do you have an opinion?" He smirked. "Ah, but that's like asking a porcupine if he has a point, isn't it?"

She squared her narrow shoulders. "I don't believe you murdered her. Tell me, who did?"

Talking of Maggie annoyed him. "I thought you were going up top."

"Aren't you going to answer me?"

"No, I'm not. You're the governess, and it's time you remembered that. I owe you no explanations or answers." He made his voice hard and his words clipped as he advanced toward her. "Now that I've gathered my good senses again, I see that you're right. We shouldn't let our emotions rule. You'd only end up crying and hurt, and I'd have to scout for a new governess." He expected her to move aside and let him pass. When she didn't, he gritted his teeth and wanted to lash out at her. Damn it all, why didn't she act like other women? Any other woman would have retreated, but not her! Oh, no. She stood there as if she'd sprouted roots. "Excuse me, mam'selle," he drawled. "You are blocking the doorway."

"Why would I end up crying and hurt?"

He stared deeply into her eyes—dark brown, lustrous eyes that made his insides weaken. "Because I can see through you, and I see that you have a heart of glass. A man like me would shatter it."

A smile lifted one corner of her lush mouth. "I bet your heart is just as fragile and that you're no stranger to tears."

He mirrored her smile and leaned down until his nose nearly touched hers and his eyes could see every nuance of hers. "Would you bet your life on it, *chérie?*" he rasped, snaking a hand around her to give her buttocks a good squeeze.

Finally she moved. Bounded backward, rather. He laughed deep in his chest and strode toward the ladder and the waning light of day. Standing on the rolling deck, he felt more himself, but still completely out at sea when it came to her and the feelings she evoked in him.

Damn, damn, damnable woman!

Chapter 15

S taring at the hat, Julienne was at a loss for words.

"Well?" Buccaneer prodded. "Will you accept it, or shall I give it to Selena? I'm sure she'll be properly grateful."

"I ... Yes, I'll accept it." Julienne admired the peacock feathers decorating the crown. "When did you ... Did you buy this in Key West yesterday?"

"No, in New Orleans."

Julienne looked at him. "And you waited until now to ... Did you buy it for another woman and decide to give it to me after I lost mine yesterday?"

"I bought it for you," he said, his words clipped. "I just took my time in giving it to you." He held up a hand, palm out. "Let's not beat a dead horse, shall we? My timing is of no importance."

She examined the hat again. "It's just that ... I'm trying to understand you."

"What are you trying to understand about me?"

"How you feel about me ... or don't feel about me."

"I think you're a fine governess." He strode to the open French doors and looked out at the broad expanse of lawn that sloped to the sea's edge.

"That, I do understand," she said behind him, her thoughts returning to a passage in Maggie's

diary about how loving and attentive Buccaneer
could be and then how he could resort to brutality
in the blink of an eye. He'd often left Maggie with
bruises on her arms and legs. Maggie had moved
out of their bedroom and into the Bride's House
shortly after Alissa's birth, but that hadn't stopped
Buccaneer from enjoying her when he took a notion. Pages and pages of Maggie's diary burned
with descriptions of his lovemaking, much of it
rough-and-tumble, some of it spurred by his anger
and resentment toward her. After the display of
Buccaneer's temper yesterday, followed by his
kisses that had left her dazed, Julienne wondered
if Buccaneer was showing his true colors—those
Maggie had known so intimately. If he possessed a
streak of evil, could her love vanquish it?

The silence became oppressive and he glanced
at her over his shoulder, his eyebrow lifting in a silent query.

"What I'm puzzled about is why you kiss me
and then try to push me away with your talk of
murder," she said.

"No more puzzled than I am." He leaned his
back against the doorjamb and ran a hand through
his midnight hair. "I suppose I don't want to ruin
you. One of the things I like best about you is
your innocence. I fear that I'll take that from you
and not be able to forgive myself."

His honest admission touched her, and she
moved closer to him. He'd come from the fields,
and he smelled of sunlight and moist soil. His
shirt laces were loose, his collar open. She could
see the bulge of his chest. His skin looked dark in
contrast to his white shirt. Dark and delicious. She
moistened her lips with her tongue, recalling the
taste of him, and she knew a fine craving.

"You forget that, while I am innocent in some
things, I've not been kept under glass. I'm a
woman who knows herself and her own mind."

"Do you now?" Amusement sparkled in his gray eyes. "A woman of the world, are you?"

"Not that, but I've suffered through my share of hardships. I tell myself that being anything more than a governess here is wrong, but then I betray my own sense of propriety by daydreaming about you and by . . . trying to catch and hold your eye. It's true, I know little of men and their ways, but I know what I feel, and I feel so wonderful in your arms. Wonderful and . . . sometimes frightened."

"Perhaps you should heed the fear, dear governess."

"I'm not frightened of you," she amended.

"Then of what?"

"Of letting my heart rule my head. Of doing the wrong thing and making you regret your interest in me. You *are* interested, aren't you? You're not just playing with me? To learn that you're only amused by me would surely break my heart."

"You do amuse me . . ." He watched the shadow of pain flit across her face before he added, "But you also make me hard with wanting." Buccaneer drew in a long, filling breath. Damn it all, how to make her understand his mercurial moods when he was with her . . . Or should he explain? Perhaps he should simply tell her to—

"I want you, too. In fact, I think I'm falling in love with you, Buccaneer LaFlamme."

He brought up a fist and slammed it into the doorjamb. "Don't say that, Julienne. You're not falling in love with me. You're talking about a schoolgirl infatuation and I—"

"Do I look like a schoolgirl to you?" She thrust out her chin and breasts, and her smile was supremely confident. "I know what I feel, and I don't need you denying it!"

"You just told me that you don't know about men and their ways—"

"But I do know that I felt something special for you the moment I heard your name."

He barked a laugh. "Which only proves my point. You fell in love with a name and your image of who was attached to that name, but not with me."

"You're wrong. After I met you, I tried to keep my distance, just as you've tried to distance yourself from me, but it's impossible. We're drawn together just as the day is drawn to the night and the surf is drawn to the sand and—"

"Stop, stop, I beg of you. Your purple prose amuses me, mam'selle, but it has nothing to do with reality. What is real is that I am a man who has had two wives, both of whom have drowned, and one of whom was most certainly murdered. I don't wish to ensnare you in the uglier aspects of my life. I think you should concentrate on Alissa and keep me at arm's length."

"You make that sound so easy."

"It is."

"Then why don't you practice it? You're the one who kisses me. I don't recall grabbing you and forcing my tongue into your mouth!"

He stared at her, surprised by her bald statement. "Your honesty is a product of your youth. It's another thing I would surely destroy, because I am, alas, quite jaded. Life does that to you."

"Don't you want me to be honest with you? I want it. I must have it. Wasn't Magdalena honest and true?"

"Why must you keep bringing her into this?"

"Because she is the yardstick by which I'm being measured."

He flung her a bitter glance. "Don't talk nonsense."

"Is it nonsense? You said that she's still around . . . in your head or heart or whatever." She gestured, indicating the Bride's House. "This was her territory, as well as the first wife's. I'm reminded by Rosa on a daily basis that I'm a glass bead in comparison to Magdalena's diamond facets. And every time you get close to me, you use Magdalena's name as a sticking point, pricking me, prodding me, pushing me away from you. She owns you. Even from the grave, she owns you."

"Shut up, damn you!" He didn't know he was yelling until the sound of it hurt his ears. He hadn't yelled at a woman since . . . since Maggie. Blast it all! Why did Julienne insist on driving him wild! "She doesn't own me, but I am reminded often enough that she would be alive today if not for me."

Julienne bit her lower lip. "Are you saying that . . . You didn't kill her. I know you didn't." Indecision shimmered in her eyes. "Did you?" she asked in a hoarse whisper.

A wicked grin tempted one corner of his mouth. "Ah, she doubts. How can you love a man you think murdered his wife?"

"I don't think—"

"But you don't *know* for certain that I'm not a murdering monster, do you? Perhaps Maggie has a grip on me by way of my conscience, eh? Yes, yes, that sounds romantic and mystical. Just the sort of thing you'd like to tackle." He straightened from the doorway and moved toward her with a catlike grace. "I have nightmares because I keep reliving the moment when I placed my hands about her neck, thus." He slipped his hands over her white skin, his palms pressing against her fragile throat. He felt her swallow convulsively. "Then I squeezed and squeezed, shutting off her voice, her air, until her eyes rolled back into her head and she passed out. But still I wasn't satisfied. I'm a monster, yes? So I squeezed harder until I broke her pretty neck. The rest was easy. I thought of my first wife and how she looked floating out on the reef like a water lily, and wanted to see Maggie out there. I took her to Spirits Cove and dumped her on the rocks out in the sea. She floated so prettily." The past overtook him, forced him to continue, although his heart was aching fiercely and he could see the fear leaping in Julienne's soft, brown eyes.

"The next day when I went to the fields, I took a detour. Later I told people it was destiny that made me take that different route. Something guided me to the cove that day, and that's when I discovered Maggie's body. People say I put on quite a show. That my face was pale and my cheeks tearstained as I carried her wet and bloated body into the house. Quite a performance, they say behind my back." He applied pressure to the pulse leaping in her throat. "Before you tell me you love me again, little jewel, picture yourself floating out there like a limp, lifeless lily."

"Let go of me." Her lips barely moved, but the words were distinct, if a bit strangled by the pressure of his hands.

He smiled, wanting to make her see that she wasn't in love with him. Couldn't be. "Answer me. Do you still love me, little jewel?"

She moved quick as a snake, stomping his boot with her heel and wrenching free of him. She still clutched the hat he'd given her, and she used it to thrash him about the head and face. He brought up his hands, defending himself without harming her. She continued to hit him with the hat. Her knuckles connected twice with his cheekbone, sending a burning sting through his nose and eyes. Finally she ran out of steam and staggered backward. With one last effort, she flung the hat at him. He caught it, crushing it against his chest.

"Get out of here," she said, her breath coming in gasps, her bodice heaving with exertion. "I hate you for mocking me!"

The smile tightened on his lips, and self-loathing sickened him. "Ah, that's better." He glanced at the ruined hat. "Pity you've mauled this. Selena would have been ever so grateful to get it, and love would have never entered into it." With another smirk he marched from her quarters. When the door was shut securely behind him, he released his breath in a long, shaky rush. Knowing that he'd done the right thing didn't ease his heartache.

His hands closed on the hat and ripped it in half.

The next day Julienne left the Bride's House and hurried upstairs to Selena's room. The door was ajar, and she tapped lightly on it before pushing it open. The bed was strewn with clothing. Shoes littered the floor. A steamer trunk sat on the floor, its lid flung back. So it was true.

"Selena?"

Selena's head popped up from the side of the bed. Her eyes narrowed when she saw Julienne. "What do you want?"

"Alissa just told me that you're going back to Cuba tomorrow. I hope nothing has happened." The timing seemed askew to Julienne. Last night Buccaneer had insinuated that he was going to seek Selena's attentions, so why was Selena leaving now that Buccaneer had decided he would take her up on her blatant invitations?

Selena stood and tossed a pair of shoes on the pile of others. She untied the belt of her wrapper. Under it she wore a matching nightdress of pale blue with indigo lace. "Don't act as if you're sorry to see me go. I know that you are relieved. I am leaving you to Buck."

"I'm not relieved that you're going. You're Buccaneer's guest, not mine."

"That is true, and it would do you good to remember it. He will have you, but he will not love you. He cannot. Magdalena took what heart he had and stomped it to dust."

Julienne shrugged. "Perhaps you're right, but I'm not here to catch Buccaneer LaFlamme. My concern is Alissa."

"Hah! You are a little liar." Selena pulled her arms from the wrapper and tossed it onto the bed. "I must have my bath, so why don't you take yourself from my room?"

Julienne thought the discolored places on Selena's arms were shadows at first, but they didn't shift with the light when Selena moved. Julienne sucked in her breath.

"What is wrong now?" Selena asked crossly, then realized what had startled Julienne. She ran her hands up and down her arms. "Get out, I said. I am busy."

"How did you get those?" Julienne demanded, advancing on her. She grabbed Selena's hand and straightened out her arm to examine the numerous bruises. One circled her wrist like a bracelet; another spotted her shoulder. There were three bruises on the other.

Selena snatched her hand from Julienne's grasp. "How do you think I got them?" Mockery glinted in her eyes and a cunning smile curved her lush lips. "I fell."

"Don't lie to me."

"I am dishing out what you served me." Selena sniffed with disdain. "Coming in here acting upset because I am leaving, when you and I both know you hate me for standing in your way with Buck."

"That's not true, Selena. Did Buccaneer give you those bruises?"

Selena's smile was supercilious. "What do you think?"

"I want you to tell me."

"Go to hell." Selena sat on the bed and unrolled

her stockings to reveal even more bruises up her thighs.

"Oh, dear Lord!" Julienne came around to stand in front of her. "Selena, who has done this? What happened? Were you ... Did someone violate you?"

"It is my own fault." Selena gave an uncaring shrug. "Maggie warned me that he doled out pain with his pleasure. I knew what I was getting into, so I have only myself to blame. I don't regret it, I tell you." Her black eyes snapped with sudden anger. "Do not pity me! I don't want your pity, orphan girl. To be with him, I would do it again. These bruises are the price I paid to enter heaven for a few minutes." Her eyes and mouth went soft. "The other times were heaven, but this last time he was an animal. I touched his anger. He found another me and he ..." She blinked and the haziness left her eyes. "As I said, it was my fault. Now, get out." She threw the stockings into a pile of clothing and marched, nearly naked, to the door. "Ursula, get your lazy backside in here and draw my bath!"

Julienne stood rooted by the memory of something she'd read in Magdalena's diary about Buccaneer accusing her of having a lover and then getting so angry when she denied it that he ordered her to move out of his bedroom and into the Bride's House. Had he displayed another jealous rage with Selena?

"I can't believe that he would do this to you," Julienne said, shaking her head.

Selena pointed out the door. "This way, please." She spotted Ursula and gave the maid a jejune expression. "At last! Where have you been all morning? I want my bath and then I want you to pack my things. Hurry up. While you're at it, show the governess to the door. She is having trouble finding her way out."

Julienne coshed her mounting irritation and took her leave. "Good-bye, Selena. Have a good journey home."

Selena slammed the door behind her. Julienne stood for a moment in the hallway, going over what had been said and what had not been said. She heard a door close around the corner and went in that direction. She approached the door with its fancy carving of a ship's anchor and tapped on the white wood in time with her accelerated heartbeats.

It swung open on smooth, silent hinges, and Buccaneer stood before her, his shirt pulled from his waistband, the laces dangling to expose half of his brawny chest. One thick, inky lock of hair curled on his forehead. His eyes were bloodshot, hooded, gray as thunderheads. Julienne felt her mouth hang open and her stomach muscles quiver with yearning.

"*Oui?*" His lips formed the word as they would a kiss, and Julienne found she preferred the French affirmation to the English one just because of that.

"I ... I ..." For a moment, she completely forgot herself.

He made an impatient gesture. "You ... you ... what? What is it? I am in the middle of changing shirts and then I must meet Cesare at the dock."

She saw that his shirt was filthy, smeared with green and brown. Vegetation and soil. "What's happened? Why are you so dirty?"

"Wireworms," he said, then cursed in French. "They attacked a bed yesterday and destroyed the whole thing. We're having to tear it up and replant."

"Oh, no." She had no idea what wireworms were, but they had destroyed some of Buccaneer's crop, so she hated them. "Is it bad?"

"Bad enough. The temperature dipped last night

and brought them up out of the ground." As he talked, he grabbed the tail of his shirt and hauled it up and over his head. He balled the shirt in his hands and flung it near the foot of the bed, then strode to the wardrobe cabinet.

Julienne managed to tear her gaze away from him for a few moments to inspect his quarters. They were smaller than she'd thought they'd be. Much smaller than hers. The double bed was draped with a mosquito net, its headboard and footrails of beechnut. The rug beneath her feet was royal blue with a broad red stripe running through it. The matching draperies of blue velvet were drawn back from the windows to let in ample sunlight. Julienne was glad for that, because it allowed her to clearly see the magnificence of Buccaneer's muscled chest and arms and shoulders. His teak-colored skin looked tough, but warm and supple. She wondered what it would be like to take one of his flat, brown nipples into her mouth.

"What do you want? Something about Alissa?" He shook out a folded shirt.

"No ..." What had she wanted?.... Oh, yes. "Selena is leaving."

"So I've heard."

She averted her gaze to find her courage. "Did you give her those bruises?"

"What bruises? What the hell are you babbling about now? I told you that I am busy and I—"

"She has bruises up and down her arms and on her legs. Do you know how she got them?" Julienne was proud of herself for getting the question past her lips, and relieved that it was over and done with. It was difficult to talk to him when her eyes wanted to worship his body, and her own skin yearned for his touch. Oh, the contradictions! That's what made it hellish to be around him. Part of her desired him and part of her feared him.

Hadn't she read that same description in Magdalena's diary the other night?

"Bruises . . . hmmm." He scowled, then his brows shot up. "I recall something about . . . Ah, yes. She and Lorenzo had a spat the other night. He must have gotten rough."

She wanted to believe him. "Lorenzo? You're saying that Lorenzo bruised her like that?"

"I'm saying only that they quarreled. He accused her of having another lover, I think." He pulled the clean shirt down over his head. "She's leaving in the morning, I'm told."

Julienne grabbed hold of her courage again. "Did Maggie take a lover?"

He was tucking in his shirt, but he paused a fraction of a second before finishing the task. When he lifted his gaze to hers, his eyes were as cold as granite. "I believe so."

"Were you jealous?"

"Wouldn't you be?"

"Were you?" she persisted.

"*Oui*, very jealous." A sinister glint sparked in his eyes. "Do you think that is a good reason for a man to kill his wife?"

She shook her head. "I won't try to answer that again. It gets me nowhere." She turned to leave, but saw a jewel-encrusted dirk displayed in a black velvet case on the wall. She paused to admire it. "Was this part of the treasure you found in Spirits Cove?"

He came to stand directly behind her. She could feel his breath patting the back of her neck. "I inherited that from Black Pierre."

"It wasn't part of the treasure you found?"

"I told you that there were rumors of treasure buried at Spirits Cove. I never said I uncovered any."

"So you're saying that you've never found any treasure at the cove?"

He sighed and his breath tickled her nape. "Do you need the wax removed from your ears? Can you no longer understand my French-accented King's English?"

She turned to face him, her gaze searching for a lie.

He propped his hands at his hips. "No, mam'selle, I have found no treasure at Spirits Cove."

Disappointment caved in on her heart, and it must have shown on her face, for Buccaneer's gaze sharpened.

"What's wrong? Are you gold-digging, little governess? Hoping to get a glimpse of my wealth so you can better determine if I'm worth all the trouble? I thought we had an understanding yesterday. We're back to being the captain"—he splayed a hand upon his chest—"and the little governess." He touched the tip of her nose with his forefinger and smiled. "It is far safer that way, I assure you."

"Please don't lie to me. Did you put those bruises on Selena in a fit of jealousy?"

He stepped away from her as if her eyes were suddenly shooting fire. His own eyes darkened to near black. "How can you stand there and accuse—" He pressed his lips together, cutting off his own speech. His hands flexed at his sides as if he desperately wanted to thrash her. "Yes, yes, of course it was me who put them there!" His voice rolled out of him like thunder. "I am a brute, is it not so? You believe it. I know you do. Selena, just like Maggie, told me she had taken Lorenzo as her lover, and I bruised her flesh and forced myself on her. I hurt her as I hurt all the women in my life." He moved toward her, and Julienne stepped back in sudden fear. Buccaneer placed the back of his hand against her shoulder and shoved her to one side so that he could stride out of the room. "Excuse me. I have another battle to wage that is much more important than this one."

Julienne listened to the booming of his boot heels on the floor and then the stairs and then the foyer. She put her hand against the doorframe and leaned her forehead against it. She closed her eyes as weariness consumed her.

Heaven help her. No matter what he said, no matter how he acted, no matter what vile thing he admitted of himself, she still wanted to love him. He had twisted her as he had Maggie and Selena. He blurred the line between love and hate. Was she the next to fall victim to the moody master of Moonspell?

Chapter 16

⌒⌒⌒⌒⌒

Two days later Julienne left the Bride's House,
where Alissa was busy coloring in the countries of the world and memorizing their names,
and made her way toward the kitchen. Alissa had
been such a diligent student, she wanted to re-
ward her with milk and cookies before nap time.
She fetched the snack herself and was returning to
the Bride's House when a snatch of conversation
waylaid her outside Buccaneer's study. She recognized Cesare's voice.

". . . dead on your feet, Buck."

"I know." Buccaneer's voice reflected profound
weariness. "But we've replanted and, God willing,
we've killed all those damned wireworms."

So that's where he's been the past two days, she
thought, inching closer to the door to hear better.
Eavesdropper, she called herself, but she strained
to catch each syllable. She'd wondered if he was
avoiding her or off somewhere, possibly to Cuba
with Selena. She hated to admit, even to herself,
that she was relieved to hear that he'd been working in the tobacco fields. Cesare said something
she couldn't quite hear, and Buccaneer grunted.
After glancing up and down the hall to make sure
she was alone, Julienne pressed an ear to the door
to make out Buccaneer's words.

". . . strain on our friendship."

"Not at all," Cesare said. "I try to keep this great beak of mine out of your private affairs."

No one spoke for a minute or two. Julienne was about to straighten and continue toward the Bride's House when Cesare's voice arrested her again.

"I am sorry for your troubles, my friend. Perhaps you should put it all behind you and take what life offers you now."

"I can't, Cesare. The past won't let me be."

Magdalena, Julienne thought with a slight frown. He's talking about his devotion to her.

"Life is not tidy," Cesare said. "Some things cannot be tied into a neat bundle. Some puzzles are never solved. If you find another, then you shouldn't let the past hold you back. You're a man and you deserve—"

"Not until I'm free of her," Buccaneer interrupted, his voice hoarse. "I can't let go, don't you see? And I can't make promises for the future while I'm stuck in the past."

"Buck, it is not good for you, this . . . what is the word? Obsession, *sí*?"

Julienne heard someone ahead of her, heels clicking on the foyer tiles, and she straightened and moved away from the study, afraid she'd be caught listening in. From the sound of the footsteps, she suspected she'd run into Rosa, and she did in the foyer. The severe housekeeper stared up at the pots of gloriously colored blooms. Julienne tensed, preparing herself for another of Rosa's disparaging lectures. She'd been careful to tend the pots and pick up every fallen leaf and petal from the floor, but she suspected that Rosa would find something to complain about, nonetheless. Rosa's black eyes lowered to find Julienne, and while she didn't smile, Julienne didn't feel the woman's usual hostility.

"The flowers are pretty," Rosa said, shocking Julienne to the soles of her feet. "You have a green thumb."

"I . . . thank you." Julienne held the tray a little higher. "I'm taking Alissa a treat for being such a good student this morning."

"It is almost time for her nap. I will come get her in a little while, unless you want to put her to bed."

Julienne knew the woman resented Julienne taking over the care of Alissa, and since Rosa had given her a crumb of kindness, Julienne decided to reciprocate. "You can put her down for her nap, if you wish."

The lines around Rosa's eyes and mouth softened. "I will collect her soon." Her heels clicked smartly on the floor as she crossed the foyer and went toward the kitchen.

Julienne stared up at the pots. Had Rosa actually decided to be civil to her? It was too good to be true, but Julienne embraced the sliver of hope. She hated being hated, especially when she felt it was undeserving.

Alissa had finished coloring the map when Julienne returned with the snack tray.

"Look what I've brought you, ladybug." Julienne set the tray on the table. She picked up Alissa and sat her in one of the wing chairs flanking it, and then sat in the other. "You've worked so hard today that I thought you deserved a cold glass of milk and a couple of Rosa's thumbprint cookies."

"Goody!" Alissa grabbed a cookie of the silver tray. "I love these. You want one?"

"No, thank you. They're all yours. Enjoy them while I put these things away." She gathered the school supplies. "I'll be right back. We've run out of drawing paper, and I have a new packet in my room somewhere."

"Okay." Alissa wiped away her milk mustache.

Julienne left the parlor and went into her bedroom, where she'd packed away school supplies. She located the packet of paper and started back into the parlor, but stopped on the threshold when she heard Buccaneer.

"And what else have you learned today?" he asked. He sat in the wing chair Julienne had vacated minutes ago.

"Rome is the capital of Italy," Alissa recited. "And Paris is the capital of France. Wasn't *Grand-père* born there, Papa?"

"Yes, just outside of Paris." He stifled a yawn behind his hand. "What is the capital of Greece?"

"Athens!"

"Very good. You are going to be smarter than me before the year is out. You make me proud."

Julienne watched the exchange, noting how easily the two talked together and wondering why it couldn't always be so. Fatigue lined Buccaneer's face, and his clothes were wrinkled and smudged with dirt. Mud caked his boots.

"Papa, is it your nap time, too?"

He smiled and ran a fingertip down Alissa's cheek. "*Oui*, it is past my nap time and I'm tired."

"Poor Papa." Alissa patted his suntanned hand. For a few moments she and Buccaneer traded sweet, heartfelt smiles that renewed Julienne's hope for them.

Someone knocked sharply on the open door. Julienne stepped farther into the room until she was able to see Rosa standing just inside the parlor. Alissa's hand slipped away from her father's and she hunched her shoulders. All the joy and tenderness died in her eyes, and the smile vanished.

"It is time for your nap, Alissa. Come with me." Rosa held out a hand, and Alissa slid out of the wing chair and ran across the room to take it. She didn't even glance back toward Buccaneer as Rosa led her from the Bride's House.

Julienne swung her gaze to Buccaneer in time to see the disappointment on his face. Couldn't he see that Rosa was the difference? Once Rosa had entered the room, Alissa had abandoned her father. Julienne had seen it with her own eyes and surmised that Rosa must be the bad influence on Alissa. She wouldn't be the least bit surprised to discover that Rosa had filled Alissa's head with tales of death and made her doubt Buccaneer's unconditional love.

Buccaneer picked up the last cookie and ate it in two bites. He lounged back in the wing chair as if he hadn't the energy to rise from it. His gaze drifted over her, and she wished it were tender instead of saturnine. She cleared her throat nervously and clasped her hands behind her as she ambled closer to him. She noted the shadows under his penetrating eyes and the thick curl of his black lashes. Dark stubble covered the lower half of his face. She hadn't seen him since their angry confrontation about Selena.

"Did Selena make it to Cuba safe and sound?"

He nodded, but said nothing, his gaze continuing to slide over her as if she were a statue to be studied instead of a flesh-and-blood woman.

"You've been out in the tobacco fields working? All day and all night?"

Again, a nod. Nothing more.

"I suppose you miss Selena's company."

He arched a brow.

Julienne mirrored the facial expression. "Are you so weary, you can't bring yourself to speak?"

"What would you have me say? It seems that you enjoy putting words in my mouth, especially when we're talking about Selena. Do you want me to say that I've been pining for Selena and that I've thrown myself into my work just to fill the hours now that she's gone?"

She sighed and tapped one foot. "I want you to speak the truth. Is that asking too much?"

"In truth, I'm glad she's gone." He ran a hand down his face. "The longer she stayed here, the more trouble she caused."

"Trouble? Seems to me that trouble found her. Those bruises looked painful."

"Ah, yes. The bruises I placed on her."

Julienne eyed him, trying to see through his thick layer of sarcasm. "Who do you think put them there?"

"I told you, but you didn't like the answer."

"Lorenzo."

His broad Gallic shrug spoke volumes.

"She said she didn't regret it."

"Did she tell you I bruised her?"

"She didn't say it wasn't you."

His smile brimmed with bitterness. "Guilty by suspicion." He pushed himself up from the chair with great effort. "I'll get out of your way."

"You're not in my way," she protested, reaching out to snag his sleeve. She didn't want him to go, although she'd rather eat a plate of nails than admit to him that she'd missed him the past two days. "But I suppose you're bone-tired and need to rest." Her hand fell away from his sleeve, and she stared at his muddy boots.

"Is there something you'd like to talk to me about?"

Her gaze lifted to his face, and she wanted to stroke his stubbled cheek and push the lock of hair back from his forehead. His hair was dusty with dirt, his face streaked with grime. He was the sexiest man she'd ever seen.

"I overheard you talking with Alissa. Did you notice that everything was fine between the two of you until Rosa interrupted? Do you think she might be making Alissa doubt your love?"

He frowned. "Of course not. Rosa adores Alissa."

"But does she adore you? Wasn't she closer to Magdalena than to you?"

"Yes, she and Maggie were quite close. What are you trying to say?"

"Maybe she intends to turn Alissa against you because she thinks—well, that you killed Magdalena."

"She doesn't."

"How do you know? Has she said as much?"

"Rosa wouldn't stay here if she thought I'd killed Maggie. She'd hate me with every bone in her body if she thought that. She's told me that she wants whoever is responsible to pay with his life."

"And she's ruled you out?" Julienne persisted, feeling that something wasn't quite right. While Buccaneer insisted he had Rosa's devotion, Julienne wasn't so sure.

"She has, but you haven't." He scratched absentmindedly at the center of his chest, then looked down at himself and sighed. "I'm filthy. I must bathe and grab some sleep."

Julienne glanced toward the fireplace, where Maggie's thoughts and intense feelings were tucked away. "You still miss her. You haven't laid her to rest." Her smile felt stiff on her dry lips.

"You mean Maggie?" he questioned. When she nodded, a wry smile touched his full lips. "Maggie is unforgettable. She had a way of getting under a man's skin and staying there like a burning itch."

Why couldn't he think of *her* that way? Why couldn't she get under his skin and find out what he was really made of, instead of having to be satisfied with only what he chose to reveal to her?

"Like tobacco poisoning," Julienne said, a bit spitefully.

He chuckled. "Yes, like tobacco poisoning, except the itch lasted a lot longer than a day."

"You still itch?"

"Sometimes." His gray eyes moved slowly, taking in her face, her shoulders, her breasts. "Although I'm not sure I have a burning itch for her or for a woman to take her place."

"Any woman will do."

"Well, that would make life less complicated, but ultimately less challenging."

Julienne turned sideways, averting her gaze from him. She was afraid he'd read the disappointment in her face. Oh, why did he long for Maggie? Was this the shadow Carmella the witch had spoken of? Was she going to have to fight off Magdalena's ghost to win Buccaneer's affections?

"What's wrong? Are you afraid that, with Selena gone, I'll devote my attentions to you? Have no fear, dear governess. I can always sail to Key West to satisfy my lusts."

She was still staring at the fireplace, but she flinched at the thought of him sailing all the way to Key West for female companionship. She couldn't believe that he didn't sense the tumult of her feelings for him. Yes, he infuriated her, and yes, he sometimes frightened her, but he also must know that he made her quake with longing whenever he kissed her, too.

Maggie had written in her diary that her moving into the Bride's House had damaged Buccaneer's pride. He felt the failure of the marriage acutely, she'd written. Two marriages, two mistakes. The later passages revealed an even darker side of Buccaneer. He'd made Maggie suffer, and she had loved it. Theirs had been a twisted emotion, having no kin to love at all. Julienne preferred to believe that Maggie exaggerated, because she couldn't imagine Buccaneer being so cruel, so demeaning, toward his wife. Even if she had been unfaithful.

Julienne whipped her gaze around to him, suddenly wanting him to share her pain of being misunderstood and unappreciated.

"It's too bad that the mistresses of Moonspell were both so unhappy that they moved in here. Are you so impossible to live with?"

If she hadn't been looking hard at him, she would have missed the flicker of pain in his eyes and at the corners of his mouth. Immediately she felt contrite.

"You place the blame for my failed marriages squarely in my lap. So typical of the female." A sardonic smile slanted across his lips. "For your information, my wives were the ones who made most of the mistakes and ruined the marriages. Not me."

She thought he sounded impossibly arrogant. Days of irritation, confusion, and sexual frustration suddenly exploded within her. She'd read Maggie's lovemaking exploits and boiled with envy. At night she had dreamed of Buccaneer making love to her—softly and gently, not savagely as he'd done with Maggie. After their argument about Selena, Julienne had alternately decided to apologize to him and keep her distance from him. But more than anything, she had confessed her love for him. A hopeless, unrequited love that festered like a boil within her.

"Are you saying you're blameless?" she asked.

"Do I detect disbelief in your voice?" he rejoined, his mouth twisting with derision.

"Mother Superior often said that stubborn jackasses learn few lessons, and listening to you has made me fully understand that bit of wisdom," she lashed out. "Like every other man I've met, you see yourself as flawless and beleaguered by the weaker sex. I think you should stay away from women, since they are such a bad influence on you, your saintness." She curtsied, pleased with herself and her lecture. The boil had been lanced and she felt much, much better.

She saw his temper break over his face like a thunderstorm a moment before his hands bit into her upper arms and his mouth came down hard on hers. He parted her lips roughly and his tongue rushed in, taking her breath, making her moan with a mixture of fear and fury. She thought of biting him, but she knew the retaliation would be fierce. Too fierce. So she suffered through the kiss that was meant to dominate, not seduce. She pushed against his chest and finally tore her mouth from his. He laughed at her, although she knew he felt no humor. Domination was his game. It was, so often, his favorite gambit. She hated him for that, but she was learning from it. The more she was around him, the more she knew about him, and the more she knew about him, the more she understood the power she could exert over him.

He stared down into her wide, dark eyes. A cocky smile claimed his mouth.

"You are hurting me," she said, evenly, coldly. "I know you are used to hurting women, but I am not used to being hurt. I will not suffer my bruises as gladly as Isabelle, Maggie, and Selena."

His hands sprang off her as if her flesh had burst into flame. "I'm sorry." Then his eyes darkened with anger. "No matter what I say, you think . . ." He shook his head and bit his lower lip.

"I want to believe you, but your actions speak more loudly than your words." She rubbed her arms, working the blood back into them.

"Don't tempt the devil, if you can't stand the flames," he grumbled, starting for the door again.

"Your problem is that you think every woman is

tempting you. Has it ever occurred to you that I might like talking to you without being mauled?"

"Mauled? You think I *mauled* you?" He reared back to glare at her, his injured male pride clenching his jaw, tightening his lips.

"You think all you did was kiss me just now?" Julienne countered. "That wasn't a kiss, Captain. That was an attack. Once again, your aim wasn't to seduce, but to humiliate, to put me in my place. Is that what drove your wives into this house? Did they get tired of being beaten down by what you passed off as love?"

"Enough!" he bellowed, so loudly that she stumbled backward. He stared at her, then shook his head slowly. His shoulders slumped with fatigue. "You provoke me, Julienne. You goad me and nettle me and make me act a fool over you."

For a moment she heard a smidgen of hope in what he said. Was he telling her that she did get under his skin . . . like a burning itch, like Maggie?

He swayed on his feet, caught himself, and tried to square his shoulders. "I shan't touch you again." He pivoted, wavered, then strode from her quarters.

Julienne reached out, clutching thin air. "Oh, Buccaneer, that's not what I want," she whispered. She wanted his touch. She wanted his love. Was that impossible?

Why wouldn't he lower his shield long enough to let her get close to him and love him the way she knew he wanted to be loved? Long and slow and deep. She trembled and closed her eyes. Yes, yes. Long . . . and slow . . . and deep.

Buccaneer stood on the balcony outside his room, wearing nothing but a pair of trousers, left unbuttoned. The ocean breeze soothed him and dried his wet hair. After sleeping most of the day, he'd taken a late supper in his room and a long bath. Clean and rested, he felt better, but he still felt like a brute.

"Jackass," he snarled, that being one of the kindest words he'd directed at himself since leaving the Bride's House earlier that day.

While his body felt rested, his soul was tired. Tired of being alone, of wrestling with the past, of the deprivation of a woman's care. He was so very tired of fighting off his growing attraction for Julienne Vale.

Why did he always act like a beast around her? Was his heart too deadened to allow himself to love a precocious angel like her? Could he ever love again? A jolt of awareness passed through him. Had he ever been in love before?

With Julienne, *love* seemed to be a word that fit. It cropped up in his mind whenever she smiled at him. It wove itself through his dreams when she was in them. It lay heavily on his tongue when he looked at her or when his mouth touched hers.

But he had sworn not to touch her again. One corner of his mouth quirked. Promises had never been his strong suit. Words were words. What was important were deeds. He knew as surely as the stars lit the night that he would touch her again, that he would break his vow at the first opportunity.

His gaze sharpened as a dark-haired figure strolled the grounds below him. He smiled. That opportunity might just be at hand. Without giving a thought to how he was dressed—or undressed—he flung a leg over the balcony, felt for the ledge with his bare foot, and swung his other leg over. He grabbed on to the sturdy vine clinging to the wall and descended. When he was a few feet from the ground, he let go and landed like a big cat on the lawn. The breeze sighed over him, reminding him that he was nearly nude.

"Ah, Christ," he gritted out, buttoning his trousers and looking up at the balcony. Should he go back up for a shirt and then ... No. She'd seen him without his shirt before. She wouldn't faint at the sight of his bared skin. He padded across the lawn in the direction he'd seen her go.

It was a moonless night, but the sky blazed with stars. He crept on cat-feet along the path toward the wash of the shoreline. He was beginning to think he'd lost her when he heard something behind him.

"Why do you keep following me!"

He whirled to regard her flushed face, her wide eyes. She was frightened. "Keep following you?" he repeated. "When have I followed you before now?"

"I ... I thought you were someone else."

"Who?" He narrowed his eyes. "Lorenzo again?"

She shook her head. "I don't know for sure. It's just that ... well, sometimes I feel as if someone is watching me—following me. I got that feeling a minute ago, but I didn't actually see anyone."

His gaze feasted on her. Even in her plainer house dresses, this one a shade of dark wine, she enticed him. The bodice fit like a glove, accentuating her high breasts and trim waist. Satin-covered buttons marched down the front to the knife-pleated full skirt. He smiled, wanting a truce, wanting to bite off each button. "Maybe it's a ghost."

She shrugged. "Maybe it's that wolf."

"You've heard it again?"

"No. Have you?"

He shook his head. "And it's not a wolf." He saw a change in her expression and realized that she was embarrassed again—uncomfortable with his lack of proper dress. "Forgive me, but I—" He ran a hand down his chest. "It's a warm night."

"Yes." She swallowed hard and fanned herself

with one hand. "Quite hot. So you *were* following me? What for?"

What for? he repeated to himself. Yes, good question. Well, he couldn't tell her the truth . . . "Have you heard about the wedding party that's being planned for the week's end?"

"Yes, I did. Ursula told me that two of the field workers are to be married."

"Cesare brought the lovesick woman from Cuba. The man she's to marry works for me, and he promised he'd make enough money someday to send for her, but she was tired of waiting." He chuckled and tucked his hands in his trouser pockets to keep from touching her. He wanted to hold her very badly. He wanted to kiss her until all defiance left her face, and her body molded itself to his. "Anyway, he was glad to see her and they decided to marry right now, money or no."

She smiled suddenly, and to Buccaneer's eyes her smile rivaled the blaze of stars overhead. "That's true love. Money shouldn't be a consideration, nor any other worldly thing."

"Spoken like a starry-eyed romantic," he whispered, watching the twinkles in her eyes.

She shrugged one shoulder. "I suppose that's what I am. All I know of love between a man and woman is what I've read in books. It seemed romantic and sweet and . . . oh, like something that could only be created by angels."

He laughed at that. "Yes, it is that way sometimes. Other times it seems like you're being guided by the devil himself."

She glanced around as if realizing they were alone in the middle of the night and that one of them wasn't fully dressed. "Well, I had better go back inside. Good night, Captain."

When she started past him, he caught her hand in his. "I liked it better when you called me Buccaneer."

She moistened her lips. "But we decided to be prudent and—"

"Yes, but is that realistic, considering how we can't seem to keep our eyes or hands off each other?"

She seemed to wilt and her forehead rested against his shoulder. "Please, don't do this. You are the master of these games, and I'm but a novice. It isn't fair."

"I'm not toying with you. I honestly can't seem to keep away from you, Julienne. Although I should—God knows I should. You deserve far better than me. I swear I'll bring you nothing but heartache, and yet I'm a selfish bastard and—"

"Hush." She pressed her cool fingertips against his warm lips. "You've listened to too many rumors about yourself."

"You haven't listened?" He moved his lips away from her fingers and probed her eyes with his. "Can you honestly say you trust me implicitly?"

She didn't blink. "Implicitly."

"Ah, Julienne." He kissed her forehead. "You are such a trusting soul. It's one of the things that draws me to you. Evil is always attracted to good, if for no reason than to sully it."

"Not always, and you're not evil."

He smiled at her and smoothed his hands over her glossy hair. "What am I, if not evil?"

"Sad and lonely and haunted by the past."

He released her slowly, shocked that she had seen so much of his heart, his deepest feelings. He tried to smile, to make light of her intuition. "Those romantic novels you read are filling your head with nonsense."

Her gaze played over him, taking in his bared chest, lingering on his nipples. He burned. He ached. How he kept from taking her in his arms and kissing her was beyond him. She blinked as if coming out of a daze.

"I should ... I'll see you in the morning." She glided past him, unhindered this time. "Buccaneer?" He turned to face her. "Will it be all right if I attend the party after the wedding?"

"Of course."

"I thought I'd take Alissa."

"No." He rejected that quickly, selfishness overtaking him. "It will be past her bedtime. I'll be your escort. Wear one of your new gowns and leave your hair down."

She captured a lock of her hair and wound it around her fingers. "You like it down."

"Yes."

"I might consider honoring your ... request if there was a 'please' or a 'thank you' somewhere in it."

He folded his arms across his chest, amused by her lesson in manners. "Please wear your hair down and thank you for being so beautiful."

She caught her breath. "Beautiful? Me?" She laughed lightly. "I should always speak with you at night, for the dark is obviously becoming to me."

"Yes," he agreed. "The stars have found homes in your eyes, and the night air has painted soft color across your cheeks. But you are as beautiful in the daylight when the sun draws out the fire in your hair and coaxes more freckles across the bridge of your nose."

"I believe you've read your fair share of romantic novels as well." She sent him one more smile, then turned and hurried toward the house.

He watched until he could see her no more, but still she lingered. In his heart, she lingered.

Chapter 17

Wearing one of the lovely dresses Buccaneer had requested, Julienne stood before the full-length mirror and wondered if she was a moth trying to pass herself off as a monarch butterfly. She ran one hand from the heart-shaped neckline to the draped bodice. The skirt was long and slim, the color midnight blue. She left her hair loose. Wispy strands curled at her temples, and a vigorous brushing had trained the rest to fall in soft waves around her shoulders. Ursula had lent her a pair of filigree earbobs that glittered through the strands of her hair.

Julienne had applied a touch of rouge to her cheeks and lips and had splashed herself with rosewater. The wedding had been held that afternoon. Cesare had captained one of the sloops to Key West and brought back a priest, who had performed the ceremony. Julienne could hear the patter of steel drums outside and the soft strumming of a guitar. The reception was beginning. She drew in a shaky breath and released it. Nerves fluttered through her on a million wings.

I'm dressing for him, wearing my hair the way he likes it, putting on cosmetics to catch his eye. I'm in love with him.

Her eyes widened. That had been so easy to admit, it shocked her. What now, now that she knew it to be true, now that her heart had been won? She had uttered those words and he had pushed her away and told her not to tell him such things, but she didn't believe he didn't want her love. She sensed that he didn't think he deserved it—or any woman's love. Something was holding him back, or rather, *someone* was holding him back. Magdalena.

Their love had been so powerful that Magdalena could reach from the grave and command him. She remembered him standing before Maggie's portrait and toasting it. He'd said something about Maggie still controlling the monster in him.

"But he's not a monster," she whispered vehemently. "It's just that all this tragedy has jaded him."

"Señorita?"

Julienne jumped, startled by the voice. She turned to find Rosa lurking in the doorway. "Yes, Rosa?"

The woman's mouth twitched. "You look very pretty."

Julienne stumbled backward, shocked by the compliment. "Why, I—uh, thank you."

"The captain, he will be most pleased." She came farther into the room. "He waits for you outside."

"Oh. I shouldn't keep him waiting, I suppose."

"*Sí*, but first I have something for you."

"For me?" Julienne couldn't keep the wariness from her voice as Rosa dipped a hand into her apron pocket. She fully expected the housekeeper to pull out a snake or an evil charm, but instead she held a necklace of shells out to Julienne. "What's this? Did you make it?"

Rosa shook her head. "You wear it. It will look pretty with that dress. Go on. Take it. No, no. Turn around and I will clasp it for you."

Julienne hesitated, so Rosa stepped around her

and looped the necklace around her neck. The shells felt cool and light against her skin. A strand of fishing line held them together in a fascinating flower design. She looked in the mirror. Rosa was right; the necklace was perfect, adding just the right something to the neckline. She touched one of the tiny shells of pearly pink.

"It's simple, almost primitive, but I like it."

Rosa looked at her mirror image. "You wear it for Captain Buck."

Suspicion niggled her. "Why? Why loan this to me?"

Rosa shrugged. "I have been unkind. You wear this and it will make me happy. It will do my heart good."

Julienne couldn't argue with her. The old crow *had* been unkind. The teachings of the Sisters guided her and she nodded. "Very well. Thank you. I'd be happy to wear the necklace."

"Good." Rosa moved away. "You better go. Captain Buck will want to see you."

"Yes, thanks again." She waited for the housekeeper to leave before turning back to the mirror. The necklace had many colors—pink, brown, purple, blue, red, yellow. Like a rainbow from the sea, she thought. She admired it another few moments, her thoughts on Rosa and this offering of peace. Had the housekeeper seen that Buccaneer was falling in love with the governess, so she had decided to become more friendly with who might be the next mistress of Moonspell?

Julienne frowned and shook a finger at her reflection. "Don't put the cart before the horse, girl. Buccaneer has said nothing remotely to do with marriage—or even love, for that matter."

But he *had* asked her to this wedding reception and he *had* requested that she wear a lovely gown and let her hair down. She remembered his kisses and shivered. A yearning, deep and keen, burned within her, and she knew that only Buccaneer could douse the flames.

She straightened to stand tall and proud. It would be best, she decided, to put Magdalena out of her mind. Don't even think of the diary, she told herself. Be yourself. Don't try to be like her. Make him love you for yourself, not because you're trying to act like his lost love.

Armed with her own good advice, she turned from her reflection and went toward the French doors. A shadow passed over the sheer curtains covering them, stilling her heart for a few moments. Had someone been watching her again? Was it Buccaneer? She hurried across the room and threw open the doors, but no one stood there. Stepping out onto the patio, she glanced around nervously. A striped tent had been erected halfway between the house and the coastline. The smell of roasted meat tantalized her, and she suspected a buffet had been laid out on tables under the tent. A big bonfire blazed nearby, lighting the area with a golden orange hue. Music filled the air with happiness. It was easy to spot the newlyweds, for the bride was still in her white dress and veil, the groom in his dark suit and bow tie. They danced under the stars, alone at first, then others joined in.

"*Bonsoir*, little jewel."

Julienne smiled, loving the timbre of his voice, then turned slowly toward Buccaneer. He looked magnificent in snug black trousers, white shirt, and black vest. His eyes glittered like sunstruck silver.

"*Bonsoir*, Captain LaFlamme. I trust I meet with your approval?" She enjoyed having his full attention. Pleasure lit his eyes, but then something changed in his face. His eyes clouded and his mouth thinned to a bitter line. He stepped toward her, then stopped himself, his hands balling into fists. A cold fear gripped her heart. She had displeased him, but how?

"Where did you get that?" he asked, his teeth clenched in rage, his gaze pinned on her throat.

Julienne touched the necklace. "It's . . . You don't like it?"

"Like it? I'd like to grind it to dust! Take it off, damn you!"

She gasped in surprise and offense. "Buccaneer, what's wrong? What have I done?"

"That necklace belonged to Magdalena. Where did you get it?"

"Magdalena?" Her fingers curled around the largest shell as the import of what he was saying struck her. Duped! She'd been duped by that old crow. Oh, why had she trusted Rosa?

"Her lover gave it to her. She preferred those to the jewels I gave her." His upper lip curled. "And now you wear them, too. Where did you find them? I thought they'd been buried with her."

"I'll take them off immediately. I only meant to please you, Buccaneer, not bring you pain."

He turned his back on her. "Yes, take the damned thing off. I can't stand to look at it and remember . . ." He strode away toward the dancing shadows cast by the bonfire.

Julienne struggled with the clasp and finally had to go back inside and twist the necklace around so that she could see it in the mirror. Her fingers were numb and shaking, and she had a devil of a time getting the clasp to work, but finally the necklace slipped from around her neck. She stared at it, amazed that such a little thing could cause such pain.

Magdalena's lover had given this to her, and she'd preferred the primitive arrangement of shells to the beautiful gems Buccaneer had commissioned for her. Maggie's colors, he'd called them. Black, green, red. He'd promised those jewels to

her in exchange for her castanets. She remembered
the pride in his voice when he'd told her about the
necklace. And Maggie had traded it for shells.
Worthless shells strung together by her lover.
Lorenzo? Was he the man who had taken her from
Buccaneer and then, perhaps, murdered her?

Her heart felt heavy, dark. So much for dispel-
ling Maggie's shadow, she thought derisively. She
sensed she wasn't alone and looked up to see
Rosa standing in the doorway a second before
she darted out of sight.

"You old crow," Julienne shouted, gathering the
necklace in her hand and pitching it toward the
doorway. Some of the shells shattered as it skittered across the hardwood floor. "Take it and
choke on it. I'll never trust you again, and you will
regret this, Rosa! I swear, you'll regret it."

She felt like a fool, but she fought off her tears
of humiliation. She wouldn't let the evil in this
house win. She just wouldn't! Nor would she allow it to destroy her chances with Buccaneer. Deep
inside, she knew that he needed her love. He was
lonely and distraught, although his stubborn pride
kept him from showing it or admitting it. But she
knew. She'd been lonely, too. Someday perhaps
she could gain his trust, his love.

Whirling toward the French doors again, she
went outside, her head held high and her confidence brimming. The Sisters had always said
she was buoyant, and she held to that claim. She
wouldn't let anyone keep her down. She knew she
could be good for Buccaneer if only he'd open his
heart to her. If only she knew as much about men
as Maggie had . . .

She squared her shoulders and moved toward
the bonfire. Lorenzo stepped directly into her
path, a wide smile splitting his handsome face, a
chain of tiny shells looped twice around his neck,
tight as a collar.

"Good evening, señorita. May I have this dance?"

"No." She hitched up her chin, refusing to be intimidated by him again. "Excuse me."

"You look ... mmm-mmm ... good enough to eat. With Selena gone, I am so lonely." He spread a hand over his smooth chest, bared by his open shirt. "She was amusing, but it is you I have had my eye on. I like a good chase. Makes my blood boil."

"There are some swift jackrabbits on the key, Lorenzo. Chase one of those." She whisked past him, dodging him when he reached out to detain her.

Spotting Buccaneer standing near the bonfire, she made her way to him. He glanced at her, the light and shadows playing over his brooding features. She couldn't read his expression or his current mood.

"Buccaneer, please don't be angry. I'm innocent."

A smile twitched one corner of his mouth. "Yes, I know."

"What I mean is, Rosa talked me into wearing that necklace." She turned sideways, looking at him, spreading her hands out in abject appeal. "I should have known something was rotten. That woman has never shown me the slightest kindness, except for the other day when she told me I had a green thumb."

"I suppose she meant well."

Julienne sputtered for a moment before she could form words. "Meant well? She tricked me!"

He folded his arms across his chest and shifted his weight to one leg. "She doesn't think it's wise for us to become involved with each other. She's trying to look out for me."

"She's sticking her nose into things that are none of her business," Julienne said hotly, amazed that he would try to justify Rosa's actions. "Why don't you dismiss her, Buccaneer?"

He shrugged. "She's been here for ages. Where would she go?"

"Why do you care?"

"I don't know." He sighed. "I'm sorry for shouting at you. I was caught off guard and I . . . Well, I'm not angry at you. Seeing that necklace brought back memories."

Julienne clutched his arm. "Teach me to dance, and those memories will fade into nothingness."

"Teach you? You mean, you don't know how to dance?"

She wrinkled her nose. "Now, when would I have had a chance to dance in my life? On Key Largo with my father? At the orphanage with the good Sisters?" She laughed, coaxing a smile from him. "You'll be my first dancing partner." *My first love, too,* she thought, her smile brightening. "Can we dance to this song? Is it appropriate?"

He listened for a moment and nodded. "It will do." Facing her, he placed one hand at the side of her waist and held out his other. "Take my hand and put your other on my shoulder. That's right. No, don't look down. Look in my eyes."

"Your eyes? But I'll stomp your poor feet. I must watch where I'm going."

He shook his head. "Just look into my eyes and concentrate on the music and the feel of my hands. I'll guide you. Trust me."

She relaxed. "Implicitly, remember?"

Smiling, he nodded to the beat, then on the next "one" count, he stepped back and she stepped forward. The going was awkward at first, and she trod on his toes a couple of times before she managed to follow his lead. He kept the steps simple, and his hands and eyes directed her. She loved the feel of his muscles sliding under his clothes and warm skin. His eyes spoke to her, telling her he was pleased with her, proud of her. He looked darkly dashing, almost making her forget the earlier faux pas. How could Maggie have turned him away and fallen into another man's arms? she wondered. How he must have loved her—still loved her, although she'd been dead a year. Would he ever feel so strongly again, or had Maggie bruised his heart too deeply?

If only he'd give me a chance, Julienne thought, her hand moving across his shoulder and around to the back of his neck. His hair felt like silk against her fingers, and she would have liked nothing better than to push all ten fingers through his hair and bring his mouth down upon her own, their breath and tongues mingling.

Give me a chance, Buccaneer, her heart begged. *I can heal you. I can chase away Maggie's ghost.*

By the end of the second song, she was floating in his arms and laughing with him as he spun her around and then dipped her dramatically over his arm.

"You dance divinely, little jewel," he said, still laughing as he straightened. "You must have had a wonderful teacher."

"Oh, I did," she agreed. "He could be quite charming when he put his mind to it."

He raised one brow, but before he could respond, someone near the tent caught his attention. "Ah, the chef is preparing to call people to the buffet, and I must go inspect the buffet table. Excuse me a moment?" He bowed over her hand and kissed the back of it. "When I return, I'll put my mind to charming you right out of your corset."

She gasped in delight and sent him away with a bright smile. As she strolled to the bonfire, her footsteps felt light, almost as if she were still dancing. Oh, it had been everything she'd dreamed of, she thought, recalling how lovely it had been to be in Buccaneer's solid arms, moving as one to the beat of the music. Smiling to herself, she closed her eyes for a moment, seeing herself dancing with Buccaneer under the stars, with the steel drums keeping time with their own wild pulses.

When she opened her eyes, she found herself staring across the flames at a pair of opaque eyes. She sucked in her breath, startled by those strange eyes and Ootay's thick, orangy-blond hair and brows. She waved at him. No response. Was he unfriendly or shy? Firelight played over his ropy muscles. He was only a few inches taller than Julienne, but he was sturdily built, reminding her of a tomcat. How old? she wondered. Surely a few years older than herself, but younger than Buccaneer. She moved around the fire to him, thinking that nothing happened on this key that Ootay didn't know about. He saw everything with those strange eyes.

Might he know something about Magdalena's death? She walked with more purpose toward him. He watched, but that was all. Even when she stood next to him, his expression was taciturn, his eyes unreadable.

"Hello, Ootay. I haven't seen you since that day I visited your grandmother. How have you been?"

No reply.

"Your grandmother is an interesting woman. What happened to your parents?"

His gaze drifted to the bonfire. After a minute passed, Julienne realized he wasn't going to answer.

"Do you happen to know who killed Magdalena LaFlamme?" she asked baldly, trying to jolt something out of him, if only a twitch of muscle in his impassive face. He blinked slowly and brought his pale eyes around to her again. She shivered, finding his whole demeanor as threatening as a sky full of black, rolling clouds. His pink tongue darted out to moisten his tan lips.

"Same one gonna kill you, little jewel."

Her heart jerked in her chest. "Wh-What . . . That's not the least bit clever." She grabbed hold of her composure. "I think you know this key like no other, and you might have heard or seen something." She waved aside the subject, perturbed by his unwavering gaze and mocking smile. "Never mind. I hope you enjoy yourself tonight, Ootay." She started to move away from him, but he grabbed her hand and flipped it over to stare at her palm. She tried to pull away, but he was strong, his grip almost bone-crushing as he peered intently at the crisscrossing lines. She forced herself to relax and not panic. "Do you read palms, too?" she asked, placing a smile in her voice.

His glassy eyes focused on her face. "Life, it has echoes."

She shook her head. "I don't understand you."

"Echoes, repeating over and over. You got an echo here. I see the same thing in Maggie's hand that I see in yours. You walk in her footsteps. You follow her path."

"No, you're wrong." She wrenched free of him and retreated. "I'm not Maggie, and I don't believe in palm reading or any other such foolishness."

He smiled, showing perfectly straight teeth. "Don't have to believe. Tides come in and go out whether you believe they will or not." He shrugged with his shoulders and arms and hands, looking for a moment like a great copper bird getting ready to fly. "I do know what go on in the big house." He jerked a thumb over his shoulder, indicating the estate. "And I know what go on in the little house." He smiled sluggishly, and she knew he meant the Bride's House.

Suddenly his eyelids drooped and his powerfully strange eyes glittered. Julienne would have turned away, but she couldn't. Something passed from him to her, making her heart beat erratically and her breathing shallow.

"Gotcha."

"What?" she whispered, dazed by the strange sensation.

"A velvet chain connects me to you. Want me to give it a little pull, just to let you know it's there?"

She started to shake her head and move farther away from him, but he brought up one hand, wrapped it around an imaginary length of chain, and gave a jerk. Something in the center of her bowed outward and tightened. She gasped. Ootay threw back his head and laughed. He dropped his hand, and Julienne felt the release. She hurried away from him, fear blinding her for a few moments so that she ran straight into Lorenzo before she actually saw him.

"Oh, I'm sorry." She regained her balance and glanced over her shoulder at Ootay, but he was gone. Vanished.

"What's wrong?" Lorenzo said.

"Nothing."

"Good." He circled her waist with one arm. "Dance with me."

"No."

"Sí. You must learn to use that word more often. Sí. It is such a nice word. Say it for me." His laughing eyes penetrated her cold fear, and she wriggled, gaining a measure of freedom.

"Lorenzo, I don't wish to dance with you. I'm looking for Buccaneer."

He frowned. "Always him. He's no good for you. He goes through women like most men go through boots. Every few years he tries on a new pair, and every few years he gets himself a new bride. He lies to women and makes promises he means to break. I will not lie to you, pretty one.

When I tell you that you are like a fire in my body, you can believe—hey!"

Buccaneer spun Lorenzo around to face him. "Keep your hands off her."

"Or what?" Lorenzo sneered. "You do not own this woman, LaFlamme."

Buccaneer thrust his face closer to Lorenzo's. "The lady doesn't want your attentions, so pull up anchor and sail away while you're still seaworthy."

Julienne moved to stand beside Buccaneer. She touched his shirt sleeve, but he kept his gaze riveted to Lorenzo. "Buccaneer, let's go get something to eat. I see that the buffet is—"

"You want to say something to me?" Lorenzo challenged, puffing out his chest and stepping closer to Buccaneer. "You been saying it behind my back; why not be a man and say it to my face!"

"Why, you sleazy, spineless—" Buccaneer charged, his hands gathering Lorenzo's shirt collar as he drove him backward against a tree.

Julienne shrieked, appalled that she'd have to break up yet another fight. She hung on to Buccaneer's arm, trying with all her might to dislodge his hands from Lorenzo, but she might as well have been struggling with a marble statue. He didn't budge. In fact, she didn't think he was even aware she was hanging on to him.

Lorenzo began to scramble, kicking, fists whirling. Julienne released Buccaneer, knowing that in another second the scuffle would be a full-fledged brawl and she might get hurt. She looked around, but no one seemed interested in stopping the fight. Cesare broke through the crowd, parting it easily by waving a flaming piece of firewood. He swept the torch down, neatly dividing Buccaneer from Lorenzo. Instinctively the men avoided the smoking fire and Cesare stepped between them. He looked from one murderous scowl to the other and tossed aside the fiery stick.

"Can you not think of anyone but yourselves and your manly pride? This is a celebration of a holy union," Cesare reminded them, his face flushed with anger. "I will not let you ruin this for the young couple. You want to fight, go someplace else." He looked hard at Lorenzo, then at Buccaneer. "Are you going to be thugs or gentlemen?"

"Gentlemen," Julienne answered for them, taking one of Buccaneer's hands and threading her fingers through his. At her touch, she felt his fury diminish and his muscles relax. She smiled. "If you want to impress me, feed me."

He laughed, more at himself than at what she'd said, and draped her hand in the crook of his arm. Without giving Lorenzo or Cesare another glance, he walked with Julienne toward the tent. The wedding guests followed them and formed a line. The tables were laden with fruit and meat and vegetables. The centerpiece was a three-tiered cake. Buccaneer handed a knife to the bride and groom.

"Please, won't you do the honors?"

The guests crowded closer to the tables. Buccaneer pulled Julienne to one side.

"Forgive me."

She looked at him, surprised to see that he was serious—even contrite.

"I behaved badly again," he whispered in her ear.

She squeezed his hand. "Yes, but you're forgiven."

"I'll make it up to you later."

She looked up into his face, wondering what was behind that promise. "What are you planning, Buccaneer LaFlamme?"

He leaned closer. "A midnight sail on the *Golden Conch*. Just the two of us."

"You can captain that ship all by yourself?"

His lips brushed her temple. "You will be my first mate. Together we will set sail for a journey few have known." His husky, suggestive laugh tickled her ear and started a fire in her heart. His arms tightened and he nuzzled her hair. "No more fighting. No more pushing you away. You've been warned, Julienne. I'm no prize. You'd be smart to tell me to release you now and stay well away from me."

She leaned her head against his shoulder and closed her eyes as a delicious quiver arrowed through her body. Buccaneer's arms came around her, molding her back to his front.

"You have nothing to say about this?" he asked.

Julienne smiled, feeling more feminine and more alive than she ever had in her life. "Do we have to wait until midnight?"

Quietly, urgently, they slipped out of the tent and raced across the lawn toward the waiting, restless sea.

Chapter 18

They were an hour out at sea before he dropped anchor. Julienne stood at the stern of the *Golden Conch*, watching the stars drown in the black water and waiting for her life to change irrevocably. How would it be? Would he guide her into this night of love or charge forward while she struggled to keep up? Would he be understanding, or understand only his need for fulfillment? She quivered inside, frightened and excited, wanting to jump overboard and swim away, and then, in the next moment, wanting him to hurry up and take her.

She heard Buccaneer come to stand behind her. His hands settled on her shoulders and he turned her sideways. Julienne closed her eyes, knowing she would soon be enfolded in his embrace and that the girl in her would be forever lost in his kiss.

"Look there," he whispered. "That's what I've brought you here to see. It's beautiful, isn't it?"

She opened her eyes to find herself staring out at sea. For a few moments she didn't understand, then she saw the eerie glow over a patch of the dark ocean.

"Oh, it's phosphorous," she breathed.

"You've seen this before?"

"There is a cove back home on Key Largo with

a patch of water like this. I snuck out one night and went swimming in it. I thought I'd glow afterward, but I didn't."

He laughed and his arms tightened around her. "I thought the same thing when I was a boy."

She relaxed against him. "This is why you brought me out here for a midnight sail?" She tried to disguise her disappointment.

''I thought you'd enjoy it. I can watch this for hours. The glow is otherworldly. One time I saw a school of several hundred fish in that patch. Drops of water would fly up and sparkle and glow like multicolored jewels. It was breathtaking. I'll never forget it."

She laughed, suddenly feeling the foolishness in her assumption.

"What's so funny?"

"Me," she admitted. "I thought you'd brought me out here to... well, ravish me."

He was still a few moments. She couldn't even feel the beat of his heart against her back. "Would you let me?"

Her heart stopped beating for a second. She wanted to tell him the truth, but she found she couldn't admit it aloud. "Ravished ladies aren't given a choice, are they?"

He stepped in front of her and stared deeply into her eyes. Framing her face with his hands, he touched his lips to hers, ever so lightly.

"You have a choice," he whispered, still staring at her, reading her every nuance.

The shimmering out at sea was nothing compared to the glow inside her. She closed her eyes again, seeing herself standing on a precipice, one foot dangling over it. Should she or shouldn't she? If she didn't, she'd never know if she could fly, if this man could make her heart soar. Ever since she'd heard his name, she had been moving toward this moment. Somewhere in her heart, she'd known the time would come when she would be asked to make this decision. Sometimes she'd even prayed for the moment to arrive.

He took her silence for apprehension, and his arms fell away. He crossed the polished deck, where he leaned against the rail and stared out to sea. Starlight limned his profile in blue. He was so handsome, he took her breath away.

Julienne felt as if she'd stepped off the ledge and had landed on solid rock.

"Buccaneer?"

His gaze met hers and he cleared his throat. She could see the glimmer of desire in his eyes and feel it quivering in the air between them.

"Buccaneer, you're not thinking of her, are you? I *am* the one to put the dark fire in your eyes, aren't I?"

"Who else would be on my mind?"

"You know."

He frowned. "Maggie?" At her nod, he swiped the air with one arm in a vicious gesture. "Of course not! What's wrong with you?"

"I was about to ask you the same question. You brought me out here tonight to sweep me off my feet, but it seems that *yours* have gotten cold."

He narrowed his eyes. "God knows, you should stay away from me."

"Why?" she demanded, hands on hips. "What's so awful about you?"

"Women tend to live short lives around me."

She made a face at him. "That's an old saw. What else?"

"It might be an old saw, but it's still rapier-sharp. You should pay heed to a man's past, Julienne, and mine is certainly stained."

"I'm not interested in your past." She closed the distance between them and wedged herself between his open thighs. "What are you going to do with this moment in time, Buccaneer?"

He tipped back his head and stared at the unfurled sails and star-pocked sky. He lowered his gaze to hers, and the naked longing in his eyes and on his face made her blood roar in her ears.

"What are you going to do?" She could hardly believe she was taunting him like this, pressing herself to his most private part, challenging him to take her virginity. Spellbound, she thought. He's cast a spell over me, and I'm not myself anymore. I'm who he wants me to be.

"God forgive me, but I've got to have you." His voice was rough-edged, but touchingly vulnerable, with the slightest tremor running through it. "If it means that I'll roast in hell, then so be it. At least I'll have known heaven in your arms."

She knew in that magical moment that she would remember those words until her dying day. And if she were allowed to take a memory with her to the great beyond, this was the one she'd take. This was the memory she'd keep for eternity.

In the space of a heartbeat she was in his arms, and his mouth moved urgently against hers. Intense love poured through her, and she wondered how she'd ever lived without him. She drove her fingers through the blue-black waves of his hair, cooled by the ocean breeze. She sealed her lips to his. He tasted of salty spray, and his tongue was warm and questing in her mouth. The breeze kicked up, blowing her skirt against him, around him. His shirt billowed against her hands. She pulled it free of his waistband and slipped her hands up under. His skin felt like hot silk. She moaned into his mouth, and her tongue danced wildly with his.

All her fantasies, her imaginings, her dreams of being swept off her feet by a dashing, dark pirate, were suddenly real. Gloriously, impossibly real. She peeled off his vest and tipped back her head to give him access to the full length of her throat.

His mouth was hot on her skin, leaving a trail of fire to where the gown's heart-shaped neckline dipped at its farthest point. He lifted his head, his eyes locking with hers. His hands moved to her back and he unbuttoned her dress slowly, surely. For an instant she saw deviltry in his eyes, and her blood ran cold. Was he going to be rough, as he had so often been with Maggie?

She clutched his shoulders. "Buccaneer, I've never been with a man before. Please, be careful."

Desire glazed his eyes, but an instant later she saw comprehension grip him. "The first time is often uncomfortable," he told her, driving his blunt-ended fingers through her hair and watching it shimmer over the backs of his hands. "One must experience pain before one can truly appreciate pleasure."

His words didn't console her. She trembled. He smiled and then slanted his mouth over hers again in a kiss that made her forget her fear of the unknown. As he worked the dress off her shoulders, she grew impatient and began helping him remove her clothes. He thrust his hands up under her skirt and massaged her soft buttocks. She'd never thought such handling of her body would be erotic or that she'd allow it, but it was and she did.

Within another minute, he had her stretched out on the deck, her clothing scattered beneath her. She wore only her loose drawers and white cotton chemise, flimsy stuff in his big hands. He pulled down her chemise, and his mouth covered one of her breasts. She gasped as he sucked until her nipple grew as hard as a stone. His tongue scraped over it and she thought she might die.

"Buccaneer . . . oh, oh." She couldn't find the words, she didn't know what she should do other than babble and stare up at the sea of stars while she writhed in soulful longing.

She parted her thighs, and his body slipped between them. His weight startled and thrilled her. She ran her hands across his bare shoulders and back, experiencing the suppleness of his muscles and skin. He felt like a sleek animal. He moved with a restlessness that instilled the same in her. She tore at the buttons on his trousers, murmuring under her breath in frustration until, finally, she could push aside the clothing.

He fastened his mouth on her other breast, letting the cool breeze dry the one that he'd left wet and throbbing. The more he suckled her, the more her body yearned for the ultimate fulfillment. Instinct guided her. Her knees knew to bend, her thighs to open wider, her hands to lock on his hips, her pelvis to lift.

Buccaneer threw back his head and stared at the moon. "Ah, Julienne, you're killing me."

"Make me yours," she pleaded. "I want so much to be yours."

He reached down between their bodies. She felt the heat of him immediately, even before she felt the tip of his stiff member against her thigh. He slid her drawers off her legs, caressing them, kissing them, tonguing the sensitive skin at the back of her knees. He shifted her slightly, adjusting her so that he could enter her. She tensed at the invasion. He bent over her, his tongue flicking her earlobe. She hissed in a breath.

"Buccaneer, stop."

His mouth came down on hers, smothering her protest, engaging her lips and tongue and mind while he drove past the thin shield inside her. For a moment the pain eluded her, but then burned through her like a fiery arrow. Tears filled her eyes. She realized that Buccaneer had gone quite still. While he began to move again, she was swamped with a confusion of feelings. He kissed her eyelids and gathered up her teardrops with the tip of his tongue.

"Is it over? Are we finished?"

He smiled tightly. "No. It hasn't even begun." His eyes glimmered with amusement. "Relax, my precious. Relax."

"I can't. I'm not good at this."

"Shhhh." He rested his forehead against hers and closed his eyes. "Hold tightly to me, my little jewel. I swear that before the night is over, you shall plead for me to stay inside of you."

She gripped his shoulders, tensing for ... for what? What would happen? Could she endure it? Would she disappoint him?

He plunged deep and pulled back. Something changed inside her. She grew moist and more pliant. He lifted her legs higher. She gave herself over to his manipulations. His hips rocked forward, driving deeper. She grasped his smooth shoulders, afraid of the new feelings stirring inside her; deep, deep inside, where his member touched and probed. He took one of her pink nipples between his lips, and those nebulous stirrings increased to a near tumult. When his fingers slipped into her private folds, she gasped, then gasped again when his thumb passed over a hard nub.

"You like that," he said, smiling against her breast. "Want me to leave you alone now?"

"No, no," she panted, moving her head from side to side. "More, I want more."

His laughter rumbled. His breath fanned the pale skin of her breasts. "I knew you'd be like this. Once a wild child, always a wild child."

The deck rocked beneath her and the world became bright and hot and all awhirl. She floated over the precipice and felt the wind under her wings. Lifting, soaring, sailing, out of control.

"Oh, no," she moaned against his shoulder.

"Oh, yes," he groaned back at her, massaging the nub and making her writhe in passion's grip. "That's it, Julienne. Give yourself to me. Tell me you want me inside you. Tell me."

"I want you! Please, please."

Pleasure blazed through her like lightning and she arched up, her mouth seeking his, her hands clutching, her arms circling. He molded his body to hers, thrusting ever deeper, ever harder, until she thought she might die with the rapture of it all. He trembled against her and then his muscles went rigid a few seconds before his hips bucked in her groping hands. His release splashed against her walls. Groaning, he kissed the side of her neck, his breath coming in short gasps, his hair-silky chest rubbing her breasts.

When he withdrew from her, she sighed her satisfaction. Her body twitched, inside and out. She felt vulnerable, but all aglow.

He combed her hair back from her face with both hands. "How do you feel?"

"Like a woman."

He kissed the tip of her nose. "Are you cold?"

"No, but this deck is rather hard."

"Poor darling." He gathered her into his arms and stood, lifting her, holding her against him. "Let's go below and I'll take care of you."

She rested her head on his shoulder, feeling shy and unsure of what she should do next. "I'll just wash up and get dressed while you steer us back to Pirate's Key."

"I'll wash you, but you won't be getting dressed yet. I'm not finished with you, little jewel."

"Not finished?" She shivered, looking over his shoulder at her scattered clothing on the deck. Second thoughts crowded her mind. "My clothes, Buccaneer."

"I'll fetch them later when you need them."

"I need them now."

He paid her no heed, but descended the ladder and strode along the narrow corridor toward the captain's quarters. Her shoulders brushed the walls and she had to tuck her feet up tight against him to clear the other wall. He kicked open the door and went directly to the bed, where he draped her like an exotic spread. He stood back to look at her, and Julienne realized that she could, in turn, look at him.

When had he shed every stitch of his clothing? She looked from his misty gray eyes down to his bronze, sinewy chest and finally to the dark pelt of hair below his navel. From that patch sprang his member, so unlike anything she had on her own body. She found herself staring and, finally, admiring.

He placed his hands at his waist and stood with his feet apart. "Well, have you gotten an eyeful yet, woman?"

She wrapped her hand around him. He moaned and almost crumpled. Julienne smiled, realizing that she'd made his knees buckle with a mere caress. He grabbed a handful of her hair and tipped her head back. His mouth descended, claiming hers in a drowning, whorling kiss. She fell back on the bed and he slid on top of her, his body warm and alive. He felt slick and erotic under her wandering hands. Her fingers found him again and he groaned and nipped at her shoulder.

"You drive me mad," he confessed. "When you touch me, I lose myself completely."

"Lose yourself in me," she commanded, guiding him to that magical entrance.

"No, wait." He slipped off the bed and went to the pitcher and bowl on the table.

"What are you doing?" She propped herself on her elbows, feeling abandoned and all quivery inside. "Come back here and finish what you started, Captain."

"I intend to, but first let me wash you." He held a damp rag in one hand and a bar of soap in the other.

Julienne curled into a ball. "No! Please, don't." She felt her face flame with embarrassment.

"It's too late for modesty, mam'selle. I have tasted you and touched you. Now, quit simpering and let me at you. You're bleeding."

"I am?" She straightened out her legs and looked at herself. Thin threads of crimson stained her inner thighs. "What's wrong with me?"

"A slight tear, *ma petite*," he reminded her, sitting on the side of the bed and forcing her hands away so that he could press the cloth to her sensitive white skin. "Nothing to worry about."

"Not for you anyway," she rejoined with a touch of self-pity and more than a touch of self-recrimination. What had she done? Now that she wasn't a virgin, she had no place to go. Even the Sisters wouldn't take her in.

"There, there," he said, his voice soft. "Every woman goes through this, but now it's done."

"Now it's done," she repeated, feeling as if she'd lost something precious.

"Please, no regrets." He tossed aside the washcloth and slid on top of her again, as agile and fluid as an ocean wave overtaking the beach. He framed her face in his big hands and made her look him in the eyes. "No regrets, Julienne. You wanted me as fiercely as I wanted you—as I still want you. Can't you feel me hot and hard against you? Ever since I took over this cabin as the captain, I have longed to have just the right woman in here with me. I finally have that woman."

Tears filled her eyes anew. She raised up to cover his mouth with hers. She slipped her tongue between his firm, full lips. He tasted better than succulent fruit or rich dessert. He tasted of temptation.

She needed little instruction or guidance this time. Wrapping her legs high and tight around his hips, she held on as he advanced. She cried out his name while her body shuddered around his pulsating shaft. He trapped one of her nipples in his mouth and sucked hard and fast, then treated the other the same. She dug her fingers into his shoulders and panted his name over and over, falling into the cadence of his thrust and parry. Her whole being readied itself for some tumult that her mind couldn't grasp and her imagination couldn't conjure. It crashed on her like an ocean wave, drowning her in a sea of exploding light and mindless pleasure. She thrashed beneath him, her breath sawing her throat raw.

He growled her name and his hands cupped her buttocks, holding her against his grinding pelvis as his own pleasure rained over him. His release came in long, hard shudders, leaving him limp and panting. He pulled out of her slowly and fell to one side with a moan of utter satisfaction.

"The French call this the little death," he whispered. "And I do believe I've died and gone to heaven."

She laughed and flipped onto her side. Flinging a leg and arm over his brawny body, she sandwiched one of his dark nipples between her lips and teased it with the tip of her tongue.

He wrapped her hair around the fingers of one hand and pulled her mouth away from him. "You're torturing me, woman. You have drained me and I have nothing left, so now you torture me."

"I liked it more this time, Buccaneer. Let's do it again and see if it gets better and better."

He opened one eye to peer at her. "If it's any better, we'll kill each other!"

She made a face at him. "No one has died of pleasure."

"No one you know of, anyway," he countered, his fingers gently massaging her scalp. "Rest awhile, little jewel."

"I don't want to rest!" She left the bed and danced over to the porthole. She had to push with all her might to open it, but it was worth the effort. The sea breeze sailed over her heated skin, and the scent of the ocean romanced her. "Buccaneer, this is the most wonderful night the world has seen. I wonder if others are wasting it." She whirled to face him again. He had propped himself on one elbow, and one leg was bent at the knee. She was reminded of Roman statues of the male physique. She'd always thought they were embellished by the artist's kind interpretation. She'd been wrong. Her gaze drifted to that telling part of him and she saw it lift ever so slightly, its tip glistening. She moistened her lips. His taste lingered in her mouth. Was it her imagination or had that lovely member that had given her so much pleasure risen an inch higher?

She realized he was appreciating her nudity as much or more than she appreciated his, and she was glad that only starlight painted the cabin. He patted the empty stretch of bedding and crooked a finger at her.

"I thought you were drained."

"You've divined another drop or two I missed."

Julienne dashed to him and snuggled into the circle of his embrace. She flirted with his mouth, nestling her tongue in the corners and biting gently on his lower lip.

"Have I released an unsatiable tease?" he asked.

"Maybe. I admit I don't even know myself tonight. I'm doing things I never, ever dreamed of!" She lay back, waiting for him to cover her again with his long-limbed body.

He shook his head. "You do the work this time."

She glanced at him from head to foot. "What do I do?"

Buccaneer spread a hand over her thigh and pulled her on top of him. "Sit up and straddle me." He shifted and his thumbs moved inward toward that kernel of flesh that seemed to hold more nerve endings than any other part of her body. His eyes were dark gray and his sooty lashes shadowed them. "Touch me, Julienne. Make me hard."

She wanted to control him, wanted to satisfy him in the most complete way possible. Holding him, she caressed and stroked, then bent over to kiss the tip. He drove his head into the pillow, and his teeth glistened in the dark as he ground out a French oath. His fingers dug into her flesh, and she knew that he wanted to be inside her. She lifted herself up and over him. He thrust once, hard, and released a long, jerky sigh along with his seed. His hands came up to cup her breasts, and his thumbs chased her nipples round and round until she covered his hands with hers and shivered atop him.

"I never knew I was so sensitive there," she admitted.

"Here, too, hmmm?" He rubbed his pelvis against her and set off a series of sharp, blazing tremors that turned her muscles to water. She drooped forward upon him.

Buccaneer slipped out of her and kissed her damp forehead. Wrapped in each other's arms, they fell into that dreamless, peaceful sleep known only to satiated lovers.

Julienne left the bed and tiptoed to the porthole an hour before dawn. She stared at the blackness and felt all aglow. Yet dissatisfaction nudged her heart. She was no longer an unplucked flower. What did the future hold for an unmarried woman who had been with a man?

Behind her, she heard Buccaneer's feet land on the floor and he padded to her. His arms enfolded her and he rested his chin on top of her head.

"You're beautiful. Like a dream."

She smiled and crossed her arms on top of his. "I feel beautiful when I'm with you." She caught her lower lip between her teeth as doubt stabbed her. "Buccaneer, this means so much to me. Do you understand?"

"Of course. It means the same to me." He peered around at her. "What's troubling you?"

"I was just thinking . . ."

His arms tightened. "When a woman thinks too hard, trouble brews."

"I must think of my future, Buccaneer. If things don't work out here, then I'll have to find somewhere else to—"

"Things are working out fine here."

"Yes, but it might be different someday. You might find a woman you respect enough to marry, and she might not want me hanging about."

He whirled her around to face him, his hands landing heavily on her shoulders. In the blue starlight, his irritation was evident in the blaze of his eyes and the downward pitch of his lips. "Respect enough? You think I don't respect you? You think I bedded you as I would a common whore? Is *that* what you're thinking?"

She tried to fight back her tears of self-pity and confusion. "I don't know what to think! I . . . I've never done this before." The tears filled her eyes and she pressed her face to the center of his chest and held on to him. "Forgive me for being such a . . . oh, I don't know, a spoiler. Women aren't supposed to discuss these things after the fact, I suppose."

His hands gentled on her shoulders, and he made her look at him.

"I can't even go back to the Sisters now, can I?" she asked in a small voice.

"Ah, sweet jewel, you don't have to go back to the Sisters."

"But someday I might—"

"Never. You'll never go back there," he repeated firmly, then his brows shot up and a strange light entered his eyes. "We'll sail back and be married."

"Married? You—you want t-to marry me?" She swayed, suddenly dizzy-headed. "We can't do that."

"Yes, we can. The priest will still be at Moonspell. Cesare isn't taking him back to Key West until after breakfast. We have time to sail home and have him marry us. But we can't waste a minute."

The word "married" rooted her in place. Marry. Was he actually going to marry her? Just like that?

"Buccaneer, are you sure—"

"I'll get our clothes. Once you're dressed, come help me with the riggings." He kissed her, his lips stroking hers, his tongue warm in her mouth. He laughed at her stunned expression. "Don't look so flummoxed. Didn't you think I might do what's right by you? I do have a heart, you know."

"I never doubted that, but are you certain this is what you want?"

"I want you. Don't you want me?"

"Yes. Oh, yes." She knew her face reflected her devotion to him, because his mouth twisted with emotion and he swallowed hard. She ran her fingertips over his stubbled cheeks and rock-hard jawline, then down over his chest, bulging with muscle. "I have wanted you since the first moment I saw you . . . even before that. When I heard your name, I fell in love with you."

"And I've wanted you since that day on the beach."

"Which day?"

"The day you were swimming."

She stepped back. "You saw me?"

He grinned.

"So you *have* been following me." A spurt of anger stiffened her spine. Why hadn't he told her before? If she'd known it was him, she wouldn't have been so frightened.

He shrugged. "I happened to come along and see you, that's all."

She felt herself blush. "You acted as if you hadn't seen me."

"But I did, and it was all I could do not to make love to you right there on the beach." Cool air swept in through the porthole, combing his hair and drawing attention from her to the piece of horizon visible through the round window. The sky had changed from black to gray. "I'll get our clothes and pull up anchor. With any luck, we'll be married before the sun burns off the morning mist."

Chapter 19

"You may kiss the bride," the priest intoned, his face wreathed in smiles.

Julienne turned toward Buccaneer, and his cool lips touched hers, reverently, tenderly. He straightened, and his beaming smile alleviated her wedding nerves. Buccaneer shook the priest's hand and then accepted congratulations from Cesare and the field hands who had stayed for the ceremony. Dazed by the swift progression of events, Julienne smiled as the priest spoke encouragingly to her, and Ursula wrapped her in a huge hug. Over the maid's shoulder, Julienne spied Rosa, and she didn't need a mind reader to tell her how the housekeeper felt about the marriage. Hatred blasted from her black eyes, and it seemed that her whole, black-clad body quivered with disapproval.

Buccaneer hadn't given anyone time to protest or question his decision to marry Julienne. He'd taken charge in his usual way, rounding up the priest, telling Julienne to wear something as bridal as she could find, and then positioning himself outside the house, near the tent that had been erected for the other wedding party. The sun had spread rosy light over the dewy grass and sugary sand as witnesses had gathered and the priest had performed a traditional ceremony. Julienne had selected the cream-colored gown, simply cut and elegant. She put her hair up and had positioned five tiny white tea roses among the mahogany strands. Buccaneer, in a dark suit and white shirt, had stood tall beside her, his expression confident, his voice firm, when he answered the priest.

"Julienne? Julienne?"

Julienne drew back from Ursula and looked down to see Alissa, dressed in her white nightgown. Julienne picked the child up in her arms.

"What are you doing awake at this hour? You're usually a sleepyhead and never open your eyes before nine bells."

"I woke her up," Ursula confessed in a whisper. "Rosa said not to, but I thought Alissa would want to see her papa marry. You're happy about it, aren't you, Alissa?"

In answer, Alissa placed her arms around Julienne's neck and hugged her, then planted a sloppy kiss on her cheek.

"Are you really Papa's wife now?"

"Yes, princess, I am." Julienne chucked Alissa playfully under her chin. "And I'm your new mother, but you don't have to call me that."

"I'm afraid to."

"Afraid to call me mother?" Julienne looked from Alissa to Ursula, but the maid looked confused, too. "Why would you be afraid?"

"If you're my mother, you might die."

"Hush, Alissa. You know that's nonsense." She tightened her arms around the child, warding off such horrible thoughts and images. "This is a happy time. I thought you'd be glad I married your father."

"I am," Alissa said, her voice small and muffled against Julienne's shoulder. "I love you."

Ursula patted Alissa's back. "You take it from me, child. Things are going to get better and better around here. I think the new señora is just what this gloomy place needs."

Julienne looked at the two-story house and the Bride's House attached to it—not conforming, not belonging. Just like its residents, Julienne thought with a touch of sadness. "I hope you're right, Ursula. I want to make a difference here. I want to bring love to this place."

Ursula stepped closer. "You will have to make Rosa step aside. She does not like this marriage."

"I noticed." Julienne shrugged. "Alissa approves, and that's all that matters." Julienne kissed the child's cheek again. "Thank you for coming to my wedding, princess."

"What's this? Royalty at our wedding?" Buccaneer stood at Julienne's elbow, his gaze on his daughter's shy smile. He bowed. "Princess Alissa, this is an honor." His playfulness provoked giggles from her. "Does Your Highness approve of the new queen mother?"

Julienne laughed with Alissa, happy to see Buccaneer in such a good mood, and praying that it would last. She'd married him hoping she could enhance his life and give it a turn of good luck. It was important that she make a difference or she feared her life at Moonspell would not be a pleasant one. Alissa pressed her cheek to Julienne's.

"I'm glad she's going to stay. Make her stay forever, Papa. I don't want her to leave like Mama left."

A shadow passed over Buccaneer's face, but it was gone in an instant. He took Alissa from Julienne and kissed her button nose.

"Your wish is my command, princess." He examined her cotton nightgown. "What's this? Were you roused out of bed and not allowed to dress for this momentous occasion? Have you had your breakfast? No? Then we shall all breakfast together—our first meal as a family." His warm gray eyes searched out Julienne. "Papa, Mother, and Lissa."

Julienne nodded, but placed a hand on his arm. "Take her inside, and I'll be along in a moment. I want to speak with Rosa. I don't think she's handling this well."

Buccaneer scoffed. "She'll come around."

"Yes, but I want to talk to her."

He shrugged. "Don't be long. Tell her we'll want breakfast within the hour. Ursula, you may help me get the princess here bathed and dressed properly for this wedding day." He brushed his lips across Julienne's temple before he took Alissa to the house.

Rosa stood in front of the trellis where Julienne's moonflower and morning glory vines were beginning to flourish.

"I can tell that you think the captain and I have made a mistake in marrying," Julienne said, cutting to the heart of the matter. "But what's done is done. I'm the mistress of Moonspell now, and you'll have to answer to me, Rosa. I hope that doesn't become too unpleasant for both of us. It doesn't have to, you know. We could decide to become friends instead of enemies."

Instead of answering, Rosa chose to turn away from Julienne and start for the house. Julienne grabbed her arm and moved to block her way.

"Is this what you want? You prefer hostility to friendship?"

"He will never love you."

"I believe he already does. He married me."

Rosa made a chiding noise. "He married that Isabelle, too."

"He was no more than a boy when he married Isabelle. She was chosen for him, and that union was a mistake."

"This one, too. He still loves Magdalena. He will always love her, because I will not allow him to forget her. Magdalena is Alissa's mother, not you!"

She tried to barge past, but Julienne held on to

her, and there was a brief tussle before Rosa stood still, resentment blazing in her eyes.

"Magdalena is dead, Rosa. How can you love Alissa and insist that she never have another woman in her life to love her as every child deserves to be loved? As for Buccaneer, he has grieved long enough for Maggie. It's time for him to move on with another wife ... with me."

"I will never accept you as the mistress of this house."

Julienne realized Rosa would not yield, so she released the woman and stood aside to give her access to the house. "Very well. However, you *will* serve breakfast within the hour. Captain's orders," she added with a tight smile. "And you *will* call me Señora LaFlamme from now on. You're dismissed."

Rosa's face looked as if it were carved from stone. Only her eyes glittered with malicious light. The skin above her upper lip was white and taut with anger, but she said no more. She went into the house that she guarded like a zealot. Julienne looked up at the peeling white facade and the black ironwork around the porch and upper terraces. The place needed a thick coat of whitewash, she decided. And more flowers and trees. Benches would be nice close to shore, where she and Buccaneer could sit and watch the sea. Perhaps a fountain could be placed in front of the house. She'd plant rosebushes around it, attracting honeybees and songbirds. By next year, Moonspell would look entirely different. It would reflect the love she felt for its owner, and all its ghosts would be gone.

She twisted the wedding ring on her finger, then held up her hand to admire the square-cut smoky topaz surrounded by pearls and diamonds. The colors of Julienne? she wondered, smiling. Buccaneer said the ring had been in his family for two generations. Pirate loot, he'd told her, knowing she would find romance in wearing the spoils of privateers.

Lifting her chin higher, she ascended the outside steps and walked proudly into the foyer. The mistress of Moonspell was home. Home at last.

Her eyes filled with tears and she gazed up at the skylight, that patch of blue surrounded by the pots of blooms she'd so lovingly tended.

"Do you see, Papa?" she whispered to the only other man she had loved with all her heart. "Can you see how happy I am and that I've found another home in our beloved keys?" She felt a glow in her heart, and smiled. "I thought so. I knew you were near during the ceremony."

She closed her eyes, at peace with her father's death. She would always miss him, but Buccaneer had filled the emptiness inside her. She sensed she wasn't alone and she opened her eyes to find that Buccaneer stood at the top of the stairs. He extended a hand to her, and his smile, so gentle and meant just for her, made her heart brim with such devotion that it hurt.

"Come up here, Señora LaFlamme. Your husband and daughter need you."

She ran up the stairs and into his embrace. "And I need you. Both of you." Julienne lifted her face for his kiss.

I'm your willing slave and you are my master.

Those words circled through Julienne's mind as she pulled aside her diaphanous wrapper and stared at the shadow of bruises on her upper arms and buttocks. A strawberry stain had bloomed on her shoulder, and she blushed when she recalled Buccaneer biting her there just before he'd climaxed that last time on the sloop. Selena had been bruised—could Buccaneer have . . . ? She shook off that vision and adjusted the white wrapper over her matching nightgown with its pale pink lace and ribbons decorating the front.

She faced herself in the mirror. Did she really know herself? She'd never thought of herself surrendering to a man before marriage, but she'd done it. Not only surrendered, but handed herself over to him willingly. In the bedroom, he was the master and she was his eager pupil. She'd done things with him that made her blush.

Julienne thought of Maggie's diary and the disturbing entries about dominance and submission. Was this the beginning? Would Buccaneer eventually be as rough and insulting as Maggie had described him in her diary?

Shutting off the torturous speculations, she focused on her reflection again and saw Buccaneer behind her, bare-chested and virile. He wore only a pair of loose cotton trousers with a drawstring waist. Padding quietly to her, he placed his hands on her shoulders and bent his head to kiss the side of her neck.

"I was observing the damage just now," she said.

He lifted his head. "What damage?"

She separated herself from him and dropped the wrapper off her shoulders and arms. "These bruises on my arms and my ... my backside."

His smile was wicked. "Ah, the marks of lust."

"Must I be marked? Can't lovemaking leave one unharmed?" She swept her gaze over him. "I don't see any bruises on you."

"It's a wonder, what with your nails digging into me and your teeth sinking into my skin."

When she would have put on the wrapper again, he gathered her into his arms, and the cover-up slipped from her fingers. He kissed her shoulder, the curve of her neck, the tip of her ear.

"Are you sore anywhere else?" he whispered.

She knew exactly where he meant. In truth, she

was tender there, too, but she couldn't bring herself to say that. A traitorously weak part of her
was afraid such an admission would keep him
from her—and she wanted him. This was officially
her wedding night, and she had no desire to
spend it chastely. She shook her head, and her hair
spread over her shoulders, over the backs of his
hands.

He grabbed handfuls of it and pulled her head
back, exposing her tender throat to his seeking,
moist lips and the abrasiveness of his whisker
stubble. That now familiar weakness stole through
her and she knew, beyond a doubt, who was in
charge. Him. He conducted her as one would an
orchestra. Every nerve ending, every heartbeat, every breath, was controlled by him. Was it like this
for Maggie, too? Was this the LaFlamme legacy,
this innate ability in the LaFlamme men to bring
women to their knees?

Buccaneer retreated from her, a sly grin slanting
across his full lips, his gray eyes heavy-lidded and
sexually frank. He sprawled on the bed, looking
ever so dark against the white linens. Crooking a
finger, he summoned her.

Julienne found a sliver of self-control and managed a haughty hitch of her chin. "You curl a finger at me and I'm to obey, is that it?"

He nodded and patted the mattress, then gestured
again to her.

Make him wait a minute, she told herself, bending over to pick up her sheer wrapper. She saun-
tered toward the massive bureau and opened the
double doors where Buccaneer's clothes had been
pushed to one side to accommodate hers. Julienne
hung the garment on a hook and started to close
the doors when she spotted the leather riding
skirt. She touched it, wondering how it had gotten
among her clothes, then gasped when she noticed

other things that weren't hers. Dresses, shirtwaists, hats. Spinning around, she glared at Buccaneer.

"What's going on here? Am I to dress in her things now? Well, I won't!"

His dark brows dipped. "What the hell are you talking about?"

"These clothes." She flung a hand toward the bureau. "Magdalena's clothes have been placed in here with mine."

"To hell, you say." He sat up and squinted at the bureau. "How did those get in there?"

"I won't wear them. True, I borrowed this riding skirt once, but I—"

"You don't have to wear them. I don't want you to wear them." He ran a hand down his face. "I suppose Rosa or Ursula put them in there, thinking you might—"

"Rosa," Julienne interrupted. "It was Rosa."

"Forget it. Come to bed."

Julienne wished it were that easy to forget that Rosa meant to thwart her at every turn. She stared at the clothes mingled with hers and wanted to find Rosa and order the old crow to remove Magdalena's clothing at once! She hung her head, feeling petty and defeated. Could she find happiness here with such hostility present?

Buccaneer bounded off the bed and swept her up into his arms. She gave a squeak of protest, which he cut off with a burning kiss. He laid her on the bed and stood at the side, looking at her, his eyes darkening to ash.

"Take off your gown and let me look at you. Slowly. Very slowly."

Timidity overcame her and she shook her head. His gaze flickered over her, hot and seeking. He waited, a slight frown appearing between his eyes, and she knew his will was stronger than hers. Her hands trembled as she eased the sheer material off her shoulders. When she exposed her breasts, she noticed a pulse beating stronger in his temples and he shifted as if he'd become uncomfortable. From the size of the bulge between his legs, she didn't doubt his discomfort in the least. Her new-found power won her over, and she brazenly pushed the material down over her hips. It whispered over the length of her legs and wreathed her feet. She wore pantalets and she didn't have to be told to remove those also—slowly, tantalizingly, all the while noticing the building of desire in him.

His gaze moved from her to the knotted cord around his waist. When he looked at her again, she knew what he wanted. Kneeling on the mattress before him, she worked at unknotting the belt, her fingers clumsy and trembling. A part of her was shocked at her actions, but a larger part of her was titillated. Her heart hammered, sending blood coursing through her veins and singing in her ears. She breathed through her mouth, almost panting with expectation as she finally untied the cord. He was ready for her, lifting into her waiting hands, proud and erect. He released a long, shaky sigh of relief and closed his eyes. His lashes curled on his cheeks, long and sooty black. Any woman would have envied them.

"You're beautiful," Julienne whispered.

His eyes opened and his hands closed on her upper arms. With a flip and a surprising economy of motion, he flung her onto her back and pressed his body on top of hers. His mouth fastened on her breast, demanding and teasing her nipple. He removed his trousers and threw them aside, then came to her again, passion raging in him and sweeping her up in a tidal wave of emotion.

"You're mine," he told her fiercely, and then entered her swiftly, lifting her hips off the bed. "Mine, mine, mine," he said in time with his thrusts.

She moved her lips in silent protest. It was too

fast, she thought. Too brusque. But then the undulation of his hips touched a secret part of her and all protests died. She grabbed on to his shoulders and matched her motions with his, getting the most of each entry, each withdrawal. It seemed he was taking her soul, then giving it back, taking, giving . . . then it was all giving as her climax showered over her, blotting out everything but the roar of blood in her ears and the helpless sounds bursting from her throat.

His own release came in short, deep jabs. He quaked from head to foot, spilling into her, filling her with the wonder and power two people can create together. He collapsed on top of her, his lips moving lazily against the curve of her neck. She caressed his shoulders, then began kneading them. Sensing his relaxation, she eased out from under him. He lay on his stomach and she straddled him to begin a languid, talented massage of his shoulders and back. He moaned appreciatively, stretching out, his arms above his head, his legs parted wide.

The only light in the room came from the oil lamp on the bedside table. It was turned down low and cast a golden sheen over Buccaneer's swarthy skin. Muscles rippled and bulged beneath skin that was tough as leather, but supple as suede. She fitted her thumbs on either side of his spine and worked them down the length of it, dropping kisses along the journey to the dip just above his tight, compact buttocks. Julienne rocked her hips, sliding herself over the hill of his smooth backside to sit across the back of his powerfully built thighs. She massaged the cheeks of his butt, her fingers showing no mercy.

Finally her hands ached and she slid her body up to lie, outstretched, on top of him. She flattened her breasts against his back, her nipples hard with desire. His eyes were closed, but she knew he wasn't sleeping. She could feel his arousal all over him—in the bunching of his muscles, in the heat of his skin, in the shallowness of his breathing, in the rock-hard set of his jaw. She caught his earlobe between her teeth and tugged gently. That was all. That was enough.

With a heady groan, he flipped over and sat up, his back against the headboard. Pulling her onto his lap, he connected with her. She gloved him in her slippery, hot sheath of skin and liquid muscle, then tightened her hold. His face became taut with concentration as he tangled his hands in her hair and slanted his mouth hungrily over hers. His tongue filled her mouth while he drove deeply into her body, his hips thrusting, bucking, dominating her.

Buccaneer lifted his mouth from hers and stared into her glazed eyes, satisfied that she was in the grip of passion and had lost all sense of timidity or modesty with him. Gratified, he rocked his hips forward, getting a gasp of pleasure from her. Her lips glistened and he kissed her again, suckling gently on her small, agile tongue, growing more aroused when she whimpered and moaned softly.

He felt his own rising passion and held it off for another minute while he tongued her pearly nipples and made her shiver in his arms.

"Buccaneer, please, please," she begged, nearly incoherent.

"Open your eyes and look at me," he commanded, and her lashes lifted. Her eyes were softly brown, unfocused, full of the love she reserved just for him. "Say my name again."

"Buccaneer," she whispered.

"Again."

"Buccaneer, my love. My dearest, darling love."

He climaxed in a long, hard shudder, never letting go of her gaze. She trembled, taking what he gave, squeezing him inside her, holding him in her tight, hot grip. He panted as if he'd run a mile in the sun's zenith and he felt light-headed, light-hearted. She relaxed and crumpled forward, her face nestled in the curve of his neck. He hugged her against him, reluctant to relinquish his hold ... or her hold of him.

"Buccaneer, will it always be like this?"

"God willing."

She gave a little sigh that feathered his skin and stirred the damp hair on his chest. "I don't know ... Can people die of too much pleasure?"

He chuckled, resting his head back against the headboard. "Would you trade it for a longer life of restraint?"

She was quiet a moment, then sealed herself more completely against him. "No. Life without you would be no life at all."

The confession should have made his heart soar, but it didn't. He closed his eyes, haunted by his past and the woman who used to share this same bed. Would she ever let him go? he wondered a little desperately. Deep in his heart, he feared that he'd never be able to love Julienne with complete abandon unless he could put Maggie's memory to rest, once and for all. He just hoped he hadn't placed Julienne in danger by his rash decision to marry her while he was still mired in Maggie's persistent aura.

Much later, Julienne awakened and stared into the gray darkness. She sensed that she was alone in the bed, and squinted toward the window, where night light spilled forth.

Buccaneer sat there, his head cradled in his hands. She started to ask if he was ill, but something in his posture stopped her. His shoulders shook slightly and then a name rumbled from his lips, the sound of it full of anguish and pain.

"Maggie."

Julienne shut her eyes and felt her heart shudder and shrink from the onslaught of pain.

Maggie. So she's still here, Julienne thought, bitter tears forming in her eyes as she buried her face in the pillow to keep her misery hidden, should Buccaneer glance her way. She was glad the dark shielded her from him when he finally rejoined her in bed. He didn't reach for her, but turned his back. Julienne stared at the wedge of his shoulder, his gleaming, broad back, the hair curling thickly against his neck.

I love you so much, she told him mentally. *Why can't you love me and forget her? How did she put a lock on your heart?*

Until she understood his relationship with Maggie, Julienne knew she'd never truly know her husband. The key to that lock on his heart was Magdalena. In fact, she thought with sudden clarity, Maggie was the key to solving all the mysteries of Moonspell.

Chapter 20

Struggling under the mound of clothing, shoes, and hats, Julienne moved blindly into the kitchen, sensing her way toward the table, and dropped the load on top of it.

"Just what do you think you're doing?" Rosa demanded. She stood by the cookstove, where something bubbled in a big pot. She held a dripping spoon in one hand. "Get those clothes off the table."

"These aren't mine. You put them in my bureau, so you can do something with them." Julienne aimed a challenging glare at Rosa. "Are you going to lie and tell me you didn't put Magdalena's clothes in the bureau yesterday?"

A smugness settled over Rosa's narrow face. "You think you can take her place, *sí?* You sleep in her bed, give yourself to her man, so why not wear her clothes? Maybe Captain Buck can imagine you are her when you are dressed like her."

"The captain married *me*, Rosa. He doesn't have to imagine any other woman, and I'm not interested in taking Magdalena's place. I've taken my own place here at Moonspell." She indicated the clothing with a brisk flick of her hand. "No more of these childish tricks. They won't make me leave. I'm here to stay."

Rosa shrugged with contempt, unflappable and haughty. "What should I do with the clothing?"

"Whatever you want. I just don't wish to see it again." She glanced at the fine gowns, beautiful day dresses, fancy hats, and footwear. Yes, she'd been tempted to keep a few of the things, but she'd resisted. She needed no reminders of Maggie, especially for Buccaneer. His moaning of her name last night still made her want to cry in frustration. Starting out of the kitchen, she paused, remembering another sore point. "By the way, I won't allow you to poison Alissa's mind toward her father anymore either."

Rosa cut her dark eyes at Julienne. "What do you accuse me of now?"

"You heard me. I know you're the one who has been feeding Alissa all kinds of lies about her father. You've made her wary of him. You've made her afraid of storms and the sea and heaven knows what else!"

"Why would I do such things?" Rosa scoffed.

"So that Alissa will look to you for support and comfort," Julienne answered. "I'm wise to your game, Rosa, and I want you to stop it immediately. You've damaged Alissa's relationship with Buccaneer, but no more."

"Alissa misses her mother. You can't stop that."

"I can help her get past it as long as you stay out of my way."

"I have not spoken ill of Captain Buck to Alissa. The child is afraid of the dark and storms because her mother was lost on a black, rainy night. Are you going to blame all troubles and woes on me? If so, then I shall tell Captain Buck I must leave and seek other employment."

Julienne held on to her temper, realizing that Rosa didn't want to leave Moonspell, but also realizing that the wily housekeeper would dearly love to go whining to Buccaneer about how badly she was being treated. "That won't be necessary as long as you don't keep playing these childish tricks." She pointed at the clothes, then left the kitchen.

Mean old crow, she thought crossly, recalling the fight over the flowerpots, the thorny twig tucked in her clothing right after her arrival, and that night when she'd thought she'd seen someone at the top of the stairs. She was almost certain it had been Rosa, sneaking around and trying to scare her or make her think that Maggie's ghost was trailing her. Rosa was probably the one sneaking around behind her, although her sixth sense told her it was Lorenzo. Now that she was married, she expected that to end.

Her thoughts guided her to the parlor, presided over by Magdalena's stunning portrait. She could suggest to Buccaneer that the oil painting be taken down in honor of the new mistress of Moonspell, but she would rather he do it without any prodding on her behalf.

Life's routine had reinstated itself this day after her wedding. Buccaneer had promised a honeymoon after the tobacco crop had been picked, cured, and shipped. It so happened they'd married during a crucial time for the crop. The tobacco had grown and some of the beds would be picked soon, then the drying and curing process would commence, all of which Buccaneer would oversee.

The morning after her wedding, Julienne had tutored Alissa in the Bride's House as she had nearly every morning since her arrival at Moonspell. After the midday meal, she'd sent Alissa to her room for a nap and had browsed through more of Maggie's diary, which had only made her feel insecure. She'd put the diary back in its hiding place, vowing not to read it again, because it wasn't helping—it was hurting.

"*You* hurt him," she accused the woman in the

painting. She recalled the descriptions that didn't quite compare to the man she knew Buccaneer to be.

He's a strutting, roaring lion, vain in the best sense of the word. When he climaxes, he is noisy and scary. Sometimes he hurts me, but the pain is real. When I weep, he loves me all the more. He says that pleasure is never any good without pain.

"That's sick," Julienne whispered, staring hard at Maggie's face. She tried to see a hint of demons in the woman's eyes. Buccaneer had been so different with Magdalena than he was with Julienne. Did Maggie bring out the worst in him? Did he sense that she wanted domination, so he became a swaggering, unfeeling bully for her?

He certainly was aggressive in bed, but Julienne couldn't imagine him inflicting pain on purpose. Did he enjoy Maggie in bed more? she wondered, then firmly told herself not to compare herself with Maggie. She only hoped he refrained from comparisons, as well.

She longed for the day when the painting would be taken down and stored. As long as it hung in this room, Julienne couldn't help but feel overshadowed by the woman's memory.

Turning her back on the portrait, she was suddenly filled with a longing to see Buccaneer. She went upstairs and changed into her blue gown. Buccaneer had told her he'd take her to Key West soon to buy more clothes, so she needn't hoard the others he'd bought her. He'd confessed that he hated her dark clothes, given to her by the nuns, and she'd promised not to wear them anymore, other than for gardening work.

Choosing a straw bonnet with bright blue and red feathers stuck along one side, she checked her appearance in the mirror before going to Alissa, who had just awakened from her nap.

"Get up and put on these play clothes," Julienne

said, pulling a tan shirt and dark green jumper from the bureau and handing them to Alissa. "I'll get you a hat and some shoes. We're going to visit your father in the tobacco fields."

"Why?"

"Because; that's why." Julienne reached for Alissa's straw boater and older, brown shoes. "These will do for now, but I'm going to ask your father to buy you some boots and a riding habit."

"What for?" Alissa asked, letting Julienne help her put on the clothing.

"It's more comfortable to ride in."

"I don't ride horses."

"Not until today." Julienne pulled the jumper over Alissa's face and smiled at the child's wide eyes. "That's right. I'm going to put you on Dumpling today, and we're going to ride to the fields. It's time you learned to sit a horse."

"I can't! I'll fall off and die!"

Julienne pressed a finger to Alissa's rosebud mouth. "I will not hear any more rubbish about dying, Alissa LaFlamme. I have ridden a horse since I was barely able to walk, and I haven't even come close to death because of it." She looked Alissa squarely in the eyes. "Does Rosa tell you these foolish things?"

"She's afraid I'll die."

Julienne nodded, not in the least surprised. "Put on your shoes and hat, then come downstairs. I'll go ahead and tell Danny to saddle our horses for us." She shook her finger when Alissa started to whine. "Where's your pirate's courage?"

Alissa sucked in a breath and trembled with the effort not to cry.

"That's better," Julienne commended her. "Your father will be so proud of you."

Gathering in a lungful of the pungent air, Julienne smiled. "I think I'm cut out to be the wife of a tobacco farmer. I love the smell of it, don't you, Alissa?" She cut her eyes at the child riding beside her and clamped her lips together to keep from laughing at Alissa's huge eyes, chalky skin, and the death grip she had on the reins and saddle horn. "Alissa?"

The girl gave a jerky nod.

"You'll enjoy the ride more if you just relax."

"If I do . . . I'll fall off and k-kill myself!"

"Hardly that. We're riding at a snail's pace on two gentle horses that have no intention of rearing or bucking." She looked ahead. "My, my, the crop has grown so much since we saw it last. Remember how they were little things? They're knee-high at least!"

The plants under the tents were deep green and leafy, spreading out over the furrowed rows. Workers dotted the area, bending over the plants, carting barrels of water, hoeing around the stalks.

"You going to get sick again?" Alissa asked.

"You mean the tobacco rash I got last time? I hope not. Buccaneer says you usually get it only once. There's Buccaneer. See, he's over there by the third shed."

Alissa squinted into the sun. "Is Cesare with him?"

"Yes, and Lorenzo." Julienne frowned, wishing she didn't have to see Lorenzo. He gave her creepy skin and made her feel like an object instead of a human being. "Sit up straight, Alissa, and don't look so frightened. We want your father to be surprised and pleased that you're a grown-up girl riding all by yourself."

They rode up to where the men stood talking. Buccaneer had his back to them as he dunked a red handkerchief in a bucket of water. He turned as he tied the dripping piece of cloth around his neck, and his expression reflected his surprise and pleasure, not only at seeing them, but at Alissa astride the white pony.

"I don't believe my eyes." He blinked, closed his eyes, and looked again. "That can't be Alissa astride a horse!"

Despite her trembling fear, Alissa giggled. "Julienne made me."

"I didn't force you," Julienne corrected. "I persuaded."

Buccaneer smiled. "And I know how persuasive she can be. What brings you out here?"

"We wanted to see how the crop's doing. And we wanted to see you," Julienne tacked on. "We miss you."

Buccaneer stepped closer and laid a hand on her thigh. "We or you?"

His hand felt warm from the sun. Julienne laid her hand over his. *My husband*, she thought. *My handsome husband.*

Cesare cleared his throat. "Lorenzo, you come with me and let's inspect the other sheds. We should give the newlyweds some privacy."

"By all means." Lorenzo bowed deeply, his dark eyes glittering with innuendo. "It is a pleasure to see you, señora. Your man should count himself lucky to have won your hand."

"Her man does," Buccaneer snapped, then presented his back to Lorenzo, shutting him out. "Let me help you down from there, Alissa." He swung his daughter from the saddle.

Julienne dismounted and handed the reins to Buccaneer. She noticed his green-stained fingers. "What have you been doing?"

"Suckering."

"What's that?"

"Pulling the buds and blooms off the plants."

"The plants have blooms?" Julienne faced the field, her interest in it expanding. "What color . . . and why in the world would you want to pick off the buds? I bet they'd be beautiful. The crop itself is lovely, but flowers would make the fields burst with color!"

Buccaneer laughed softly. "We're growing tobacco, not bouquets. The blossoms are large and sweet-smelling. They range from nearly white to a deep pink."

"Why not let them flourish?" Julienne persisted.

"Because the plants should nourish their leaves, not their blossoms. We pick off the flowers and buds so that the leaves will grow larger and lusher."

"Don't the buds have the seeds?"

He nodded. "We save enough seeds from them for next year's crops." Reaching into his shirt pocket, he pulled out a white handkerchief and opened it carefully. "I put some seeds in here." He held it out for Julienne and Alissa to see.

Julienne stared at the tiny black pellets. "They're nothing but specks."

"*Oui.* One tablespoonful can sow one hundred square yards of seed bed." He folded the handkerchief and pushed it back into his pocket. "This is a new strain I've been experimenting with this year. They aren't as vulnerable to the weather and insects." He tugged at the brim of Alissa's hat. "But this is boring to you ladies, I'm sure."

"Not to this lady, and I think it's good for Alissa to know about the cash crop on her family's land."

Buccaneer's smile made her glow inside. "You're an amazing woman, Julienne Va— LaFlamme," he corrected himself.

For a few moments they stared into each other's eyes. Julienne hoped he was seeing a happy future in hers. She saw a chance of it in his, given time and luck. Eventually she felt that she could make him forget Magdalena and take her into his heart.

"Who lives in the little houses, Papa?"

Buccaneer refocused his attention on Alissa.

"Those are drying sheds, princess. After we pick the leaves, we air-dry them in those buildings."

"When do you pick the leaves?"

"Not for a while yet. They'll be picked green and then dried, fermented, and aged."

"Quite a production," Julienne observed. She'd started strolling toward the tents, and Buccaneer and Alissa joined her. Alissa slipped between them, and they all held hands in the natural link of family.

Walking hand in hand, Julienne experienced a profound sense of belonging. She looked at the tented fields and felt possessive of them and of the man and child beside her. When she had married Buccaneer, she had also joined this land and this child. She had mingled her history with his, her future with his. Emotion burned her throat and she looked to him, finding his gaze on her. He furrowed his brow, questioning the moisture glimmering in her brown eyes. She smiled, shook her head, and directed her gaze toward the fluttering tents again. She ducked underneath into the cooler shade where several dark-skinned men were bent double, their fingers working rapidly as they plucked buds and blooms and tiny top leaves. One looked up and flashed a big grin. She recognized him from the night when Buccaneer had so unnerved her with his knife dance. She returned the man's smile and he resumed his work, his dark hands flying over the tops of the plants.

"The worms didn't cause too much damage?" Julienne asked, recalling Buccaneer's concern with wireworms.

He sighed. "They destroyed two fields, but we saved enough of the crop to have a respectable harvest." He glanced down at Alissa. "How do you like riding, princess?"

"It's scary."

"At first, but after a few days you'll be begging to go riding every day, all day."

Alissa shook her head. "Nuh-uh. I can get hurt riding horses."

Buccaneer exchanged a glance of irritation with Julienne. "Alissa, you can get hurt doing almost anything. I think it's useful that you're learning to ride. It will give you independence." His attention was drawn away from them by the jingle of harness and the squeak of wagon wheels approaching. "That's the load of fertilizer I've been waiting for all morning."

Julienne gave him a gentle push. "Go back to work. We don't want to get in your way."

"Are you sure?"

She nodded. "Alissa and I should be getting home. She has her afternoon piano lesson. But before you dash off, do you know if there are any other flowerpots around the house? I asked Rosa, but she evaded the question."

He worked his panama hat more securely onto his head. "You might check the shed out back of the house. The decrepit-looking one. Isabelle used it to store her gardening tools and whatnots."

"Thanks."

"It hasn't been cleaned out for years. Might be some wasp nests in there." He started to leave, but second thoughts sent him back to them. He tipped Alissa's head back and bent to kiss her puckered lips. "See you later, princess." Then he brushed Julienne's lips with his in a caress that was sweetly lingering. "I'm glad you've been missing me this morning. Miss me this afternoon, too."

"I will," she promised, then let him go back to his precious crop of leaves.

As they made their way to the tethered horses, they passed near Cesare and Lorenzo. Cesare waved, grinning broadly.

"You horsewomen go with God!" he teased for Alissa's benefit.

"Sí, be careful," Lorenzo called. "We would be so sad if anything happened to you."

Julienne returned their wave, but didn't acknowledge Lorenzo's warning. Everything about that man rankled her. Even his attempt at concern sounded more like a threat than a caution.

It was early evening by the time Julienne found time to investigate the shed in back of the main house. Approaching it, she realized that it was indeed decrepit. She moved cautiously, listening for angry buzzing or darting insect bodies. The outside of the building was nearly void of paint, with only flecks left to suggest it had once sported a thin coat of white. The roof had been attacked by termites and was as holey as Swiss cheese.

Surprisingly, the door hinges weren't rusty and the crossbar on the outside was thick and heavy. Julienne lifted it and stood it to one side of the door. Grabbing hold of the handle, she pulled the door open slowly, still listening for buzzing. She heard the lazy drone of wasps and crouched a little, shrinking into herself as she opened the door all the way. Her eyes slowly adjusted to the dusky interior of the shed and she spotted a large wasp nest in one corner next to a quarter-sized knothole. The place was full of holes, some two inches wide, but mostly buckshot-size. Evidently the shed had been a favorite during target practice. The door swung shut behind her.

Shelves lined one wall, and the top three were full of clay pots, old gardening tools, gloves, and watering cans. Stepping inside, Julienne kept an eye on the wasp nest. The shed was narrow, so she could stand in the center of it, stretch out her arms, and touch the walls. It was also stifling, full of dust and heat. Not wanting to tarry, she sorted through the pots, finding six that weren't cracked or broken. That would be enough, she thought, imagining them filled with mums and gardenias, which she would place on the balcony outside Buccaneer's bedroom—no, *their* bedroom.

She smiled to herself, thinking how strange it sounded. Buccaneer's bedroom—only two days ago completely off limits to her—was now theirs. *Theirs*. Oh, it was a lovely word. Ours. Us. We. Lovely, lovely words.

Humming to herself, she forgot the wasps and the dirty interior as she examined the garden tools and small gloves. Gloves so small that she couldn't get her hands into them. Isabelle must have had hands like a child's! She wondered what Buccaneer's first wife had looked like. Tiny, evidently. What color eyes? Was her voice soft? Did she speak English at all?

Something thumped outside. She stilled, listened, but then resumed her inspection of the items on the shelf. The light shifted ever so slightly and Julienne glanced up, puzzled. Fading light spilled through one of the larger holes, no more than five inches above her. Another bump and then something long and menacing shot through the hole at her. Julienne shrieked and doubled over, dropping the pot she held and flinging her arms over her head in a protective posture. Peeking upward, she saw a broom handle sticking through the hole. She reached up to grab it, but it slipped out, disappearing. Julienne straightened.

"Hey, out there! I'm in here, so stop that!" she called, angry. Something darted past. Through the buckshot holes, Julienne could only see well enough to know that someone moved swiftly around the shed.

The broom handle attacked again, slipping through a hole behind her and jabbing her painfully in the back. She spun and grabbed hold of the shaft of wood, but it was jerked from her hands, leaving splinters in her palms.

"Stop it!" she cried, lunging for the door. She pushed and the breath rushed out of her. "Let me out!" Julienne threw her weight against the wood and heard the crossbar rattle in its rack. Someone had barred the door! "Who is out there? Rosa? Rosa, is that you? This isn't funny."

Another hole filled with the wooden menace, which struck her hip. She cowered in a corner. Something bounced off her cheek. She batted at it, then realized she was directly under the wasp nest. Screaming, she stumbled to the opposite corner, her hands flying around her face and head, fighting off the buzzing bodies. One wasp penetrated her frantic shield and sank its stinger into her forearm.

Shrieking, she slapped at the place and squashed the insect against her arm. Panic rose in her quicker than the pain of the stings and she stomped the insect into the ground while looking around frantically for another attack. The wasps circled their nest, but stayed in their corner away from her.

The broomstick punched her shoulder and knocked her away from the wall. Julienne dug in her heels and managed to keep her distance from the agitated wasps. She whirled, tried to grab the broom handle, but it was yanked out of the hole. It protruded through another opening, pounding her temple and sending a bright, hot pain through her head.

Defeated and nearly mindless with panic and pain, Julienne crumpled into a sobbing heap in the middle of the shed. She covered her head with her arms and waited for the next vicious attack of wasp or wooden handle. Sweat rolled down her back and sides and face. The heat pressed in on her and dust filled her mouth and lungs as she gasped for breath. The furious sound of the insects began to fade as minutes ticked by and the sunlight changed from orangy gold to pale yellow.

Slowly, fearfully, Julienne lifted her head and looked around at what had become her torture chamber. She crawled to the door and sagged against it, sobbing and praying that someone would come and raise the bar, releasing her into the world again.

She gasped when the door swung open, dumping her out of the shed and onto the beaten path leading from the house to the shed. Julienne scrambled to her feet, but assumed a crouched position as she looked around, ready to fight or bite or kick whoever threatened her. A mockingbird hurried through his imitations of a crow, a jay, a whippoorwill, and a chickadee. Julienne blinked away her tears. Could it be that all was right with the world again? Had the danger passed? In the near distance she saw a man leaning a shoulder against a tree, his back to her. Buccaneer. She started running, arms outstretched, needing his shelter. She wanted to call out to him, but her throat was raw, and her voice scratchy and weak. When she was almost on him, her toe struck something in the long grass. Stopping, she stared down at the broomstick.

Buccaneer turned, and to Julienne's tear-washed eyes, his smile seemed to mock her.

"You ... you ... How could you?" she rasped.

"Looks like you've run into a spot of trouble," he observed, his smile beginning to slip.

Snatching up the broomstick, Julienne attacked him with a fury born of fear and heartbreak.

Chapter 21

Ursula worked the last splinter from Julienne's palm and dabbed the bleeding nick with alcohol. As she blew on the stinging place, she glanced warily at Buccaneer, who stood in front of the window, his back to the bed where Julienne lay and Ursula tended to her superficial wounds. The splinters had been removed, the wasp stings painted with soothing paste, and much ado had been made over the round bruises on her shoulders, hip, and head where the broomstick had struck.

"Thank you, Ursula," Julienne said, lying back against the fluffy pillows. "You can leave now. I'm fine."

"Ring for me if you need anything."

"I will."

Ursula slipped from the room and closed the door softly behind her. Julienne stared at Buccaneer's imposing back and knew it was her place to apologize for attacking him with the broom handle and accusing him of terrorizing her in the shed. He had turned her over to Ursula and hadn't joined in with the commiserating. He's furious, she thought. No, he's hurting inside. I've shown him that I don't completely trust him. But that's not true! Is it? She gnawed softly on her lower lip, struggling with her traitorously vague

310

feelings. Of course Buccaneer wouldn't do such a thing to her. It was sheer lunacy to think otherwise.

She drew in a deep breath and plunged ahead, anxious to breach the sea of misunderstandings stretching between them. "Buccaneer, I know you're angry at me, and you have every right to be. Please, look at me. I'm so sorry. Don't stay angry."

"I'm not angry." He faced her slowly, his expression giving away nothing. "I'm confused and disappointed, but I'm not angry." He moved closer into the lamplight, displaying the bluish shadows under his eyes and the taut set of his mouth. "You believed that I'd lock you in that shed and try to hurt you, frighten you."

Shame scalded her neck and cheeks. "I didn't think ... I was half-crazed when I got out of the shed. I saw you standing there and the broomstick was lying on the ground near you and I ... I just lost my head, that's all. I didn't harm you, did I?" She vaguely recalled that he'd taken the blows on his forearms and had easily wrenched the broomstick from her hands. He had withstood her pummeling fists against his chest until she'd worn herself out and had collapsed at his feet. She thought he'd carried her to the house, but it was a blur. She might have even fainted. She recalled being placed in this bed and Buccaneer shouting orders to everyone.

His eyes were darkly gray. His mussed hair fell over the tips of his ears and curled on his forehead. "You didn't harm me ... physically."

He didn't need to expound. The pain in his eyes, the bitterness in his voice, the flexing muscles in his jawline, said it all. Julienne raised her hand to reach out to him, but he turned aside. She examined the two sting punctures on her forearm and the swelling around them instead and tried not to break down in front of him. He could be so cruel, she thought, glancing at him through her lashes and wondering if she'd ever really know him. Had her fantasies of pirates and romantic love blinded her so that she had never seen the man behind that wonderfully fanciful name? She'd convinced herself that he'd been a bully with Magdalena because that's what Maggie had wanted. Maybe she'd been wrong. Maybe Buccaneer forced Maggie into those wickedly demeaning games.

The silence became oppressive. "You were right about the possibility of wasps in the shed," she murmured, realizing that was one of the reasons she'd leaped to the conclusion that Buccaneer had locked her inside it. He'd suggested that she look in the shed, warning her of the wasps, and then he'd been standing nearby with that broomstick lying no more than two feet behind him in the grass. He hadn't seemed that upset when he'd turned to look at her either. However, she reminded herself, he'd rushed her into the house and marshaled Ursula and Rosa to calm her down and see to her scrapes and bruises. Her suspicious mind won out.

"Buccaneer, didn't you hear me screaming and crying? You must have heard me. I was loud enough to wake the dead."

A derisive smile touched his mouth. Aggravation narrowed his eyes. "In other words, you believe that I heard your screams and did nothing." His laughter was as bitter as jimsonweed, his eyes dark as the night outside the windows. A flash of irritation passed over his face. "How can you ask me that?"

Emotion blocked her throat for a moment. She swallowed and plucked restlessly at the band of lace edging the sheet. "I'm sorry."

"So you've said."

"I am!" Her gaze bounced up to him, challenged

him. He looked away first. "I was just wondering how—"

"I was walking from the stables to the house and I paused to light a cigar," he said, his tone full of resignation. He strode toward the windows and pushed aside the heavy draperies to survey the moon-splashed night. "The next thing I knew, you were standing behind me with a club in your hands. If you were screaming before, I didn't hear you."

She closed her eyes and thought back on those terrifying minutes in the shed. After the attack, she had knelt in the shed crying softly, waiting for her attacker to strike again. If what he said was true, he wouldn't have heard her.

"I'm surprised someone in the house didn't hear."

"Ursula was in the washroom doing the laundry, and Rosa was up here and heard nothing."

"Rosa." Julienne sat up in bed. "I bet she's responsible."

"Didn't you hear me?" Buccaneer glared at her over his shoulder. "I told you that Rosa was up here at the front of house, and that's why she couldn't hear you."

"So she says. She hates me, Buccaneer. It's just like her to do something like this."

"For what purpose?"

"Because she's mean! Hateful people don't need a reason."

He scowled at her and faced the window again. "You should rein in your imagination."

"Someone locked the door and terrorized me, Buccaneer."

"The door wasn't locked."

"It was at first. Maybe she saw you coming and unbarred the door, then dropped the broomstick. She sneaked back into the house and made up that story about being in here and not hearing a thing."

He stuffed his hands in his trouser pockets, drawing the material tightly against his muscled buttocks. "It wasn't Rosa."

"Who, then?" She glared at him.

"I don't know, and I resent your implication that I should!"

His anger stunned her and she stared at him, speechless. Eyes blazing, he made a chopping gesture, dismissing her shock.

"I don't like being questioned. Why would anyone want to scare you like that? It doesn't make sense." He sat in the chair near her bed and ran a hand down his face. "Other than Rosa—and me—do you suspect anyone else?"

"I don't think you had anything to do with it."

"You're repeating yourself."

"If you refuse to consider Rosa, then perhaps Lorenzo?"

Buccaneer angled a glance her way. "Lorenzo? I don't recall his leaving the fields, but he might have." His glance sharpened. "He's been pestering you again?"

"No, not really." She knew a moment of guilty pleasure to have aroused even a tiny bit of protectiveness in him. "Rosa's the only one who is openly hostile."

"I won't believe she'd do such a thing."

"I can't believe you think her incapable of it. My first day here she put a thorny twig among my folded clothing so that I'd prick myself on it."

He leaned back in the chair and drove all ten fingers through his hair. "Julienne, don't be ridiculous. Did she admit to this?"

"I didn't tell her about it. Why give her the chance to gloat?"

"Therefore, I take it, you have no proof that she's done anything against you."

"I have proof! That day she came tattling to you, she called me names."

"Referring to someone as a strutting hen isn't a threat or even blasphemy." He clasped his hands behind his head and sent her a grimace of mockery. "I think you're still a bit hysterical. Maybe you should get some rest. You'll be thinking more clearly tomorrow."

"I'm not crazy."

"I didn't say that."

"And I'm not hysterical."

"You're tired. I'll leave you alone so you can sleep. I need to check on Alissa anyway."

"I didn't imagine being in that shed," she said, slamming her fists into the mattress at her sides. "I didn't imagine these wasp stings or the splinters or the bruises!"

He sat on the side of the bed and grasped her shoulders. "Don't get worked up, Julienne."

"You're acting as if this is all a dream!"

"I know it's not a dream. I know someone did this to you. I just have trouble believing it was Rosa. I will find the person responsible and I'll make him regret it. But for now, you rest." He pressed her back against the pillows and brushed a kiss over her forehead.

Julienne grabbed the sides of his leather vest before he could get away from her. "I swear to you, Buccaneer, I don't think you had anything to do with it. I was ... blinded by fear. I struck without thinking. Forgive me, please."

He covered her fists with his and pried her fingers open. She tried to find forgiveness in his eyes, but couldn't. He seemed eager to leave her. She wanted to beg him, to insist that he stay beside her until she was sure he was hers again ... if he ever had been, that is. Looking into his impassive gray eyes, she wondered if she had mistaken desire for devotion, passion for love.

"Don't worry yourself over it." He patted her

hands and then stood up and moved away. "I'll have a dinner tray sent to you later."

"You'll be back?"

He was at the door. His smile was brief and unconvincing. "Sleep well." Then he closed the door.

Julienne stared at the light and shadows mingling on the ceiling for a long time before her eyelids grew heavy. She went over the horrible time in the shed, trying to find a clue to the identity of her tormentor. Nothing substantial emerged to enlighten her. Could it have been Lorenzo? He'd certainly been following her ... or she suspected as much. Suspicion. That's all she had. She suspected Lorenzo and Rosa. Before Selena had left, she'd thought Selena had been following her, especially that night when she'd seen someone standing at the top of the stairs. But she had no evidence.

She'd been married less than two days, and already trouble brewed between her and Buccaneer. Had it happened like this with Isabelle and Magdalena? Was it happening all over again? Would this insidious circle of suspicion and tragedy ever be broken?

By the end of her second full week as the mistress of Moonspell, Julienne had recovered from her scare in the gardening shed, although no culprit had come forth or been found out. Buccaneer had slept in one of the other rooms for two nights, telling her he wanted her to rest. Finally on the third night he had returned to their marriage bed and had fallen on her, making love to her with furious intent. She'd been stunned and terrifically aroused, which had bothered her later. Was she going the way of Magdalena? If so, was there any way to save herself?

But his lovemaking later in the week had gentled. He brought her body to a fever pitch, tenderly, thoughtfully. And he was holding back a piece of himself. Ever since she'd accused him of locking her in that shed and menacing her, he had withdrawn. He didn't talk *with* her, he spoke *to* her. He didn't reach out to her except in bed. Their intimacy had suffered, and she couldn't see a way to mend it.

Two weeks, she thought, after checking in on Alissa, who was busy playing with her dolls. Two weeks of married life. She should be the dreamy-eyed wife, but her marriage was unorthodox. Maybe Buccaneer had wed her only to ease his guilty conscience for taking her virginity. Maybe he regretted his gentlemanly gesture. Or perhaps he wanted another mother for his child and merely changed her from governess to Mama Julienne.

Restless, she decided she needed to get out of the house. She went to her room and changed into her new riding outfit, a khaki split skirt, gauzy white blouse, and royal blue jacket. Her new boots pinched a little, but she figured they'd be a perfect fit once she'd broken them in.

Out in the stables, she told Danny to throw a saddle pad and bridle on Seabiscuit, then she was off, taking a fork in the riding trail she and Buccaneer had traversed once before. She rode slowly, enjoying the smell of growing things and the warmth of the sun slanting through the tree branches. She removed her hat and ran her fingers through her hair, craving freedom in whatever form she could obtain it. Lately she'd felt closed in by invisible walls. If the truth be told, she'd been afraid to leave the estate since that afternoon in the shed. She had hoped that her tormentor would be caught and she could leave the house without looking over her shoulder all the time.

Julienne glanced back, peering at the shadows at the far end of the trail, straining her ears to pick up any sound. Then she faced forward again, aggravated with herself for being edgy, even though she had every right to be. Someone had locked her in a shed with a hive of wasps and had poked at her with a broom handle while she screamed and cried and begged him to stop. If this was funny to someone, then what hilarious thing would that someone do next?

She coaxed Seabiscuit into a canter and enjoyed the smells and scenery a little less. Someday, when the danger had passed, she wanted to explore every foot of Pirate's Key. She wanted to know it intimately, every trail, every shortcut, every landmark. She'd introduce herself to all the residents, and then it would feel more like home to her.

Her heart scoffed at her meager plans. This would never feel like home until she could convince Buccaneer that she trusted him. How could she do that when this terrible voice inside her head kept questioning his motives, his personality, those stupid descriptions of him in Maggie's diary? Oh, she wished she'd never found that journal.

The trail bent around a grove of papaya and forked again. Seabiscuit veered right without guidance and trotted confidently along the more narrow path. Chickens pecked along the side of the road, and one squawked and fluttered into thick brush. Julienne laughed to herself when Carmella's shack came into view. No wonder this path had looked familiar and Seabiscuit knew it so well.

Carmella stood in the doorway and leaned heavily on a cane. She was dressed in a tangerine-colored shift and had tied a gaudy green scarf around her white hair. She motioned for Julienne to come inside, then disappeared into the blackness within. Julienne hadn't planned on stopping, but she realized she had little choice. Dismounting, she tied Seabiscuit securely to a tree, not wanting to be stranded in this odd place with the witch of Pirate's Key.

The hut was hot, dark, and dusty. The chattering monkey leaped from chair to chair, from table to shelf, and irritated the parrot and owl. Carmella sat at the table and poured tea into two cracked cups. Melted candles sagged over wooden candlesticks. A cricket in a small, black cage chirped loudly. Carmella laid a hand on top of the cage, and the cricket fell silent. Julienne shook off an onslaught of goose bumps.

"Sit down. We'll drink and then I'll read the leaves." Carmella's voice was marbled with age.

"Not my palm this time?" Julienne rejoined, smiling and trying to seem nonchalant.

"Leaves. The leaves be strong today. Your life, it's changing too quick, and the lines in your palm cain't keep up. Takes years for the lines to change. The leaves change hour to hour, day to day. Sit. Hurts my neck to be looking up at you."

Julienne took the chair opposite her. "My life *has* changed. I married Captain Buck. I guess you've already heard that."

"I be knowing you would marry him when you sat here the last time." She smiled, showing off the gaps between her teeth and her pink and black gums.

"I don't recall any mention of it. All I remember is your predicting doom and gloom. Something about a shadow on my life."

"You happy as a clam, are you?" she asked, her watery eyes denouncing Julienne's outward calm. "I hear tell you got yourself penned up in a shed and 'bout went crazy."

"I did not go crazy! Someone barred the door and tried to frighten me. It was a childish prank, and when Buccaneer finds out who did it, that person will be very sorry indeed."

Carmella waved a blue-veined hand. "Cap'n Buck got bigger fish to fry. He ain't gonna find nobody. He cain't even find the one that done killed his wives. Maybe he need only look in a mirror, eh?" She cackled, then laughed even louder when Julienne glared at her. "Drink your tea. No need you being so touchy."

Julienne sipped the tea. It was bitter with no sugar, milk, or lemon to cut the taste. She wrinkled her nose, affronted by the stench in the room. It smelled gamy, what with the animals coming in and out. The owl blinked slowly, then closed its eyes and dozed. The monkey had found a half-eaten potato and munched on it, its bright eyes almost glowing in the dim light.

The chipped cup was small, and two more sips emptied it enough for Carmella to see the leaves. Julienne pushed it toward the woman, wishing she'd hurry up with her hocus-pocus so that Julienne could be gone from the hot, smelly place. She sniffed and caught the scent of yeast in the air.

"Have you been brewing whiskey?"

Carmella snickered. "Maybe. You be wanting some?"

"No. Have you been sampling your brew?"

"You think maybe I be drunk?" Carmella shook her cottony head. "I be sober as a high mass. I hardly ever touch the stuff. Just make it to sell. The mens love it and pay good money for it. Sometimes they trades goods for my liquor. One of them gave me a pig last year, and I fattened it up and butchered it this spring." She eyeballed the scattered leaves in Julienne's cup, turning it this way and that and making *tsk*ing sounds. She set the cup down to vigorously rub her eyes, then she refocused on the leaves again. Lines deepened in her forehead and sunken cheeks, and her mouth turned down at the corners.

"I take it you don't like what you see," Julienne

said, guarding herself against the old woman's superstition.

"You been keeping a secret," Carmella accused in her raspy, reedy voice. "You got something hidden away that don't belong to you."

Despite herself, Julienne flinched and felt as if she were five and had been caught stealing a watermelon out of the neighbor's patch. The diary. Could she be talking about the diary? She chided herself for even entertaining the notion that the old woman could read such details in a wad of wet leaves. It would be best if she escaped right now before Carmella could disturb her even more.

"Well, if that's it, I should be on my way," she said as cheerfully as possible. "Thanks for the tea and the reading."

"You wait." Carmella's hand shot out to capture Julienne's wrist. Her fingers were dry and dusty-feeling, like powdery parchment. "Danger be following you because of this secret thing. You shouldn't be holding onto this secret thing. It don't belong to you. It belong to another woman."

"Magdalena," Julienne said, then wished she could bite her tongue. Too late now, she thought, sighing away her plan to escape. "I have Magdalena's diary—or, rather, I know where it's hidden."

"You been reading it?"

"Yes." She looked down, ashamed at revealing her weakness. "I don't know if Buccaneer knows she kept a diary or not. I shouldn't have read it, but I thought I might learn more about him through it."

"It be cursed."

Julienne made a face. "Posh! Next you'll be telling me that Maggie's ghost locked me in the shed." Even saying it sent a chill up her spine.

"As long as you got that diary, you be cursed.

Your life got that shadow on it because of that secret you be keeping."

Julienne frowned. "You're right about part of this. I shouldn't have been looking through the diary. It's none of my business. I thought to give it over to Buccaneer the moment I found it, but I kept making excuses why I shouldn't." She placed her hands flat on the table. "I'll give it to him tonight."

"No, no!" Carmella waved her hands in agitation. "That will only give him the curse. That diary got to be destroyed. It holds bad things."

Julienne nodded. It was true that Maggie's diary had done nothing to help her, had only served to confuse her about Buccaneer. Julienne wouldn't want it to land in the wrong hands.

"You bring it to me," Carmella said. "I can handle curses. I take off the curse, and then you don't have to worry no more. You can give it to Cap'n Buck then."

"There isn't a curse on it," Julienne stated, not wanting the old woman to think that she believed in such things.

"You bring it here. Cap'n Buck don't need no more pain on him."

Julienne considered the old woman's advice and decided she could be right. The diary might only inflict more pain on Buccaneer by dredging up the past. While she didn't believe in curses, she did believe that some things were better left alone.

"You go now and be careful. As long as you got that diary, you got plenty of trouble."

"Carmella, don't tell anyone else about this."

"You don't have to tell me that. I don't spread curses. I stop them. You be a pretty woman and you be good for that Alissa child. I want you to be happy, but you can find no happiness while you got that secret a-hauntin' you."

"Thank you for your advice, Carmella." Julienne

escaped the steamy hut, her clothing sticking to her moist skin.

She mounted Seabiscuit and turned to wave at the old woman, but she was nowhere to be seen. Brush rustled off to one side, and Julienne thought she saw a flash of reddish blond hair as she placed her hat on over her own dark auburn hair. Ootay, no doubt. He saw everything that went on. She wondered if he might have seen who had locked her in the shed. Next time, she'd ask him. Of course, catching him long enough to talk to him wouldn't be easy. He was like an ocean wave, here and gone.

Thinking over Carmella's uncanny intuition and advice, Julienne urged Seabiscuit into a lope back to the estate. She left the winded horse in Danny's hands and went to the house. Once she stepped inside, she felt something different. The quiet was deafening.

Julienne walked into the kitchen, but it was empty. She went upstairs and changed from her riding clothes into a summery dress of white with printed cabbage roses on it. She located Alissa in the backyard where she had persuaded Buccaneer to hang a rope swing from the oak tree. Alissa didn't bother to stop the swing, but flew out of it and landed lightly on her feet.

"Papa came home, but he's gone now."

"Where is everyone? I didn't see Rosa inside." She bent and kissed Alissa's cheek.

"Rosa's in her room."

"Is she ill?"

Alissa shook her head, making her dark ringlets bounce. "She's just sad today."

"Why? What's happened?"

Alissa's gray eyes were solemn as she looked up at Julienne. "Everybody's 'membering."

"Remembering what?"

"When Papa married Mama."

Julienne crouched in front of Alissa. "What about when Papa married Mama?"

"It was today that he married her. Rosa talked to Papa when he came home a while ago, and he got sad and left again. Rosa's eyes were full of tears, and she said she had to go to her room. She's real sad."

Julienne closed her eyes for a moment, slightly sickened as Alissa's meaning washed over her. "Their anniversary. Today's their anniversary."

"That's it. Anna-ver-sorry. When Papa married Mama. But it was a long time ago, wasn't it? Years and years. Before I got here."

Julienne ran a hand over Alissa's soft, black hair. "That's right. Get on the swing and I'll push you."

Alissa hitched herself onto the plank seat and held on to the ropes as Julienne stood behind her and sent her off toward the blue sky. Her giggles grew as the swing soared higher. Julienne looked toward the horizon and wondered if Buccaneer had gone back to the fields or was off somewhere remembering his other wife—the one he had called magnificent.

She couldn't even have a wedding date that wasn't tainted by Magdalena's memory. Only two weeks separated her anniversary from the one Buccaneer had shared with Maggie.

"Alissa, do you remember your mother's birth date? When was it?"

Alissa looked back at her as the swing sailed upward. "I 'member. Two days before Christmas!"

Julienne smiled bitterly. There goes another happy holiday at Moonspell. She glanced at the blue sky and wondered if someone up there was having a good, long laugh.

Chapter 22

Sitting in the front parlor with the pages of Magdalena's diary in her lap, Julienne finished reading the last entries Maggie had penned. Fear emanated from each sentence. Maggie had known that she'd fallen into a trap and that she couldn't get out of it by herself. She needed help, she'd written, but she had nowhere to turn.

I thought of confiding in Rosa, but I don't want her thinking bad of me. To dear Rosa I am flawless, and I so enjoy being perfect in someone's eyes.

He was angry last night when I spurned him. I know he will seek revenge on me. He can no longer trust me with his dark secrets, and he will try to insure my silence. I should tell someone. Perhaps I will speak to my uncle, although that old man could do little or nothing if challenged by a younger, ruthlessly stronger man. My only hope is my own fatal charm. I've been able to control him, and I might still exercise some power over him. Maybe even enough to save me from him.

"Julienne?"

The voice jarred her to her soul. Julienne stuffed the papers between the chair's cushion and arm even as her gaze flew to Cesare. His eyes questioned her.

"I startled you. Forgive me." Cesare walked closer to her. "What are you doing in here? Reading?"

"Yes. Yes, I was . . . reading some letters." She winced, hating herself for lying. "Has Buccaneer returned?"

Cesare sat on the footstool near her. "No. You shouldn't wait up for him."

"I'm worried. He's never missed dinner before." She looked toward the windows, covered with heavy drapes. "He could be out there injured. Maybe his horse threw him."

"More likely he is off somewhere drinking." Cesare shook his head at her look of concern. "It is a male reaction to memories once thought buried. Don't worry about him. He will return. It is best that he is away from you while he licks his wounds." Cesare reached out to pat her arm. "Why not go to bed. He will be here come morning."

She smiled, but wasn't in the least comforted by his conjecture that Buccaneer was off somewhere getting roaring drunk. "Cesare, before Maggie died, did she seem afraid or depressed?"

He frowned. "Not that I recall." He glanced up at the woman's portrait. "She was high-strung and nervous as a Thoroughbred filly. It was difficult to know what was going on behind those green eyes of hers." Memories softened his smile. "That was one of her gifts, I suppose. The mystery of her attracted many a man."

"Was she often afraid of Buccaneer?"

"Afraid of Buck?" His gaze swept back to Julienne. "I don't believe this is so. They fought, but I don't think she was afraid of him. Magdalena was a confident woman and was convinced she could handle any man—even Buck."

Julienne leaned forward and lowered her voice. "Cesare, do you think he killed her?"

Cesare sat back as if she'd spit in his face. "You think I would work here, side by side with a man I thought murdered my own niece? Worry for him has addled your brains, Julienne. You should get some rest. You are not yourself. You don't believe such a thing of him, do you? Your own husband?"

Julienne scooted back into the wing chair, letting it curve around her like a protective shell. "Someone killed her."

"*Sí*, but not Buck. You married him thinking he killed his wife?"

She shook her head. "No, of course I don't ... didn't ..." She sighed. "You're right. I'm not thinking straight. Forgive me." She tried to smile, but her lips felt weighted. "I think I'll read awhile before I retire, but you go on to bed, Cesare."

Cesare shrugged one shoulder. "Very well. Good night, Julienne."

"Good night." She rested her head against the back of the chair and closed her eyes, listening as Cesare's tapping boot heels faded. Her fingers touched the pages of Maggie's diary, but she didn't pull them out of their hiding place. She'd read it all now and was more confused than ever about what happened between Maggie and Buccaneer.

Cursed diary, she fumed, wishing she'd never discovered the vile pages. They'd served only to weaken her belief in Buccaneer and strengthen her feelings of inferiority. She opened her eyes and stared at Maggie's portrait, trying for the umpteenth time to discern something in the mixture of paints that created the perfection of Maggie's face and figure. The woman in the portrait seemed to be smirking tonight, not smiling. Julienne tore her gaze from Maggie's beautiful face and stared at the necklace Maggie dangled from her fingers. The colors of Maggie. Red, black, and green. What colors would be appropriate for Buccaneer? Julienne wondered. Black for his hair, silver for his eyes, and gold for the moments she shared with him.

He had the power to make her feel every inch a woman.

"Did he make you feel that way, too?" she whispered to the portrait. "Why did it go wrong with you? Was it his fault or yours?"

She'd give Buccaneer one month to remove Maggie's portrait, and if he hadn't done so by that time, Julienne decided she'd take it down herself. One month, she thought, glancing at the portrait, and then Magdalena won't be smirking down at me anymore.

Curling her legs into the chair, she snuggled more deeply into its confines and closed her eyes. She would wait for him, she thought before she fell into a light, dreamless sleep.

When she opened her eyes again, he was standing in front of her, but he wasn't looking at her. He was looking at Maggie. His raw, impassioned expression twisted her heart.

"Buccaneer, are you all right?" she asked, struggling up from her slumped position in the chair. "I've been worried about you."

"Have you now?" His gaze chilled her to the bone. "You know what day it is, don't you? Someone has told you by now, I'm sure of it."

"Yes. Your and Maggie's anniversary."

"That's right. I'd forgotten until Rosa reminded me earlier." Some dark emotion twitched the corner of his mouth. "Then it all came back to me."

"Your love for her?"

He tipped back his head and closed his eyes. "My love for her," he repeated, but it sounded hollow, as if coming from a bottomless well. "And you were worried about me."

"Of course. You didn't come home for dinner."

"Did you think I was off somewhere pounding some defenseless woman with a broomstick?"

She cringed from his wicked intent. "Let's not

quarrel." She reached for his hand. "Let's go to bed."

"You go on. I'll sleep in here."

Julienne glared at him, and her resolve to wrench him free of Maggie's hold intensified. She stood up and pressed herself against his side. "If you want to sleep in here, so be it."

She went toward the archway and pulled out the pocket doors on either side until they met in the middle. Glancing once over her shoulder to make sure he was watching her, she flipped the tiny latch into place and then turned to face him.

"I know what you need."

He lifted his brow in that devastatingly debonair way that always made her heart pound. "You do, do you? And what is that?"

"Me. All of me." Julienne stood before him, expecting him to touch her, hold her. When he didn't move a muscle, anger fired her courage and singed her pride. She wrapped her arms around his neck and kissed him, openmouthed, the way she knew he liked it.

For a few moments he didn't respond, and despair blasted through her, but then she felt his arms go around her waist and his tongue speared her mouth. He tasted of whiskey, and she realized he'd been drinking even as he swayed slightly, the liquor and the passion playing havoc with his equilibrium. Julienne stepped back and began unbuttoning the front of her flowered dress. His intense gaze and his ragged breathing restored her self-confidence.

"You want me, Buccaneer? Do you want me?"

His eyes were all smoke. "Every inch, and I want you to take every inch of me."

He grabbed either side of her dress and yanked, sending the covered buttons bouncing to the floor. Julienne gasped, her mouth falling open in surprise, and then his tongue filled it, driving all rational thought from her head. She stroked his tongue with hers and pulled at the collar of his shirt to loosen the crisscrossed ties in front. Finally she slipped her hands under his shirt and caressed his smooth back and broad shoulders. He palmed her buttocks, rubbing and pulling her closer to him. He moved his thigh against her mound, up and down until she felt herself grow moist. She tore her mouth from his to cry out his name, and he branded the length of her throat with hot, urgent kisses.

He propped one of his boots against the edge of the coffee table and shoved it against the fireplace grate, creating room in front of it to lay Julienne down on the soft wool rug. Before he joined her there, he tugged off his boots and socks, then stood astraddle her while he unbuckled his belt and unbuttoned his fly.

Julienne trembled, anxious to have her hands on him, to melt her mouth upon his, to clutch him to her as she would a treasure. She pushed her dress off her shoulders and untied the ribbons of her chemise. Slowly she bared her breasts to him. She arched her back, offering up her tight, throbbing nipples. He came down on one knee and cupped her breasts in his hands. His mouth was a flame on her sensitive skin, and his tongue circled her nipples until she almost sobbed with rapture.

Frantic, she worked his trousers off his hips and took him in her hands. He was impossibly hard, and the mystique of his masculinity cast its spell over her. She parted her thighs, and his hand slid under her skirt and up her leg to the pulsing heart of her. He stroked her, slipping two fingers inside while his thumb teased the tiny crest of passion until she begged him to stop. She lay back and pulled him on top of her. He entered her swiftly, and she closed her eyes as the pure pleasure of having him inside her again astounded her.

God, how she loved him! She tried to telegraph
her feelings through her hands and lips and
tongue. He moved inside her, setting off ecstatic
contractions. Julienne hugged him with her legs
and stroked his bowed back. His tongue bathed
her nipples and he impaled her over and over
again. Each plunge into her body took her breath
and sent her closer and closer to that white-hot
peak she wanted. He reared up, his arms sliding
under her back, and lifted her as he thrust hard.
He bared his teeth and closed his eyes, gripped by
his own powerful release. She felt him pump inside her twice before reaching her own vortex. She
sank her teeth into his shoulder and sucked hard,
drawing the taste of him into her mouth. He
kissed her nape, and his body was slick against
hers. Their crumpled clothing stuck to them,
bunched between their bodies. Some of her senses
returned. The first thing she noticed was that he
was still hard in her. He still needed her, and she
still burned for him.

Her mouth found his and her tongue breached
his lips. He courted her tongue as he sat up and
pulled her into his lap and onto his stiffening organ. She trailed her fingers through the mat of
hair on his chest. He leaned back, giving her room
to explore, and she settled the circle of her lips
around one of his brown nipples. When he sucked
in a noisy breath, she bit him gently, just enough
to make him flinch. His hands came up behind her
and he grabbed her hair, forcing her head back.
His mouth flowered on hers and he thrust his hips
forward, rocking into her, his forearms flattening
against her shoulder blades. Her passion-heavy
breasts rubbed his hairy chest and her nipples responded, tightening from the friction. She wound
her fingers in the hair that curled against his neck
and flung back her head. Her bones liquified and
she lost herself in the wild ride as he bucked be-

neath her and his breathing sounded like a bellows in her ear.

"*Oui, oui, oui,*" he rasped with each desperate lunge. "Take me. Take me. All of me."

"Now, please, now," Julienne whispered before a moan broke loose and trembled on her lips. She felt the hot tip of him ram into her center core. Again she climaxed in a shuddering, trembling tumble. Her hair spread over her shoulders, across her flushed cheeks, her trembling chin, and into the moist corners of her mouth. Her heart sounded like a drum in her ears.

When the passion had ebbed enough to give her back her mind, she realized that he was still inside her, but he was spent. She opened her eyes and slowly, slowly righted her head to look at him. He was staring past her shoulder, and she didn't have to follow his line of sight to know what he was looking at. Maggie's portrait.

Julienne scrambled up, flipping her skirts down and tugging her chemise together. Her breasts felt bruised, swollen. Fury pounded her, hammering her temples and her heart.

"You bastard."

He blinked up at her.

"How dare you make love to me and think of her! I won't have it, you hear? I'm tired of trying to be her, of trying to make you forget her! I'm sick and tired of it."

He tugged his shirt down over his chest and stuffed himself back into his trousers. "What in hell are you talking about? You've got no right to complain. You reached the peak so many times, I lost count."

"I'm not talking about that. I'm talking about you and your insane obsession with your dead wife." She pointed at the portrait. "Her. It's her you want."

He pushed himself to his feet. "You're the one

who sounds insane, not me. I wanted you just now."

"Of course you did," she said with a bitter laugh. "But you were thinking about her while you were inside of me. You've used me for the last time, Buccaneer LaFlamme. I thought I could drive her from your heart, your head, your soul, but I can't. I give up." She turned to glare at Maggie. "You win, Magdalena. He's yours. All yours. I guess he's never been mine, except in my dreams."

"Using you?" He hooked a hand on her elbow and spun her back to him. "Stop talking to that damned painting and talk to me! What do you mean, I've been using you? I've never said I was still in love with my dead wife. You got that inside your head all by yourself, so don't blame me for your own foolishness."

"And don't treat me like an imbecile," she returned, flinging off his hand. "You only married me to give your daughter another mother and to give yourself a female body that you could imagine was Maggie's. You never saw me. You never loved me."

"What brought this on? That scare in the shed? You still think I did that, don't you? You think I'm crazy as a loon." He grabbed her arms and brought her up on her tiptoes. "If anyone is crazy, it's you!" Then he shoved her away from him so abruptly that she stumbled and fell into the chair.

Julienne heard the rattle of papers. Maggie's papers. "I can't live in her shadow anymore, Buccaneer. I can't be her for you." Her fingers slipped past the cushion and touched the edges of the papers.

"Why, you ungrateful little wench," he ground out, coming toward her, his fisted hands swinging at his sides. He rounded the chair to stand behind her, and she could feel the searing heat of his anger on the top of her head. "You dare to accuse me of using you when I have done everything but fall to my knees before you in abject adoration."

Julienne stared straight ahead, one hand clutching the chair arm while her other slipped farther beside the cushion where Maggie's papers rustled. Buccaneer's hands suddenly circled her neck and his fingertips pressed against her throat. Julienne gasped and trapped her breath in her chest. His fingers moved, tightened, and she swallowed convulsively. He leaned over to whisper in her ear.

"I could strangle you for being so blind."

She swallowed again. "You're not frightening me."

"I'm not trying to frighten you, you little fool. I'm trying to get your attention." He craned around to see her face. "Do I have it?"

She nodded.

"Good. Then listen carefully. I tried to bare my heart and soul to you, but you were too busy looking for ghosts to see what I wanted to show you— only you." His fingers moved, caressing her now and slipping to her shoulders. "Maybe my heart and soul are so black, you couldn't see them. That's possible. Entirely possible." His hands fell away and he sat in the chair across from her, dejected and gloomy.

Incensed by his scare tactics and his nightmarish moods, Julienne sprang up from the chair. She fished the diary papers from between the cushion and chair arm and shook them in his face.

"This is where your heart and soul reside, Buccaneer. Not with me." She flung them in his lap. They scattered, some falling like dead leaves around his feet. "Read them and weep for your long-lost love, but don't you dare come to me later and fall on me like a starving man. It's not me you hunger for; it's her. It's always been her." She choked back a sob and wrestled for her dignity.

Buccaneer stared at the pages and lifted one slowly, his eyes moving from side to side as he read. "This is Maggie's handwriting."

"It's her diary."

He hitched himself higher in the chair, his gaze sharpening. "What? Her diary? I didn't know she kept one. Where did you get this?" he demanded, glaring at her.

"I found it in the Bride's House. It was hidden in the fireplace."

"When did you find it?"

"Right after I arrived." She lifted her chin to deflect his accusing scowl. "I should have given it to you straightaway, but I decided to read it and see if I could glean some insight to you ... how to please you, how to attract you." She pulled her lower lip between her teeth. "I wanted you to fall in love with me."

He looked through the pages and picked up the ones off the floor. "You've read all of it?"

"Yes."

"And you kept it from me?"

She pulled at her clothing, suddenly aware that she was half-dressed and that part of her body pulsed in the aftermath of him. She managed to pull the sides of her dress over her breasts and fastened the one button that was left.

"Well? Have you nothing to say?" he bellowed, soaring up from the chair, the papers gripped in his tight fists.

"Why are you so angry? You should be happy now, Buccaneer. You have your Maggie again—at least, you have her thoughts and her memories." She looked past him to the portrait. "You can gaze upon her beauty and you can read her glowing descriptions of you."

His eyes narrowed to slits. "If you've finished insulting me, you can get out of my sight."

Strangling a sob that clawed at her throat, Julienne turned away from him and went to the doors. She tore at the latch and then pushed one of the doors back far enough so that she could slip through. Tears blurred her vision and she let instinct guide her. She ran through the quiet house, along the dark corridor to the door that opened into the Bride's House.

She could get no farther than the center of the parlor before her legs gave out and she crumpled in a heap of misery. Her emotions poured out in a wash of hot tears and wrenching sobs. Her stomach ached, her throat burned, but it felt good to finally surrender to the dismal shambles of her life at Moonspell. She'd been living in a dream, thinking that Buccaneer loved her. She was glad to burst through into the real world again, however painful, however depressing.

Shame and despair coated her. She had bared herself to him, given her all to him and taken all he gave, only to discover that he had felt nothing for her. He had been thinking of Magdalena. He had been making love to Maggie in his mind and heart. Julienne buried her face in her hands, ashamed to have displayed her passion and her body to a man who wasn't the least bit interested in her.

A foreign sound broke through her sobs and she lifted her face to stare wildly around the parlor. Dazed, she realized she was in the Bride's House. Not the room she had shared with Buccaneer. Her heart had brought her to these quarters where all broken hearts of Moonspell had come to mend.

The handles on the French doors leading outside rattled. Julienne shrank back and clamped down on the scream rattling in her throat. Who . . . Buccaneer? Lorenzo? No, no. A woman, her sixth sense warned her.

"Magdalena?" Julienne croaked out the cursed name.

Suddenly the doors burst open and the sea breeze scurried in, not fresh-smelling as usual, but sour, stale. Julienne cried out and lifted a hand to ward off the inky shadow that loomed in the doorway and spilled across the rug.

338   Constance Laux

Her library until noon. Then he finished then on
much. That's when mamma. She wanted more to

Chapter 23

"**H**ush your mouth, silly girl!" Carmella advanced on Julienne, her face set in unrelenting lines of disapproval. "You wake the whole house if you don't be careful. What you screeching like that for anyways?"

Julienne recovered herself and bolted to her feet. She wiped tears from her cheeks and puffy eyes. "What are you doing coming in here like you own the place? You should have knocked."

"I been looking for you and I seen you in here. What you crying for? That curse be giving you troubles, I reckon." She squinted her strange eyes and peered around the dark parlor. "Where you keeping that diary of the dead woman?"

"It was over there." Julienne pointed toward the fireplace, and the old woman started for it. "But it's not anymore."

"Where is it?" Carmella demanded. "You supposed to give it to me, remember? I got to lift the curse off it."

"Buccaneer has it."

Carmella widened her eyes and planted a hand over her heart. "He found it?"

"No. I gave it to him."

The old woman moved with surprising zest as she rounded on Julienne, her bony hands grasping her by the shoulders to give her a sound shaking.

"You want that man cursed? You thinking you kill him and get all this for yourself?"

"No, of course not. Take your hands off me." Julienne wrenched free and retreated from the wild-eyed woman. "I told you I should have given it to him when I found it. It wasn't mine to read, and I'm paying the consequences now." She warded off another bout of self-pity by crossing to the open French doors. A shadowy figure darted from tree to tree. "Who is out there?"

"Ootay, probably. He followed me here." Carmella stalked her, thrusting her wrinkled face close to Julienne's. "You know what you've done? You gave that curse to the cap'n. No telling what will happen to him." She poked her fingers in Julienne's shoulder. "Better go get that diary back if you don't want his troubles on your head."

"Stop that," Julienne complained, angling away from the woman's blunt fingers. "I don't believe in curses and all that hocus-pocus you're so fond of."

"You gonna die just like them other brides," Carmella predicted, her watery eyes blaring with evil intent. "I seen that in the tea leaves, but I didn't say nothing 'cause I thought I could help you. All you had to do was give me that diary, but you done nailed your coffin shut. Cap'n Buck's, too. You done made that child of his an orphan."

"I won't listen to another word." Julienne pushed the woman through the open doors. "Get out and leave me alone. And next time, come to the front door and knock. I won't have you sneaking around and breaking into this house." Julienne spied the lithe figure slipping across the shadowed lawn. "And take Ootay with you."

Carmella hitched her patchwork shawl more tightly around her humped shoulders. "You be sorry, Key Largo girl. You be sorry. Better get that diary from the cap'n while you still can."

"Good night, Carmella." Julienne closed the

doors and locked them. Crazy old witch, she thought as she walked stoically through the parlor to the bedroom. She looked around at the furniture that used to hold her belongings. "Well, I'm back," she whispered, emotion gathering behind her eyes and in her throat. The Bride's House had claimed her once again. Was it destiny?

Drained by the events of the night, she removed her ravaged dress and underclothing and slipped into a cotton nightgown. She lay on the bed and missed the sound of Buccaneer's breathing and the weight of him on the mattress beside her. The pillow under her cheek was damp with her tears before she fell asleep.

Again Julienne awakened to find Buccaneer standing beside her, his bare chest gleaming in the semidark as if it had been oiled. She sat bolt upright in bed and flung her hair back from her face. Her eyes felt gritty with the aftermath of her tears, and a dull headache invaded her temples. Buccaneer held the pages of Maggie's diary in one fist. His chest rose and fell as if he'd run a mile, but Julienne suspected his ragged breathing was the result of his tumultuous emotions. She could read anger and betrayal and remorse on his handsome face and in his enigmatic eyes. Impulsively she reached out and lightly touched his forearm. The black hair covering it was as soft as down, but his arm was hard and warm like sun-baked granite.

"You've read it? All of it?"

He flung the papers at her, and they scattered across the rose-colored bedspread. "She duped you just as she duped everyone else around here."

"What do you mean? Are you upset with what she wrote about you?"

"I'm hardly even mentioned by her."

Julienne laughed, thinking he was making a joke. "Don't be silly. You're on virtually every page." She began gathering them up off the bed and thought what a lovely fire they'd make.

"I am not," he said, teeth gritted as if he were in pain. "The few times she writes about me, she calls me by name."

Julienne glanced through the pages in her hands and shook her head, looking at Buccaneer again. "But she—"

"When she's writing about her *lover*," he said, cutting her off with a voice that shook with suppressed rage, "she refers to him as 'he' or 'him' to protect his identity should her journal fall into the wrong hands. Namely, mine." He held out his big hands and clutched at the air in front of Julienne's face. "I had sworn that I would discover his identity and kill him. Maggie knew I meant it." He leaned forward to lock gazes with Julienne. "I still do."

"You mean . . ." She swallowed hard.

"Yes. I mean to kill him."

Julienne shook her head and sat back on her heels. "Don't talk like that, Buccaneer. I don't like it when you sound so . . . so—"

"Savage? Barbarian? You've called me that before. Well, dear wife, I *am* a barbarian!"

"No." She clutched his forearm with both hands. "You're not that."

He yanked his arm from her grasp. "You thought she was rhapsodizing about me, didn't you?"

Julienne nodded meekly and peered at him through her lashes. Shame built inside her until she thought she'd be sick. "You don't know who this man is that she wrote about?"

"I've always suspected Lorenzo, but Cesare swears that Lorenzo would never dally with a married woman." His lips curled in a sarcastic snarl. "I don't share Cesare's faith in Lorenzo's rules of conduct. I think he'd bed any woman, married or otherwise, if he decided he wanted her."

"If you suspect him, why not dismiss him? How can you stand to have him around if you think he cuckolded you?"

"Because if I send him away, then I'll never know for certain if he was the one or not, and I must be certain. Someday Lorenzo will make a fatal mistake . . . he will talk to the wrong person or confess something to Cesare . . . and I will have him." He closed his hand into a fist. "I'll have my revenge at last!"

"You . . . you think he killed her, too, don't you?"

He nodded. "Her lover killed her. Who else could it have been—other than me, of course?" His smile taunted her, fairly asking her to contradict him.

Julienne clamped her lips together, refusing to be led into another fight about not trusting him. He propped his fists on the edge of the mattress and leaned into her. His eyes glittered like quicksilver and he still smelled faintly of liquor, though she didn't think he was drunk. He seemed quite clearheaded and sure about what he wanted—although she hadn't a clue.

"You thought all this time that he was me, didn't you?" he asked, his voice dipping to a hoarse, slightly menacing whisper. "I bet you're disappointed to discover the awful truth—that you've been courting the wrong man. You've tried to be like Maggie, tried to act like her, and you *are* like her in one way. You both fell hard for the man in that diary. Not with me."

Julienne shook her head, but couldn't find her voice. A trembling began in her center and spread outward to her extremities. She was suddenly aware of the thin material of her nightgown and that her nipples showed through. His gaze hadn't drifted there, but she knew he was also aware of those pink peaks poking against her white gown. She was also aware that his pride had taken a battering and there was little she could do at the moment to right the wrongs done him.

"I'm not him, but I am the man you married, and I retain my rights." He straightened and his hands went to his waistband. "I'm glad you're not wearing anything under that night shift. Take it off."

His intent slammed into her. Julienne recoiled and stared at him, noting his wolfish grin and his exaggerated breathing. He was going to take her! After their argument, after the tears, after the revelations of the diary, he was going to brand her his in anger and retribution. A traitorous part of her tingled with anticipation, and her heartbeats accelerated. Despite everything, she wanted him, too. But like this? No, not with revenge burning in his eyes.

"No, Buccaneer. Not now. Not when you're feeling this way."

"Are you going to remove that nightgown or must I rip it off you?"

She knew he would and she also knew that fighting him would serve no useful purpose. He meant to have her, with or without her cooperation. But she wouldn't surrender completely to him, she vowed as she sat on her knees and pulled the nightgown up over her head. She wouldn't give him the satisfaction of responding to him. He meant to teach her a lesson, but she would be the teacher. She would show him that anger would not melt her resistance. She would respond only to love and gentleness.

Flinging her nightgown aside, she glared at him, hoping to singe his pompous attitude with the damnation in her eyes.

"You are my lord and master and I am your willing slave," she recited with brassy contempt.

"Why, you little—" He bit off the rest and grabbed a handful of her hair, jerking her head back for his kiss. He pushed his trousers off his hips with his free hand and placed a knee on the mattress beside her, using his weight to press her onto her back.

She struggled briefly, her heart galloping, her senses blooming under his hands and mouth. His lips ground hers against her teeth and then his tongue plunged, a velvet dagger piercing her iron will. He plundered the slick walls of her mouth and tamed her rigid tongue, making her respond to his sleek caresses. When his mouth finally released hers, she was breathless and near collapse. Don't surrender, a voice inside her head screamed. Don't bend to his will.

His mouth continued its rampage, traveling down her throat to the valley between her breasts. He nuzzled her and flattened his tongue along the side of her left breast to the rising peak, across it and down the other side. She trembled and grasped the side of the headboard in both hands to keep herself from clutching him. Oh, how she wanted to caress him, to guide his cursed mouth to hers again! But pride prevented her from giving him that sign of surrender. Her fingers curved around the sleek wood of the headboard and her nails bit in, leaving their half-moon marks.

He moved to her other breast, giving it the flat of his tongue, licking her nipple like a big cat lapping up cream. Julienne increased her grip on the headboard and sank her teeth into her lower lip to keep from moaning in ecstasy. One of her nails broke, but she barely noticed. Her head reeled and her heart thundered in her ears. Oh, the power of him! She knew she couldn't take much more. His mouth . . . his wicked, wonderful mouth ravaged her.

Lower now. His lips caressed her quivering stomach and her inviting navel. The tip of his tongue dipped inside that crevice and traced the oval, dancing around and around until her head was spinning. His hands spanned her waist and tightened there as he kissed the skin below. Three more kisses and he was there—between her thighs and into the soft, moist folds of her. His cunning tongue found her most sensitive spot and pushed at it, lifted it, raced around it.

Julienne squeezed her eyes shut. God, how she wanted to cry out his name. Another fingernail broke. He blew hot breath against the damp curls. Julienne moaned low in her throat. Another nail snapped, to the quick. The flash of pain was quickly smothered by a tidal wave of pleasure. She could stand no more.

She released the headboard and clasped his head in her hands, holding him in place while his wickedly marvelous mouth sucked on her, osculated against her wet flesh to drink her in. She made low curring sounds in her throat. The flash of desire took her, shook her, made her cry out his name. His glorious name.

Buccaneer lifted himself, straining above her, his body a muscular, brown-skinned bow of taut restraint. He pushed her legs farther apart and aimed his stiff arrow of hot, satiny skin and turgid sinew. The tip of him breached her and then, slowly and methodically, he went deeper and deeper, his flesh widening her flesh, his muscle dividing her muscle, his will conquering her will. She ran her hands up his chest, her fingertips rasping through the slick black hair. Hooking her hands over the tops of his shoulders, she gained leverage to meet his driving motion. She wrapped her legs around him, above his hips, and crossed her ankles. She took him, all of him, and he smiled in utter satisfaction.

"You're so wet, so tight," he said, almost groaning the words. He bent his head, worshiping the sensations bombarding his body, his mind, his throbbing organ. He closed his eyes, ready to release the pressure building inside him. Then he thought of that diary. Of that other man she had been trying to please.

He opened his eyes and looked into her face—a face infused with passion, lips swollen with his kisses, eyes dark with desire. He rocked his hips, rubbing against her, knowing the friction would send her over the threshold. It did. She thrashed helplessly, garbled sounds filling her throat, her eyes tightly closed, her legs trembling around him but never letting go.

He slid a hand up her back, slick with perspiration, and gathered her dark auburn hair in one fist. Her eyes popped open.

"Say my name," he commanded. "No, don't say it. Yell it. Scream it to the heavens. Shout it to the devil."

"What . . . Please, do it. Come to me. Now. Please, now."

He jerked her hair, and she questioned him with those melting brown eyes that he found so captivating. "Shout my name so that there will be no mistaking who you want, so that heaven and earth and hell will know that I'm the one inside you, that I'm the one you're begging for. Do it, or I swear I'll pull out of you and empty myself on these bed linens." He thrust his face closer to hers. "Who am I, little jewel? Who is making you writhe and groan and quiver inside and out?"

"Buccaneer," she whispered, her eyes rolling back in her head. He tightened his grip in her hair, and her eyes focused on him. He eased out of her an inch and he saw panic rise in those brown depths like a storm on the horizon. She gathered in a great, gulping breath. *"Buccaneer! Buccaneer LaFlamme!"*

Her drove in to the hilt, lifting her hips off the bed and holding them aloft by cupping her soft, small buttocks. He fired into her in three short, powerful bursts, followed by one long flare that lit up his body and melted his bones. In the dim, intuitive recesses of his mind, he felt certain he'd impregnated her. Gradually the rest of his senses returned and he pulled out of her with a soft, moist sound of separation. She gave a little sob of farewell.

Buccaneer sat on the edge of the bed and rested his head in his hands. Damn her to hell, he couldn't hate her. Even though tonight she had filled him with dismay and self-loathing and self-doubt, he couldn't despise her for it. That diary. That's what he should hate. Those glowing sentences about another man that had not only wrested Maggie from him, but had seduced Julienne as well.

She moved behind him and he looked over his shoulder to see that she lay curled on her side, her knees drawn up to her chin. A smudged line of crimson stained the sheet near her hands.

"Did I hurt you?"

She shook her head. "But I hurt you."

"Yes, but I'll live." He stood up. "There's blood on the sheet."

"It's nothing. From my fingernail. I broke it."

He padded to the shuttered window and pushed it open, letting in a breeze that dried the vestiges of her from his body.

"Carmella was right," she said.

Buccaneer ran a hand down his chest, wiping away drops of sweat clinging to the tips of the black hair. "What made you think of her?"

"She was here tonight."

"Here? Where, here in the Bride's House?" He leaned a shoulder against the window frame and looked at her. She nodded, her cheek rubbing against the sheet. "When?"

"Earlier. She said that the diary had a curse on it and that it would bring trouble to whoever kept it. I should have given it to her instead of you. She said I placed the curse on you when I handed it over. She was very upset with me."

"You can't blame that old woman for the trouble between us."

She sat up in the center of the bed and gathered the sheet in front of her, hiding her pale breasts, belly, and thighs from him. She already knew his favorite parts, he thought with a self-mocking smile.

"But if I had given it to you the night I found it, things would be different between us."

He shrugged. "Perhaps. Who's to say?"

"You said you read all of it."

He nodded.

"Did you see how frightened she was at the end? She was sure someone was going to do her harm."

"And you thought that someone was me."

"It never occurred to me that she'd write so . . . so passionately about any man other than her husband. I knew she had moved into these quarters, but I thought you were still . . . well, sleeping with her every so often."

"Like I did with you tonight."

"I haven't moved out of our bedroom."

He waited until her gaze tracked to him. "But you will."

Her lips trembled. "Is that what you expect?"

He laughed, loving her naïveté and hating it also. "You liked it tonight, didn't you?"

She blanched. After a moment, she shook her head, her eyes cautious, wary.

"You like it rough like in the diary."

Julienne sucked in a breath, her eyes now wide with affront. "No!"

"I think, yes." He smiled at her murderous expression. "And I think the rough play has its place, but that's where it stops with me, my poor little jewel. I won't lower myself to the behavior described in Maggie's meanderings." He took a step toward the bed, and she gathered the sheet higher under her chin as if the flimsy linen could defy him for more than a moment's time. "I won't tie you up and tickle you with rushes and then beat you with thin strips of suede that leave ribbons of swollen flesh," he said, reciting from the diary. "And I won't gag you so that you can't scream. I won't sail embers over your body or rub burn weed over your nipples."

"I don't want that!" She let go of the sheet to plant her hands over her ears. "I never wanted those things done to me!"

He grabbed her wrists and forced her hands away from the sides of her head. "You were trying to provoke me into that behavior the night of the knife dance. You quoted from that damned diary and did so again tonight, so don't deny your baser desires. They've been revealed."

She struggled and somehow escaped his hold. Clutching at the sheet again, she stood up and backed against the headboard. "Get out. I mean it, Buccaneer. Get out or I'll scream my lungs out. I don't want you if you think such vile things of me."

He stared up at her, transfixed by her beauty. Flags of color rose in her cheeks, and her eyes burned with a pulsating fire. The sheet covered the front of her, but left exposed the long, shapely length of her legs. He felt himself begin to stiffen. He looked down at his naked body and then back up to her. She'd seen it, too. She shook her head.

"No. No more. We're no good for each other like this. Carmella's right. We have a shadow across us that has darkened our souls and distorted our feelings for each other."

"You can't blame the diary or Carmella or any stupid curse for what's happening to us. You never trusted me. Never. I couldn't figure out why you'd marry me if you thought I could lock you in a shed and try to frighten you to death or if I could murder two previous wives and get away with it. But then I read that diary and I figured it all out. You were hoping I'd turn into him and give you a good scare. You liked being in the shed. I should have made love to you after I got that broomstick out of your hands. That's what you wanted."

"Get out!" She picked up a heavy crystal vase from the bedside table and cocked her arm. "You sicken me with such talk!"

"We have one thing in common, my lovely jewel. We've both been chasing ghosts."

She went limp, falling to her knees and letting go of the vase. It thumped to the floor and rolled across the thick rug. She closed her eyes and a shining tear escaped from the corner of one eye and wet a path down her cheek. It hung on her chin, refusing to let go.

"I loved you, Buccaneer. Oh, how could I have ever loved you?"

Her words drilled his heart. He grabbed his trousers and retreated from her. In the parlor, he stepped into the pants and yanked them up over his hips. He felt punch-drunk as he swiveled his head and his gaze collided with his reflection in the full-length mirror. The man looking back at him was hollow-eyed, with a day's growth of stubble darkening his cheeks and chin. His hair was wild, finger-tossed, and lay in tangles against

his neck. Buccaneer could see only failure and fu-
tility in every line of his face.

I loved you. Oh, how could I have ever loved you?
How, indeed.

Chapter 24

The narrow band of sand edging Spirits Cove sparkled like sugar in the sun. Julienne leaped from rock to rock, holding up her skirts in front with one hand, until she reached the rock near the shipwreck. She sat on it, her feet dangling in the water, and stared at the ruins of what once had been a seaworthy beauty. It was a fitting study, she thought, on this morning after the storm that had wrecked what had been beautiful in her life.

Folding her knees up tight against her chest, she stared over the tops of them at the rippling sea, all blue and white and translucent green. Guilt nagged at her for dismissing Alissa's morning lessons and letting her tag along with Ursula, who was setting off for a neighboring homestead to buy beeswax candles and lye soap from an old woman there. Sensing the trouble brewing in the house, Ursula had been quick to invite Alissa along, and Julienne had been as quick to permit it. She would have been a worthless teacher today, she thought, since nothing but questions buzzed in her head in search of elusive answers.

For instance, what kind of taciturn patience did it require to work side by side, day after day, with a man one thought might be a murderer? How did Buccaneer do it? Why did Lorenzo continue on at Moonspell, knowing that his boss was living for the day when he could snuff out his life? And what of Cesare, knowing that the two young men he valued were headed for a duel that would leave one or both dead?

Staring out to sea, she remembered standing on this rock with Buccaneer. He'd reminded her so much of a swaggering, dangerous pirate that day. A chill tapped its way up her spine when she relived those horrible minutes in the cave ... touching skin ... someone's skin, and thinking it was Buccaneer. Who had been in the cave with her that day? She looked over her shoulder at the shore and the dark mouth of the cave. Lorenzo? What had he been doing, following them? Was he the one who howled like a wolf to frighten her?

She faced front again and the sea breeze washed over her, pushing her hair back over her shoulders as other memories tumbled in her mind. She had presumed that one person was responsible for the disturbances she'd suffered at Moonspell, but that didn't seem feasible now. Perhaps Rosa and Lorenzo were working in tandem. Rosa had never made any pretense of liking her, and Lorenzo had dogged her at every opportunity. Where did Buccaneer fit into all of this?

He doesn't, her heart spoke up, and Julienne smiled. She turned her cheek against her knees and closed her eyes against the sun. She was glad the man in the diary wasn't him. That man had frightened her and made her doubt that she could ever satisfy him without losing herself and the notions of romance she held dear. Her heart had known all along that Buccaneer couldn't be the man described in the diary. He'd shown no bent for such cruelty. He was moody, yes, but not maniacal. While he could be forceful, he was capable of surprising tenderness and—

Hot color washed up over her neck and cheeks as flashes of last night's wild coupling crashed through her. She had been furious with him for seeking revenge through lovemaking, but in the light of a new day she saw that she had done the same thing to him earlier when he'd come home after moping over Magdalena all day.

Magdalena. Julienne glared at the wreckage near her feet, and hatred pumped through her veins. How in the name of God could she fight that woman's ghost? She couldn't look at her portrait anymore without wishing for a knife with which to shred the canvas to ribbons. To win Buccaneer's love and then squander it on some demon who abused her and reduced her to a groveling slave was sheer madness! If only she could secure Buccaneer's heart, Julienne thought, she would never, *ever* jeopardize that treasure.

Treasure . . . Now, that was another puzzle. Magdalena had found buried treasure with the man in the diary here at Spirits Cove. Julienne had mentioned it to Buccaneer, and he had acted as if he knew nothing about it. Had Magdalena kept the discovery from him?

The questions numbed her mind, and she closed her eyes and drifted. The night's turbulence and her wakefulness sapped her energy, and she dozed on the warm rock with the ocean air caressing her skin, combing her hair, and whispering in her ears.

When she opened her eyes again, she sensed a change in the air and smelled rain. She lifted her head and examined the approaching clouds blotting the horizon. Raising her hands above her head, she stretched and twisted from side to side, unkinking muscles and reviving nerve endings. One of her feet had fallen asleep, and she tapped it against the boulder until it tingled from a thousand pinpricks. She supposed she should be getting back, but she was loath to face that imposing house again with all its dark secrets. She must speak to Buccaneer about giving the old place a new look.

If she remained at Moonspell, that is. Even that was at question. She knew one thing for certain— she didn't want to move back into the Bride's House. If he suggested it, she would absolutely refuse to follow meekly in those other wives' footsteps. To her mind, that had been their downfall. Once they had been ensconced in that attached structure, they had ceased to be part of the household or of its master. They had become islands, with no protection against the storm-tossed environs of Moonspell.

She stared at the sharp coral visible through the glassy sea and thought of the hidden dangers and how they could rip right through life before one could steer a different course.

The waves kicked up, drenching her booted feet and the hem of her forest green skirt. She inched back, and two small crabs scuttled backward with her onto drier rock. One of them bumped into her hand and reached out a claw to give her a pinch.

"Oh, no you don't," Julienne said, removing her hand from easy reach. "I have as much right to this rock as you." She stood and wrung seawater from her skirt's hem as she examined the encroaching storm. Well, it's coming, she told herself, so there's nothing left to do but take yourself home ... such as it is.

Pivoting, she gained her balance and prepared to leap to the next rock. She looked toward shore to make sure that Seabiscuit was still tethered to the leaning palm tree. The big gelding rubbed his side against the tree, scratching himself. Satisfied, Julienne jumped to the next rock, teetered, then held fast to her balance. She wished for Buccaneer's strong arms and solid bulk.

Thunder rolled, startling her, and her left boot slipped out from under her, driving her down on her right knee. She moaned as hot pain exploded around her kneecap. Seabiscuit whinnied. Julienne looked toward him, hoping he wouldn't bolt. He stood steady. Her gaze sharpened on something that moved through the swaying palm trees. A shadow. A ghost of a figure, crouching . . . or was that a rock?

"Hey, there! Anyone there? Buccaneer, is that you?" she called, cupping her hands around her mouth. The first raindrops plopped on her forearms and the crown of her head. She'd have to hurry to beat the storm.

She took the next rock without mishap, although her knee pained her something fierce. She paused to lift her skirt and examine it. Nothing was broken, but it was definitely bruised. The color was already changing from blotchy red to faintly violet. Lovely. She curled up her lip and dropped her skirt. The next boulder was flat and wider, and she stood on it a few moments to get her breath.

Directing her attention to the shore again, she saw that the crouching shadow was gone . . . No, it had moved. Farther down the beach, closer to her, it squatted among the palmetto. A man. She knew it was a man and not an apparition.

"Buccaneer?" she called again. "Lorenzo?" she whispered, and a trickle of fear slipped down her spine. She shivered and sent up a quick prayer, then jumped to the next rock and the next. She took the shore at a run, heading straight for Seabiscuit.

The horse swung its head, watching her approach. Julienne reached out, ready to grab the reins. The reins . . . they looked funny . . . short. A shrill whistle pierced the air and Seabiscuit tossed his head. The short reins flew up as the big horse whirled and bolted along the beach.

"No! Seabiscuit, whoa! Stop!" Julienne ran a few

paces before she realized that giving chase was futile. Seabiscuit was already a dot in the distance. "Blast your hide!" she shouted after him.

Laughter, low and sinister, rumbled behind her. Julienne whirled, expecting to find Lorenzo grinning like Carmella's monkey at her. Nothing. No one. She whipped her gaze to the place where the man had been hiding, and of course, he was no longer there.

"Who is it?" she demanded, fear rising in her like the approaching storm. A raindrop plopped on her shoulder. Another splashed upon her cheek. The laughter sounded again, not as distant this time. He was getting closer. "Coward! Show yourself."

A wolf howled, no more than six feet from where she stood. Julienne didn't bother to look. She didn't want to see. Lightning flashed and thunder cracked, and she made a wild dash through the underbrush in the general direction of the bridle path.

To her ears, her breathing sounded as loud as hurricane gales. She thrashed through tall grass, low shrubs, and finally located the bridle path.

Damn that horse for bolting and leaving her to be stalked by some wolf-howling madman! She tried to listen for footfalls behind her, but heard nothing except her own pounding heart and raspy breath. Rain dotted the dirt path and thunder grumbled, making the air vibrate with expectation.

Julienne made herself stop. She spun about to face her terror and stared, wild-eyed, at no one, nothing, save a darting lizard. Listening to her own booming heart, she waited and watched. Nothing still. She spotted a fallen branch at the side of the path, small enough to carry and big enough to cosh someone. Moving cautiously, she went to it and bent slowly, ever watchful of an ambush. Through the tall grass and lacy ferns she saw a flash of reddish brown and the soft thud of hooves on grass. She forgot the branch and stumbled toward the horse. Her gaze fell on the reins—long reins, not sliced in half—and then the saddle with its high pommel and fancy braided trim. The steed turned its white-starred face toward her. Wrong horse.

"Hey, there, little señora!"

Julienne faced her attacker with fisted hands and murder in her eyes. Lorenzo retreated a step, his own eyes bulging.

"What's wrong with you? The devil giving you chase?"

"You demented worm!" Julienne pushed him hard, making him stumble. "I know you've been following me and howling at me like some ... some animal. No more! Do you hear me? No more!"

Lorenzo's black eyes snapped with fury. "You loco, lady? What's with you? I done nothing to you but say hello."

"Hello, my foot!" She faced him with a courage that went only skin-deep. Inside, she trembled. "I'm telling Buccaneer this time. I've tried not to stir up trouble for you, but you've gone too far." She grabbed the horse's reins and swung up into the saddle.

"Hey, what you think you're doing with my horse?" Lorenzo started toward her.

Julienne dug her heels into the horse's sides, and it reared. "I'm taking it since you spooked mine. Get away or I'll make sure this horse leaves its hoofprints all over your back."

The horse settled on all fours again, and Julienne nudged him with her boot heels again. This time the big gelding shot forward, taking the bridle trail at a fast gallop and leaving Lorenzo to yell Spanish obscenities at the top of his lungs.

Good! she thought with malice. Hope you choke

on those words, Lorenzo. Spooking horses, howling, tracking. She'd tell Buccaneer and let him handle Lorenzo. She hoped Buccaneer banished him from Pirate's Key forever. She reined the horse to a brisk walk and relaxed. Her heartbeats slowed to normal, and she rolled her shoulders. A few minutes ago, she'd dreaded returning to Moonspell, and now she looked forward to it. She prayed that the rest of her day would be utterly dull and boring in comparison.

Buccaneer examined the leaves in the drying shed and then checked on the fire. A boy, no older than fourteen, sat near the door and fanned himself.

"How are you doing today, André?"

"I doing okay," the boy answered in heavily accented English.

"Your father tells me you're saving your money to buy some netting and crab pots."

He nodded. "I open me a fish market someday."

"Here on Pirate's Key?"

"Mebbe so, if you let me, Cap'n Buck."

Buccaneer cuffed him playfully on the shoulder. "I'm glad to see you're making plans for yourself. No wonder Jean-Michel is so proud of you. Why, he can't hardly pick a bent without stopping to brag about you."

"How many bents he pick yesterday?"

Buccaneer shrugged. "A lot, but I don't know the exact number of rows he traveled. Why?"

"Oh, he telling my mama he done picked ten, eleven bents, but a big old dragonfly done flied up his nose and made him lose count. Says all's he could do was start over with the number first."

Buccaneer grinned at the grand lie. "The number one, André," he corrected. He leaned a shoulder against the doorframe and appreciated the sight of tobacco leaves sewn to laths for curing. Cesare had brought in additional crew last week, Cubans and a few Jamaicans. The waiting was over and the monotony had changed to industry. In the fields, pickers worked in tandem, plucking the leaves and placing them in baskets, held by other workers called "draggers."

Instead of being paid by the week, now pay was by the bent picked, a bent being the space between two posts on a single row. The shading tents were no longer white, but had turned gray from dirt and wind and rain.

"Good crop, Cap'n?" André asked, breaking into his musings.

"Not bad. We were hit hard by worms and we were lucky that it was early in the season so we could plant again. We had to leave one field fallow, though, because the worms were so bad."

"Them wireworms, they is a plague."

"I should move on and check on the other sheds." He inspected the fire pit. "You could use some more fuel here, André."

"I know, suh. Señor Lorenzo gone to fetch it."

"When was he here?" Buccaneer heard the sharpness in his voice and saw that the boy had noticed the change in his tone, too. He'd meant to keep an eye on Lorenzo, but had lost sight of him hours ago.

"Not long. Short of an hour, mebbe."

Blaze whinnied, and Buccaneer turned to peer outside into the day that had grown gray with encroaching rain. His heart bolted to his throat when he saw a riderless Seabiscuit, his reins dangling and broken.

"What the hell is this?" he muttered, barging outside and grabbing Seabiscuit by the mane. "Whoa, son." He examined the horse and then the reins. Cut. Sliced neatly with a knife or sword. "Son of a bitch!"

"Whose horse is that, Cap'n?" André asked from the doorway of the shack.

"My wife's."

"She get throwed, you think?"

"Doesn't look like it." Buccaneer tied a lead rope to Seabiscuit's bridle and then mounted Blaze. "If she comes along, tell her to wait here for me."

"Will do, suh."

Buccaneer tracked Seabiscuit's course, alert to flattened grass, broken twigs, and hoofprints in the dust. He tried not to think the worst, but worry knotted his stomach and cinched his gut. Not again, his mind kept repeating. Not again. Not my jewel.

Time crept by as the day grew darker and raindrops splattered his shoulders and thighs. It seemed like an eternity before he heard movement ahead of him and spurred Blaze onto a narrow track connecting drying sheds. Lorenzo walked along the path. He waved wearily, but surprise flitted across his handsome features. To Buccaneer, he looked guilty as hell.

Buccaneer propelled himself from the saddle and plowed a fist into Lorenzo's face, knocking him off his feet. "Goddamn you, you murdering son of a bitch! What have you done to her?"

Lorenzo sputtered, spitting blood and cursing floridly in Spanish. He scrambled to his feet. "You loco, man?" He dabbed at his bleeding lips and grabbed the hilt of the knife protruding from his belt. "You stay away or I will cut you, man. I will slit your throat."

"Not before I slice off that pitiful noodle dangling between your legs and stuff it down your gullet. Where is she?"

"She, who? That wife of yours? She's as loco as you, man."

Buccaneer planted a boot, then another, closing

in. Lorenzo stepped backward. "You know where she is."

"I know where she *was*," Lorenzo corrected, tilting a head in the opposite direction. "I ran into her back there and she took my horse from me." His gaze skittered to the big bay. "You found hers, I see. She thought I'd spooked her horse. *Dios mío,* what's going on around here?" He swiped at the blood dribbling from his mouth onto his chin.

"*You* tell *me* what's going on."

"*Sabe Dios!* I was going for wood, minding my own business, and your woman came out of nowhere and took my horse. Then you come along and loosen my teeth, and for what? What have I done?" He spread out his arms in a grand shrug.

"Murder. Remember that? Remember Magdalena, you swine?"

"You talk crazy again. What have I got to do with Maggie?"

"And Selena. You would have killed her if I hadn't told her to leave."

"I have killed no one. You are the one everybody points to when that comes up. The murderer of Moonspell is what they call you."

Buccaneer lunged and grabbed Lorenzo by the collar. The man was quick and had the point of his knife against Buccaneer's throat before Buccaneer could react.

"I don't want to cut you," Lorenzo said. "You let me go. I will help you find her. She took my horse, I tell you, and she is probably back at home by now."

Buccaneer forced himself to open his hand. Lorenzo retreated, but didn't return his knife to its sheath. He stared at Buccaneer a few moments as thunder sounded overhead and raindrops tapped against leaves and fronds. Lorenzo shook his head slowly.

"*Está loco por ella,*" he muttered.

"Maybe I am crazy for her, but I'm not crazy. I know that you and Maggie were lovers and that you killed her."

"Me and Magdalena?" Lorenzo jabbed a thumb into his own chest and gave a short laugh. "Cesare told me you had this in your head, and I could not believe it. Me and Maggie?" He laughed again. "She treated me like all the other field workers— dirt under her feet. You were always blind when it came to her."

"Not always. Now, tell me what you've done with Julienne."

"You deaf, man? I told you that she took my horse." He paused, struggling with something, then added, "She looked scared, like something had happened to her."

Buccaneer balled his fists, ready to reduce Lorenzo to bloody pulp. "If you've harmed one hair on her head, I'll—"

"Cap'n Buck, Cap'n Buck!"

Both men whirled toward the screeching voice. Carmella emerged from the thick underbrush, her white hair in wild disarray, her orange dress torn at the neck. She practically collapsed in Buccaneer's arms. He carried her to a fallen tree and set her on the ground, propping her crooked trunk against the tree's straight one. Carmella gasped for breath, her mouth opening and closing, air wheezing in and out of her laboring lungs.

"She needs water." Lorenzo bent over the old woman and smoothed her hair from her face. "Go easy, old woman."

Buccaneer fetched the canteen from his saddle supplies and tipped the bottle to the crone's cracked lips. She drank and gurgled, then pushed the bottle aside.

"You gotta do something 'fore it's too late, big Buck," she implored, latching on to his forearm and digging her short, dirty nails into his skin. "She gonna be next."

"What are you babbling about?" Buccaneer asked. "I can't be bothered with this now. Lorenzo, see to her. I'm going back to the house to see if Julienne's there."

"He gonna kill her, Cap'n Buck. He gonna take another bride from you this day. I seen it in his eyes and in the leaves. I seen it."

Buccaneer swiveled around to her again. "Who are you talking about?" He glanced at Lorenzo. "Him? You know something about Lorenzo here?"

Lorenzo had sheathed his knife, but he rested a hand on its hilt again, ready to draw it out if needed. "You got your mind stuck, Buck."

"I know nothing of no Lorenzo," Carmella said. "I speak of the boy."

"Boy? What boy?" Buccaneer crouched in front of her. "Try and make sense, old witch."

"Ootay! Ootay and Maggie, they sinned together, so I said nothing. Let them burn in hell, I think. God will judge. But this little jewel, she be no sinner. The leaves tell me she has pure heart and should not die. She love you, big Buck, and she true to you."

"Ootay?" Buccaneer soared to his feet. "Ootay and Maggie?" He clamped a hand to his throbbing forehead where his beliefs shifted and toppled and visions of Ootay with Magdalena reared up. "I never knew her," he whispered, stunned. "Maggie with Ootay? My God! I never knew anything about her."

"That's right," Carmella piped up again. "Ootay think that Key Largo girl done figured out it was him in the diary. That he's the one that found that treasure with Maggie."

Treasure? Buccaneer spun away from the old woman as Lorenzo made her drink more water. He ran a distracted hand over his face and tried to grasp this startling turn of events. Maggie had chosen Ootay as her lover. Ootay. He shook his head, finding it hard to accept since it proved that he had lived with a woman for years and had never really known her. All this time Ootay had been right under his nose, and Buccaneer had never seen him, never suspected him of anything but laziness. He looked at Carmella again, recalling his last visit to the old witch. While she had read Julienne's palm, he had noticed a few expensive-looking items on a side table, conspicuously out of place. Had Ootay raided the *Seaworthy* wreck?

"You said something about a treasure. Is that what you and Ootay have been living on?"

She nodded, trepidation quivering on her lips. "He found it in Spirits Cove. He tell Maggie he dug it up, but she no fool. She know he gets it off that wrecked ship. He got ugly with Maggie later and she tells him she gonna tattle on him to you 'bout taking all them coins and gold stuffs. She goes along with his lie 'bout where them things come from, but one night she gets mad and tells him them things really belong to you, big Buck, seeing as how they be buried on your land. Ootay, he beat her, and she tell everyone she fell off a horse. But Maggie no shut her mouth after that. She keep telling Ootay she gonna say something 'bout the things Ootay found. She keep wagging her tongue 'bout it, and it gets Ootay real mad."

The truth speared him, through and through. "He killed her to keep her mouth shut."

Carmella's pale eyes filled with tears. "Him did. I shoulda said something, but they was both sinners. This one, though. This one is a jewel, big Buck."

"Julienne." Panic clouded his mind for a blinding moment. Crashing thunder overhead shook him loose of it. "Which way did she go, Lorenzo?"

"That way." Lorenzo pointed to a break in the trees. "Toward the house. Vamoose!"

Julienne let the big horse have his head, and he settled into a comfortable canter. The first few drops fell, making her clothes damp, but the rain held off. She glanced up, catching a glimpse of dark gray cloud through the canopy of green branches. She might just be able to make it to the house before getting drenched, she surmised, guessing that she was less than a mile from the estate grounds.

She fumed and plotted her revenge on Lorenzo. She'd let Buccaneer deal with him, and she would deal with Rosa. If things were ever going to get better at Moonspell, she and Rosa had to come to an understanding for the sake of Buccaneer and Alissa. The way she saw it, she had two choices. She could dig in at Moonspell and carve out a place for herself in it or she could pack her bags and return to St. Augustine, where nothing awaited her. The choice was easy. Moonspell and its master.

Her anger subsided and peace began to filter through her veins again. Even the misty rain felt good on her face and arms. She heard the groan of the tree branch above her a split second too late. Ootay was on her before she could even scream.

Chapter 25

At first all she could see was rain falling in silvery sheets, and all she could hear was her own gasps for breath. Opaque eyes swam into view, and Julienne blinked to bring them into sharper focus.

"Ootay?"

He grinned, showing two rows of straight, white teeth. Julienne's senses returned. He'd ambushed her! He'd been waiting for her, clinging to one of the branches that stretched across the bridle path, and then slipping off it to sweep her from the saddle. He straddled her, pinning her hands to the ground on either side of her head and anchoring her legs with his body.

"Let go," she ordered, struggling. "Let me up."

"You know about me, don't you? You been reading all about me. Get you hot? Make you dream of me, pretty one?"

"I don't know what you're talking about. Get off me. You're hurting me." She tried to sound cross, but inside her blood had turned to ice and a knot of fear expanded in her stomach.

He laughed, deep in his chest, and his strange eyes reminded her of foggy glass. "I would think you meant it if I didn't be knowing that you been reading all about me and wild Maggie. We had good times, me and her. Still be having them if she hadn't tried to boss me. I be the boss man. She shoulda remembered that."

He released one of her hands and filled his palm with a knife. He split Julienne's dress open from her throat to her waist. She shrieked and swung a fist, hitting him in the side of the head. Ootay moved with the speed and fluidity of a jungle snake and had snatched the handkerchief from around his neck and stuffed it into Julienne's mouth before she could scream again or land another blow. The material tasted of sweat and dirt, and she tried vainly to spit it out.

"You be recalling how I cast my spell over you that night by the bonfire? I made you mine." He laughed, the sound higher, more insane. "I done staked my claim on you that night, and now I'm gonna plow my field and plant my seed. You won't be no good to any other man once I be done with you."

Ootay's hands on her bare breasts revolted her. Julienne thrashed and bucked and screamed against the rag. Ootay pinched her nipples hard and she jerked. Hot tears flooded her eyes. God, he was going to rape her! She tried to talk him out of it with all she had left—her eyes. He laughed at her beseeching demeanor and ran the tip of his knife along her cheek, stopping short of drawing blood.

"You gonna like this, but you gonna like it more if you obey me. I be your master and you be my slave, woman. You hear?" He leaned over her until his nose touched hers and his eyes filled her vision. He squeezed her breasts again as if they were lumps of bread dough, and she whimpered and shook her head in futile denial of what was happening to her.

The helplessness of it all hurt more than anything physical he administered. His rough hands and pinching fingers were mild annoyances in

comparison to the shriveling of her soul and the
destruction of her dignity. He planted her wrists
above her head and held them in one hand while
his other worked its way up her skirt and tore vi-
ciously at her underwear.

"You feel sweet and tight," he said past his
sneering grin as his hand cupped her. "Bet Cap'n
Buck been enjoying sinking his rod in this honeypot. Wild Maggie told me he was good at
humpin', but he didn't understand her needs. I
understand. I know women be wanting a man to
be a man. Won't have no woman around me that
don't mind and don't show me the proper respect." He grabbed her chin in one hand, his fingers biting into her skin and bruising her. "I want
you to worship me with your mouth. If you don't,
I gonna slit your throat. I want you to kiss me and
suck me and drink me dry. Then I think it be nice
if I try myself in all your tight places. If I don't fit
at first, why, I'll stretch you out until I do."

Julienne screamed against the filthy cloth in her
mouth and struggled, but she couldn't move more
than an inch. Ootay sat on her legs and he tightened his hold on her wrists. He bent over her and
took one of her nipples in his mouth. Julienne
screamed again, her pain and outrage muffled by
the gag.

"I'd like to keep you around, but I do think
you'd go running to Cap'n Buck, and I can't be allowing that. You be fun to diddle with here in the
rain—" He shook his head. "No, I be watching
you ever since you landed here, and you all bug-
eyed for big Buck."

He threw back his head and howled. Julienne's
body broke out in chill bumps, and black spots
swam before her eyes. Lorenzo wasn't the shadowy wolf dogging her every footstep. *It was Ootay.*

"You be blabbing to big Buck about me and that
treasure I found. Just like wild Maggie. Women

don't have much sense. They be dumber than animals. That Selena woman, she wanted some of what I got, and I gave it to her good. But she all talk and she don't know how to be respectful. I taught her a lesson she won't be forgetting, though."

He gazed at Julienne's heaving breasts and slapped them, laughing when she sobbed. He held the knife to her throat and she went limp.

"That better," he murmured. "Now, you stay that way. I'd rather hump you while you're still breathing, but I'll do it with you dead, too, if you make me. Your body will stay warm for a while afterwards. Maggie's did." He dropped the knife and fumbled with the front of his pants.

He killed Maggie and then he raped her . . . dumped her in the ocean . . . She was dead and he raped her . . . Oh God, oh God, oh sweet Jesus God . . . help me . . . Buccaneer . . . please.

A bloodcurdling war cry split the air, and the world blurred out of focus. Weight fell off her and Julienne rolled and came up on all fours, looking around wildly, trying to defend herself from danger at every turn. Two men grappled on the soppy ground. Ootay and . . .

Buccaneer! She sobbed and reached out, wanting him to make the terror go away and shelter her in his arms. Julienne pulled the foul-tasting rag from her mouth and breathed in and out, exchanging stale air for rain-freshened. She wiped rain and tears from her eyes and tried to think of something she could do to help Buccaneer.

The men rolled, grunted, and punched. Buccaneer surged to his feet, pulling Ootay with him and smashing his fist in the man's mouth. Julienne looked around for a rock or a club of some sort as fists flew and blows landed. Blood streamed from Ootay's mouth and from Buccaneer's nose. It seemed that Buccaneer was gaining, winding

Ootay with body blows and staggering him with his huge fists. The rain made the footing precarious, and they both slipped as the mud sucked at their feet.

It wasn't until Ootay lunged that Julienne saw the glinting knife in his hands. She glanced wildly about and realized he'd snatched it from the ground when she hadn't been looking. His arm arced and the sleeve of Buccaneer's white shirt split open and bled crimson. Julienne scrambled to her feet, losing her logic in a moment of desperation. Buccaneer's glance speared her.

"Stay back," he warned. "Run, get out of here. Go to the house!"

She planted her feet, refusing to leave him to the knife-wielding maniac.

Ootay made another pass with the knife, and Buccaneer danced backward. Ootay laughed. Buccaneer smirked.

"You gonna die, big Buck."

Buccaneer nodded. "*Oui*, but not today." He circled Ootay and ducked behind a tree where Blaze stamped the wet ground.

"You running away?" Ootay shouted. "You had enough?" His pearlized eyes went to Julienne. "So much for your rescue." He shrugged and cut a big S through the sheet of rain with his knife. "Come to your master, doggie. Get on your knees and crawl to me."

"Never," she vowed. "Except in your demented dreams."

"Your man done gone, silly bitch. He gone for a posse, but by that time I be done with you and hid. Once I'm hid, nobody can find me. Don't be looking for him. Big Buck is hightailing it to Moonspell. His horse is back yonder and he done left you to—" He whipped his head around as if a thought had struck him a stunning blow.

Buccaneer reappeared, a curving cutlass in his

hand. Savagery glinted in his eyes, and Julienne knew he meant to kill Ootay. "Now we'll fight even. Care to test the strength of my blade on your breastbone?" He swiped the air with the weapon and smiled. "Drop your knife and save your life, boy."

It seemed that everything stopped. Even the rain. And then everything moved at once. Thunder boomed, the rain came in stinging needles, and Julienne witnessed true madness in Ootay's milky eyes. He and Buccaneer circled each other, darting in and out, looking for that one fatal misstep. Buccaneer's advantage became obvious within seconds, Ootay's short-bladed dirk being no match for Buccaneer's cutlass.

"You're not going to get away," Buccaneer told him. "So you might as well lay down your knife. It's over for you."

Ootay grinned, the madness glimmering in his eyes like diamond dust. "Maybe you be right, Cap'n Buck, but I'm not afraid of you. You can draw my blood, but you can't kill me. I got the magic in me, don't you see? You want my blood painting your blade? You got it."

A moment after Ootay thrust out his chest and squared his shoulders, Julienne realized what he was about to do. A garbled sound of distress bubbled from her throat. Buccaneer must have discerned Ootay's intention, too, because his expression changed to disbelief.

"No, you fool!" Buccaneer shouted, even as Ootay threw himself at the deadly blade.

Buccaneer dropped the cutlass a few inches, trying to thwart Ootay's attempt at suicide. Instead of tearing through Ootay's heart, the steel slid into his belly as if he were made of butter, and curved out his side. Horror twisted Buccaneer's face, and he withdrew the weapon quickly. Ootay's face reflected a shock of pain, a flicker of discomfort, a

grin of absolution. He wobbled and sank to his
knees, then pitched forward as the breath gushed
out of him and his body convulsed, then lay im-
mobile.

"Buccaneer, is he dead?" Julienne whispered.

Buccaneer's gaze swept from the fallen figure at
his feet to Julienne. Rain poured down Buccaneer's face in rivulets and plastered his hair to his
head. Blood trickled down his sleeveless arm and
dribbled from his nose and the corner of his
mouth. His eyes, dark and unfocused, looked
bruised by life ... and by death.

Julienne closed the distance between them in
three running steps and threw herself against him.
He took her full weight and, holding her with one
arm wrapped around her waist, dropped kisses
over her face with feverish abandon.

"Are you all right?" he asked, letting go of the
cutlass to run his hands over her, checking, searching.

"Yes, I'm fine ... I'm scared."

"It's over. I'm here. I won't let anything happen
to you." He held her face between his hands and
stared at her so hard, she thought he could see
into her mind and heart and soul. "You mean everything to me, do you know that? If I lost you, I
don't think I could go on living."

"Hush ... let's not talk of—Buccaneer!" She
pushed at him, fear clouding her mind again as
Ootay loomed up like Satan escaping the confines
of hell.

Buccaneer pushed her behind him and snatched
up the cutlass, but Ootay was already gone, disappearing into the thick brush. Buccaneer gathered
Julienne close again.

"Let him go. I don't give a damn what happens
to him. All I care about is you."

She shivered, drenched by the rain and beaten
by her own fear. "I'm so c-cold." Julienne clutched

at the shreds of her clothing, trying to cover her breasts and stomach.

"I must get you home and out of this weather." He picked her up in his arms and carried her toward Blaze. He set her on her feet and climbed into the saddle, then pulled her up.

"Ootay killed M-Maggie," Julienne said, settling in front of him.

Buccaneer nodded. "Hold on to me." Then he set his heels into Blaze's sides and they plunged through the rain, making haste for Moonspell.

Cupping his hands around the match, Buccaneer bent over the feeble flame and lit the blunt tip of the cheroot. He puffed furiously until the tobacco leaves caught and glowed. The aromatic smoke shocked and soothed him all at once. His head cleared. His nasal passages burned. His lungs expanded. He breathed out and lipped the cheroot to the side of his mouth, clamping it in place with his teeth. Staring at the glittering sky and hearing the murmur of the ocean, he marveled that such a peaceful night could follow such a frightful day. He stood on the front porch and enjoyed the cheroot and his lightness of heart. Julienne was safe. Maggie was gone. Almost.

He heard Lorenzo's approach, but didn't acknowledge him. An apology was in order, but he wasn't sure he could give it. His pride rebelled. Hating Lorenzo had been easy. Giving up that hatred would take time, even though he knew he must.

Lorenzo propped his boot on the bottom step leading to the porch. "How is she?"

He knew Lorenzo was talking about Julienne. "She's sleeping. Ursula says she's fine. Only a few cuts and bruises."

"I just got back from Carmella's. Ootay is dead."

Buccaneer squinted at him through a curl of smoke. "You're sure? You saw him?"

"I checked him over myself. He made it to Carmella's, but died minutes after he stumbled through the doorway. He had lost so much blood, he was nearly white. I helped Carmella bury him."

"How is she holding up?"

"Strange, but Carmella did not seem too distressed. She said she saw Ootay's death in the tea leaves and in her visions." He looked toward the ocean. "The old bat knew he had killed Magdalena, but she kept quiet."

"She thought they deserved what they got."

Lorenzo swung his gaze back to Buccaneer. "All this time you thought I killed her."

Buccaneer blew a long, thin line of blue smoke. "I convinced myself of it."

"Why me?"

"I knew you had slept with her."

Lorenzo bowed his head and shook it slowly. "Never. You are wrong, Buck. Cesare told you over and over again that this could not be, but you wouldn't listen to him."

"You deny sleeping with her?"

Lorenzo's eyes glittered like wet onyx. "She flirted with me, but that is all. I don't sleep with married women. I am the result of such an ill-fated union, and I swore many years ago that I would not knowingly sport with another man's wife. I have seen the suffering this can bring—my own mother was treated like dirt by my father because she turned to another man while Papa was at sea for months on end. He never respected her after I was born and he never accepted me. We were outcasts in our own home." His face contorted with resentment. "If you had asked me, I would have told you this a long time ago."

"Why wait for me to ask?"

"Because then I would know you are ready to listen."

Buccaneer shrugged one shoulder, conceding the truth. "I never in my wildest moments suspected Ootay. Maggie and Ootay." He contained a shudder. "God, it still seems impossible."

"Perhaps he was the only one who really knew her."

Buccaneer nodded. "I certainly didn't." He drew on the cheroot. "You staying or going?"

"Now? You want to be alone, then I will—"

"Here," Buccaneer interrupted. "Are you going to stay on here?"

Lorenzo tipped back his head, eyes shining. "Ah, so you think you have insulted me so hugely that I can no longer remain on your payroll? I have tolerated your bad side for more than a year, but now you know better. Why would I leave when you must make amends?" He grinned at Buccaneer's sharp glare. "Maybe I will begin by asking for more wages or a new roof on my house so that I don't have to dodge drips when it rains. There are so many things I want that you can provide."

Buccaneer gauged the mischief in Lorenzo and let go of his anger. "If I pay you more wages, you can thatch your own damned roof."

Lorenzo dipped his head. *"Muchas gracias."*

"Why have you stayed on?"

"For Cesare."

"Cesare asked you to put up with me?"

Lorenzo pulled a pouch from his pocket, dipped in a finger and thumb, and then placed the smidgen of tobacco at the back of his mouth. "Cesare is like a father to me. He took Magdalena's death hard, and I wanted to bring her killer to justice to put his mind at ease." He shoved the pouch into his trouser pocket and angled a glance at Buccaneer. "I thought you murdered her."

Buccaneer smiled at the tables being turned on him. "You and most of Key West and points beyond. So while I watched you, you watched me. No wonder neither of us saw anything suspicious about Ootay."

Lorenzo hesitated, then stuck out his hand. "Truce, boss man?"

Buccaneer studied the man's hand a few moments before giving a grand shrug and shaking it. "Truce. Just keep away from my wife."

Lorenzo smiled. "You like this wife very much, eh?"

"Very much," Buccaneer agreed. "So very much that I'll slit any man's throat who lays a finger on her."

Lorenzo chuckled. "I got enough women chasing me. I got no problems there."

"Yes, but the women don't linger long with you. Selena couldn't wait to get back to Cuba after rubbing up against you."

"Me?" Lorenzo spread a hand over his chest. "I admit I tried to get under that one's skirt, but she brushed me aside. She was seeing someone else, she said. At first I thought it was you—" He held up a hand to ward off Buccaneer's denial. "Sí, I know better now. The man who made Selena run home to Cuba was Ootay."

"Ootay? Selena was messing with Ootay, too?" Buccaneer shook his head. "God, it's too much. I thought you got rough with her and she ..." His voice trailed off with his jumbled thoughts as he tried to piece together the puzzle.

"Not me. We yelled at each other, sí. I was mad that she would chose another man over me. I thought she was jumping in your bed, and this made me so furious, I wished I could strangle her. But it wasn't you. I see this now. It was Ootay. She told me she was tasting Magdalena's leavings, so naturally I thought ..."

"That she was talking about me?" Buccaneer finished with a wry smile. "Maggie left me for Ootay. At the time, I thought she left me for you, of course. I told her she had to choose. I knew she had a lover, and I wouldn't share her. Him or me, I told her." Bitterness crowded his heart. "She moved into the Bride's House."

"What's wrong with these Gomez women that they wanted that crazy man instead of us? I never hurt a woman in my life! But Selena wanted to be slapped around, I guess." He scratched his head and let loose a stream of tobacco juice. "Makes no sense to me."

"I guess it runs in their blood," Buccaneer hazarded a guess. "Maggie took everything to extremes." He shrugged off the memories. "Is Cesare checking on the tobacco sheds?"

"*Sí*. The drying and curing is going well. We will soon be sailing to St. Augustine and New Orleans with our first loads. I must make the rounds as well. *Buenas noches*, boss man."

"*Buenas noches*, Lorenzo."

Buccaneer watched Lorenzo until the darkness swallowed him up. He dropped the cheroot and ground out the embers with the heel of his boot, then went into the quiet house. He looked up at the second landing and saw Ursula.

"How is she? Still resting?"

Ursula nodded. "She has asked for you."

He started to head for the stairs, but caught himself. She'd been through so much ... and he still had some sorting out to do before he could think straight. He knew for certain he wouldn't think straight if he looked at her. He never did. She always cast a spell over him. "I'll check on her in the morning." He moved toward the parlor.

"Captain Buck?"

He stopped and looked up at the maid again. "*Oui?*"

"Alissa is asking for you, too."

"She's awake?" He jogged up the stairs. "I thought Rosa got her settled." What Ursula had revealed brought him up short, and he paused halfway up the flight. "Did you say that Alissa was asking for *me*? She actually asked for me?"

Ursula smiled. "*Sí*, for *you*. She wants to see her papa. All that has happened tonight has upset her, and she needs her papa to give her a hug and tell her everything is fine."

Buccaneer patted the maid's shoulder as he passed behind her and headed for his daughter's room. "Thank you, Ursula."

He paused outside Alissa's room and held on to his private joy a few moments. His daughter had asked for him. He prayed this was a turning point. He wanted Alissa's love and trust. Ever since Maggie had died, his child had kept him at a safe distance. He'd often wondered if she could see something hideous in him that he refused to acknowledge.

Buccaneer opened the door on soundless hinges. A flickering candle at Alissa's bedside sent pulsing light across the room. Alissa sat up, her eyes wide, her hair a profusion of dark curls around her face.

"Papa, is that you?"

"Yes, princess." He sat on the edge of her bed and smoothed her black hair from her forehead. "Why aren't you asleep? It's late."

"Papa, is Mother Julienne sick?"

"No. She's fine. She's tired and you can see her in the morning."

"Something bad tried to get her, didn't it? But you stopped it."

He smiled. "Yes, that's right." He kissed her cheek and lifted the covers. "Snuggle down and go to sleep."

"Papa, you'll keep bad things away from me, too, won't you?"

"Yes, princess. That's what papas are for." He tucked the sheet around her small body and thanked God for the blessing of her. "I love you, Lissa."

She held up her arms in a simple, trusting gesture that flooded Buccaneer with sweet emotion. He leaned down for her hug and her smacking kiss on his lips.

"I love you, too, Papa."

Buccaneer didn't trust himself to speak. He blinked and his eyelashes grew wet with tears.

"Papa, how come you let the bad thing get Mama?"

He breathed deep to alleviate the tightness in his chest. "Your mama didn't want me to keep it from her. If she had wanted me to help her, I would have. I tried, Lissa, but Mama didn't think she needed me to protect her."

"But she did need you."

"She needed both of us, but she found that out too late." He kissed her nose and her eggshell-thin eyelids. "I'll protect you with everything I have in me, Lissa. You're the most important thing in the world to me."

"Even more than Mother?"

Her new name for Julienne startled him, but then he smiled. "Always remember that I loved you first." He patted her small hand on top of the coverlet. "*Bonsoir*, princess."

"*Bonsoir*, Papa," she whispered, her French surprisingly good.

"Have you been studying French with your new mother?"

Alissa nodded. "Spanish, too."

"Shall I leave the candle burning?"

Alissa turned onto her side and yawned. "I don't care."

"You don't care?" he repeated, thinking he'd heard her wrong.

"The dark is God's nightgown."

He tilted his head to one side, studying her angelic profile. "God's nightgown, you say?"

"Jul ... Mother says. God wears a dark blue nightgown. He drapes it around himself at night. It's got diamonds all over it, and that's the stars." She yawned again. "We don't have to be afraid of the dark anymore, Papa. It's only God's nightgown."

He smiled, amused by the whimsy and how it worked magic on his child's imagination. "I'm relieved to hear this." He kissed her again, then blew out the candle. God's nightgown enfolded them.

Everything would have been perfect if not for one nagging bit of truth. While he had fallen in love with Julienne, it seemed that she had fallen in love with the man in Maggie's diary. That pained him. To be a consolation prize wasn't his idea of perfection.

Perhaps she loved him a little bit. Given time, she could forget that phantom lover and love him with all her heart, and he would give her that time. Forever, if she needed it. Because only one thing scared Buccaneer LaFlamme—and that was life without his little jewel.

Chapter 26

❦ ⎯⎯⎯⎯ ◯◯ ⎯⎯⎯⎯ ❦

The full moon drew her to the window. Julienne stood there for a minute, admiring the moonlight and the distant shimmer of the ocean.

"Where is he?" she asked the moon. She glanced over her shoulder at the empty bed. "Where is he?"

Snatching up her ochre satin wrapper, she slipped it over her sheer nightgown and belted it. She opened the door and almost collided with Rosa.

"You need something?" Rosa asked. She carried a book and candle and was dressed for bed. Her brown velvet wrapper had seen better days. The elbows, cuffs, and collar were worn slick. "I checked in on Alissa and was retiring, but if you need—"

"No." Julienne started to retreat, but reconsidered. She laid a hand on Rosa's sleeve. "Come into my room a minute. I won't keep you long, but I would like to talk to you."

Rosa nodded and moved stiffly into the bedroom. Julienne closed the door for privacy, and Rosa glanced nervously at her. Her skittering gaze bounced around the room.

"He's not here. I suppose he's downstairs somewhere or perhaps in the Bride's House." Julienne smiled, knowing that Rosa was looking for Buccaneer. "I was going down to look for him."

"It has been an eventful day and evening," Rosa said.

"You thought Buccaneer killed Maggie, didn't you?" Julienne blurted out, and the candle in Rosa's hand wavered. "What did you hope to gain by turning Alissa against him?"

Rosa set the book and candle on the bedside table. She turned slowly to face Julienne, her hands clasped in front of her, her expression shuttered. "I did think he killed her and his first wife, too. I was wrong. As for Alissa, I didn't want the child to love the man who murdered her mother. I didn't want the captain to have even one shred of happiness after destroying my beautiful Magdalena. I never had children, you see. Magdalena was like a daughter to me. I suffered greatly upon her death and I wanted Captain Buck to suffer just as horribly, so I set out to take Alissa's love from him."

Julienne nodded. "You never suspected Ootay?"

Rosa's lips thinned. "Never. I still find it nearly impossible to picture my beautiful Magdalena with that . . . that pale-eyed *demonio*." She closed her eyes for a moment, and Julienne knew she was shaking inside. "What drew her to him . . ." Rosa shook her head in confusion.

Julienne started to tell her that Maggie had a streak of perversion that Ootay had fed, but she thought better of it. Why inflict more pain on the poor woman? "Did you try to thwart me at every turn because you didn't want Buccaneer to marry me?"

"I saw that you were special to him," Rosa acknowledged. "And it was another opportunity for me to make him miserable." She bowed her head. "Of course, I am ashamed of myself now. I must apologize to the captain—and to you," she added in a whisper, and her gaze rose to find Julienne's.

"If you want me to leave, I will do that. If you allow me to stay here at Moonspell, I will give you my allegiance and try to mend what I have tried to destroy."

Julienne couldn't imagine ever being close to the woman. However, tolerance was good enough, she supposed. "Go on to bed, Rosa. Tomorrow's another day and a new beginning. There's no need to apologize to Buccaneer. He never doubted your allegiance to him." She smiled at the woman's momentary shock. "Believe me, I tried to make him see that you weren't to be trusted, but he wouldn't listen." She went to the door and opened it for Rosa. "I'm glad we found out who murdered Maggie. Maybe everyone at Moonspell can rest easy tonight."

Rosa picked up the book and candle again and walked to the door. "Good night, Señora LaFlamme." Kindness flickered in the black depths of Rosa's eyes.

Julienne smiled, acknowledging the woman's proffered olive branch. *Señora LaFlamme.* It sounded wonderful. "Good night, Rosa."

Rosa made her way toward her own room in the east side of the house as the grandfather clock struck twelve bells. Julienne went downstairs to the foyer where the tall clock stood sentry. Its metallic ticking paralleled the beat of her heart. She heard something else . . . in the parlor . . . a shuffling followed by a whispered French oath. Aha! She'd located her prey.

Julienne slid open one of the pocket doors. Buccaneer stood on a step stool and carefully lowered Magdalena's portrait from over the fireplace. Propped against the mantel and at easy reach was an oil painting of Buccaneer's prized schooner, the *Treasure Chest*, battling a storm-tossed sea.

"You should be in bed asleep," he said without turning around.

She closed the door behind her. He looked good to her eyes in his brown twill trousers and clean white shirt. A wide belt circled his trim waist, but no cutlass hung from it. She smiled, remembering how she'd threatened to shoot him that first day when she'd thought he was going to hurt Alissa. After looking in his eyes, she'd known how wrong she'd been. If that diary hadn't put stupid ideas in her head, she would never have doubted his goodness, his integrity, his devotion to his family.

"Is something wrong?" he asked, still not looking at her.

"How did you know it was me?"

"I smelled you. Rosewater and scent of Julienne. It reminds me of the sea and the sun and the wind after a spring rain."

Her heart tripped over itself. "So you're taking Maggie down."

"It's time."

"Because you found her murderer?"

"Exactly." He hung the other oil painting. "How does this look to you?"

"Almost perfect. The left lower corner needs to go up a quarter of an inch. There! That's it."

He stepped off the stool and stood back to admire the new painting. "Yes, that will do."

Would her portrait ever grace that space? Julienne wondered. Would he think to commission one?

"Isabelle painted this."

She sucked in her breath and examined the painting more minutely. "Isabelle? She was an artist?"

"Among other things. She was quite creative."

"The painting is lovely. You know, I like her. I believe we would have been friends."

"Me, too. She had a good heart. Just like you. Do you think Maggie would have been a friend of yours?"

She considered the proposition a moment. "No, I don't think so. I think Maggie was self-centered. She wouldn't have liked me, either."

"I agree. Strange that you both liked the same man, being so different from each other."

She nodded. "Where will you hang her picture now?"

"I'll place it in storage for Alissa. She might want it someday." He turned the portrait around so that it faced the wall. "I've put her to rest . . . finally." He sat on the sofa and propped his bare feet on the stool. "How are you feeling?"

"Relaxed. It's good to know that the evil on this key has been vanquished." She sat on the other end of the sofa. "Ootay's been the one following me, and he locked me in that shed and tried to hurt me." She shrugged. "His idea of fun, I guess."

"I always thought he was touched in the head. When he worked for me, he slipped around like a damned ghost."

"He and Maggie uncovered a treasure. I think he quit your employ and lived off what he could make from selling pieces of it."

"Yes, so I gathered. I suspected something that day we visited Carmella. I noticed a rather expensive goblet and bowl on a table, and I wondered where she'd gotten them."

"She's all alone now," Julienne murmured, feeling pity for the old woman.

He glanced at her. "You heard that Ootay is dead?"

"Ursula told me. He was buried near Carmella's?"

"*Oui.* Lorenzo buried him."

"Have you talked to Lorenzo? I mean—"

"We've made our peace," he said, intercepting her question. His gaze drifted to Maggie's portrait. "I couldn't get on with my life until I could avenge Magdalena's death. Everyone talked, you understand. How could Alissa grow up strong and healthy with everyone whispering that her own father killed her mother?"

"I understand, Buccaneer." Julienne felt a moment of intense jealousy. He had loved Maggie so much that this quest for revenge had become his obsession. Could he really put it all behind him now? Would he be able to love her as much as he'd loved Maggie?

"Why are you looking so sad?"

She forced a smile, not realizing her expression had revealed so much. "Oh, I was thinking how deeply your love runs for Maggie. You've spent this whole year anguishing over what happened to her and why it happened. I think it's ... well, admirable and romantic in a way. Every woman dreams of being loved so completely."

"What love I felt for Maggie died long before she did."

Julienne gasped. "You don't mean that."

"Ah, but I do. I sought Maggie's murderer for two reasons—to clear my own name and because I owed it to Alissa. Besides, I felt certain that whoever murdered Maggie was still on Pirate's Key, and I couldn't rest knowing that."

"Buccaneer, I know you loved her. You don't have to—"

"I did love her," he interrupted. He sat forward, propping his elbows on his bent knees. "In the past ... in the very beginning. I was infatuated. She was wild and free and unlike any woman I'd ever known. The first time I saw her, she was dancing, clicking her castanets and wearing a dress that fit her like a second skin. Even back then she had a reputation for being unpredictable. Cesare warned me not to get involved with her, that she wasn't what I was looking for, but I didn't listen. I was caught in Maggie's spell. It was only after we married that I realized she had a vicious streak."

"You were thinking of her on our wedding night. I saw you sitting by the window ... I heard you whisper her name."

He rounded his shoulders, and pain pinched the skin at the corners of his eyes and wide mouth. "You misunderstood. Yes, I was thinking of her and wishing to hell I could find her killer and get on with my life—my life with you. The only good thing Maggie gave me was Alissa, and she never appreciated our child."

Julienne wanted to enfold him, shield him from the memories, but she also needed to know what had happened in his marriage. She clasped her hands tightly in her lap to keep from reaching out to him.

"If Maggie didn't get her way, she struck like a cobra," he went on. "It wasn't long before my infatuation with her waned and our marriage began to hit rocky places. I wanted children and she didn't. When she was pregnant with Alissa, things went from bad to worse. Maggie hated being with child. She felt ugly and awkward."

"Was she a good mother?"

"She turned Alissa over to Rosa and didn't spend much time with her other than when she was nursing her. When Alissa began walking and talking, Maggie took more interest in her. She read her stories and they took walks together. But we weren't a happy family. I soon realized that Maggie had taken a lover."

"And you thought it was Lorenzo?"

He nodded. "Maggie wouldn't tell me who, because she knew I'd kill him—or try to, anyway. She moved into the Bride's House, which was no great loss to me. We hadn't made love for months. Whenever I touched her, she pulled away."

"I can't say I admire her taste. Choosing Ootay over you is incomprehensible to me."

His mouth quirked at one corner. "She found someone as twisted as she was. Maggie liked it rough. She once asked me to spank her, and I wouldn't. Then she tried to provoke me into a fight—a physical fight. I wouldn't strike her, and that made her furious. From her diary, I gather that Ootay obliged her—and more." He brushed his hair back off his forehead with both his hands in a gesture that spoke of weariness. "But that's all behind me now. Thank God."

"I should have given you that diary straight-away," Julienne confessed.

"Yes, that would have saved you from making a grave mistake."

"What mistake?"

He made a scoffing sound. "Marrying me. Poor Julienne. You fell in love with a dream and married a nightmare."

Julienne rocked backward, stung by his assessment. "That's not true, Buccaneer. I did not fall in love with the man in Maggie's diary."

"I know it's hard to admit it now that you know it was Ootay, but you were trying to entice the man Maggie described."

"Only because I thought he was you. I wanted you. The man in the diary disgusted me, and I was afraid you might suddenly start treating me as that man treated Maggie. Buccaneer, are you listening to me?" she demanded, since he'd closed his eyes and turned his face from her.

He stood up suddenly. "Look, I was going to talk to you about this tomorrow, but tonight is as good a time as any." He took a deep breath and exhaled the next words. "You can move into the Bride's House. We'll keep up appearances for Alissa's sake, but I won't hold you to a real marriage."

Julienne surged to her feet and rounded on him. She clutched his shirt sleeves and gave him a good shaking. "Listen to me! I will not move into the Bride's House."

"Julienne, I'm giving you a way out. You're young and I took advantage of your inexperience—"

"Buccaneer, I believe it was the other way around. I practically threw myself at you."

"I don't remember it that way," he said, frowning. "In any event, given time, you might learn to love me and—"

She clamped a hand over his mouth. "If you don't want to share our marriage bed, then you can move your things in there. Your other wives might have followed your instructions, but I won't." She removed her hand and rested it on his wide shoulder. His gray eyes reflected the flickering lamplight. She ran her hand down his shoulder and felt the bandage under the shirt sleeve. "Did he cut you deeply?"

"Cesare had to stitch it up." He shrugged. "It doesn't hurt." He smoothed a hand over her hair. "Alissa is so very fond of you. You've filled a void in her life. Maybe I'm being selfish by asking you to stay on here. I admit I'm thinking of Alissa. She'd take it hard if you left."

"Buccaneer, I married you for better or for worse, in sickness or in health, for richer or poorer—"

" 'Til death us do part," he finished. "I remember."

"Do you also remember the night on the *Golden Conch*? Do you recollect our evening on this very rug?" She glanced down and felt warmth flood her cheeks. "I couldn't have given myself with such abandon or responded with such intensity to a man I only hoped to love someday. Buccaneer, I do love you. Right now. Right this moment. The only way you'll get rid of me is when we're old and gray and this body no longer can contain my soul. And even then I'll reclaim you in paradise."

His breath caught in his throat. "Thank God!" He gathered her into his arms, lifting her off the floor. Her feet dangled and she tipped back her head and laughed with joy.

"You scared me for a minute, Buccaneer," she confessed, winding her arms around his neck. "I was afraid I couldn't break through your stubbornness."

"No one has until you. I've never loved anyone like I love you. I love you so much, I want the best for you. That's why I suggested you move into the Bride's House. I didn't want to subject you to my attentions if you didn't want them." He grinned crookedly. "Of course, I don't know how noble I'd be or for how long. Eventually I'd have to come to you—be with you."

She lowered her mouth to his, and desire zigzagged through her like lightning. "I want you, Buccaneer. Now and forever."

He rained kisses over her face and swung her up into his arms. "Do you have any idea how happy you've made me? All my life I wanted a woman to believe in me and love me despite my past, my heritage, my many faults."

"I love everything about you. Even your stubborn pride."

He carried her upstairs to their bedroom. Setting her on her feet, he opened the windows to the sea-freshened air. A breeze swept in to stir the mosquito netting draped around the big bed. He stared at her for a long minute.

"I can't believe my good fortune. I fully intended to sleep alone tonight—and for many nights to come."

She untied her belt and shimmied out of her wrapper. She knew he could see the outline of her body through the sheer white nightgown. She shook her head to scatter the ends of her hair over her shoulders. Folding back one corner of the coverlet, she angled a glance back at him. He was removing his wide belt with one hand while unlacing his shirt with the other.

"Buccaneer LaFlamme, from this night forward you shall never sleep alone again if I have anything to do with it."

Grinning, he pulled his shirt up over his head and flung it aside. Two strides brought him to her, and she pressed her body fully against his. His mouth plundered hers, and his tongue was a welcome conqueror. Julienne fell back and he lowered her to the bed. She unbuttoned his twill trousers, and he pushed them down his hips and powerful thighs.

"Is every man as beautiful as you?" she asked, her eyes full of him.

He chuckled. "No. You must believe that no man holds a candle to me."

She laughed at his teasing, then did what she had seen him do to her more than once. She crooked a finger and patted the mattress beside her. "Come hither, my master of Moonspell. Your eager pupil awaits her next lesson in lovemaking."

He shook his head. "You don't need any lessons. You have mastered the art of lovemaking and taken it beyond anything I've known."

"I hope your actions speak as potently as your words."

He smiled with smoldering intensity and ran his hands from her slim ankles up her legs and under her nightgown. He slipped her underpants off her and removed his own. She wasn't surprised to see that he was already erect and glistening. His arousal matched her own and she parted her thighs, eager for the union that always surpassed her anticipation.

He kissed her lips softly and his nimble fingers danced over her breasts, flickering like flames over her nipples. She wrapped her legs around him and rubbed the backs of his with her heels. Arching against him, she felt his hard length on her belly.

"Buccaneer, I love you so much," she whispered, reaching down to guide him inside her. He filled her, stretched her, answered her deep craving. "I want to love our children, too. Tell me that you want more children. Our children."

"I do," he rasped, lunging against her, driving himself toward the ultimate satisfaction. "I want to fill this house with love and laughter, and I can only do that with you, my little jewel. Only with you." He released his life-giving seed into her womb and chanted her name as if it were a prayer.

Julienne trembled with her own tumultuous release. She accepted his soft, moist kisses and ran her hands through his inky black hair and over his smoothly muscled shoulders. Her fingers danced lightly over the bandage, and she gave thanks that they'd escaped Ootay to live and love another day. Many, many days.

He kissed her tender breasts, and she closed her eyes to glimpse her future with him. She laughed.

Buccaneer raised his head. "You laugh after I make love to you?"

"I was laughing at the picture I just imagined."

"What?"

"I saw us raising a passel of little pirates and princesses."

He laughed with her and fell onto his back. He put an arm around her and brought her against his side. "Pirates and princesses," he repeated. "I can hardly wait." He caught his breath in his chest when her mouth moved down, down, down ... over his chest and belly. "Julienne? What do you think ... *Mon Dieu!*" He groaned in a seizure of ecstasy.

"Why wait?" she whispered against his hot, pulsing skin. Her eyes met his and twinkled with mischief. "Hoist the sails and raise your flag, Captain. Our journey has just begun."